CRIME, ORBITAL STYLE

The days flew by, with each man counting the days until Sam showed up at the airlock with another few videos. We stopped eating ice cream so that we would have plenty to give him in return.

But then Sam sprung his trap on us. On me.

"Listen," he said as he was suiting up in the docking chamber one day, preparing to leave. "Next time, how about sticking a couple of those diamonds you're making into the ice cream."

I blinked with surprise and automatically looked over my shoulder at the technician standing by to operate the airlock. He was busy admiring the four new videos Sam had brought.

"Impossible," I said. Softly.

Sam seemed to accept defeat. "Okay. It's a shame, though." He pulled the helmet over his head. But before sliding down his visor he asked, quite casually, "What happens if Zworkin finds out what's on those videos you guys have been watching?"

My face went red. I could feel the heat in my cheeks.

"Just a couple of little diamonds, pal. A couple of carats. That's not so much to ask for, is it?"

—From "——*mond Sam"*

Also by Ben Bova
published by Tor Books

BEN BOVA
FUTURE
CRIME

A TOM DOHERTY ASSOCIATES BOOK
NEW YORK

FUTURE CRIME

Copyright © 1990 by Ben Bova

A TOR Book
Published by Tom Doherty Associates, Inc.
49 West 24 Street
New York, NY 10010

Cover art by Colin Hay

ISBN: 0-812-53241-4

First edition: August 1990

Printed in the United States of America

0 9 8 7 6 5 4 3 2 1

Acknowledgments

To my fellow "road warrior,"
Ralph Arnote.

Contents

Foreword

In 1866 Fyodor Mikhaylovich Dostoyevsky published *Crime and Punishment*.* The collection of stories now in your hand, while making no claim to be on a par with that great Russian novel, might be thought of as "Crime and (Possible) Correction."

For these stories are science-fiction tales, and they deal not merely with the fact that crime and criminals will exist in the future as they have in the past: they deal also with possible ways that thinking human beings might be able to protect honest citizens against crime, and even turn criminals into upright, productive men and women.

When I first started reading science fiction, back when *Astounding* was the only magazine I could find

---

*Don't worry if you haven't read it. Neither have most science fiction fans. For that matter, neither have most of the modern generation, thanks to our modern educational systems.

on the newsstands and space flight and the atomic bomb were regarded as utter nonsense, except on its pages, my young and naive soul was shocked to find stories about crime and criminals in the future. Surely this could not be so, I thought. In the beautiful future that science was to build for us, certainly crime would be eradicated.

Now I know better.

Criminals, like the poor, will always be with us. And very often the criminals will come from the ranks of the poor.

To some extent we are dealing here with a matter of semantics, and of comparative terms. There is an absolute "poor" and a comparative "poor." Being absolutely poor means being destitute, starving, lacking the physical resources to survive. Being comparatively "poor" means that the "poor" person does not have as much wealth as a "rich" person.

I have seen absolute poverty both at home and abroad. I was born in the midst of the Great Depression of the 1930s, and I know what it is to be hungry, to be sick, and to be afraid that there is no way out. I have also seen absolute poverty in places like Turkey, Ireland, Grenada (before its socialist revolution and the subsequent American conquest of that tiny island), and elsewhere. Most Americans who are regarded as "poor" live far wealthier lives than the poor in other countries. Most American "poor" are comparatively, not absolutely, poor.

Most, but not all. There are hard pockets of absolute poverty in the wealthiest nation of the world. It is in these ghettos and backwaters that most of the violent criminals are bred. But criminals also come from the upper echelons of society; in today's complex society, many criminals have gone through law school or (God help us) even computer schools.

As a newspaper reporter who covered the police beat, more than thirty years ago, I was fascinated to find that the criminals and the police usually came from the same neighborhoods. Often they grew up together, went to school together, and knew each other fairly well. The difference between them was that those who opted to become police officers wanted an assured, secured future for themselves and their family. Those who became crooks wanted to get rich quickly.

Now, being a police officer may not seem like a very safe or secure lifestyle. But as a public employee, the police officer receives a steady wage, predictable benefits, and a secure pension. Even if killed in the line of duty, the police officer's family is "taken care of."

The criminal disdains such security in the quest for big money fast. The risks are greater, but—to the crook's eye—the rewards are worth the risks. There is even a bit of folk wisdom among the professionals: "If you can't do the time, then don't do the crime." If the penalty (prison sentence) for the prospective crime is more than you think you can bear, then don't take the risk.

But they take the risks. The average criminal is not deterred by the thought of being caught and punished. The death penalty does not stop professional hit men. Disgrace and prison do not deter embezzlers or stock manipulators.

What of the future?

There will always be criminals among us, because there will always be a few men and women who want to bypass the accepted rules of their society, who want to try to break the Second Law of Thermodynamics and get something for nothing—or at least, get something for far less work than they would have to exert to get it legally.

In this book, we examine a variety of criminals of

the near and far future. Murder, arson, revolution, youth gangs, and extortion are all subject matter for these stories. But, since we are dealing here with science fiction, and since science fiction is a *hopeful* kind of literature (when it's done right), these stories also show some possible ways of dealing with crime and criminals.

For example: Since the end of World War II, youth gangs have grown dangerously in size, firepower, and viciousness in cities all around the world. In the U.S., youth gangs that once "rumbled" over "turf" (i.e., had hand-to-hand fights over territorial rights in their neighborhoods) now shoot it out on the streets over control of the retail narcotics trade.

City of Darkness—a complete novel—looks at street gangs from a slightly different point of view. Here, youth gangs are examined as a response to a problem, rather than the problem itself. For the truth is that street gangs are an attempt by uneducated social outcasts to build some form of viable society for themselves. When family, school, and the normal modes of society fail, the kids form their own societies—just as our primitive ancestors did. And they use many of the social techniques that Stone Age tribes did, to the anguish and delight of the few anthropologists who have taken the trouble to examine the phenomenon.

I suppose I am the only person who regards William Golding's *Lord of the Flies* as a hopeful, uplifting novel. Most people see the schoolboys who are cast away on a deserted island reverting to savagery and mutter the common wisdom: "How thin is the veneer of civilization that covers our brutish true nature." To which I reply, "Garbage!" The schoolboys, thrown on their own resources on the island, quickly revert to Stone Age behavior—because they either learn how to live that way or they die. They do not have electricity or grocery markets to serve them. They adapt to their primitive surroundings. They drive out the weaklings. The group survives. Perhaps Golding did not intend for this to be read into his novel, but to me the book is a hymn to human adaptability and survival. Just as Golding's cherubic schoolboys became Stone Age savages, so do many of the youngsters in today's urban ghettos revert to tribalism and form gangs as their way of surviving in a hostile environment where no other help seems available to them.

Then there is the question of how we treat criminals once they are behind bars.

"Out of Time" and the short novel *Escape!* raise questions about the way the criminal-justice system attempts to rehabilitate criminals, once they are sentenced to prison. "Out of Time" deals with a technological fix: If you don't know how to rehabilitate a convict, and you believe that crime is basically a social maladjustment, then freeze the poor sucker until such time in the future that scientists have learned how to "fix" such antisocial deviants. *Escape!* presents a much more humane possibility, in which technology and wisdom work hand in hand to remold the outlook of a young offender.

"Brillo," which Harlan Ellison and I co-authored, deals specifically with the differences between the average person's piously expressed views on law enforcement and what we *really* want from our police officers. Not only is this a story about crime and law enforcement, it is a story that landed Harlan and me in a Los Angeles law court, suing some very large entities for plagiarism!

Of the remaining stories, "Vince's Dragon" is an out-and-out fantasy, and while arson is anything but funny, the story is meant more to amuse than anything else. "Test in Orbit" is completely different: a realistic presentation of an encounter that very well might occur before the next decade is out. "Stars, Won't You Hide Me?" takes us to the distant future, the ultimate crime of genocide, the ultimate drive for survival.

Will crime always be with us? Yes, in the sense that every society sets down rules of conduct, and there will be members of every society who are not content to live within those rules.

The important question is: How do we deal with such criminals? Execute them? Freeze them for future generations to consider? Or use our best powers to change them into useful, honest citizens? These stories examine some of those possibilities.

Ben Bova
West Hartford, Connecticut

City of Darkness

INTRODUCTION

If you have read my short story, "The Sightseers,"* *you know about the origins of this novel. Just as Arthur C. Clarke's magnificent* 2001: A Space Odyssey *grew from an earlier short story, "The Sentinel," so did* City of Darkness *evolve from that brief tale of mine.*

The idea that a city as mammoth and important as New York might be abandoned—even deliberately closed down and evacuated—seems madly extravagant to most people. Especially to New Yorkers! To us, "civilization" is virtually defined as "living in cities."

Yet Western civilization has gone through at least one period when most cities were abandoned either completely or partially, and the majority of the population lived in the countryside or in small villages and towns. We call that period the Dark Ages, the time between the fall of the Roman Empire and Charlemagne.

*Published in *Battle Station*, Tor Books, 1987.

In today's era of instant, easy electronic communications, cities may be becoming redundant. There is no longer any need for most people to live in a city. They can work at home, or in a much smaller community, and have a much better lifestyle doing so. As we watch "urban sprawl" covering up the countrysides surrounding today's cities, we often forget that today's cities are growing around their edges. And dying in their cores.

The Roman Empire was physically destroyed by invading barbarian hordes. Today we are growing barbarian hordes in the cores of our decaying cities.

Thereby lies the tale called City of Darkness.

Oh beautiful for patriot's dream
That sees beyond the years,
Thine alabaster cities gleam
Undimmed by human tears . . .

America the Beautiful
Katherine Lee Bates (1911)

Save the people!
Save the children!
Save the country!
NOW!

Save the Country
Recorded by the Fifth Dimension (1970)

"And the girls . . . wow!" said Ron Morgan.
"What about them?"

"How'd they look?"

Ron was sitting on the edge of the swimming pool, his feet swishing in the heated water. It was a cool, clear, late summer night. Eight of his buddies were clustered around him on the astroturf of the back yard. The only lights were the pool's underwater lamps, which threw strange shimmering shadows on the boys' faces.

"New York City girls are something else," Ron told them. "It's hard to describe. They're not prettier than the girls here at home, but . . ."

"But *what*?" Jimmy Glenn squeaked in his cracking voice. "Don't hang us up!"

"Well . . ." Ron searched for the best words. "They sort of—well, for one thing, they dress differently. Sharp. Like they want to be seen. I guess that's it. They know what it's all about, and they like it!"

"Not like Sally-Ann."

"That dimwit."

Ron went on, "They want guys to notice them. They even stare right back at you when you look them over."

One of the boys laughed. "Man, I'm going to talk my dad into taking me to New York City before the summer's over."

"Your dad must be okay, Ron—taking you to the City."

"Hey, he likes it too, you know," Ron answered.

"Is the City really that great, Ron? I mean, for real?"

Ron smiled. He had an even-featured, good-looking face. Like all the boys around the pool, his teeth were straight, his eyes were clear, his lean teenaged body was strong and unblemished, thanks to a lifetime of carefully-regulated diet, vitamins, exactly eight hours' sleep each night, and the school's physical-fitness programs.

"It's the only city they open up, isn't it?" Ron answered with a question. "All the other cities have been closed down, haven't they?"

"There's still a couple cities open out West," said Reggie Gilmore.

"They're just little ones."

"San Francisco's not so little!"

"Yeah, but Mr. Armbruster in Social Consciousness class said the Government was going to close down San Francisco next year, too. They had an epidemic there this summer."

"It's a lot better out here in the Tracts," one of the boys said. "We're safer and healthier."

"You get an A for social consciousness, Leroy!"

All the boys laughed, except Leroy, who knew that all believed the same way he did, even though they kidded him for admitting it openly.

"New York is wild," Ron said, taking over the conversation again. "The streets are jammed with people. You can hardly walk. Stores everyplace. Not just shopping centers, but all over the place! You can buy anything from clothes to stereo TVs without walking more than a block."

"But it's real unsanitary, isn't it?"

Ron nodded. "I'll say! The streets are filthy. How can you keep them clean, with so many people pushing around everyplace? And they've got old-fashioned gas-burning cars in the streets. The pollution! And the noise! The cars and horns and people talking and shouting . . . it's crazy. No wonder they only keep the City open during summer vacation. It's too unsanitary for people to live in New York all year 'round."

"Where do all the people go, after the summer's over?"

"Back to the Tracts, dumbhead! Just like Ron and his dad, right?"

"That's right," Ron said. "They close the City after

Labor Day and everybody goes back to their homes. Then the next spring they open it up again, for the vacation season.''

''Man, I'd like to spend a summer there!''

''Can't. They only allow you to stay two weeks, at the most.''

''Two weeks, then. Cheez!''

The boys were silent for a few moments, and the night was silent with them. No crickets, no mosquitos, no sounds of life at all. Nothing except the darkness and the softest humming of the methane-fueled generator, which provided electric power once the sun went down.

Ron splashed at the water with his feet.

''The girls are really terrific, huh?''

With a laugh, he answered, ''More than that. They've got something they call bedicabs driving around along the streets. With a meter and everything.''

''What's that for?'' Jimmy asked.

The other guys hooted at him.

''Ohhh!'' Jimmy finally got it. ''Okay, so I'm a slow learner. Do they charge by the mile or the hour?''

After they quieted down again, Ron resumed, ''When you leave Manhattan Dome and start out for the train station to go home, they put you on a special bus—it's sort of like an ambulance. They take off all your clothes and get rid of them. Then they make you shower and they cleanse you with all sorts of special stuff. You have to stick a tube down your nose and all the way into your lungs—''

''Yuck!''

''Yeah, but you've got to get rid of the carcinogens you breathed in while you were in the City. And the germs. You pick up enough germs to start an epidemic back home, the medic told us.''

''Well, cancel my trip. I'm not going through *that*.''

"I am," Ron said. "I'm going back to New York City before they close it for the winter."

"You are?"

"Yep. And this time I'm going alone, without my dad. There are a lot of things to see and do that he wouldn't let me into. He always thinks he knows best . . . treats me like a kid."

Jimmy asked, "Does your father know you're going back alone?"

"No. And don't anybody tell on me, either."

They were still talking about New York City when the ten o'clock whistle went off.

"Damn!"

"Curfew time already?"

"I bet those security cops ring it early on us."

"They can't. It's automatic."

The boys got up slowly, grumbling. Ron pulled himself to his feet.

Jimmy came over beside him and asked softly, "Are you really going back to New York City?"

Nodding, Ron said, "You bet. I don't know how I'm going to do it, but I'm going."

"There's only a week or so left before Labor Day. Don't they close the City after that?"

"Yep."

"Wish I could go, too."

"Come on along!" Ron said, enthusiastically. "It'd be terrific, the two of us."

"Naw, I can't. My folks wouldn't let me."

"Don't tell them!"

Jimmy scuffed at the astroturf with a bare foot. "They'd kill me when I got back. Naw . . . I just can't."

Ron didn't know what to say. He just stood there.

"Well . . . g'night," Jimmy said.

Ron shrugged at him.

The boys filed through the back gate in the fence that surrounded Ron's house. They fanned out, each heading for his own house. All the houses on the long curving broad quiet street were the same. Each had a broad back lawn of astroturf with a swimming pool and the same low, imitation-wood fences. In each of the houses, the parents sat watching TV, like good citizen consumers.

The Tract houses went on, street after street, row after row, for as far as Ron knew. The only break in their ranks was the big shopping center, where all the fathers worked in offices on the upper floors of the store buildings. The train station was next to the shopping center, underground, beneath the parking lot. The train ran through a deep tunnel, so Ron never saw where the Tracts ended and the City began.

Ron stood beside the pool for a long while and looked up at the stars. The sky was completely clear of clouds. The Weather Control Force wouldn't start the nightly rain for another couple of hours. Up there now in the blackness he could see sparkling Vega and brilliant Altair. And there was Deneb, at the tail of the Swan—the stars of the Swan stretched halfway across the summer sky in a long, graceful cross, slim and beautiful.

If only Dad could see how beautiful it all is, Ron thought. *If only . . .*

Then he remembered the National Exams. The tests that settled what your career would be. The tests that fixed the pattern of the rest of your life. If you did poorly, the chances were that they would put you in the Social Services, or worse, in the Army. But if you did well—incredibly well—maybe you could get to spend your whole life studying the stars.

They'd tell him how he scored on the tests tomorrow.

Tomorrow was going to be The Day.

Tomorrow.

A movement of light caught his eye. Far down the row of houses, a silent patrol car was gliding along the emptied street. The security patrol, making certain that nobody was out past curfew.

Ron shook his head and headed for the house. He knew that his parents were watching TV: Dad in his den and Mother in her bedroom. Mother never felt very strong, so they seldom had friends over. Ron went straight up to his room without bothering either of his parents.

Before they close the City down, I'm going back to New York, he told himself again. *No matter what the National Exam results are, I'm going back.*

Ron woke up.

His eyes snapped open and he was awake. Not groggy at all. Eyes wide open, mind clear and sharp. He could hear the morning music and news coming from his alarm stereo, the newscaster's soft voice purring along in cadence to the "easy listening" music. The sun was streaming through his bedroom window. Very faintly, Ron could hear the water circulating in the solar-powered pumps between his bedroom ceiling and the roof.

A moment ago he had been sleeping, dreaming something ugly and scary. Now he was so fully awake that he couldn't even remember what his dream was about. He lay on his back, staring up at the ceiling. He had painted patterns of stars up there on the blue paneling: Orion, the Dippers, the Lion—

The Exam results, he suddenly recalled. *Today's The Day!*

Forever Day.

He got out of bed and walked quietly to the sanitary stall. The needle-spray shower felt good. The hot-air blower felt even better. Ron looked at his face in the stall's mirror. He had never been very happy about his face. The nose was too big and the eyes were too small. Ordinary brown eyes. Brown hair, too. Just ordinary.

He had seen a few guys in New York with long hair, really long and flowing. It looked weird at first. Ron stared at his own short-clipped hair. Nice and trim. Everybody wore it that way at home. Easy to keep clean. Sanitary. Ordinary.

He wondered how it would look if it were long, long enough to flow over his shoulders. Then he pictured what his father would say. Or scream.

There was some dark brown fuzz on his chin, so Ron rubbed in a palmful of shaving powder and rinsed it all off. Now even his mother would agree that he looked clean and sanitary.

Pulling on a jersey top and shorts, Ron noticed how quiet the house was. The alarm stereo had shut off, of course, as soon as he'd gotten up from the bed. *It's early,* he told himself. His mother stayed in bed most of the time; doctor's orders, she said. Dad didn't have to leave for his office for another hour. Ron slid his feet into his plastic sandals and went downstairs.

His father was already in the kitchen, sitting at the breakfast counter with a cup of steaming coffee in front of him, watching the morning news on the wall TV.

"You're up early," said Ron's father. "Nervous?"

Nodding, Ron answered, "Guess so."

Mr. Morgan was nearly fifty years old. His hair was gray and thin, with a bald spot showing no matter how he combed it. Ron had seen photos of his father when he had been much younger—he had been tall and trim and he was grinning happily in those pictures. Now he was heavy, almost fat. And he seldom smiled.

Someday I'll be just like him, Ron thought. *Rich and overweight and old. Unless . . .*

The wall TV showed a handful of soldiers walking

slowly, painfully, through some jungle growth. They looked all worn out: shoulders sagging, mouths hanging open, shirts dark with sweat, eyes red and puffy. One of them had a blood-soaked bandage wrapped around his middle. His arms were draped over the shoulders of two buddies, who were half carrying, half dragging him along. All but two of the soldiers on the screen were black. The only black people Ron had ever seen were on TV.

The TV newscaster was saying: ". . . and only sixteen Americans were lost in this skirmish near the Amazon River delta. Fifty-four enemy dead were counted and verified, and . . ."

He sounded so damned *cheerful*! Ron stared at the soldiers. He knew they were his own age, or maybe a year older, at most. But they looked like old men—old, old men who had seen death so often and so close that nothing else mattered to them.

The TV picture suddenly snapped off. Ron felt himself jerk back a little in surprise. His father had turned it off.

"You don't have to worry about things like that," his father said.

Ron looked at him. "If I didn't do well in the Exams—"

"You won't be drafted, don't worry," Mr. Morgan insisted. "Even if you funked the Exams, I can buy your way out of the draft. The draft's not for kids like you, anyway. It's for those poor slobs—those bums who couldn't hold down a decent job even if you handed it to them on a platinum platter."

"But—"

"Don't worry about it, I'm telling you." The older man's voice went up a notch, which meant he wasn't going to listen to anything Ron had to say on the subject.

"Okay, sure." For a moment Ron stared at the now-dead TV screen. He could still see the young-old soldiers.

Then he went around the breakfast counter and pulled a package from the freezer. The cold metal foil made his fingers tingle. He put the package in the microwave cooker and thirty seconds later, out slid the package, sizzling hot. Ron grabbed it and put it in front of his father quickly, before the heat could get to his fingers.

Mr. Morgan peeled back the metal foil to reveal steaming eggs, pancakes, and sausages. He looked up at his son. "Where's yours?"

"I'm not hungry," Ron said.

His father huffed. "You ought to eat something. Get me some juice, will you? At least have a glass of milk. You shouldn't start the day on an empty stomach."

Ron got the juice and the milk. He drank half a glass of ice-cold milk and watched his father eating. But he kept glancing at the clock on the wall, next to the TV screen. *The call will come at nine o'clock,* he knew. *They always call at nine sharp.*

An hour and a half to go, and the seconds-counter on the digital clock was crawling like a wounded soldier dragging himself through jungle mud.

"I . . . I'm going out to the garage," Ron said.

His father stared at him a moment, then said, "All right. I'll call you when the Examiner phones."

"You're not going to work today?"

With a tight smile, Ron's father said, "I'll wait until the Examiner calls."

Ron nodded and headed for the back door.

It was cool and pleasant outside. The night's rain had washed the sky a clean and cloudless blue.

The garage was really more of a workshop than anything else. The family electric car always stayed out on the driveway, where the neighbors could see how big and new it was. It took so much electrical power to run it that Mr. Morgan had to keep it plugged in to the garage's special power-charger all night. Once he had backed out of the driveway without disconnecting the cable. It snapped across the windshield like a whip, crazing it into a million spiderwebs of cracks. Mr. Morgan spent an hour hopping up and down on the driveway next to his car, screaming at everybody about everything except his own forgetfulness.

Ron had fixed the cable and the plug. He had also wanted to try to put in the new windshield, but his father wouldn't let him. Mr. Morgan took the car to a repair shop, where they charged him six times what Ron thought the job was worth. But Ron did change the socket in the car, so that it would automatically disengage and release the cable when the car began to move.

"That's pretty good, son," Mr. Morgan had said, with genuine astonishment in his voice.

So Ron clanked around in the garage workshop for more than an hour. He deliberately avoided looking at his wristwatch. Instead, he worked on the electronic image booster that he was building for his telescope. It would allow the instrument to pick out stars that were far too faint for an unboosted telescope to register. With this electronics package, Ron's telescope would be almost the equal of the big reflector in the school's observatory.

"Ron!" His father's voice.

He suddenly felt hot and cold at the same time. His guts seemed to go rigid, and he could hear the blood pounding in his ears. Stiffly, Ron walked back to the house. Through the back door into the kitchen, across the dining area, and into the family room.

His father was sitting on the big plastic sofa. The full-wall TV screen was connected to the phone, so the

Examiner's face looked out at them, huge and frightening.

But he was smiling. The Examiner had a thin face, with absolutely white hair that was cropped so close to his slightly square skull that it looked like baby fuzz. But his face wasn't a baby's. It was lined and lean and leathery.

But he was smiling!

"Ahh . . . and this is our young man," said the Examiner.

He hadn't been smiling when he'd handed out the test sheets to Ron and the other sixteen-year-olds. Nor had he smiled when they had left the Exams, eight grueling hours later.

"Ron, you kept the Examiner waiting," his father snapped.

"I'm sorry . . . I was out in the workshop . . ." *But you knew that,* Ron thought.

The Examiner said, "Perfectly all right, although I am rather pressed for time. Ronald Morgan, I have the pleasure of announcing that you scored in the top three percent of the National Exams."

Ron felt the breath gush out of him. He hadn't realized he had been holding his breath. His father broke into a broad grin and looked up at him happily.

"Your scores were especially good in the mechanical arts and electronics. Math was a little low, but still in the highest ten percentile. All in all, one of the best Exams it's been my pleasure to score this year. Congratulations."

"Um . . . er . . . thank you, sir."

"Marvelous, son. Marvelous."

"Now then," the Examiner went on, "you are in the happy position of being qualified to choose the Career vector you desire. You are obviously too valuable a man for service in the Armed Forces—unless you choose to volunteer for officer training. With your Exam results, you could be commissioned in the Army, Navy or Space Forces quite easily.''

Ron's father said, ''I don't think—''

''No, no, no,'' said the Examiner. ''The decision must not be made right now. You must take your time and decide by the end of the month. You must think over many different sides of the problem.''

''Of course. Excuse me.''

Turning his gaze back to Ron, the Examiner went on, ''In addition to the Service vector, the next choice of Career vector is in the Business community. You can enter the Business college of your choice, with these Exam results behind you. There are several fine schools in this State that are free. There are even better private Business schools, if you so choose.''

Ron nodded.

''The final choice open to you is the University vector. Your high scores in science and the mechanical arts show that you would enjoy a career in science or engineering. You'd need to work a little harder on your math, of course.''

''Yes,'' Ron agreed.

''There are very few career openings in the sciences, you must realize. Only a young man with as brilliant an Exam as yours can even think of trying for the sciences. On the other hand, there is a great need for engineers—men who can make machines work properly. If I were making a recommendation, that's what I would pick for you.''

The Examiner stopped talking and looked at Ron. Not knowing what to say, Ron simply mumbled, ''Thank you, sir,'' again.

''Very good,'' the Examiner said. ''Well . . . talk it over. Think about it very carefully. Remember that the choice you make will determine your Career vector for life. This is the most important choice you will ever make, young man. Good luck. I will expect to hear from you by the first . . . no, no, there's the Labor Day holiday. I will expect to hear from you on the Tuesday after Labor Day.''

"Thank you," Mr. Morgan said.

The TV screen faded into grayness.

"Son, I'm proud of you!" Mr. Morgan pulled himself up from the sofa and stood before his son, with his hand outstretched. Ron grasped it, grinning and feeling a little sheepish.

His father pumped Ron's hand hard. "You've done very well. Very well indeed."

"Thanks, Dad."

"Come on, let's go up and tell your mother."

Mrs. Morgan was quiet and frail. She lived on pills and long talks with doctors on the TV phone. She seldom left her bedroom. When Ron and his father entered her bedroom, she was sitting up in bed, her lounging robe buttoned up to the neck. She smiled and nodded when they told her of the Examiner's call. Then she called Ron over to her side and hugged him.

"I knew you would make it, Ronnie dear," she said.

After a few moments of her fussing over Ron, Mr. Morgan took over and pulled him away from her. He towed Ron by the arm out of her bedroom and into his own den. It was a darkly-paneled room, part office and part hideaway. Mr. Morgan closed the door firmly and pointed to the chair in front of his desk.

"Sit down, son."

Ron sat while his father went behind the desk and pulled a little booklet from one of the drawers.

"This is from Getty College, where I went to school," Mr. Morgan said, sliding the booklet across the desk toward Ron. "I knew you'd do well in the

Exams. I've already enrolled you in Getty's business school—the same course that I had as a freshman!''

And now Ron knew why he had been scared. It wasn't that he had been afraid of flunking the Exams, of going into the Army to fight in South America. It was this. He was afraid of his father.

''Dad . . .'' His voice was so low that he could barely hear himself. ''Dad . . . I, uh . . . I don't know if I want to go to business school. Maybe I ought to try science. The Examiner said—''

''Science?'' Mr. Morgan's face went hard. His brows pulled together in a frown. ''Science? What good is that? Spend the rest of your life in some dumb university, teaching kids useless stuff? No, that's not for you.''

''But it's what I like best. The Examiner said—''

''I was there!'' His father's voice got louder. ''I heard what he said. He said he'd recommend engineering, not science. But I'm telling you that you're going into business. That's where the money is.''

''But I—''

''Don't argue! I'm your father and you'll do as I say!''

Ron said, ''It's my life, Dad.''

''And you think you're old enough to run it for yourself? You're only a sixteen-year-old snot! Who the hell do you think you are to turn your nose up at a business career? Nine-tenths of the kids in this Tract would sell their sisters for the chance to go to Getty! You just don't know what you're doing.''

Before Ron could think of anything for an answer, his father went on, but in a gentler voice, ''Listen, son, I really know a lot more about the world than you do. The business career is best, believe me. Once you—''

Ron stared at the carpet and shook his head.

His father pounded a fist on the desk so hard that the desk lamp tumbled over. Ron jerked back and looked up at the old man—he was red-faced and snarling.

"You're going to Getty whether you like it or not!" he shouted.

No I'm not, Ron said to himself. *I'm going to run away. I'll go to New York!*

It was easy.

So easy that Ron could hardly believe it. It took him all week to work up the nerve. Then, on Saturday morning, while his father was out with his usual golfing foursome, he told his mother that he was going to spend the weekend with some of his friends who lived in the next housing Tract, a few miles away.

"Don't go on the freeway with your bike, Ronnie dear. Stay on the secondary roads—they're safer."

That's all she said.

Ron went up to his room and put on a clean one-piece zipsuit. *I can get throwaway clothes in New York,* he thought. *Don't have to carry anything else with me.* He took his credit card and all the cash he had in the house, about thirty dollars. He walked his power bike out of the garage, started its tiny electric motor, and hummed down the driveway and into the street.

Fifteen minutes later he was in a sleek air train, whizzing along at three hundred miles per hour through a deep tunnel. The bike was locked in a stall at the train terminal. He would pick it up on the way home.

The train was packed. Ron sat in a four-passenger compartment, but six people were jammed in there. All adults, all men his father's age. They all looked grim. They were going to New York to have one last good time before the summer ended, even if it hurt.

Nobody talked. The only sound was the noise of air whistling past between the outside skin of the train and the tunnel wall. The compartment was painted a pleasant bright green, with clever little decorations spotted here and there along its paneled walls. There were no windows and nothing to see outside except the bare tunnel wall rocketing past. There was a blank TV screen on the partition wall in front of Ron, but he didn't feel like watching TV. Besides, he got the feeling that his five cramped compartment-mates would object if he turned on one of the shows that he liked.

Ron saw his own face reflected in the dead screen. He was frowning. Thinking about what was going to happen when he returned home. It was Labor Day weekend. He had today, Sunday, and most of Monday to be in the City. Monday night he'd have to go back home—and face his father.

Okay, so I'll go to business school. I can always make astronomy my hobby. But he hated it. He hated being forced into something he didn't want to do. He hated having to give up what he wanted most. And he hated the feeling that there was nothing he could do about it.

Well, you've got this weekend, he told himself. *Make the most of it.*

It was only a little past noon when the train pulled into Grand Central Station. Stepping out of the train's clean plastic shell and onto the station platform was like stepping from an art museum into a riot.

The noise hit Ron first. There were thousands of people bustling around the station platform, all of them talking, shouting, arguing at once. Policemen in black uniforms and white hard helmets were directing people into lines that surged up moving stairs. People were struggling with luggage. One old man—Ron's father's age—was screaming red-faced at a porter in a ragged uniform who had dropped a suitcase. It had popped open and all sorts of clothing were scattered across the filthy platform floor. People were trampling over the clothes, paying absolutely no attention to the man's yowls.

Ron got into line behind a fat woman who was

clutching a six-year-old girl by the wrist. The child was scared and whimpering.

"I don't like it here, Mommy. I want to go home."

The woman jerked the child's arm hard enough to lift the kid off her feet. Bending down to push her puffy face into her daughter's, she said: "Listen, you little brat. It cost plenty to get here and I didn't have to bring you in the first place. Now you behave or I'll sell you to the first meat grinder I see."

The child's eyes went wide with terror. For a moment she tried hard not to cry, but it was too much for her. She burst into a wild, high-pitched scream. Tears poured down her cheeks and past her open mouth.

"Shut up!" her mother hissed at her, glancing around at the crowd. Ron saw that everybody on the moving stairway was looking the other way, trying hard to ignore them.

Ron wanted to bend down and tell the little girl that she didn't have to be afraid. But he didn't know if he should or not. So he just stood there while the child cried and the mother glared and threatened. He felt confused and sad, and a little guilty about not doing anything to help the child.

At the top of the long moving stairway the crowd was broken into smaller groups by still more policemen and set up into dozens of lines. The woman and her child disappeared somewhere in the confused, chaotic mass of people. Ron found that the line he was shunted into wasn't terribly long, only about twenty people ahead of him. But it moved very slowly.

It was hot and Ron felt sweaty. The noise that pounded in from everywhere in this huge cavern of a room made it feel even hotter. Echoes bounced off the vast ceiling, high overhead. It felt as if all the people in the world were in there, shouting at each other and heating up the station to the boiling point.

Ron leaned out to see around the people in front of him. The line ended at an entrance booth. He remembered the entrance booths from the time before.

People jostled and grumbled and looked at their watches and wiped their brows and complained. But the line moved slowly, slowly. Finally Ron was standing at the booth. He slid his credit card and ID card across the counter to a tired-looking man with narrow, bloodshot eyes and tight, thin lips.

"Fullamnt?" the man mumbled.

"What?" Ron asked.

Looking disgusted, the man said more slowly, "Full amount? Ya want the full amounta cash dat the credit card covers? Dat's two towsan dollahs."

"Oh." Ron finally understood. "Yes, two thousand dollars, please."

The man touched a button and a neatly wrapped package of bills popped up from a little trapdoor in the counter.

"Y' alone?" the man asked.

"Yessir."

"How old are ya?"

Ron suddenly noticed the sign on the back wall of the man's booth: CHILDREN UNDER EIGHTEEN NOT ADMITTED UNLESS ACCOMPANIED BY PARENT OR GUARDIAN.

"Uh . . . I'm eighteen."

The man's sour face turned even more sour. "Fifty bucks," he said.

"What?"

"Fifty," he pronounced carefully. "Gimme—give me fifty dollahs."

Ron tried to remember if his father had paid anything at the entrance booth. "But why?"

"Look kid, you ain't eighteen. Ya want me to believe

you're eighteen, gimme fifty. Otherwise, go home. Now c'mon, you're holdin' up the line.''

Ron blinked at him. ''But that's illegal! You can't—''

''Ya wanna get in or ya wanna go home? C'mon, there's lotsa people waitin'.''

Ron looked around. The people in line were glaring at him, angry, hot, and impatient. There was a policeman nearby, tall and official-looking in his uniform and helmet. But he was carefully looking in the other direction.

Ron tore the plastic wrapping off his package of bills and pulled out a fifty. He slid it across the counter.

''Welcome t' Fun City,'' said the man in the booth in a flat, totally automatic way.

The little gate at the far end of the booth clicked open and Ron stepped through. He was now officially in New York City.

''Watch it!''

A porter in an electric wagon piled high with luggage zipped past him. Ron had to jump back to get out of the way.

Ron pushed through the crowd and made it outside to the street. The throngs here were even thicker and noisier, pushing and shouldering along the sidewalk. Everyone was going someplace. Someplace important, too, from the busy looks on their faces. At the curb was a line of cabs, and people poured into them. Cars were charging down the street. They pulled up short when the traffic light turned red, then roared for the next light as soon as it flashed green again. Bumpers banged but nobody seemed to care or even notice.

These cars weren't the safe, quiet electrics that were used in the Tracts. These smoked and went *vrooom!* when they started up. *Unsanitary*, Ron told himself. *They make a terrible amount of pollution*. Still, he yearned to drive one.

Down the street he rushed. He couldn't walk slowly because the crowd pushed him along, move, move, move. Doesn't matter where you're going or why. Just keep moving or they'll trample over you.

A little old lady with a sweet smile and an umbrella passed him, heading the other way. She was holding a leash that was attached to the collar of the biggest dog Ron had ever seen. Walking a dog, on a public street! In the daytime! Back home, you couldn't take a dog out on the street at all. You could only walk him in the park, or on your own property, and then only at night.

It wasn't until after the lady with the dog had passed that Ron thought about her umbrella. It took him a minute to figure out what the odd-looking thing was. Back home, with the Weather Control Force in charge of everything, you always knew well in advance when it was going to rain. And here, under Manhattan Dome, why would anyone need an umbrella at all?

He glanced upward. Yes, the Dome was still up there. He could see its gray steel framework, like a giant spiderweb, far, far above. It was almost lost in the haze of smog that hung above the street.

Two blocks down the street Ron found a clothing store. The windows looked great. Real live models walking up and down inside the windows, talking to one another, tossing a ball around, laughing and waving to the crowd. A bunch of people had gathered in front of the window to watch them. Ron fought his way past the stream of people walking down the street and got to the edge of the crowd at the window. He was tall enough to see over the heads of most of them.

The girls were fantastic! Shorts and little sleeveless tops that barely covered their figures. Not at all like the girls back at the Tracts, with their shapeless prefaded sloppy clothes and their constant challenging in the classroom and the athletic field. Ron grinned at these girls and they smiled right back. Every few minutes a new model would come into the window and one of the others would leave. *To change into a new outfit,* Ron guessed.

The window must have been soundproofed, because Ron could see the models moving their lips, talking, but he couldn't hear them at all. The people in the crowd were yelling things to them, but they paid no attention. Some of the things that the grown men said to those girls . . . Ron was surprised at first, then he got sore. *Dirty old cruds,* he said to himself.

Ron began to notice the clothes that the boys were modeling. Wild. Leather, and macho-looking real metal zippers. Snug-fitting. Boots. Stripes. Glancing down at his own loose, pale green zipsuit, Ron started to feel like a real country boob. A plastic imitation. He nodded once to himself and then pushed his way through the crowd to the store's entrance.

Inside it was much quieter. And cool. The air felt pleasant and clean. It even smelled good.

And there were human people in there to wait on you! Not the automatic machines like they had in the stores back home. Instead of talking to a dumb computer, there were people here to listen to you and make suggestions.

They were men, mostly. Some of them were young, in their twenties. But most of them were older. Gray hair, getting heavy, but smiling and ready to help a dumb kid from the Tracts.

They measured Ron: arms, legs, chest, waist, neck. They fussed all around him and brought out some of the models from the window to show him different kinds of outfits. A few of the girls from the window hung around, watching and smiling.

When Ron strutted out of the store, he was dressed in a black polyester suit with silver emblems on the shoulders. His boots were real synthetic leather. He felt about eighteen feet tall.

He was also three hundred dollars lighter. Under his arm he clutched a plastic box that contained another entire outfit, plus his old green zipsuit, wrinkled and tossed in only for the trip back home.

Now I look like a real New Yorker, he told himself as he strode down the street. Everyone else was dressed in very ordinary clothes. Tourists. Visitors. Ron noticed how they all stared at his outfit. He grinned. He pictured himself as an Executive, one of the men who used to live high up in a skyscraper before the City was closed and evacuated. His grin widened.

Further down the street was a movie theater. It was showing old-time films. The big signs flashing above the entrance said: MURDER! FIGHTS! WAR! SEX! There were no theaters at home. TV was everything, and kids weren't allowed to watch anything more exciting than the six o'clock news.

It cost another twenty dollars, but Ron didn't care. He sailed right into the theater. It was completely dark inside, and he bumped into several chairs and people before he could find an empty seat for himself.

For four hours he watched exactly what the signs outside had promised. Blood and fighting. Beautiful girls and handsome men. War and all sorts of thrilling adventures. One of the films starred two guys named Redman and Newford, or something like that. They were terrific.

People got up and left and other people came in. Ron ignored them, his eyes locked on the screen. He watched people shoot each other, make love, fight wars that were much more exciting and fun than the warfare in South America. He saw doctors, policemen, killers, and each girl was better-looking than the last one.

Somebody stepped on his foot.

"Oh! Sorry."

Ron looked up at the person who had done it. She came into the aisle and sat in the seat next to his. In the changing, colored light from the movie screen, Ron could see that she was about his own age. And kind of pretty.

"I'm awful sorry. Hope I didn't hurt your foot."

"No, it's all right."

She didn't say anything else, and Ron went back to watching the screen. But he kept glancing at her. She was *very* pretty. And dressed sharp, too. He wanted to talk to her, to say something, anything, just to start a conversation. But his tongue was frozen. He didn't know where to begin.

He was watching her now, not the movie. She was looking straight ahead, at the screen, and smiling slightly.

She doesn't even know I'm sitting next to her. Ron felt miserable.

Then all of a sudden she turned to him. "Live'n th' City?"

Ron's throat was so dry it took him three tries to say, "Uh . . . no. I'm from Vermont."

"Oh. From yer clothes, I thoughtcha lived here." She spoke fast, blurring her words together. Ron had to listen hard to understand her, especially with the movie's sound track blaring at them quadraphonically.

"No . . . no . . . I'm just here . . . for a few days."

She nodded and smiled at him.

"Um . . . where are you from?"

"Noo Yawk."

"I mean, after vacation time. Where do you live then?"

She said, "Right here. I live'n th' City alla time."

"But you can't!" Ron said. "The City's closed down after this weekend. Nobody lives here after Labor Day."

"Don't let 'em kid ya," she answered.

By the time the movie was over, Ron learned that the girl's name was Sylvia Meyer. She kept insisting that she lived in New York City—in Manhattan—all the time.

"I never been Outside," Sylvia told him as they walked slowly out of the movie theater. "I was born here."

The blinking, bleary-eyed people pushing out of the theater merged into the faster-moving noisy crowd on the street. It was still bright and muggy outside, even though the Dome blocked off any direct sunshine. Cars growled and honked in the streets. People hurried along, their faces grim.

"You alone?" Sylvia asked.

Ron nodded. Out here in the better light, he could get a good look at her. She was beautiful! Long dark hair falling over her shoulders, gray eyes with a bit of an oriental look to them, and a figure that made his pulse start throbbing. She was wearing a microskirt and white boots and a kind of loose-fitting short-sleeved blouse that didn't hide anything.

"Nice rest'rant a few blocks down th' avenya," she said.

"Thanks—I was thinking I'd eat at one of the hotels. I've still got to find myself a room for the weekend."

"Cripes, you ain't got a room yet?" Sylvia shouted over the noise of the crowd. "Ya'll never get one in th' regular hotels. City's jammed."

Ron felt like an idiot. "Oh . . . then, what—"

She grinned at him. "Don't worry. I know a place where you can get a room. An' it'll be a lot cheaper'n dese big hotels they stick visitors in. Right? An' there's a good rest'rant on th' way. Right?"

Grinning back at her, Ron said, "Right. Let's go."

They fought across the stream of people walking down the street, went around a corner, and started down a cross-street. The crowd here was a little thinner, and it was easier to walk.

"Lousy tourists," Sylvia muttered. "Think they own the City."

The restaurant she led Ron to was quiet and dimly lit. It was nearly full, but it wasn't noisy and nervy like the restaurants Ron's father had gone to. Like most places in New York City, the restaurant had real live waiters. No automatic selector dials with their rows of buttons. No robot carts rolling your food tray up to your table on silent rubber wheels. Real waiters, in funny suits. Men who spoke with far-away accents and bowed and stood waiting for you to make up your mind.

Ron let Sylvia order dinner, since she knew the place. When the waiter left, she smiled at Ron and asked, "Where ya from? I don't know nothin' aboutcha."

So while they ate, Ron talked. Sylvia listened and hardly said a word. Ron jabbed on and on. It was the first time anyone had asked him to tell much about himself, and he found that he enjoyed telling the story of his life. Especially to such a fantastic-looking girl.

By the time they left the restaurant, Ron felt warm and full and happy. And also sleepy. It was dark outside now, the street lamps were on. Not all of them, Ron saw. Many of them were broken, the bulbs shattered and sharp edges of glass hanging uselessly from their sockets. There were only a few people walking on the street now, and they all seemed to be hurrying as if they were afraid that something was following them. Something terrible.

Ron shifted his package of clothes from one arm to the other. "I still don't understand how you can live here all year long when—"

Sylvia laughed. "Forget it. Don't worry about it. Hey, c'mon . . . we gotta getcha a room. Right?"

He started to follow her down a street. But it looked dark down in the direction she was heading. Glancing back over his shoulder, Ron saw that the bright lights of the main avenue seemed to be behind them.

"Wait . . . shouldn't we be going the other way?"

Sylvia reached for his free hand. "Naw—that's where all th' tourists stay. Dose big dumps charge ya five hunnerd a night for a room th' size of a rat's nest. And they're all full-up by now. Right? C'mon down this way."

She seemed to be in a hurry.

"What's the rush?" Ron asked.

For a moment Sylvia's face looked strange. Like she wanted to tell him something but was afraid to. The light from the street lamps made everything look weird, shadowy, off-color.

"C'mon," she repeated, with a smile that was starting to look forced. "This is a great hotel. You'll like it."

Shrugging, Ron let her lead him down the street, into the deepening darkness. They crossed one avenue and started down the next block.

"Hey Sylvie."

She stopped as if she had hit a steel barrier.

Ron turned to see a guy about his own age and height step out of the shadows of a doorway. He was grinning, but there was no fun in it.

"Been waitin' fer ya," he said.

"I'm busy, Dino," Sylvia said. Her voice was suddenly flat and hard, nothing like the way she had talked to Ron.

"Yer *supposed* t'be workin'," Dino said. "I been waitin' here for a half-hour, maybe longer."

"Some other time," Sylvia said. But she didn't move.

Dino looked Ron up and down. Without taking his eyes off Ron, he asked Sylvia, "Who's th' dude? You goin' out on yer own again? You know what Al's gonna say when he finds out."

"You don't hafta tell him."

"Get ridda th' dude," Dino said, still looking at Ron.

"Flash off, Dino," Sylvia said. "I'll see ya later."

Dino pushed Ron on the chest with one hand. "Get humpin', dude. She's seen enough of you."

Ron took a half-step backward, but he could feel his anger rising. "Now wait a minute—"

"I said get humpin'!" Dino swung an open-handed slap at Ron's face.

Without thinking about it, Ron dropped the box of clothes, blocked Dino's slap, and countered with a right to his midsection. Dino's eyes popped wide and he went *"Oof!"* and folded almost in half.

But when he straightened up again there was a knife in his hand. Long and slim and glittering in the light from the street lamp.

"Dino, don't!" Sylvia screamed.

"Shuddup!" he snapped. "You get yours next."

Ron felt hot with anger. This guy was going to hurt Sylvia; he meant it. *But first he'll have to stop me.*

Strangely, Ron felt no fear. Almost like karate class back home. Calm. Even his anger was helping him to see things clearly. Dino was about his own height, yes. But he was skinny, almost frail-looking. His eyes looked weird. And he moved slowly. That slap he had aimed at Ron had been so slow that the kids in karate class would have laughed at it.

The knife made a difference. But Ron remembered his instructor's words: *Never wait for a man with a weapon to make the first move.*

So Ron faked a punch at Dino's face. Dino reacted just the way Ron expected: he jerked back a little and raised his knife hand higher. Ron kicked at his midsection with enough strength to crack a cinderblock. Dino went completely off his feet, doubled over, and landed with a thud on the sidewalk next to the building wall. He lay there in a heap of dirty, ragged clothing, not moving.

Sylvia stood by the curb, her mouth open, her eyes looking very scared.

"Quick," she said, staring at Dino's slumped form, "we better get away from here."

Ron kicked the knife into the gutter. Then he bent down and picked up his package of clothes.

"He was going to hurt you," Ron said.

She was really shaking. "He . . . he talks too much. Al wouldn't let him hurt me, an' he knows it."

"Who's Al?"

"He's—a friend of mine."

Now that the fight was over, Ron felt good. He was excited now. High. He had fought to protect her and he had won. Like Saint George against the dragon.

"Here's th' hotel," Sylvia said.

They stopped at the hotel's main doorway. It looked small and shabby. There was a little canopy over the doorway, with a row of lights around its edge. Most of the lights were missing.

Then he found that Sylvia was clinging to his arm. "Hey," Ron said, "you're not scared that that guy will try to follow you home and bother you again?"

She shook her head. "I dunno. He's kinda crazy sometimes. He gets stoned and goes wild."

Without even thinking about it, Ron said, "Well look, why don't you come up to my room with me? Then you can go home later on, when it's safer."

Looking up at him, seeming very small and frightened, Sylvia said, "Okay, Ron."

They went into the lobby. There was no clerk, just

an automatic sign-in machine. Sylvia held his package while Ron wrote his name on the plastic strip that stuck out of a slot in the machine. A recorded voice said: "Fifty dollars please."

Ron put a bill into the slot next to the plastic. They both got sucked inside as quickly as an eyeblink. He heard the faintest click of a camera shutter, then the same slot spit out a key that clattered into a bin in front of the machine. He reached into the bin and took the key.

He and Sylvia rode the automatic elevator up to the forty-second floor and together they walked down the long, shabby hallway, searching for the room whose number was on the key. The hallway carpet was threadbare, the walls covered with decorations that were so old you couldn't tell what they had been before they faded. The lights were dim.

He noticed that Sylvia was staying very close to him, holding his free hand and trembling.

"It's all right," he whispered to her. "He won't hurt you."

She didn't answer.

They found the right door at last and Ron unlocked it. The lights in the room went on by themselves as the door swung open. Sylvia walked in slowly and looked all around the room. Then she placed Ron's package carefully on the bench that stood at the foot of the bed.

Ron closed the door and clicked the safety latch. Turning, he saw that the room had one big bed, one night table next to it, and a long piece of low-slung furniture with some drawers in it. There was one window that you couldn't see out of, it was so grimy, one mirror above the bureau, and a wall TV screen next to it. No chairs. The only place to sit was on the bed.

It looked seedy, used. Not exactly dirty, but worn out. The room even smelled funny.

"It's not much for fifty dollars," Ron muttered to himself.

Sylvia came over to him. "Ron—you were so brave out there, against Dino. So good and strong . . ."

She slid her arms around his neck. For a flash of a second, Ron felt as if he wanted to run away. But then his arms curled around her and he was kissing her and he forgot about everything else.

Ron woke up slowly. For a groggy moment he didn't know where he was. Then he remembered—the hotel, New York, Sylvia.

He sat up in the bed. She was gone!

"Sylvia?" he called out.

No answer.

He padded barefoot to the tiny bathroom. The door was open and the room was dark. Nobody there.

She's gone.

Glancing toward the window, Ron could see that it was still dark outside. His wristwatch said two o'clock.

She must have gone back to her own place. But where does she live? Why did she leave without telling me?

He looked all around the room for a note, but there was nothing. Then he remembered Dino, and he started to worry.

Maybe she left just a few minutes ago. Maybe I can catch her out on the street. She shouldn't be out alone with that nut around.

He pulled his clothes on quickly and dashed out of the room. Down on the elevator, wishing it would go faster. Out through the empty lobby. Out onto the street.

Something hit him *thunk!* behind the ear and he went sailing slow-motion through the air. No pain, not yet. He just saw the pavement tilting sideways and rushing up closer, closer—and then he hit the cement, face and hands together. He could feel skin scraping off.

"Wha . . ."

A pair of filthy bare feet stepped in front of his eyes. Ron tried to prop himself up on one arm but somebody kicked the arm out from under him and he cracked down on the sidewalk again. He could feel his head throbbing now, and his face and hands felt raw.

"Don't bother tryin' t' get up, dude," a voice said from somewhere up above him. "Yer gonna be down there fer a long, long time."

Ron recognized the voice. Dino. He tried to roll over and get a look at him, but somebody kicked him in the ribs. And the face. And the small of the back. They were all over him, an army of them, kicking, pounding him. Pain flashed everywhere. Ron couldn't see, couldn't hear. And after what seemed like ten thousand years, he couldn't feel anything at all.

Sunlight. Bright glaring sunlight poked into his eyes painfully. No, not both eyes. Ron could open only one. The other was swollen shut.

They had dragged him over to the side of the hotel building and left him there, half sitting against the wall, half sprawled on the sidewalk.

It was daytime now, and people were walking by. Some of them glanced quickly at Ron and then just as quickly turned their heads away. Others never looked at him at all, even when they had to step over his outstretched legs. They kept their faces pointed straight ahead.

"Help . . ." Ron tried to say. But his mouth and throat were so raw that he could only make a horrible croaking sound.

With his one good eye Ron looked down at himself. His boots were gone, his clothes torn and spattered with blood. He felt numb all over. When he tried to move his legs, pain flashed through his whole body. One of his hands was swollen blue; he couldn't move the fingers at all. His pockets had been ripped open and everything taken out of them—keys, money, credit card, ID card, everything.

Slowly, painfully, Ron tried to push himself up onto his feet. His legs wouldn't hold him.

Got to get back . . . to the hotel . . . can't stay here . . .

So he crawled, with pain shooting through him at every movement. Hundreds of people walked past, most of them visitors like himself. But no one stopped to help. Ron crawled along the sidewalk and pulled himself into the doorway of the hotel.

He passed out on the dusty carpet of the hotel lobby. When he awoke again, he saw that the lobby was just as empty as it had always been.

He edged over to the sign-in machine.

"Help . . . me," he moaned. "Call . . . hospital . . . police . . ."

The machine did nothing.

Ron's mind swirled. Then he realized he was dealing with a narrowly-programmed machine. He took a ragged breath. "Give me . . . key . . . the key to my room." His voice sounded strange, muffled, as it came through his swollen lips.

The machine's scratchy voice tape responded, "Are you a registered guest in this hotel?"

It hurt even to breathe. Ron sat at the base of the machine and painfully nodded his head. "Yes . . . Ronald Morgan . . ."

"Your name please?" The machine asked the questions it was programmed to ask, no matter what you told it.

"Morgan . . . Ronald Morgan."

"Will you please stand directly in front of the camera so that we can compare your face against the photograph in your file. This is a protection for our registered guests, you understand.''

''But I . . .'' Ron knew it was useless to argue with the machine. It took several minutes and much pain, but he pulled himself to his feet, leaning heavily against the machine itself.

The camera clicked and the machine hummed to itself for a few seconds. *Can it recognize me the way I look now?* Ron wondered.

''Morgan, Ronald . . . Mr. Morgan, it is past checkout time. Checkout is eleven o'clock. You have paid for only one night, therefore you have been automatically checked out of your room.''

''Checked out? But—''

''You can have your room back by paying another fifty dollars.''

''They took—''

''Fifty dollars please.''

''But—''

''Fifty dollars please.''

Ron felt all the strength go out of him. Everything went black and he collapsed on the hotel lobby floor.

A voice woke him up. A child's voice.

The child was singing softly to himself. Ron saw that he was about six years old. His song made no sense. Either it was in a language that Ron didn't understand, or it was no language at all—just nonsense sounds. The boy's voice was high and thin. His face was very serious, as if the song was really important. His eyes were big and dark, his hair also dark, curly. His skin was a deep olive. He had skinny arms and legs, and his clothes were ragged. He was sitting on a floor littered with paper, cans and metal-foil containers, rags, and one old bottomless shoe. He sat with his knees tucked up close to his chin, his hands clasped around his skinny little ankles, rocking back and forth, singing.

Looking around without moving his head, Ron saw that he was in a strange room. More like a closet, it was so small. The ceiling had so many cracks in it that it looked like a road map. Huge chunks of plaster were missing from it and from the bare walls, showing crumbling lath inside.

Ron tried to prop himself up on one elbow. His head spun dizzily, but the pain was nowhere near as bad as it had been before.

"Hey! He's awake!" screamed the little boy. He jumped to his feet and raced out of the room.

Head spinning, Ron sat all the way up. He was on a grimy, torn mattress that was resting flat on the floor. A greasy-looking blanket covered his legs. The room had no windows, so he couldn't tell whether it was day or night.

There was a blurry mirror hanging crookedly on one wall. A corner of it was broken and a crack ran up its whole length. Ron couldn't tell if his face really looked as bad as it seemed, or if the mirror was making things worse than they really were. There was a huge shiner under his right eye and another big blue bruise along his left cheekbone. Holding up his left hand, he saw that it was still nearly black and swollen. But he could wiggle the fingers a little. Nothing broken.

He was drenched with sweat. The room was like an oven; no air moving at all.

Somebody came to the door that the boy had left open. Sylvia.

"You . . ." Ron began. Then he realized that he didn't know what he wanted to say.

She came over and knelt beside his mattress. "I was so scared you was gonna die."

"What happened? Where are we?"

She touched the bruise on his cheek, very lightly, just a fingertip. "Poor Ron . . . It was Dino. Him and some of his goons was waitin' fer you outside th' hotel."

It was almost funny. "And I was worried about you."

"About me?" She looked surprised.

"I was afraid he'd try to hurt you."

"Oh, Ron!" She put her arms around his shoulders. It hurt, he was still aching. But he held her there for a long moment.

Sylvia said into his ear, "I came back t' th' hotel to see if you was okay. I found you in th' lobby. I got you out just a coupla minutes before th' hardtops got there."

"Hardtops?"

"Helmet-heads. Cops." She pulled away from him. "Some tourist musta called 'em. If th' hardtops get you, they toss you in th' Tombs."

"But I'm a visitor. They can't do that."

"You got no money, no ID, nothin', right?"

"Oh . . . but still . . ."

"They woulda thought you were a gang kid. Or some weirdo got himself freaked out and beat up."

"Then—how do I get out? What day is it, anyway?"

"It's Monday, Labor Day. Th' gates close t'night at midnight and they won't open again 'til next summer. For tourists."

"I've got to get out!" Ron started to get up.

Sylvia put a hand on his shoulder. "Hold on, hold on. We'll getcha out. Al's gonna be here soon. Right? He'll figger out what t'do. You jest rest. Dino went over you pretty good."

Ron frowned. "How many of them were there?"

"I dunno," she said. "Four or five. Maybe six."

The little boy came back in. His eyes were wide with excitement. "Al's comin'! He's comin' up here *right now*!"

Then he raced out of the room again.

"Al knows what t'do," Sylvia said again.

For some reason that he didn't fully understand himself, Ron wanted to be on his feet when Al came in. He started to struggle up. Sylvia helped him.

The boy popped in again, his face red and sweaty. "He's here! Al's right here!"

Ron expected to see a tall, broad-shouldered, steel-eyed leader of men. Instead, the guy who stepped into the room was about his own age, short and wiry. He was much smaller and skinnier than Dino. There was a scar running across his chin and odd-looking wrinkles around his eyes.

"This is th' dude, huh?" Al's voice was soft, quiet.

Sylvia answered, "He's gotta be out before midnight or—"

"I know," Al said. "You an' th' kid split."

"But—"

"Split."

Sylvia gave Ron a worried glance. Then she tried to smile and said, "Good-bye, Ron."

"I'll see you later," Ron said as she went to the door.

Al looked Ron up and down. "Can you walk?"

"I think so."

"Okay. I'll give you directions t' th' nearest gate in th' Dome. It's about thirty blocks from here."

"Wait a minute," Ron said. "Before I go anywhere, I want my money back. And my ID and credit cards."

Al just stared at him.

"Well—you're supposed to know how to do things. How do I get this Dino guy? Do I have to call the police, or what?"

"The hardtops?" Al broke into a laugh. "The hardtops? Last time they was down here half of 'em never got out. They ain't been around here fer years."

"But Dino—"

"Forget it! Just be happy you're gettin' out. And alive."

"Now wait," Ron snapped, his temper rising. "Dino took more than a thousand dollars from me."

Al's face settled into a hard scowl. "Listen, punk. First off, nobody's gotta help you get out. I don't give a shit if you live or die, and nobody else does either, except that whacky Sylvia."

"What—"

"Second, whatever Dino took off ya is *his*. You want it back, you go find him and fight him for it. Only, this time he might not leave you breathin'. Catch?"

Ron felt his teeth clenching.

"An' third, Dino took yer cards and keys all right. But he didn't get any cash. Sylvia took that while you was sleepin'."

"What?"

"In th' hotel room," Al said.

"That's a damned lie!" Ron was suddenly shaking with fury.

"I got th' money off her," Al said, very calmly. "It belongs to us—"

"It's mine!"

"Not no more. It belongs to my gang. I'll help you get out—but only b'cause we got your money. Catch? Like you're buyin' your way outta th' Dome. You don't get nothin' fer free."

Ron limped down an empty Manhattan street in the hot haze of late afternoon. He passed row after row of crumbling old buildings and empty store fronts. Windows blankly staring at him. No drapes or curtains or blinds. No glass left. No people. For all he could see, he was the only human being in Manhattan. The last man on Earth.

But inside those buildings there was life, Ron knew now. Rats scuttled in the darkness of the basements, and two-legged animals huddled in the rooms upstairs.

She took my money. Ron knew it was true. He didn't want to believe it, but he knew it was true. *She seemed so scared and alone, so soft and pretty . . . And it was all a trick. A lousy trick.*

Ron's feet hurt. Walking barefoot down streets covered with broken glass, old food cans, cigarette butts, torn paper, cracked cement that was steaming hot—he had cut one foot on something, and they were both coming up with blisters. His back and ribs still ached from the beating Dino and his friends had given him. His eyes were okay now, though the bruises still felt tender to the touch. His hand was still swollen painfully.

He couldn't get the thought of Sylvia out of his head. *She tricked me. She and Dino must have been working together.* But he kept remembering how it felt to hold her, the sweaty odor of her body, the words she whispered to him.

There were other people on the streets now. Visitors, all of them. Mostly middle-aged men. There were a few couples. Nobody Ron's age. They all were dressed well, but their clothes now looked rumpled, dirty. They were all heading in the same direction, toward the gate. They all looked tired.

A car drove by, a taxi honking at the pedestrians who were strolling in the street, pushing them out of its way. The taxi was filled with more visitors. A plume of sooty smoke trailed after it.

Ron felt completely bushed. He had been walking painfully for more than an hour. Finally, far up the street, he could see a thick crowd of people swarming. And beyond them, the heavy steel criss-cross beams of Manhattan Dome came down to street level.

The gate.

There were open shops and restaurants on the street now. People buzzed in and out, doing their last bit of shopping or eating or drinking before the City closed down for the year. Everybody seemed to be rushing about even faster than usual. They looked wild-eyed, frenzied, like there were a million things they had to do before the gate closed.

But they didn't look happy at all. They didn't seem to be enjoying their fun.

Is it really fun? Ron wondered.

A pair of white-haired women came out of a shop gripping huge plastic bags that bulged with packages. They almost bumped into Ron because they were too busy talking to each other to notice him. He stepped back as they jostled past him. They stared at Ron as they passed.

"My goodness, look at him," said one to the other.

"Disgusting."

"Is that dirt or bruises?"

"What's the difference?" They headed toward the gate.

Ron stood there in the midst of the surging crowd. The people flowed around him the way water flows around an obstacle. They stared at his ragged clothes and bruised face. They talked about him. But no one spoke to him.

Above the heads of the crowd, Ron could see a policeman in his clean white helmet. For some reason he couldn't understand, Ron edged away from the gate, away from the policeman.

And then he saw Sylvia.

She was pushing through the thickening crowd, frowning and looking around. Searching for somebody.

For me? He was glad and angry and scared, all at the same time.

He made his way toward her. She spotted him and her eyes lit up. They both pushed through the crowd until they were standing face to face.

"I didn't know if I'd make it in time," she said, breathless. She had to raise her voice to nearly a shout to be heard over the noise of the crowd.

"I don't have any more money," Ron heard himself say to her.

For a moment she didn't answer. The crowd pushed at them. It was hard to stay in place.

"Al toldja I took yer money. Right?"

"Right."

She shrugged and said nothing.

"Well, did you? Or was he lying?"

Sylvia shook her head. "No, he ain't a liar. I took it. While you was sleepin' in the hotel room."

Ron didn't know what to do, what to say. He stood there while the people streamed by, jostling them. The crowd was getting bigger and noisier. His head was hurting. Cars and buses full of people were honking and growling along the street. It was hot and dirty and noisy and confused.

"Why'd you come here?" he blurted.

"T' warn ya."

"Warn me?"

"About th' gate. They won't letcha through without an ID. The hardtops'll throw ya in th' Tombs."

"What's the Tombs?"

Sylvia glanced across the crowd at the helmeted policeman. "It's like a big jail. Underground. It's real old and rotten. They toss ya in there, you never come out again. Nobody ever comes outta th' Tombs."

"They can't do that," Ron said.

"They sure can," she insisted, her eyes frightened. "I thought Al gave you back yer ID. But Dino's still got it. Gonna sell it fer fuel, he said. If you got no ID, the hardtops won't letcha outta th' Dome. They'll think yer one of us.''

She was serious. ''You really stay here in the City all year long?'' Ron asked.

''Yeah. We can't get out.''

''But . . . how come Al didn't warn me? Why would he just send me to the gate to be arrested? You told me—''

''Al don't care. He just wanted t' get rid of ya.''

''And you *do* care?''

She frowned. ''I . . . I don't wanna see nobody tossed in th' Tombs. Nobody. Ya never get out.''

Ron thought a minute. ''Then I've got to get my ID back from Dino.''

''I can get it off him,'' Sylvia said.

''How?''

''I can do it, don't worry how.''

He grabbed her by the shoulder. ''How? The same way you got the money from me?''

Pulling away from his grip, Sylvia answered, ''Yeah. Sort of.''

Ron shook his head. ''No. *I'll* get it back from Dino. I'll break him in half, if I have to. Come on.''

He started pushing through the crowd back the way they had both come. Sylvia had to trot a few steps to catch up to him.

''You can't fight Dino . . . not like you are.''

Ron said, ''I can break every bone in his body with one hand.''

''No . . . you can't . . .''

But Ron wouldn't listen. He kept walking. She stayed beside him, silent.

They walked up the street, away from the gate and the hectic crowd. They passed a hotel on the other side of the street. Men and women were leaning out of its windows, laughing and throwing things down onto the sidewalk. Somebody tossed a stuffed chair through a window, about ten flights up. It crashed through the glass and spun as it fell in a shower of glass shards. People on the sidewalk jumped and screamed as they raced out of the way. The chair hit the pavement like an explosion.

A woman collapsed and fell to the pavement. Others looked up, cursing and shaking their fists at the people in the windows. A sofa came tumbling down next, and everyone on the sidewalk scattered for safety.

A police car pulled up, its red roof light pulsing like a living heart. Four hardtops jumped out of the car and raced into the hotel.

"They must be crazy in there," Ron said.

"It's th' last night. They all go kinda flakey. Gonna be a tough night."

Ron shook his head. *And then they go home to be hard-working businessmen and loving fathers again. Until next summer.* Suddenly he started to wonder what his own father did every night while they visited the City together, every night when he left Ron in their hotel room watching TV while he went out and didn't return until Ron was sound asleep.

Smoke was coming from one of the hotel windows now. A woman was screaming, and Ron could hear the deeper shouts of angry men.

"They're all sick," Sylvia said.

They walked on. Ron forgot how tired he was, because his stomach was reminding him about how many meals he had missed. He was *hungry*. He'd never felt really hungry before in his life. It hurt.

Police cars cruised through the streets, but soon the crowd thinned down and Ron and Sylvia were in a part of the City that was deserted. They walked alone up empty, filthy, littered sidewalks. He didn't speak to her.

He couldn't. Sylvia remained silent, too, until: "You think I'm a crud, dontcha?"

"Should I be happy that you stole my money?"

"I . . ." Sylvia looked confused. "I don't know how to say it right, Ron. Like . . . I don't wantcha t' think I'm a crud."

He kept walking.

It was hard for her to keep up with him. She nearly had to run. "Okay, I clipped yer money. Right? But . . . that had nothin' t' do with whether I like ya or not. Catch? Th' money's just money. It ain't you and me."

"It was my money. And I trusted you."

"Yeah, but me and Al and the kids need it more'n you. You can get more. We can't. Not 'til next summer."

"And you needed it so much you had to steal it."

"I needed it fer Davey an' me. He's jest a little kid . . . he hasta have food all winter."

"Couldn't you get a job?"

She looked at Ron as if he were crazy. "A job? How'm I gonna get a job? All th' jobs're taken by people who live outside th' City. They come in fer two months in th' summer and make enough t' live on th' rest a th' year."

"Well, you could apply for a job too," Ron insisted. "There are employment centers where they can find jobs for you."

Sylvia stopped walking. "Ron, you jest don't unnerstand. We got no ID's. None of th' kids. We don't exist! As far as th' hardtops an' th' computers an' th' world outside th' Dome's concerned, *we don't exist*. They throw us in th' Tombs an' get rid of us whenever they catch one of us."

Ron felt his face squeezing into a frown, as if that would help his brain to understand what she was telling him. "You mean you really live here inside the Dome all year long . . . and the government doesn't take care of you at all?''

"That's right. Al, Dino, all th' gangs. Lotsa people. Some grown-ups, too. We all live here all year long.''

"But that's against the law! The Dome's closed for most of the year. New York was evacuated years ago—''

"The law!'' Sylvia laughed. "Th' hardtops leave at midnight. From then on 'til next July, there ain't no law inside th' Dome. Al's th' boss in our turf. Every gang's got its own leader and its own turf.''

It was finally starting to sink into Ron's brain. "And you live here all the time. In that—that rat hole I was in?''

Nodding, Sylvia answered, "Right. That's home fer Davey an' me an' all Al's gang. That's why I needed yer money. T' get us through th' winter. Gotta buy food and everything.''

Horrified, Ron said, "But you *can't* live there all the time. Not in there! Not like that!''

"We all do,'' she said simply.

Without even thinking about it, Ron said, "Well, you're not going to anymore.'' He started walking again. Faster than ever.

"Whaddaya mean?'' Sylvia hurried alongside him.

"I'm getting you out of here. Tonight. You can't live here. I won't let you.''

"But I *can't* get out, Ron. I can't!''

"Why not?''

She looked scared. "Ya need an ID card. I never had one. I was born here. They'll never let me through th' gates. They'll put me in th' Tombs!''

"No they won't,'' Ron said firmly. "I'll get my ID from Dino. I'll tell the police that you're with me and your ID was stolen. I'll get you through.''

"No. I can't.''

"Why not?''

"Davey," she said.

"The little kid?"

Nodding, Sylvia said, "I'm the only one he's got t' take care of him. I can't leave him all by himself."

Ron glanced at his wrist, forgetting that Dino had taken his watch. "Come on, time's getting short. We'll take Davey with us."

"You'll what?"

"We'll take Davey, too. Come on."

She kept pace beside him. "You really wanna do this?"

"Yes."

"And Davey too?"

"I'm not going to let you rot here."

"But we was born here. We make out all right."

Ron just shook his head. Sylvia looked at him in a funny way. But she stayed beside him.

The building she lived in was even filthier and more crumbled-down than Ron had remembered it. It had apparently been a factory building once, part of a long row of such buildings jammed side-by-side the length of the long city block. Most of the other buildings were ten stories high; hers was twelve stories. Across the narrow street, an empty garage yawned at them, the sidewalk in front of it stained and slick with ancient grease spills.

At the street level, the building had once had big store windows. Now they were boarded up with old, warped boards that were covered with the remains of a thousand posters and ragged, hand-scrawled graffiti that Ron couldn't understand. A handful of dark-looking boys were sitting on the low step in front of the building's main doorway as they came up. One of the boys said something to Sylvia in a foreign language. Ron had taken Spanish in school, and this sounded vaguely like

it, but he couldn't make it out. Sylvia clacked out a few
fast words in the same dialect and the boys laughed.

"What did he say?" Ron asked as they stepped
through the doorway.

"Nothin'."

They walked quickly up four flights of creaking
wooden stairs to Sylvia's room. The building was like
an oven, hot and breathless. Ron was bathed in sweat
by the time they got to the fourth floor. Her room was
bare. The only things in it were a battered old chest,
like a wooden box, sitting in one corner, and a mattress
next to it, half covered by a dirty bedspread. The walls
were grimy and cracked, with gaps in the plaster. A
few posters and pictures torn from old magazines tried
to cover up the worst spots on the walls. It was like
putting a few band-aids on a man who had fallen off a
cliff.

Ron stayed by the hallway door as Sylvia walked
through the bare little room and into the room beyond.

"Davey's not here," she said. "Wait a minute 'til I
find him. You want somethin' t' drink?"

Ron nodded. His mouth was desert-dry. He wanted
to ask if there was anything to eat, but decided not to.

Sylvia led him into the "kitchen," an even tinier
room, blazing hot, without any windows at all. There
was a shelf built into one wall and a shaky-looking
chair next to it. On one side of the shelf sat a stuffy
little refrigerator.

Sylvia opened the refrigerator and pulled out a plastic
bottle of juice. "Here, have some of this while I find
Davey."

She handed Ron the bottle. It was warm. The refrigerator wasn't working. He looked around for a glass.
There were none. The only thing on the shelf next to
him was a dead insect, reddish and ugly-looking, curled
on its back with its thin legs poking stiffly upward.

"I'll be right back. He's prob'ly downstairs, playin' with some of the other kids."

She left. Ron sat on the chair. It groaned as his weight settled on it. The juice bottle felt sticky. He got up and opened the refrigerator. There was nothing else in it.

The heat was awful. Ron felt sweat trickling down his face, his neck, his ribs, arms, and legs. He looked around again for a glass, a plastic cup, anything. No chance. Finally he rubbed the lip of the juice bottle with the torn edge of his not-very-clean sleeve. Then he took a long swallow of the juice.

It tasted funny. Different. But wet and good.

He took another drink, then walked out into the bigger room, still holding the bottle in his hand. Maybe there was a window he could open. His head was buzzing and his eyes were starting to feel very heavy.

The heat, he thought.

Ron stood in the middle of the room and stared at the posters on the walls. They were moving! Shimmering, the way water sparkles when sunshine strikes it. Ron blinked at the posters and tried to shake his head. For the first time since Dino's guys had beaten him, his body felt fine—no pain at all, everything loose and warm and good. He was floating, weightless and happy. He heard himself laughing. The posters were floating now, too. Swirling around his head, colors shifting and glowing and everything going around and around and around . . .

When Ron opened his eyes again he was sprawled face down on the grimy mattress. Some sort of red-brown bug was crawling an inch past his nose.

He jerked away from the insect and bumped into Sylvia, who was sitting next to him.

"You okay?" She looked guilty.

It took a long moment for Ron to get everything to-

gether in his head. "There was something in the drink
. . . you stoned me!"

"I had to, Ron. Honest . . . you was gonna drag me
out t' th' gate . . . you woulda just got us both tossed
in th' Tombs."

"But I was going to take you back to my home."

"They wouldn't let us through th' gate. Al was jest
tryin' t' get rid of you. I thought he was gonna help ya.
When I found out what he did I came after you . . ."

For the first time, Ron saw that there was daylight
filtering through the dirt-caked window.

"What time is it?" he shrieked.

"Morning. Tuesday morning. All th' gates're
closed."

Ron scrambled to his feet. "No, it can't be! I've got
to get out of here."

"You can't," Sylvia said flatly. She got up and stood
beside Ron. "Nobody gets out now. Not 'til next summer."

He grabbed her by the shoulders. Hard. "You did
this to me! First you robbed me and now you've locked
me up in here!"

She wasn't scared. And if his grip hurt her, she didn't
let him see it.

"I ain't gonna let nobody get me put in th' Tombs,"
Sylvia said. "I like you, Ron. I toldja that before, right?
But you was jest gonna get both of us into th' Tombs.
Them hardtops down at th' gates don't listen to nobody
that ain't got an ID."

He let her go and turned to stare at the window. "I've
got to get out of here," he muttered.

"Not now," Sylvia said. "Not 'til next summer. And
you gotta get yer ID off Dino before he sells it."

Ron looked sharply at her.

"I gotta get Davey," Sylvia said.

She left him alone in the grimy, crumbling room.

Ron walked slowly to the window. There was nothing to see through its gray-filmed panes except the cracked, stained back wall of another brick building.

His mind was spinning. *I can't stay here for a year! There must be some way out. Dad will get the police to come in and look for me. Got the National Exams . . . got to make my Career vector choice . . .*

He turned and looked toward the open door. *Sylvia! It's all her fault.* But his mind kept picturing her face, her body, how it felt to hold her, how much he wanted to be holding her right now. *She saved my life. And if the Tombs are as bad as she says they are . . .*

Then a different thought came to him. He tried to picture what his mother and father would do if he brought Sylvia home. Ron couldn't imagine what they'd do. Except that he knew they wouldn't let her stay. They'd turn her over to the police. *That's just what they'd do. Maybe she really is better off here.*

But he shook his head. *Here?* Looking around the littered, filthy, bare, bug-infested room, Ron could hardly believe it. *The jails back home are better than this.*

Sylvia came back at last, pulling Davey along with one hand and carrying a bag of food in the other. They sat on the floor together, the three of them, while she handed out rolls and cheese and plastic cups of something that was supposed to be coffee. It was warm, not hot, and it tasted like machine oil.

"Where did you get this?" Ron asked.

Sylvia munched on a bite of roll and answered thickly, "Downstairs. First floor. Al's got a big stack of food an' stuff. Leftovers from th' tourists."

Stolen, Ron knew. But it was the best meal he'd ever had.

He wolfed down the food greedily, thinking about beggars and choosers.

"We gotta get Al t' let you in th' gang," Sylvia said. "Otherwise yer gonna be in tough shape."

"The gang?"

"Al's gang. He's th' boss. He's out someplace on th' turf right now. Be back t'night."

"And what do I do all day?"

"Stay here. Dino's around, an' if he knows yer here he'll start in on you again. He likes t' lean on people."

"Dino hits hard," Davey said, in his high little voice. "He hits me when I'm bad."

Ron stared at the child, then looked up at Sylvia. "He hits Davey?"

She nodded, her face grim. "That's why I want th' two of you t' stay right here all day. No trouble if you stay here."

"And what about you?"

"I'll be around. Hafta go out this afternoon fer a while, get some food. Wish that damned 'frigerator worked. I could put food in there instead a goin' out twice a day."

Ron said, "Maybe I can fix it. Are there any tools around?"

Davey scrambled to his feet. "I know! There's big tools inna basement, next t' th' furnace. Eddie and me seen 'em when we was playin' down there!"

"Let's take a look at them." Ron started to get up.

Sylvia stopped him with a hand on his shoulder. "No—you stay right here. Davey, you go down an' get all th' tools you can carry. Bring 'em up here. But don't tell nobody Ron's up here. Unnerstand?"

Davey nodded eagerly. His big dark eyes went from Sylvia to Ron. "Okay. I be quiet." He looked very serious and excited at the same time.

So Ron spent the morning taking the refrigerator apart. It kept his mind busy, kept him from thinking about what was happening back home, thinking about his father, his mother, the Examiner. He just worked on the refrigerator and tried to keep his mind blank.

Davey squatted on the kitchen floor next to him, hardly saying a word, watching intently. He took in every move that Ron made, until Ron felt that the child could have copied everything he did, move for move.

Sylvia left in the afternoon. By then, Ron had figured out what was wrong with the refrigerator. It was simply dirt. The motor was very old, but still good. It was just clogged with dust and greasy grime. Davey found some plastic sheets that were almost as dirty as the motor itself, and they used the sheets to clean the motor, piece by piece. Davey helped, although Ron had to re-do almost every piece the boy worked on.

By mid-afternoon the refrigerator was humming smoothly and getting cold.

"We did it!" Davey shouted.

Ron grinned and rubbed a hand through the boy's curly black hair.

The afternoon heat was getting fierce. The little kitchen was like a furnace. Ron went into the other room, and for the first time he saw that there was an air-conditioner set into a niche below the window.

"Hey Davey, bring those tools in here."

It was dark by the time they finished. The air-conditioner's main problem was also dirt. But there was also a bad coil in the motor and a couple of loose connections. Ron and Davey sneaked up to an empty room on the next floor and stole pieces from the air-conditioner there.

"Now don't tell Sylvia we left the apartment," Ron said to Davey. "She'll get upset."

Davey grinned a huge grin. "Okay Ron. It's a secret. Right?"

Ron nearly got sick when he saw Davey's grin. The boy's teeth were almost all rotted black stumps.

By the time Sylvia came back the rooms were cooled off, and Ron's stomach was growling with hunger. She looked surprised as she came through the doorway, carrying a plastic bag in one arm.

"It's cool in here!" she said, delighted. "Howdja do it?"

Davey bounded up to her. "We fixed th' 'frigimader and we fixed the air commissioner. Ron an' me!"

"Wow," Sylvia said. She handed Davey the plastic bag; it was small and light enough for him to carry. She went over to the air-conditioner and stood in front of it.

"This's great. It's hotter'n hell out on th' streets."

Ron smiled. "Wasn't much."

"It's terrific." Sylvia came over and kissed him lightly. "C'mon, let's eat. Al's comin' up here later on."

Dinner was nothing more than a few pieces of cold meat and a single bottle of beer. Davey drank the beer, too. There was nothing else.

But Sylvia was planning ahead. "With th' 'frigerator fixed I can stock some food an' keep milk fer Davey. An'—hey, Ron, can you fix cookers? There's a cooker sittin' in an empty kitchen upstairs. If we can get it down here an' get it goin' . . . wow, it'll be great! Right?"

He laughed. "Right."

Davey went to sleep right there on the floor. Sylvia picked him up and brought him to the mattress and laid him down gently. Then she pulled the bedcover up over him. Both the mattress and the cover were so filthy that Ron shuddered.

"He's a bright kid," Ron said quietly.

Sylvia nodded.

There was a knock at the door, and it swung open before they could move to answer it. Al came into the room, his face dark as a thundercloud.

"So yer back," he said.

Before Ron could answer, Sylvia said, "I brought him back. You was jest gonna let th' hardtops flip him."

For a moment, Al stood there at the door and said nothing. He glanced at Davey curled up on the mattress, then quietly shut the door behind him.

"Okay. Let's sit down and talk." They squatted on the floor like three Indians.

For the first time, Ron saw that Al was tired. There was tension in his face. His eyes were bloodshot. Tight lines were etched around his mouth and eyes.

"Now lissen," Al said. "We can't feed no extra mouths all winter. That's why I hadda get ridda ya. It's tough enough gettin' food fer all the mouths we got already without puttin' on a dude from Outside. Catch?"

Ron realized that Al was trying to be honest. Maybe even fair. "What do I do, then?" he asked.

Al shrugged. "All I know is, we can't feed no extra mouths."

Sylvia broke in, "But Ron can help th' gang! He can fix machines an' stuff. Look, he fixed the air-conditioner. An' th' 'frigerator in th' kitchen. He can fix anything. Right, Ron?"

"Well, not anything—"

She went on, "I bet he can fix th' whatsit down in th' basement that always blows out."

"The generator," Al said.

"You have a generator downstairs?" Ron asked. "So that's where the electricity comes from."

"It's always conkin' out," Al admitted. "We hafta pay a guy from another gang t' fix it, or else we go without power. Costs plenty, too."

Ron nodded.

"Can you fix it?" Al asked flatly.

"I won't know until I see it," Ron answered. "But

I've fixed generators before, and motors, and lots of other stuff.''

"Guns?" Al asked suddenly. "Can you fix guns?"

Ron shrugged. "I don't know. I never tried. But if they're not too complicated . . ."

Al eyed him suspiciously. "Okay. We'll see. Come on down to th' basement an' take a look at th' generator."

They started to get up. But Sylvia stopped them for a moment. "Al, what happens if Ron can't fix th' generator?"

"Then he's out. He either knows how t' fix things or he don't. If he can fix machines, then he can help us, an' we keep him. If he can't, then he goes out onna street."

"On his own?"

"Yeah."

"But he'll die. They'll kill him. Nobody can live on th' streets by himself."

"I know," Al said. He wasn't being cruel. It was simply a flat statement of truth.

It was an old, old generator, powered by an even older diesel engine that roared and clattered and spewed a fine mist of oil spray through the musty air of the basement. A dim light hung over the machinery. In the shadows Ron could make out a half-dozen drums of diesel fuel.

"How on earth do you get diesel fuel here?" he wondered aloud.

"Never mind," Al said. "We get it. That's all you gotta know."

Ron shrugged and went up close to the machinery. The oil spray stung his eyes. He shouted over the noise, "How long does it run between breakdowns?"

Al waved a hand. "Coupla weeks. Sometimes more, sometimes less."

Ron could see that the generator was held together with little more than bubble gum and prayer. It vibrated dangerously. In time it would shake itself apart.

He stepped back to where Al and Sylvia stood.

"Can you get spare parts?"

Al said, "You show us whatcha need an' we'll get it for you."

"Okay."

"Can ya fix it?" Al shouted.

"Sure. Had one just like it in school, in mechanical repair class. Our auxiliary generator at home is a later model—"

"Okay, okay. You can stay 'til it stops runnin' again. If you can fix it, great. If you can't . . ." He jerked his thumb in an old baseball umpire's gesture that meant *out*.

Ron said, "We ought to shut it down and overhaul it, put in new parts, get it back in good shape. Then it won't break down on you."

"Shut it off on purpose?"

"Yes."

Al shook his head. "Naw, I don't like that. It stops all by itself often enough. I ain't gonna shut it down on purpose."

"But—"

Al walked away from him.

They went back upstairs. Ron could still hear the clattering of the diesel engine. His ears were ringing from the noise. His skin felt slimy with machine oil.

"Okay," Al said when they reached the ground floor. "You stay until it quits workin' again. Now go find a room of yer own. I don't wantcha stayin' with my girl no more."

Ron felt the air gasp out of him, as if someone had

punched him in the gut. *Your girl?* he asked silently. He looked at Sylvia, but she wouldn't look back at him.

"An' come see me first thing t'morrow mornin'," Al commanded. "We'll start gettin' those parts you want."

Ron nodded dumbly.

He turned and headed for the stairs. *His girl. Sylvia's his girl? Then why did she . . .* All at once it hit him. *She's agreed to be his girl to save me!*

Ron didn't sleep that night. Not at all.

He saw daylight come, slowly brightening the window of the room he had picked. With the Dome over Manhattan, you never got any direct sunlight, just a gradual brightness that had to fight its way through the dirt-streaked windows.

Ron had picked out a room on the floor above Sylvia's. It was blazing hot, but he knew he could get the air-conditioner working soon enough.

Now he lay sprawled on a mattress, hands under his head, watching the daylight come to the city. And wondering about Sylvia. Wondering and worrying.

He heard the door to the hallway creak open.

"Ron?" It was Davey's high, thin voice.

Sitting up, Ron answered, "Right here, Davey."

The boy ran in and knelt beside him. "Hi, Ron. Al says we're gonna go out on a raid t'day! An' you're comin'!"

"A raid?"

Davey nodded. He was almost trembling, he was so excited. "Th' warriors're meetin' up on th' roof. Al says fer you t' come up right away."

Puzzled, frowning, Ron followed Davey up flights of creaking steps to the roof. More than two dozen guys were already there, clustered around Al.

The roof was the highest of all the buildings in the

block. Ron could look out over the rooftops of the nearby buildings and see the gray ribwork of the Dome, dim and misty in the distance. The roof was covered with black gravel-like stuff that crunched and stung under Ron's bare feet. There was something wrong about the place, though. It took Ron a few moments to realize what it was: no wind. If he had been this high back home at the Tracts, on a building roof or a hill, there would have been a breeze. But here under the Dome there wasn't any. At least, not at that particular moment.

"Here he is now," Al said as Ron stood uncertainly near the door at the top of the stairs.

All the guys turned to look at him.

"Come over here," Al said, waving to Ron. "This's Ron," he told the others as Ron walked gingerly over the rough gravel to him. "He's from Outside an' he knows howta fix machines. We're goin' over t' Chelsea turf t' get some parts he needs t' fix th' generator downstairs."

"It ain't broke." Ron saw that it was Dino who spoke.

Dino grinned at Ron. He was wearing Ron's boots. *And he's got my ID card, too,* Ron said to himself. He took a step toward Dino.

But Al grabbed his arm. "Now lissen!" he snapped. "I'm tellin' both of ya. There ain't no room for bad blood in this gang. You guys got a beef—bury it! Unnerstand? No fightin' between gang members. We got a raid t' pull off. You wanna fight, then fight the Chelsea warriors. They ain't gonna let us come in and take what we want, just for the askin'."

So Ron stood there glaring while Dino grinned back at him. Al started to tell of his plan for the raid, pointing toward some distant rooftops to show what he meant to do.

"They won't be expectin' a raid so soon after the gates closed down," one of the guys said.

"Right," Al answered. "Now, Dino'll lead th' main force right down th' middle o' their turf"—he pointed toward a group of high, blocky looking buildings—"an' make 'em think we're goin' for their headquarters."

"They'll think we're tryin' t' grab their broads!"

"Them pigs. Erg!"

Everybody laughed.

"Okay, okay," Al said, quieting them down. "Now, while Dino an' th' main force're makin' a big fight in th' center of their turf, me an' Ron and a few other guys swing 'round to the warehouses"—Al pointed to another row of gray worn-looking buildings—"an' grab th' stuff Ron needs. We gotta do it quick, before th' Chelsea guys find out what we're up to."

As Al went on talking, Ron began to realize what was going to happen. This was going to be a raid. A real fight. Like Indians raiding a town in the old West. Like knights storming a castle. The gang was a little army. They were going to fight another gang, another army. They would kill people.

He saw that most of the guys had weapons on them. Dino had a pistol stuck in his belt. Others had pistols, rifles, knives, chains, clubs, and strange-looking things that Ron couldn't figure out.

And out of the corner of his eye, Ron noticed Davey and three other little boys. They were crouched near the door to the stairs, listening to every word, big-eyed with excitement. They watched the older guys, stared at their weapons. *They can't wait until they're old enough to be warriors*, Ron realized. *Old enough to get killed.*

"Okay, let's go," Al said.

Everybody started to move toward the door and down

the stairs. Ron stood still and let the other guys flow past him.

Dino came up to him, still grinning. "Whatsamatter, dude? You look scared."

Al stepped between them. "Knock it off, Dino. Get movin'. You're supposed t' be leadin' th' main force, not makin' chatter."

"Go hump yourself," Dino muttered. But he turned away and headed for the stairs.

Al shook his head. "He's gettin' too lousy for his own good. Gonna hafta stop him one of these days."

Ron said nothing.

"Okay, kid," Al said. "You come with me."

Ron hesitated for just a bare second. Then he followed Al to the stairs. *No use arguing,* he told himself. *You either go with them or they throw you to the wolves. You're either part of the gang or you're dead.*

Still, Ron knew that there was going to be fighting— killing—because of him.

Al led him down into the street and around the corner. A battered old Army truck was sitting at curbside, waiting for them. Al went around to the tailgate and swung himself up. Then he reached a hand out and helped Ron up into the truck. There were eight other guys already in the truck, sitting on the floor. The plastic roof and sides made it dark and cool inside. Al sat down nearest the open tailgate. Ron sat next to him.

"One other thing we got goin' for us," Al said as the truck started up with a roar and a rattle, "is we got gas to run with. Stashed a lot of it all summer long. Better'n goin' in on foot."

Shaking and lurching, the truck groaned away from the curb and started down the street. Ron couldn't see much out of the open tailgate. Just empty streets. Totally empty. Nobody on the sidewalks at all. No other cars driving by. Not even any cars parked at the curbs. The city was really empty.

Except for the gangs.

After many blocks, the truck stopped. But the driver kept the engine running. Ron felt its low, fast vibration in his bones. He tried to figure out where they were. There was a strange smell in the air; a foul smell, like the stink bomb one of his friends had made once in chemistry class.

Al sniffed it too. "Humpin' sewers backin' up already," he muttered.

"Soon's they close down th' garbage plants," said one of the guys deeper in the truck.

"Them Chelsea clowns must like th' smell," somebody said.

"They think it's perfoom!"

They laughed.

"Keep it quiet," Al snapped. "Lissen for th' signal."

They stilled down. For several minutes there was nothing to hear except the ticking of the truck's engine. Ron mentally diagnosed a sticky valve. The engine would need an overhaul soon, or at least a tune-up.

An explosion! The sudden blasting noise made Ron jump.

"That's it!" Al shouted. "Let's go!"

The driver heard him and put the truck in gear, with a horrible grinding noise. The truck lurched forward, engine roaring. Down the streets they raced, buildings whizzed by, windows blank and staring.

Al stood up. Bracing himself and holding tight to the metal framework that supported the plastic roof, he leaned out and looked around the end of the truck to see where they were. The wind tore at his curly hair and made him squint.

He pulled himself back inside and hunched down again. "Hang on tight!" he yelled.

Everybody pulled his knees to his chest and grabbed his ankles. Ron did the same.

The truck hit something with an ear-splitting crash and a jar that rattled Ron's teeth. Then they drove inside a huge building, the truck's engine suddenly sounding hollow and even noisier than before.

They stopped with a lurch that slid everybody into a jumbled heap. Al jumped out of the truck before the last echo of the engine's roar had died away.

"C'mon, c'mon, let's go!" he yelled.

Ron jumped down to the floor of the warehouse and the other guys piled out behind him. They all had guns in their hands. Two guys had automatic rifles, the rest had pistols.

The eight armed men sprinted to the doors that the truck had just crashed through. Ron looked around and saw row after row of packing crates, stacked up as high as the ceiling, which must have been at least six stories up.

"Okay," Al snapped. "Find whatcha need and let's get it packed in th' truck. Quick! We ain't got all day."

"I can't go running through a strange warehouse and pick out everything we need in a few minutes," Ron complained. "This is no way to—"

Al cut him short. "This's the *only* way yer gonna get whatcha need. Now get busy and stop yappin'!"

With a shrug, Ron turned toward the stacks of equipment. Al and the truck driver and another guy, who must have been up in the cab with the driver, went with Ron.

At least the crates were clearly marked with stenciled lettering. And further back there were smaller pieces of equipment wrapped in clear plastic, so Ron could see what they were.

He spent nearly an hour pacing up and down the rows of equipment, picking out as much as he could find. The driver and his helper carried most of the stuff back to the truck. Al stayed with Ron. He had a gun tucked into his waistband. *Is he protecting me or making sure I won't try to run away?* Ron wondered.

"Time's getting' short," Al muttered.

"Okay. I think I've got most of what I need," Ron said.

A shot echoed through the warehouse.

"They found us!" somebody shouted.

"C'mon, let's go," Al said.

He and Ron started sprinting back to the truck. The driver and his helper were already there, loading some of the equipment Ron had picked out.

But as they ran, Ron's eye caught a glimpse of the lettering on one of the big crates: CHARLESTON TURBOGENERATOR MARK VIII.

Ron skidded to a halt. "Wow! Can we get that into the truck?"

Al had to scuttle back a dozen steps. "It's big—"

"And it's heavy," Ron said. "We'll need at least six guys to carry it. But it'll be worth it."

Al glanced over his shoulder toward the truck and the smashed front gate where his eight fighters were crouched tensely, waiting for an enemy attack. Then he looked back at the big plastic crate.

"Dimmy, Lou, Patsy, Ed—come over here, quick!"

Al got the driver to back the truck up to the end of the row where the generators were stacked. Then the six of them heaved and lifted and strained to get one of the big crates onto the back of the truck. Ron and Al helped, too. Ron felt its weight against his shoulders, felt sweat breaking out on him as they struggled to get the crate high enough to slide into the truck. He wished for a powered forklift.

More shots! Guys shouting, cursing. Somebody screamed with pain.

They got the crate into the truck. Ron's arms seemed to float away from him once the load of the turbogenerator was taken away.

They scrambled up into the truck. The driver edged it out toward the gate and the other warriors who had been defending the gate against the Chelsea fighters clambered in. One of them was badly hurt. He had to be pulled in. His face and chest were covered with blood, and he moaned sickeningly.

Ron stared at him as they dumped him on the floor of the truck, next to the generator crate. The truck roared out into the daylight, and into a hail of enemy fire. Bullets whizzed by and clanged off metal. The guys flattened themselves on the truck floor. All except Al, who knelt at the tailgate and fired back with an automatic rifle. The shattering noise of the gun's blasting shut everything else off from Ron's brain.

Only when the gun stopped firing could Ron open his tight-squeezed eyes. He smelled sharp, bitter, slightly oily fumes from the gun. He felt the wind ripping through the truck from a hundred bullet holes in the plastic sides.

Then he saw that he was lying next to the wounded boy. Ron backed away, his hands and knees sliding on the blood-slippery truck floor. Ron found that his clothes, his hands, even his face were sticky with the kid's blood.

"How's he?" Al asked.

"Dead," somebody answered.

And then Ron was leaning out of the truck, over the tailgate, vomiting. He could feel his stomach twisting inside him. All the strength left him.

Is that what it's like here? Is this the way I'm going to have to live?

* * *

So Ron became a member of Al's gang. It's formal name was the Gramercy Association, Ron found out, although no one ever told him why it was called that, or where the name came from. No one seemed to know. To each of the hundred or so members, it was simply Al's gang. Al was their leader, tough, wary, totally without a smile in him, but as fair as any leader of a pack of wild teenagers could be.

It took several weeks before they made Ron a real member of the gang. But when the generator down in the basement of their building conked out and Ron had it fixed and running again in a few hours, Al reached out his hand and shook with Ron. That night the gang's inner council met up on the roof and voted Ron in as a full gang member. Only Dino voted against him.

In the following weeks, Ron tried to get a firmer idea of where they were and just how large the gang actually was. He spent much of his time repairing things, from air-conditioners to rusted-out revolvers. In the evenings, though, he'd walk around the deserted streets and gawk at the high, empty buildings. Most of them had been lofts or factories. A few were once apartment buildings. One of the smallest in the area had a tiny plaque on it that Ron could barely make out through the grime and rust that had accumulated.

BIRTHPLACE OF
THEODORE ROOSEVELT
TWENTY-SIXTH PRESIDENT
OF THE
UNITED STATES

Every window in the four-story building was broken. Its stone front was blackened by fire.

There were at least a hundred members of the gang,

two-thirds of them male, teenaged or in their early twenties. The number seemed to shift every day. On raids, Al would never take fewer than twenty warriors, usually more like thirty or forty. He always left a fair-sized group of fighters back at their home turf to defend their headquarters and the women and children.

After that first raid, Ron stayed strictly inside Gramercy turf. Al announced that Ron was a mechanic, not a warrior. He was too valuable to risk in fighting. Al had Ron repairing everything the gang owned, from generators to guns. Especially guns.

For there were raids every week. Raids on other gangs. Counterraids by neighboring gangs into the Gramercy turf. Ron nearly got caught in one of them, one evening as he was walking alone on the streets. He had to hide in a deserted basement until the shooting was over. It was scary, because the basement wasn't totally deserted, after all: it was alive with rats.

There were raids to gain revenge for something that had happened the previous winter. Raids to get even for someone else's revenge raid. Dino took a small group of warriors out one night and brought back a half-dozen girls, none of them older than fifteen, who immediately were voted into membership in the Gramercy gang. They didn't seem to mind much.

One afternoon Ron was sitting in his room, tinkering with an automatic rifle. His room looked more like a workshop than a living place. And it was. Tools were stacked everywhere, in shelves that Ron had made himself. Not quite by himself: little Davey had become Ron's helper and almost constant companion. The only place in the room where there were no tools or pieces of equipment waiting to be fixed was Ron's bed, an old cot that Davey had found down in the basement.

Ron frowned as he disassembled the firing mechanism of the rifle. He didn't like guns and didn't like working on them. But Al gave the orders, and if Ron wanted to eat, he fixed the guns.

Sylvia walked in and stopped a few paces from the door. Even though the room was air-conditioned, she left the door open. She was wearing a sleeveless jumper and microskirt that had once been white, but would never be white again.

Ron forced himself to stay in his chair behind the work table. "Hello," he said, keeping his voice calm.

"Hi. You seen Davey?"

"He's outside playing. I told him he shouldn't spend all day cooped up in here."

"Oh. Yeah, I guess that's good . . . Howya' doin'?"

"Fine," Ron said.

"Ever'body says yer great at fixin' things."

He nodded.

She wouldn't come any closer. "Uh . . . you been eatin' okay?"

"Sure." It was a lie. Ron had been hungry from his first day with the gang. But no hungrier than anyone else. The kids just didn't have much food. They had piled up some canned and other packaged foods during the summer, when most of the gang members had either found jobs among the tourist centers or stolen food. Some of their raids on other gangs had been for the purpose of "liberating" food supplies. And there was some sort of a market uptown somewhere, Ron had heard, a black market that somehow brought in fresh food from outside the Dome and sold it for enormous prices. Al wouldn't let any of the gang members deal with the black market, however. Too expensive, he insisted. And they all obeyed him, despite their constant grumbling hunger.

"Ever'body been treatin' you okay?" Sylvia asked. "Dino or nobody givin' you trouble, are they?"

Ron put the rifle mechanism down. There was no

sense trying to work while she was in the room. "No. No trouble from anybody."

"Good," Sylvia said.

She was so pretty! For a long moment neither of them said anything.

Then finally Sylvia asked, "You wanna come down t' my place for dinner? Got some special frozen stuff Al took offa the East River guys yesterday."

Ron's stomach trembled with anticipation. But he said, "No thanks. You and Al enjoy it."

"Al's out," she said. "He's talkin' t' some other gang chiefs, tryin' t' set up a truce or somethin'. Too many raids, ever'body's hurtin'."

"When will he be back?" Ron heard himself ask.

Sylvia shrugged.

Shaking his head, Ron said, "Look, you're his girl now, and I . . ."

"So what? I still like you."

"Yes, but—well, where I come from, you stay with one guy. It could just cause trouble."

Sylvia almost laughed at him. "Cheez, you must come from a real bughouse. Is everybody uptight on the Outside like you?"

"Look, Sylvia, I appreciate what you've done for me. You saved my life and, well . . . is Al treating you all right?"

"Sure. Why shouldn't he?"

"You like being his girl?"

"Sure."

"Sure," Ron echoed.

It took a minute for Sylvia to understand what Ron meant. "Hey, I dunno what's goin' on inside yer head, Ron. But get one thing down. I *always* been Al's girl. Right? Ever since he was chief of th' gang. Even before that, I was his girl. Catch?"

Ron felt as if a truck had hit him. "But . . . but . . . you and me . . ."

"I like you an awful lot, Ron. Some ways, yer nicer'n Al. Yer awful sweet. But I'm Al's girl. Nuthin' we can do about that."

"Then—what you just said . . ."

She shrugged. "But I'm still his girl."

Al was gone for three days, and all during that time Ron stayed in his own room. Davey brought him some food, but most of the time Ron stayed hungry. And sleepless. He stared into the darkness each night, thinking of Sylvia and hating himself twice over. Once for thinking of her, and again for not doing anything about it.

When Al finally got back, he was glowing with happiness. He called a council meeting up on the roof. Ron was included in the meeting.

Al paced up and down along the crunching gravel as he talked. The other guys stood or squatted on their heels. Ron stayed on the fringes of the twelve-man council, on his feet.

"Musta been twenty-five, thirty gang chiefs there," Al said excitedly, waving his hands eagerly as he spoke. "We met in the Empire State buildin', down on th' ground floor. Y'know they's a dozen gangs livin' right inside the building? On different floors. One of 'em never comes down t' th' street at all! Grows its own food up on th' roofs. Creepy."

Ron looked at the council members. They didn't seem very impressed. None of them could think as fast or as far as Al, Ron realized. That's what had made Al the gang's leader. He could plan ahead, he could see farther than any of the others. He wasn't the best fighter among the bunch, but he could get the fighters to work together and do better as a team than they could ever hope to do as individuals.

"Why'n't we take over th' whole Empire State buildin'?" Dino asked, grinning. "Make some headquarters, huh?"

Al threw him a sharp glance. "No time fer jokes. The meetin' was serious business. All th' chiefs got together t' figure out some way t' stop all the raidin'. The gangs're cuttin' each other up too much."

"We're doin' okay," somebody said.

"So far," Al answered. "Y'know those Muslims uptown . . . they're all bunched up t'gether now in one big super-gang. Got a leader they call Timmy Jim."

"Them black bastards."

"Yeah," Al agreed. "So far they been pretty quiet. But if they start movin' all together, and us white gangs're all split up, the way things are now—we're dead meat."

Everyone started muttering.

"So we gotta start workin' t'gether," Al said.

Dino shook his head. "How we know we can trust the other gangs?"

"How they know they can trust us?" Al shot back. "I'll tell ya how—we're gonna start out small. We're gonna let Ron start fixin' stuff for some of the other gangs. And th' Chelsea gang agreed t' let us use th' stuff in their warehouses. Ron can go there an' they'll let him take what he wants. No more raids on 'em. And they won't raid us."

"That don't smell right," someone else said. "Them Chelsea rats always been hittin' us. Ever since I was a kid."

Al said, "Well, we're gonna try and see if we can get along together. It's worth a try."

"It's a trap," Dino said. "You got suckered by some sweet talk."

Al walked straight up to Dino. He was shorter and skinnier than Dino, but it was Dino who backed a step away. "Lissen speedie," Al said, "you wanna fight so bad, go uptown and fight th' Muslims."

Dino's face went red. "Aww . . . don't get hopped up. I was only—"

"You was shootin' off yer mouth," Al said. "As usual. Only time you keep it closed is when it's fulla pills."

Dino said nothing. But his face went dark with hatred.

And that was that. Ron started fixing machinery for other gangs, working longer hours and sleeping even less than he had before. Most times the other gang members would come into Gramercy turf under a white flag of truce, carrying the equipment they wanted fixed. Soon, when they saw how well Ron worked, they began asking him to come to their turfs to fix equipment that was too big for them to carry.

Ron began to move around the area, going into different turfs. Al put only one restriction on him: He was not allowed to fix guns for any other gang. Wherever Ron went, he was always accompanied by at least one other gang member. A warrior. And, usually, by Davey as well. He fixed generators and freezers, heaters and stoves, truck engines and street lamps. Once he even repaired an old movie projector in an empty, crumbling theater for a gang that had films to show.

Each of the gangs was very much like the Gramercy Association. Teenaged guys and girls, a few smaller kids. Hardly any older people; no one over thirty. The City hadn't been closed, officially, long enough for the gang kids to get that old. Also, gang life wasn't conducive to old age. Everyone was poor, dirty, without education, without decent food, without medicines—it was like living in the Middle Ages. The constant raids had also helped to kill off many of the youngest and strongest warriors. But Al was working desperately to maintain the shaky truce that he had helped establish among the gangs.

One day Ron was walking back from an area called the East Village, after fixing a building's heater. He passed a dozen kids Davey's age playing on a littered, cracked sidewalk. They were running and laughing, making lots of noise, breathless happy grins on their dirty faces.

How can they be happy? Ron wondered. *In the middle of all this, how can they laugh?* Then he realized that the children didn't know any other world. *They're like kids everywhere. All they want is a chance to live.*

Then he saw that they were playing a war game, fighting a make-believe battle with sticks or fingers for guns. Feeling sick inside, Ron knew that none of those children would ever see thirty.

There were adults in the city, Ron discovered. Up in the market area, along Broadway above Times Square. You could buy food there, and clothes, and other things. This was the black market, with stalls set up on the sidewalks offering goods smuggled in from outside the Dome.

Walking along Broadway, under the sagging blank theater marquees, Ron passed long wooden counters heaped high with canned foods, clothes new and used, gadgets of all sorts, and even some jewelry. Behind the counters were adults, men mostly. Some of them were really old, Ron saw. As old as his father. He bought tools that he needed from some of these aging men. He saw that they all carried guns and had young assistants at their sides all the time; the assistants were also armed.

You needed money in the market. No bartering, no trading. Just cash. That's why the kids worked so hard for money during the summer. The only way to get food after the city was officially closed for the year was to buy it at the market, or steal it from another gang. No gang had enough money to buy all the food it needed, not when a tiny can of peas cost five dollars. Ron suddenly realized that somebody on the Outside was getting rich off the teenaged gangs.

They smuggle food into the City and make a fortune doing it, Ron told himself. *It's all carefully organized and smoothly operated. Everybody profits . . . except the kids.*

And the kids were almost always hungry. Ron knew that he was losing weight, getting as skinny and mean-looking as Dino or Al or any of the others. Even Sylvia was beginning to look gaunt, and she ate better than most. It wasn't yet winter, either.

Ron had heard stories about gang raids on the market area. Soldiers had suddenly appeared inside the Dome, killing mercilessly, burning whole sections of the City where the gangs lived. *Even the Army is part of the system.*

Ron saw Sylvia just about every day. She smiled at him, talked with him, let it show very clearly that she liked him. But Ron never touched her, never even let himself get within arm's reach of her. He wanted to hold her and love her again. Instead, he kept his distance.

When they talked, it was mostly about nondangerous topics. Like Davey.

"He's helping me a lot," Ron would say. "He'll be a good mechanic someday."

And she would reply, "You oughtta see his room. He's got it filled with stuff. Looks like th' junkyards down by th' river."

True to Al's word, the Chelsea gang let Ron roam through their warehouses and take anything he wanted. But when Ron couldn't find things he needed there, he had to go up to the market area and search for them. If he could find what he wanted, he had to pay cash for it.

Dino didn't like that at all. "He's spendin' money we need for food!" he complained.

Al snapped back, "We get th' money back from th' gang Ron buys the stuff for."

Dino shook his head and muttered something.

"We gotta work t'gether with the other gangs, an' stop fightin' among ourselves," Al repeated to the gang council. The kids sat on the gravel of the rooftop in the evening darkness. They didn't say much, and it was too dark to see their faces and figure out if they really agreed with Al or not.

Doggedly, Al went on trying to convince them. "Those Muslims uptown are *organized*. We gotta be jes' as strong as they are or they'll come down here and pick us off, one gang at a time."

"Bullshit," somebody said in the darkness. It sounded to Ron like Dino.

"That's the way we're gonna do things," Al said firmly, "as long as I'm runnin' this gang."

The meeting broke up soon after, and the guys started filing down the stairs to their rooms for the night. Ron went up to Al.

"Maybe I shouldn't buy things at the market. Maybe I should just tell the other gangs that if we can't find what we need in the warehouses—"

"No," Al said sharply. "Long as we're not really takin' money we need for food, why should we stop?"

"Well, Dino—"

"Dino can go suck his thumb."

Ron said, "He's going to make trouble for you."

"I know," Al answered quietly. With a shake of his head, he said, "Someday I'll hafta stop him. Before he stops me."

Then he walked past Ron and went to the stairs, leaving Ron standing there alone on the roof, wishing very much that he could be somewhere else, somewhere where he could see the stars and not be so close to death.

Al started letting Ron go to the market area alone, or with no one accompanying him except Davey. Dino protested, of course, and claimed that Ron would run away and hide. But Al overruled him.

Ron liked the market area. It was a connection with the world Outside, the safe, sane world of the Tracts and his parents and friends and the Exams and peace and plenty. *The world that supplies this black market and lets the kids stay in here and die,* he reminded himself.

The market area was busy and noisy, almost like the City during the summer tourist season, except that there were no cars or buses in the streets. And the people roaming the sidewalks were mostly kids, dressed in rags.

The adults who ran the sidewalk stands were dressed much better. Standing behind their makeshift wooden tables, heaped high with goods for sale, the adults looked well fed, even overweight. They were clean and healthy. Their eyes were clear and alert. They went home to Tracts outside the Dome every night and watched their own children growing fat and clean and healthy.

But there was one hardware merchant who seemed almost as raggedly dressed as the kids themselves. Ron got to know him fairly well, since he had the best collection of tools and machinery parts in the entire market area.

His name was Dewey, and he was an old man with a rough gray beard and a million tiny wrinkled lines around his eyes. His hair was gray too, almost white. But it was still thick and shaggy. His eyes were very light blue, and almost always looked sad. He was big and burly, with a thick, heavy body—strong not fat, powerful arms, and hands that were large and tough. Even though he seemed very old, Ron thought he could handle Dino or even Al without much trouble.

Just about every week Ron would go to the market. He'd push and worm his way through the yelling, arguing crowds of kids who clustered around the food counters and walk quickly down the side street where there weren't as many kids and everything was quieter. They sold clothes here, and tools. Finally, Ron would come to Dewey's hardware counter.

The old man was almost always perched on a rickety wooden stool, looking as if he were half-asleep. But when he saw Ron, he'd smile and talk for hours.

"Yep," he said, one afternoon, "I been watchin' you for just about two months now. Not many kids come around this end of the market. Too many of 'em working out how to kill one another, not enough of 'em caring about how to build things up."

Ron felt almost embarrassed, standing there in front of the wooden sidewalk counter. Dewey smiled back at him from the other side, leaning back dangerously on his stool.

"I . . . well, I'm really from Outside," Ron mumbled. "I got stuck here at the end of the summer."

The old man's shaggy eyebrows lifted a bit. "Oh? That so? Huh! You're not the first one to get caught in that net. Dyin' to get out, I suppose?"

Ron nodded. "Guess so."

"Wish I could help you," Dewey said. "I can't get out my—"

The rumble of a truck's engine stopped him in the middle of his words. Ron heard it, too. He turned to look down the street.

"Who's still got gas for trucks?" Ron wondered out loud.

"Muslims," Dewey said. His voice sounded funny. Not scared or even worried. Just grim.

An open-backed pickup truck nosed around the corner and drove slowly down the street toward them. Ron could see two black kids in the cab and another black standing in back with a rifle in his hands. Another truck followed the first one. And then another.

"Get back here," Dewey said.

Without even thinking of arguing, Ron went behind the counter.

"Inside." Dewey jerked a thumb toward the door of the building that his stand was in front of. "Get inside and don't come out 'til I tell you."

Ron glanced at the advancing trucks and then looked at the old man. His face was completely serious. Ron went to the doorway and pushed on the metal and glass door. It swung smoothly and Ron stepped into the shadows of the building. He found himself in a lobby, almost like the lobby of the hotel he had stayed in so many weeks earlier.

He looked back through the door and saw truck after truck rumbling past. Each was empty in back except for one black youth with a gun of some sort. Ron stopped counting after twenty trucks had gone by, but still more came.

Dewey stood behind his counter and watched them without moving. When the last truck had passed, he turned and pushed through the doorway to where Ron was standing.

"You said you're with the Gramercy gang?" Dewey asked.

"Yes."

"Well, you won't be getting back there today. Better stay with me tonight."

"If there's going to be trouble . . ."

Dewey shrugged. "The Muslims did this last year, just before summer season opened up. There was a lot of trouble then."

"Did what? What's going on?"

"The Muslims don't come into the market like you kids do. They come in force, like an invading army. They stay for a day or two, load up all their trucks with what they want, then they go back uptown. Last year they took over the whole market for a couple of days, and the white gangs went wild. They fought a big battle down on Thirty-eighth Street—"

"But why?"

Dewey made a sour face. "White and black don't mix. Don't ask me why, they just don't. These white kids just go crazy when they see the Muslims—crazy . . . Funny thing is, the Muslims treat us pretty fair here in the market. They pay fair prices for whatever they take. Of course, *they* decide what's fair, and if they think you're tryin' to cheat them . . ." Dewey shook his head.

"Then I'm stuck here for as long as they're around?" Ron asked.

Nodding, Dewey said, "It's best not to get in their way. There's bound to be trouble and you never know where it's going to start. You can stay with me tonight. I live right upstairs here."

Ron stayed in the cool shadows of the lobby all afternoon, watching the street outside.

The lobby had once been beautiful. But now its marble walls were cracked and stained. Sliding doors that had once opened onto gleaming sleek elevators now hung crookedly, halfway open. The elevator shafts were dark and empty.

Outside on the street, things were very quiet. Dewey sat on his stool for a long time, looking up the street, squinting in the slanting afternoon sunlight. Ron couldn't see what he was watching.

Then a patrol of black warriors came past and stopped at Dewey's counter. They were dressed no better than any of the white gang kids, but somehow they looked sharper, more *together*. Like they had an exact job to do, and they knew how to do it well.

Ron had never seen blacks close-up before. Not at home. No blacks lived in any of the housing Tracts he knew of. The only blacks he had ever seen had been soldiers on TV.

These kids looked serious and alert. But they weren't afraid to laugh. One of them cracked a joke that Ron couldn't hear, and it broke all of them up. Even Dewey was laughing. After watching them for a while, Ron wondered what all the fuss was about. These were ordinary guys, acting pretty much the way anybody would act. Except that each of them carried a rifle slung over his shoulder, and even Dewey seemed to fear something about them.

The long day finally ended. Ron was sitting on the steps at the end of the lobby when Dewey pushed the front door open and came in, wiping sweat from his face with a red and white kerchief.

"You'd best bunk in with me tonight. The Muslims might give you trouble if they found you in the streets."

Standing up, Ron asked, "Can I help you bring your stuff inside?"

Dewey glanced back at the counter outside, with its hardware and machinery parts scattered over it.

"No, we won't have to. Not today. That's one of the good things about the Muslims. Nobody steals when they're in the market. They themselves don't steal, and if they catch anybody else at it, they shoot him, quick and simple."

Ron let his breath out in a low whistle.

"Besides," Dewey said, "if we take the stuff in, they'll think I don't trust them. Might start a fuss." He clapped Ron's shoulder. "Come on, we've got some climbing to do."

"What floor do you live on?"

"Tenth."

Ron thought that they would simply have to climb ten flights of stairs. It wasn't that easy.

They went up the first two flights. The stairway was not lighted and there were no windows, so Ron followed Dewey as the old man trudged slowly up the steps. *He knows his way even in the dark,* Ron thought.

"Hold it now," Dewey said when they reached the foot of the third flight. "Stay close against the wall on your right. Halfway up this flight there's five broken steps. If you're not careful you'll fall through and break your back."

So they slinked against the wall. It felt rough and gritty. On the next flight they had to do the same thing, only this time they kept on the left side.

"Why don't you fix these stairs?" Ron asked. "I can do it for you if—"

Dewey laughed in the darkness. "After I worked so hard to set 'em up this way?"

"What?"

"Think I want visitors bustin' in on me while I'm asleep?" the old man said, still chuckling.

There were traps and barricades on every flight. At the eighth floor, Dewey pulled Ron into one of the rooms. By the last glimmerings of late-afternoon light filtering through a grimy window, Ron saw that there was a rope ladder hanging from a hole in the ceiling.

"It's monkey style from here on," Dewey said, as he grabbed the rope in one hand. "The stairs are out completely from here up to the tenth floor."

They went up the rope ladder. Dewey climbed heavily, slowly. Ron could hear him grunting and puffing. When they reached the top of the ladder, Dewey hauled it up, hand over hand, and coiled it on the floor.

"Here we are," he said.

The landing looked like a little fortress. There were two machine guns sitting on tripods, cases of ammunition and grenades, and a dozen automatic rifles stacked against the wall.

"Nobody gets up here unless I invite 'em," Dewey said proudly.

"Have you ever . . . had anybody . . ."

"Tried to break in on me? Sure. But not for a long while. The word gets around. All them other merchants, they all slink out of the Dome at night, like rats going back to their nests. But I stay here. I live here. All the time. And if you can't defend yourself, you'd best not try it."

Dewey's apartment was a staggering surprise. It was big, roomy, and beautiful. The lights went on as soon as they stepped into the living room, and Ron could hear the soft whine of a well-maintained generator running somewhere not too far away.

"It's like a palace!"

"Ought to be," Dewey said. "I've got the whole floor to myself. And I've spent twenty years fixing everything up just the way I like it."

There was a carpet on the floor; not as rich or as thick as those Ron had known back home, but it was clean and well kept. The living room was filled with real furniture—sofas and soft chairs. One whole wall was lined with bookshelves, and there wasn't an empty space to be seen.

"No TV," Ron muttered.

"Can't get TV broadcasts here inside the Dome," Dewey said, "except in the summer, when they pipe 'em in from Outside."

Dewey excused himself for a few minutes, leaving Ron alone to wander around the big living room. Looking at the books, the furniture, the big clean windows with real curtains on them, suddenly Ron felt his eyes filling with tears. It was like home! The home he would never see again. He had almost forgotten what it was like to be in a comfortable room with real chairs and a sofa.

Dewey came back into the living room, cleanly washed and wrapped in a gorgeous blue robe. "I have to wear my old clothes down on the street or the kids would start to get ideas about how rich I am," he explained. "But up here I can dress like a gentleman."

Ron just stood there, blinking away tears and feeling stupid.

An uncomfortable look crossed Dewey's face. "Go on in and take a bath while I fix dinner," he said gruffly.

For the first time in months, Ron sank into hot water and scrubbed himself clean. He never realized that ordinary soap could smell so good.

And Dewey's dinner was the best Ron had eaten since coming into the Dome. Even better than the restaurants. The old man drank wine with his dinner and had glass after glass of brandy afterward.

"My one vice," he said to Ron, holding his glass up crookedly over his head for a moment.

They went back into the living room and sat side by side on the big sofa. Dewey brought his glass and brandy bottle with him. He put the bottle on the table beside the sofa, next to him.

It was night outside now, but through the sweeping windows at the far end of the room, Ron could see little pinpoints of light here and there in the otherwise darkened city, like tiny stars in the unending blackness of space.

"See anything?" Dewey asked, squinting at the windows.

"Just a couple of lights," Ron said. "Don't you see them?"

Shaking his head, the old man answered, "No. I can't see very much anymore. I'm going blind."

"Blind?"

"Yup. In another year or so I'll be blind as a mole. I have to make sure I keep everything in here exactly in place, so I don't bump into things."

Ron didn't know what to say.

"The City," Dewey said, leaning back on the sofa. "She used to be ablaze with light! Outshone all the stars in the sky!" He was suddenly shouting. "Lights everywhere. The Great White Way. All gone . . . dead and gone."

There were tears in the old man's eyes.

"How did it happen?" Ron asked. "Were you here when they closed the City?"

"You never saw her the way she was, boy. You're too young. I was here. She was a beautiful city. Beautiful—but sick. Corrupt and dirty."

He took a huge swallow of brandy. "Damn city just got dirtier and sicker and sicker and dirtier. Every day was worse. People died from the poisons in the air. Nobody did their jobs, they just argued and went on strike and fought everybody else. City ran out of money, had to sell its soul to Albany and Washington. They put that stupid Dome up to make things better and it just made everything worse. Everybody was going crazy. You couldn't walk down the street without getting shot at."

He finished his glass and reached for the bottle. "Too many people crowded too close together. People started falling over in the streets, dead from pollution or mugging or just plain brain fever. The Mayor was busy running for President. The City Council was busy stuffing its pockets with money and arguing with the unions. The banks threw up their hands and said the city was a bad investment. Eight million bad investments. Then the Federal Health people came in and said the environment inside the Dome had sunk below the level needed to sustain human life. Inside of a year everybody would be dead.''

"Wow!" said Ron.

"You should have seen the rush! It was like a riot and an earthquake and a war, all at once. Went on for months. Families separated. Kids left behind. Banks closing their doors, and mobs breakin' 'em down, only to find their money'd been taken out long ago. People running every which way. When the dust finally cleared, the City was declared officially abandoned—empty, nobody here. So they sealed it off.''

"Then how did you get in? And the others?''

Dewey laughed. "We never left! I sat here and watched 'em boiling out of the City. I figured I had plenty of time. And anyway, the more of 'em left, the better for me. I'd have the whole City to myself. Pick up a few things the others had left behind.''

"Is that how—''

But the old man wasn't listening to Ron. "After a couple months, Manhattan got to be right livable, with everybody gone. I knew there was a few others like me; a couple thousand of us, at least. We never got out of the City, and as far as the Government was concerned, they wasn't going to come in looking for us. They had enough to do, handling the eight million or so who had come screaming out. So the Government wrote us off their records. Officially, I'm dead. You're talking to a dead man!''

"Not really,'' Ron said.

Dewey shrugged. "Somewhere Outside there's **a**

Government computer with my death certificate coded into its memory banks, signed and official and everything. Just like all the kids that got stuck inside here. Officially, none of us exist. No social security, no IRS identification number, nothing. We don't exist. None of us.''

But I've got an ID record, Ron insisted to himself. *They know I exist!*

''That was twenty years ago,'' Dewey said, his voice sinking to a dark muttering. ''Had a woman with me then. She was awful pretty. She died the first winter . . . got sick . . . couldn't find a doctor, no medicine . . .''

The old man slumped against the back of the sofa, eyes closed, head down against his chest, empty glass slipping from his thick fingers. Ron took the glass and placed it quietly on the table next to the nearly empty bottle.

''I'll help you to your bed,'' Ron said softly. He couldn't tell if Dewey was already asleep or not.

''Thanks, but I can make it by myself,'' the old man replied, without opening his eyes. ''Been getting myself to bed without help for twenty years now. Won't be able to do it much longer, though.'' Dewey's eyes snapped open and he stared at Ron fiercely. ''Tell you what. How'd you like to be my partner? I'm getting too old to keep alive all by myself. The eyes are getting real bad. You could live right here. We could fix a place upstairs for you, deck it out with furniture . . .''

Without even thinking about it, Ron said, ''But I've got to get back to my home. As soon as they open the gates next summer—''

Dewey put a hand on Ron's shoulder. ''Son, they're never going to let you out. You're not the first kid to get stuck in here. If you show up at a gate without your

ID, you'll go straight to the Tombs. If you're lucky, you'll end up in the Army. If you're lucky."

Ron shook his head stubbornly at the old man, but his mind whispered to him, *Forever. You're going to be stuck in here forever.* He turned and stared out the broad windows at the darkened City, where only a pitiful few glimmers of light broke the darkness. *Forever.*

Dewey showed Ron to a bedroom. The old man walked very straight and sure-footed, in spite of all he had drunk. Ron felt as if he were the one who was staggering.

"Good night, son," Dewey said, leaving Ron at the doorway to a small, clean, and well-lit bedroom.

Ron said, "If . . . if I come here to work with you— live with you—could I bring a girl with me?"

Dewey seemed to hold his breath for a moment or two. Then he let it out with a long sigh. "Some kinds of girls are nothing but trouble, you know."

"She's not like that."

"You sure?"

Nodding, Ron added, "She's got a brother, too. Six or seven years old. He's a good kid. Interested in machinery."

Dewey ran a hand through his shaggy white hair. "I ask for a partner and I get a family. Okay . . . I'm probably crazy, but—bring 'em along. We'll see how it works out."

"Thanks! Thanks an awful lot!"

"Good night. Get some sleep," Dewey said. He started to turn away, then he looked back at Ron. "You're really sure now?"

"About Sylvia?"

"About our partnership. You'll come back? You won't disappoint an old man?"

"I'll come back," Ron said firmly. "Don't worry."

* * *

Ron stayed with Dewey all the next day. Toward evening, the Muslims' trucks started to pull out of the market area. They were loaded with food and supplies. A smudge of smoke rose toward the south, somewhere downtown of the market area, in the direction of the Gramercy turf.

"Trouble," said Dewey. "One of the white gangs must have had a run-in with the Muslims."

The trouble never reached the market area, and the day ended quietly. Dewey insisted that Ron stay with him another night. Ron easily agreed. The old man's food was too good to miss. And sleeping on a real bed again was like being in heaven.

The following morning Ron started for the Gramercy turf. He passed the burned-out section. Buildings were black with smoke. Windows, doors, roofs all gone so that the daylight sifted through the still-smoldering insides of the buildings.

White warriors were patrolling the streets here and there. Either they knew Ron from his earlier trips to the market through their turf, or they didn't care who he was long as his skin was white.

Turning a corner, Ron saw a handful of kids sitting quietly on the front steps of an old brownstone house. One of them had the stump of a broken knife tucked in his belt. He couldn't have been older than Davey. The children were watching the unmoving body of a boy, about twelve years old, that lay under a swarm of flies in the gutter. The corpse lay face up, chest crumpled and brown with dried blood. His eyes were open and his mouth was twisted as if he had been screaming when he died.

Ron felt his teeth clench. *The local gang ought to clean up after themselves better than that,* he grumbled silently. *Those kids are scared half to death.* Then he thought of his own retching reaction to the first corpse he had seen, back in the truck on that first raid into Chelsea turf. It seemed like a thousand years ago. Ron realized he had changed, hardened. He wasn't certain he liked it.

The Gramercy area looked deserted when Ron got there. There was no damage, no sign that fighting had come this far downtown. But there was no one on the streets, either. Everything looked dead and emptier than usual. As he climbed the steps inside their home building, Ron wondered where everyone had gone. There was no one in the halls. No kids playing. Nobody around anywhere.

He took the stairs three at a time and didn't stop until he was pounding on Sylvia's door. She opened it and went wide-eyed when she recognized him.

"Oh, Ron!" She threw her arms around his neck. "We thought they killed you!"

He kissed her, long and warm and hard, forgetting about Al and Dewey and everything else except her.

Finally she pulled away from him. "Al's called a war meetin'," Sylvia said. "All th' gangs're doin' it. Th' Muslims made a lotta trouble yesterday an' all th' gangs're tryin' to figger out what t' do."

"The hell with them," Ron said. "We're getting out of here."

"Whatcha mean?"

"You and me and Davey. We're getting out. Right now, while they're all busy making war talk. We're going to live in the market, live like real human beings. Get Davey and let's go."

"You're crazy," Sylvia said, backing away from him. "You can't just quit th' gang."

"Yes we can. And we're going to do it right now. Where's Davey?"

But Sylvia was shaking her head. "No, Ron, it won't work. You can't quit a gang. They'll come after you and kill you. They'll find you, wherever you go. Nobody's allowed t' quit."

Ron stood in the doorway, feeling his face twisting into a frown. "Listen. Nobody owns me. Or you."

"Al went to bat for you," Sylvia said, talking more slowly now, trying to explain. "He letcha into th' gang when he coulda left you out on the street t' die. Right? He hadda go against Dino t' bring you into th' gang. If you buzz off on him now, it'll make things rough for Al. Catch?"

Ron muttered, "I don't owe him—"

"He saved your *life*, Ron!"

Ron slapped a hand against his leg. "Does that mean that he owns me? And you?"

She shrugged. "It means you can't quit th' gang. Unless he says it's okay."

"And you? If he lets me go, will you come with me?"

"Al won't lemme go." She looked away from Ron.

He reached out and touched Sylvia's shoulder. "But if he was willing to let you go, would you come with me?"

She wouldn't look at him. She stared down at the floor.

Ron lifted her chin with his outstretched hand until she was gazing right at him. "Would you?" he asked.

In a voice so low that he could barely hear it, Sylvia said, "Yes."

Ron smiled at her. "Okay. I guess I'd better get to that war meeting, then."

"Don't do anything that'll hurt Al in front of Dino," Sylvia called to him as he started for the steps.

The roof was packed with guys, warriors and others that Ron had never seen before. As Ron edged through the door to join the crowd, he could hear Dino shouting: "Them Muslims been gettin' too smart for their own damned good! It's time we taught 'em a lesson!"

"Yeah!"

"Right on!"

"Hell yeah!"

Then one of the guys standing next to Run suddenly called out, "Hey look who's here! The fix-it dude!"

Everyone turned toward Ron. Through the sea of faces Ron could see Al up at the head of the crowd. He was almost smiling, as if he was really glad to see Ron.

"Hey, Ron, we thought you was killed."

Ron wormed his way up to the front of the crowd. "No, I'm all right. I stayed . . ." *Don't tell them who you stayed with!* Ron warned himself. "Uh . . . I stayed in the market area, hid out until the Muslims left. I hear there was trouble."

"I hear there was trouble," Dino sing-songed, trying to make Ron's words sound funny. "Humpin' *right* there was trouble. And there's gonna be more. Right?"

"Right!" answered half a dozen guys.

"Cool it," Al snapped. "Ron, we thought the Muslims killed you. But since they didn't, maybe we don't have any real reason for fightin' against 'em."

"No reason!" Dino shouted. "Them black bastards gonna take over th' whole humpin' city if we don't stop 'em!"

Al made a sour face. "We ain't gonna stop 'em by runnin' crazy. Dontcha think they're ready for us right now? Waitin' for us?"

"Half th' gangs between here and th' market are ready t' fight," Dino argued. "We gonna jus' sit here?"

"Be smarter if we wait 'til *all* th' gangs between here and th' market are ready to march t'gether," Al said. "An' all th' midtown gangs, too."

"No!" Dino yelled. "I say we fight 'em now. An'

if yer too chicken t' fight, then I'll take th' gang with me!''

Al stayed unruffled. But his eyes blazed. ''Dino, you got such hot rocks t' fight th' Muslims, go fight 'em. But the Gramercy gang don't declare war on nobody without a vote.''

Dino stood there looking like a volcano about to blow its top. His face was getting redder and redder.

Al said, ''You wanna take a vote?''

''No!'' Dino snarled. ''I don't need no vote. I'm goin' with whoever starts after the Muslims. An' there's plenny guys here who'll go with me. Right?''

This time only a few voices answered, ''Right.''

''Go on then,'' Al said calmly. ''Anytime you wanna. An' you can come back anytime, too. But th' Gramercy gang ain't declarin' war on nobody. Not today.''

Dino stamped off, pushing through the crowd. He kicked the door open and disappeared down the stairs. The meeting started to break up. Guys began drifting toward the door in groups of two or three, talking among themselves.

Ron waited until everybody else had left the roof, and he was alone with Al.

Al's tired face almost smiled at him. ''I'm glad yer okay. We got plenty worried when you didn't show up an' we heard th' Muslims had taken over th' market. You see Sylvia? She was pretty shook up about you.''

Nodding, Ron said, ''I saw her.''

''Okay.''

For a moment, Ron didn't know what to say or do. There was something in Al's eyes, those old-man's eyes set into his young face, something that Ron couldn't fathom.

Finally he blurted, ''Al, I want to leave the gang.''

''Leave? Whaddaya mean?''

Ron told him about Dewey. ''I'd still work for you,

for the gang. I'd fix anything you want, anytime you want. For free.''

But Al was frowning. ''Can't letcha go. Too much stirrin' right now. Gangs ain't supposed t' let guys quit. It's a bad thing. 'Specially right now, with this Dino crap an' th' Muslims an' all.'' He shook his head. ''The answer's gotta be no.''

Ron asked, ''Suppose I stay a member of the gang, but just live in the market area, with this old guy. How would that be?''

''I dunno,'' Al said slowly. ''I gotta think about it . . . later, after all this trouble settles down.''

With a shrug, Ron said, ''Okay. Later.'' *Don't even mention Sylvia to him. Don't even think about it!*

Ron started for the door that led downstairs. Al called to him, ''Hey, don't take off on yer own, now, unnerstand? I'd just hafta send a coupla guys t' drag ya back. Don't make me do that.''

Ron nodded. ''I won't.''

Al studied him for a long, silent moment. ''I'm sorry it's gotta be this way.''

''So am I,'' Ron said.

That night Ron's sleep was filled with dreams. He dreamed of Dewey, of Al, of the dark somber Muslims walking through the streets of the market area with their rifles slung over their shoulders. He dreamed of Sylvia. Mostly of her.

He dreamed that she was crying. Then Davey started screaming.

Ron's eyes snapped open. It wasn't a dream. Davey *was* screaming!

It was still dark. Davey screamed again, a high, thin screech of pain and terror.

Ron leaped from his mattress, pulled on his pants as

he ran, and raced downstairs to Sylvia's room. The door was open, the lights were on.

Sylvia was kneeling beside her mattress with a torn sheet wrapped around her. She was crying and holding Davey in her arms. The boy had stopped screaming, but he was crying now too, with quick, panic-filled gulping sobs. Sylvia rocked back and forth with Davey's curly black hair nestled against her breast.

Ron knelt beside her. Her lip was split and bleeding. There was an ugly bruise on her throat.

Then he saw Davey. The boy's face had four straight red welts across one check—finger marks. One eye was swollen. He was trembling, shaking with terror, whimpering.

"Dino," said Sylvia. Her voice was strained, slurred. "He wanted me t' go with him. He's quittin' th' gang. Started slappin' me around when I wouldn't go with him . . . Davey tried t' protect me an' he beat up on Davey. Kicked him . . ."

Ron found that he was shaking now. He turned and found Al coming in. There were more people out in the hallway.

Barely able to control himself, Ron got to his feet and went to the door. He pushed through the growing crowd in the hallway and raced upstairs. On his worktable was an automatic pistol. In fifteen seconds he had clicked all its parts together, worked the action twice to make sure it was ready to fire, and then started back downstairs.

Ammunition was in a storeroom on the second floor. His hands steady now, his insides white-hot, Ron turned on the storeroom light and found a box of cartridges for the pistol. When he finished loading the automatic, he jammed the rest of the ammo into his pants pockets. Then he turned toward the door.

Al was standing there watching him.

"Where you goin'?" Al asked.

"Where do you think?" Ron snapped. He was surprised at how calm his voice sounded. Flat. Deadly.

Al shook his head. "No, you ain't. Sylvia an' th' kid ain't dead. They'll be okay."

"I'm going to kill that sonofa—"

"Dino'll kill you before you even know where he is," Al said. "Dontcha think he's waitin' for ya right now? He knows you'll be out after him, an' he's waitin'. With a big grin on his stupid face."

Ron stood there, smoldering like a hot ember.

"Put the ammo back," Al said, "an' put th' gun away. Dino's left an' he won't be back. That's the end of it."

"But my ID card . . ."

"That's the end of it," Al repeated, his voice stronger.

Not for me, Ron told himself. *It's not the end of it for me.* But he turned back and did what Al commanded.

It was more than a week before Al let Ron go to the market again. And when he did, he ordered two warriors to go with Ron.

"Jes' in case you meet up with Dino," Al said, "or there's more trouble with th' Muslims."

Or I try to run away, Ron added silently.

At the market, Ron told Dewey what had happened. All of it. The old man listened patiently as he sat on his stool behind the counter full of hardware. Once in a while he nodded or scratched his beard.

"So maybe I can get away later on," Ron said at last, "but not now."

Dewey's eyes looked sadder than usual. "I should've figured that the gang wouldn't let you go. Especially with all this trouble with the Muslims."

"More trouble?"

Nodding, Dewey answered, "Some of the midtown gangs tried a few raids on Muslim turf. Wouldn't be surprised if this Dino fella wasn't in on it."

"What happened?"

"Don't know, exactly. Except that a lot of kids came through here yesterday. Most of 'em were hurt pretty bad. Looked like the Muslims chewed 'em up fierce."

Ron shook his head. "I'll get free of the gang," he said, his voice low. "I promise."

"Don't take any chances you don't have to take," Dewey said. "I can wait. I waited a long time to find a boy like you, son. I can wait a few months longer."

Feeling sad and embarrassed, Ron covered up his emotions with, "Well . . . don't worry. I can take care of myself."

"Sure," said Dewey. "I know."

"I'll see you."

"So long, son. Good luck."

Life settled into a tense routine. It was getting to be winter now, and even though the Dome protected the city from the fiercest winds and bitterest cold, it got too chilly to walk the streets without a coat. The buildings that the kids lived in were heated only when they had enough fuel oil to run the furnaces. Otherwise they made wood fires at night out of furniture, doors, anything they could find that would burn. The smoke hung in the air inside the Dome, making Ron's eyes sting and his lungs burn from coughing.

Slowly, the other gangs stopped asking for Ron to repair things for them. They even stopped bringing in small repair jobs for him.

"They're runnin' low on food an' money," Al said. "Got nothin' left t' trade with."

Ron saw all the work he had done for the Gramercy

kids become meaningless. The lights, the stoves, the electrical machinery he had fixed—all were useless now. Even the generator down in the basement, which warriors had died for, was now cold and silent, without fuel. It couldn't snow inside the Dome, of course, but the winter cold seeped in, bringing at first discomfort, then pain, and finally sickness.

The bruises that Dino had put on Sylvia and Davey slowly faded away. But Davey stopped going out on the streets to play with the other boys his own age. He developed a hoarse, dry cough that got deeper and more racking every day. The child stayed close to Ron almost all the time, and even slept with him many nights, under as big a pile of blankets as they could find. Still, Davey coughed and Ron always awoke shivering.

There was no news about Dino. At the market area, there were plenty of stories about raids around the border of the Muslim turf. Sometimes it was white gangs hitting the Muslims, sometimes the Muslims raiding the whites. The fighting was bitter. Many were killed and wounded.

The shaky truce that Al had engineered among the white gangs was beginning to crumble. Kids who were cold and hungry were no longer willing to live in peace if they thought they could get the food or fuel they needed by force. There was no fighting in the Gramercy area though. Ron concluded that the other gangs respected Al too much for them to attack his gang.

Then the night exploded.

Ron was asleep when the first blast lifted him off his mattress. He bounced on the floor, completely awake and totally scared. More blasts! People shouting, cursing, screaming.

Ron's mind began to work. *It's a raid!*

Scrambling to his feet, he dashed out of the room and downstairs. A thin, oily-smelling smoke drifted up the stairwell. Guys were dashing all around down on the first floor. Ron stopped at the second floor landing. More warriors were bunched up in the doorway to the ammo room. Al was in there, shouting orders.

Ron heard glass break downstairs and then a sheet of flame *whooshed* up from the first floor. Screams of agony came up the stairs with the blistering heat and glaring white flames.

"Up on th' roof!" Al shouted. "Quick!"

They all boiled upstairs, heading for the roof. Ron still heard shouts down below as warriors pounded past him on the stairs. There was shouting out on the street. Flames were licking up the stairs now, as Ron stood frozen watching them. He heard the shouts of excited, victory-crazed guys mixed with the shrieks of those who were burning to death.

Ron could feel the heat singeing his face, curling the hair on his hands and arms. All at once he turned and ran upstairs. Not for the roof. For Sylvia's room. He pushed her door open. The rest of the guys kept on swarming toward the roof.

By the flickering light of the flames he could see her sitting huddled in the farthest corner of the room, covering Davey with her arms.

"Shh . . . shhh . . . don't cry. Davey, please don't cry."

The boy was rigid with fright. His eyes were squeezed shut and he clung to Sylvia so hard that Ron knew he must be hurting her.

"Sylvia!" he called.

She looked up. "Oh, Ron, what're we gonna do?"

"Come on. They're all going up to the roof."

He helped Sylvia to her feet. "Give Davey to me," he said.

She shook her head. "Naw, I'll hold him."

Ron stroked Davey's hair as they headed for the doorway. "It's okay, Davey. It's me, Ron. We'll be okay. Don't be scared."

The fire was roaring two flights below them and licking up the stairwell. Ron could feel its searing heat on his back as they started up the steps. They passed his own floor and were heading up the last flight of stairs that led to the roof when the shooting started again.

This time the shots came from the roof. The screaming and swearing was almost as loud as the gunfire. Ron heard heavy machine guns blasting the night air. *They were waiting up on the roof for us! It's a trap!*

The door burst open and two warriors staggered down the steps, bleeding, limping, hands empty and eyes glazed with pain and shock. Then a girl stumbled through the doorway, covered with blood. She collapsed and tumbled halfway down the stairs. Sylvia buried her face in Davey's dark hair. Two warriors pushed past Ron and headed down the steps in panic.

"My room, quick!" Ron whispered to Sylvia. Numbly, she followed him. The fire was only one floor below them now. The stairway and landing were lit by its hungry red glow. More shots rang out from the roof.

The only window in Ron's room opened onto an air shaft. There was a chance that they could get down to the bottom of it and sneak into the next building, then hide there until the battle was over.

In the flickering shadows, Ron slashed blankets and mattress coverings and knotted them together with shaking fingers into one long rope. Looping one end around Sylvia's shoulders, he lowered her and Davey out the window and to the bottom of the air shaft.

The fire was licking at his doorway, evil and hungry. The smoke was making him cough, blurring his vision. Ron tied his end of the makeshift rope to an ancient steam radiator that hadn't worked for twenty years. He hoped it wouldn't fall apart under his weight. Then, coughing and teary-eyed, he crawled out the window and edged down the side of the building.

He almost made it all the way before the rope broke. He landed hard, but on his feet, then sank to all fours. Looking up, he saw flames spurt from his own window.

He turned and saw Sylvia kneeling a few feet away from him, still clutching Davey close to her. Without a word he grabbed her and led them across the grimy, garbage-slick shaftway to the next building. Ron kicked in a window and stepped through into a pitch-dark room. He helped Sylvia and Davey through.

They groped in the flame-lit dimness away from the fire. For the first time, Ron realized that the monstrous blaze was roaring; the sound had just not penetrated his consciousness until that moment. Over its hideous roar, he could hear more shots and screams.

They made their way down to the basement and hid behind an old, broken-down furnace. Things scuttled across the floor in the darkness. Ron wasn't worried about roaches or mice, particularly. He saw the red glowing eyes of big rats, though, and knew that he wouldn't be able to sleep.

Not that he could have, anyway. From outside he could hear more shots, then nothing for a long time except the gradually diminishing roar of the fire. Then came a huge crashing groan that Ron guessed was their building caving in from the gutting flames. He heard shouting and laughing.

In the darkness, Ron couldn't see Sylvia's face or Davey's. But he heard the boy whimpering, a high-pitched thin crying sound of pure terror. Sylvia kept whispering, ''Shhh . . . shhh'' and tried to hold Davey close to her, so that his voice would be muffled. But Ron could still hear it.

As morning came, Ron saw that there were windows

in the basement, set high up in the walls. He went to one of them and carefully peeked outside, standing on tiptoe.

The street outside was covered with bodies. Warriors mostly, but there were several girls among them. Some of them were blackened with burns. Others were torn by bullets. All of them were dead.

A group of warriors was slowly coming down the street, rifles in their hands. Ron recognized one of them as a member of the Chelsea gang, a kid who had stayed with him whenever he went through the Chelsea warehouses. Striding down the street beside him, grinning happily, was Dino.

Ron's insides suddenly felt as if someone had lit a fire in him. He gripped the edge of the basement window ledge so hard that his fingernails bit into the dust-caked cement.

If only I had a gun . . . Then Ron thought of Sylvia and Davey, still huddled behind the furnace. There was nothing he could do. Nothing but watch.

The Chelsea warriors stopped at one of the bodies. It was lying face-down on the sidewalk. Dino nudged the body with the toe of his boot. *My boot!* Ron thought furiously.

Dino pushed the body over onto its back. It was Al. Ron sagged against the gritty basement wall.

"That's him," he heard Dino say. "Good."

Sick with anger and sadness, Ron made his way back to the furnace. Sylvia was sitting against its sooty black metal side, half-asleep. Davey was still in her arms, his eyes still squeezed shut, still whimpering.

Sylvia opened her eyes as Ron sat on the floor beside her. She looked completely exhausted.

"It was the Chelsea gang," Ron said quietly. "Dino's with them."

She didn't move, didn't say anything.

"They got Al. He's dead."

Sylvia looked at him. "Yer sure?"

"I saw his body."

She nodded. Nothing else. No tears, no words. Only a nod.

They sat there for a long, long time. Ron didn't know what to do. The only sound was Davey's muffled crying.

Slowly Ron realized that the boy was saying a word, one single word over and over again:

"Mommy . . . Mommy . . . Mommy."

Ron stared at the boy, then at Sylvia. She was rocking Davey now, bending her head low over his and whispering into his ear: "It's all right, Davey . . . it's all right . . . I'm here, honey . . . Mommy's here . . ."

"You're . . . you're his mother?" Ron's voice went high with shock.

She looked up at him. "Didn't you know? Al was his father."

And now there were tears in her eyes.

The day was cold. Hiding down in the unheated basement, huddling in the dust and dirt, Ron could feel the cold seeping into his bones. Sylvia was dozing. Davey was asleep at last, still in her lap, clinging to her.

Ron went to the window a dozen times an hour. The bodies were still there. The day looked gray and felt damp, as if snow were coming. Of course, inside the Dome no snow ever fell. But it *felt* like a snowy winter day.

Davey woke up late in the afternoon.

"I'm hungry," he whined.

"Shh," Sylvia said. "We gotta wait a while before we can eat."

Ron said to her, "I'll take a look around outside. Maybe I can find something."

"No!" She looked alarmed. "They'll be prowlin' around out there. Wait 'til dark."

Ron waited. It got colder and darker. Sitting there on the cement basement floor, Ron found himself shaking from the cold. They didn't even have coats. Davey had started coughing again. Ron got up and paced around the cluttered basement floor.

"It's dark enough," he whispered to Sylvia at last. "I'm going out."

He might as well have saved his energy.

The gang's main building was completely gutted by the fire. The food supplies, guns, ammo, clothing—all gone. What hadn't burned had been carried away by the victorious Chelsea warriors. Even the dead bodies had been stripped of anything useful or valuable.

There were no people around. None living, that is. The dead bodies littered the streets. And there were the rats. Ron nearly stepped on one before he realized what it was. In the dark, he heard a chittering sound, the *skritch-skritch* of clawed feet scurrying across cement pavement. And he saw the tiny, gleaming, wicked eyes.

A chill raced through him. All thought of food vanished. The previous night, the fire had kept both humans and rats terrified and cowering. Now the rats were out to claim their usual, ultimate victory over the humans. Ron raced back to the basement where he had left Sylvia and Davey. In the darkness, he tripped over a body and sprawled face down on the sidewalk. Something furry brushed against his hand.

Ron nearly screamed. He *did* scream, in his mind. But he managed to keep it silent.

He got to the basement and found them both asleep, untouched.

"Come on, we're going upstairs," Ron said as he shook Sylvia awake.

"Wh . . . whassa matter?"

"Rats."

He could feel the shudder go through her. Silently, they climbed to the top floor of the building and slept on the floor of a bare little room.

But Ron slept very little, only in snatches of a few minutes each. By the time morning started lighting the streets outside, he was wide awake and aching with cold. And he was *hungry*.

Davey was coughing again. And crying.

"Ron, he feels hot. Like he's burnin' up!" Sylvia said.

The child's face was red. Fever.

"He needs food," Sylvia said, her voice close to cracking.

"And medicine," Ron added.

Davey's eyes were still closed, but he was moaning softly, "It hurts . . . hurts . . ."

Dewey! Dewey will know what to do. He'll have food. And medicine, too, maybe.

"I've got to get to the market," Ron told her. "I can get food there, and whatever else we need."

"Th' market? You'll never make it that far."

"Yes I will. I've got to."

She reached for his arm. "Ron, don't! You'll get caught. If th' Chelsea gang don't getcha, some other gang will. They all know Al's dead by now. They won't give a damn what they do to you!"

He pulled free of her. "I can't sit here and let us starve. Davey needs food and medicine. No way to get them except at the market."

"Ron, wait—"

"I'll be back," he said. "Don't worry about me."

He was out the door before she could say anything else.

It took three days. Ron had to travel slowly, avoiding everybody and anybody on the streets. Most of the day he inched along, a block at a time, sometimes just a building at a time. Ducking into a doorway, he'd look carefully out onto the street and wait until no one was in sight. Then he'd sprint as far as he dared and duck into another doorway, praying that nobody saw him.

Twice he was spotted. Once he simply outran a pack of little kids. He ran until his lungs were aflame and his vision blurred. He raced down one block, cut around a corner, through an alleyway, up a fire-escape ladder, and down the other side of the building. When he collapsed, chest heaving painfully, the kids were nowhere in sight.

Just as night was falling he was surprised by three warriors from a gang he didn't know. Ron stepped into a shadowy doorway and the three of them were already in there. They were just as surprised as he was.

They were smoking something and didn't expect to be disturbed. For a flash of a second the three of them froze, wide-eyed, scared. Before they could recover, Ron took off, running wildly again. After a few minutes he looked back over his shoulder. No one was following.

He got to Dewey's place late that night. He nearly forgot about the traps that the old man had set up along the stairs. But he remembered them just in time.

Finally he stood under the hole in the ceiling where the rope ladder had been and yelled out, "Dewey, it's me, Ron. It's Ron! Wake up. Hurry. Please hurry!"

A powerful light suddenly blinded him. He put his hands up over his head to shield himself. The light was blazing bright; Ron could feel its heat.

"You alone?" he heard Dewey's voice ask.

"Yes."

The rope ladder tumbled down and dangled in front of Ron. In a few minutes he was standing in Dewey's living room, trying to tell the old man everything at once.

"Slow down, slow down," Dewey said. "I can't hardly understand you."

Ron took a deep breath and tried to speak more slowly. He told Dewey about Dino, about the raid, the killings, Sylvia and Davey, their need for food and medicine.

Dewey nodded grimly. "Okay. I get the picture."

Then the old man quickly moved through the apartment, pulling a worn old hiking pack from a closet, stuffing it with cans and plastic packages of food, a canteen of water, and cartons of powdered milk. From another closet he took a small metal box marked with a red cross.

"There's penicillin and bug-killers in this kit," he told Ron. "Hope they can do the job, 'cause there's nothing else we can do for him here inside the Dome."

Ron nodded gratefully.

As Ron started to slide his arms through the pack's shoulder harness, Dewey said, "You know you ought to eat something, and get some sleep. You're not goin' to get back for another day anyway, and you look mighty worn out."

Shaking his head, Ron answered, "I can't. That kid might be dying."

Dewey nodded. "I know . . . well, good luck, son."

The old man stuffed handfuls of dried food into Ron's ragged pockets and helped him down to the street. Ron waved to him from the corner, turned, and headed back downtown. He munched on a dried piece of fruit as he started out.

It took the rest of that night and all the following day for Ron to get just halfway back to the Gramercy area. He had to be especially careful now because the pack he carried contained valuable property. If anyone saw him, they would kill him just for the chance to look inside the pack. And with the pack weighing him down, Ron couldn't run or fight as well as before.

So he had to go slowly, very slowly, through the dirty, nearly empty streets. Whenever he saw someone or heard anything at all, he hid in an alley or doorway or basement. Most of the day he had to stay hidden. Twice he dozed off while he crouched in basements. Each time he snapped awake, feeling angry at himself and ashamed for being so weak.

He made better time after dark. Still, it was nearly dawn on the third day when he got back to the building where he'd left Sylvia and Davey.

But they weren't in the upstairs room where he had left them.

Ron put his pack down on the floor. His shoulders and arms creaked in relief as he got rid of the weight. The room was empty. In the gray light of early morning, Ron searched the whole floor for them. They weren't in any of the rooms.

She must have gone to look for food, Ron told himself. *Maybe Davey's feeling better and they both went to look for food.*

But he didn't really believe that.

Ron searched every floor of the building, starting at the top and working down, floor by floor, until he reached the basement. Nothing.

He climbed wearily back up the stairs to the main hallway on the street level.

"Hello dude."

Dino and four Chelsea warriors were standing in the hallway waiting for him. Somehow, Ron wasn't surprised. He almost expected it.

"Lookin' for somebody?" Dino was smiling. A nasty, yellow-toothed smile.

"Where are they?" Ron asked flatly.

Dino laughed. "Where d'ya think? Sylvia came lookin' fer me yesterday. Th' kid was sick an' they both was starvin'. So now she's my girl."

"I'll bet she's thrilled by that."

"You betcha."

Ron jerked a thumb toward the staircase. "I've got medicine for Davey. He—"

"He won't need it. He's dead."

"What?" Ron felt the breath catch in his throat.

With a sour face, Dino said, "Damn' little brat coughed his guts out all night. Died jes' about an hour ago. One less mouth t' feed."

Without even thinking about what he was doing, Ron growled like an animal and leaped at Dino. He got a glimpse of Dino's face, suddenly scared-looking, and felt the solid shock of their bodies smashing together and hitting the floor. They rolled and thrashed around, and then Ron was on top of Dino, pounding him with both fists.

"Murderer! Butcher!" Ron screamed. Dino's mouth and nose were filled with blood. "Killer! Filthy goddamned killer!"

The other guys pulled Ron off Dino. He fought back, hitting, kicking, screaming at all of them like a cornered wild beast until they clubbed him to his knees and kicked him unconscious.

Ron came to slowly.

His head throbbed painfully. His body ached and felt stiff. He found that he was lying on the cold floor of a completely dark room. He couldn't see anything at all. No window, no light. Only darkness.

He sat up, taking it easy, trying to see if anything was broken.

Not so bad, he said to himself. It hurt, but not as

much as the first time Dino and his pals had worked him over.

He thought about that time for a moment. It was almost as though the past few months hadn't really happened. Here he was again, stiff and sore from a beating by the same guys. Everything that had happened was like a dream. A bad dream. Al and Davey were dead. As if they had never lived. Nothing but memories now.

Sylvia. Ron frowned, then winced as a cut on his cheek pulled open. *Sylvia. She never gave a damn about me at all.* He almost laughed, but it hurt too much. *Did she really love Al? Or did she do everything just to make sure Davey would get fed and protected? Maybe she went to Dino just to get help for Davey. Sure, that's why she did it. I was gone for three days. She must have thought I wouldn't come back. Maybe she thought I was dead. Dino would be the only one who could help her—and Davey.*

But Ron heard his own voice whisper to him, "Then why is she staying with Dino now? Davey's dead. She doesn't need Dino's help."

He sat there, seeing her face in the darkness, hearing her voice, feeling her touch. He tried to hate her. "You never cared for me at all," he said to her.

Then he thought of Dino, and he *did* hate. Dino had led the raid by the Chelsea gang. He knew all the strong points of the Gramercy headquarters. He knew Al's defenses. Dino had planned the raid. He had triggered the trap. He had killed Al. And Davey too.

Dino was going to kill Ron now. Ron knew it. But he knew one thing more. He knew that he would kill Dino first. He didn't know how he'd do it; he only knew he was going to kill Dino. He snarled like an animal, sitting there in his blackened cage. A few months in the City and Ron had turned into a hating, bloodthirsty animal, eager to kill.

Footsteps outside.

Ron scrambled to his feet, ignoring the pain and stiffness in his body. He had to feel along the walls to find the door, it was that dark in his cell.

From the outside he heard a muffled, "Hey, what—" And then scuffling sounds. A thud. A moan. Finally, the rattling of a key in the door's lock.

Ron flattened himself against the wall, next to the door. *When they come in here, I'll jump them.*

But they didn't come in. The door opened outward and somebody flashed a light into the cell. Ron was blinded.

"Hey you! C'mon out, quick! B'fore somebody sees us." It was an urgent whisper.

Ron staggered out of the cell, rubbing his eyes. Squinting in the light from a bare bulb in the ceiling, he found that he was in a hallway. Two guys were standing next to him: strangers. A third guy, one of Dino's pals, was lying face-down on the floor, out cold.

"C'mon, dummy. Move! We're tryin' t' getcha outta here," one of the strangers whispered harshly.

Puzzled, Ron went with them. They led him down the hallway, into a tiny bathroom. They crawled through a window into an alley. Then they sprinted, all three together—Ron and the two strangers—down street after street, staying in the deepest shadows.

After a few blocks, Ron saw a car parked at a corner. The driver must have spotted them at the same moment, because the engine coughed to life.

"Okay, here it is," one of the guys said, panting for breath, as they came up to the car. The rear door swung open and the two guys more-or-less pushed Ron inside.

"Okay," said the driver in a deep, rumbling voice. He handed something to the two guys, who were still standing on the sidewalk beside the car. It looked like a plastic package of white powder.

"This better be the good stuff," one of the guys muttered.

The driver laughed. "It's real, baby. We don't cheat."

He put the car in gear and turned on the headlights. They slid slowly away from the curb and headed up the street, making as little noise as possible. In the faint glow reflected by the dashboard lights, Ron saw that the driver was black.

"What's going on?" Ron asked. "Where are you taking me?"

The driver didn't answer.

They drove in silence for nearly a half-hour, slowly, like a one-car parade. *Or funeral,* Ron thought grimly. They passed the market area heading north. Ron thought he spied the pinpoint of light that was Dewey's home, high up in one of the buildings. As they went through Central Park, Ron saw packs of dogs racing beside the car, barking furiously. He had heard stories about the dogs in the Park. When the City had been officially closed down, many people had turned their pets loose. Thousands of dogs made it to Central Park where they quickly went feral. Now the Park was their own private jungle, and people who wandered in there never came out.

As they left the Central Park area, still moving uptown, Ron saw that there was a glow in the street far ahead of them. The car seemed to be heading for the light. Soon Ron could see that there were lights—real street lights—ablaze along the streets. And people were walking along on the sidewalks. Shops were open, here and there. And every person he saw was black.

At last the car pulled up in front of a building that must have once been a church. The driver got out of the car and opened Ron's door.

"C'mon, whitey—shake it."

Ron slid out and stood on the sidewalk.

"Up this way," the driver said.

In the light of the street lamps, Ron could see that there were no people walking along this part of the sidewalk. A small crowd stood across the street, gawking at him. He shrugged and followed the driver. Ron noticed that the driver wore a sort of uniform of tight black slacks and black leather vest. Even his boots were black and highly shined. Ron felt shabby in his tattered old polyester suit and sandals. At least his clothes were black, also. Or they had once been. Now they were grimy and faded gray.

Inside the church they went. But it was no longer used as a church. The interior was long and narrow, with a high, sharply pointed ceiling and heavy old wood beams holding it together. Down on the wooden floor, benches and pews were gone. There were only a few folding chairs scattered around.

Up where the altar had once stood, there was a big carved wooden chair. Empty. Off to one side of it was a cluster of desks all pushed together. Four black guys sat there, their backs to Ron and his burly escort. They were talking to each other.

The driver nudged him, and Ron walked down the length of the church and up the three broad steps that led to the desks. Then he stood there, silently, waiting, while the blacks at the desks kept up their hushed conversation. Ron was just starting to wonder how long they'd keep him waiting, when one of the guys at the desks turned and noticed him.

"They got him," he said simply.

The others turned and looked at Ron. It was hard for Ron to tell what they were thinking. Three of the four were openly frowning. The fourth stood up and grinned.

He walked down the steps slowly toward Ron. He was tall, but very lean, spindly. His face was thin and bony. His eyes had a funny shape, almost oriental. His smile was wide, toothy. He looked friendly enough. He wore a simple outfit—vest, slacks, sandals—all sky-blue.

"They call me Timmy Jim," he said in a mild, slightly scratchy voice. "That ain't my real name, but it's what everybody calls me."

Ron blinked at the leader of the Muslims for a moment. "I'm Ron Morgan."

"I know. Know all about you. You got a good friend down in th' market—that ol' man Dewey. He got word to me you was in trouble. Tol' me I could use you. Says you're a freak with machines."

"I fix machines," Ron said.

Timmy Jim's grin got even bigger. "Okay. Great. You can fix 'em for the Muslims. More'n that, you teach some of my kids how to fix 'em."

Ron felt confused. "I didn't know the Muslims took in white people."

The grin vanished. "The Muslims do what I say. We ain't takin' you in as a member. We're gonna let you work here, *boy*. We're savin' your ass—but only because that ol' man down in the market claims you can help us. If you ain't as good as he says you are, you're goin' right back where we got you. 'Stand?"

Ron heard himself say, "In other words, I'm a slave."

Timmy Jim's mouth dropped open. Then he broke into a wild, high-pitched cackling laugh. "Yeah, baby, that's just what you are!" He laughed and laughed. The others all laughed, too.

Ron stood there, feeling their scorn bite into him. Then he thought about what Dino was going to do to him. *I don't really have a choice*, he realized.

It wasn't too bad. Most of the blacks treated him fairly. But they made it clear that he was white in a world where only black can be beautiful. The Muslims had many different shades of black, though. Some of them were the tannish brown of Latin Americans. Some were so deeply black that their skin shone with an African heat. Most were some shade between those two extremes. A few even looked like Indians.

There were more old people among the Muslims, although Ron saw little of them. Like Timmy Jim, most of the Muslim warriors were Ron's own age, or slightly older. The mechanics that Ron worked with were all in their early teens. Some of them resented taking orders from a white, but they did what Ron told them to with skill and speed.

Timmy Jim quickly set Ron up in the afternoons with even younger kids, whom he was expected to teach. They were fun. Young and eager and burning to learn about machinery. They learned fast. Ron soon had them fixing refrigerators and furnaces and even automobiles.

Once or twice some of the black warriors who always stayed near Ron gave him trouble. One guy clubbed Ron with a pistol butt once, for some reason that Ron never found out about. Two other warriors pulled him away, and Ron never saw that one again.

Timmy Jim himself was hard to figure out. Whenever Ron saw him, he seemed to be different. Sometimes he was quiet and friendly. Other times he seemed hard and mean. He could smile at Ron, talk pleasantly with him. Or he might call Ron "whitey," or "paleface," or "nigger's slave."

Slowly Ron began to understand. Timmy Jim was tough with him whenever there were other blacks watching. When they were alone, he was almost friendly.

As the weeks went by, Timmy Jim called Ron up to his private office more and more. It was in the building next to the old church. The office was bare, like a field general's tent. No decorations on the walls, except for a street map of Manhattan. No furniture, except a desk and its chair, plus a stiff wooden chair for a visitor.

"So tell me more about what it's like Outside," Timmy Jim would say.

Ron couldn't determine why he wanted to hear so much about the world outside the Dome. But he told Timmy Jim all about it, time after time.

"Wish you were back there, huh?" Timmy Jim asked Ron once.

"I guess so." Ron was surprised that he didn't feel more strongly about it. His parents, his friends, his whole life was Outside. But that was so long ago, so far away. It felt strange even to think about it. As if that life belong to somebody else, some other kid, not Ron himself.

The winter passed slowly. Ron lived in a single small room in a building that had once been a school. In fact, it was a school once again, because the Muslims used its large downstairs rooms for Ron's "classes" in mechanical repair. At least once a week, Timmy Jim had Ron up to his office to talk about the world Outside. The rest of the time Ron spent teaching the kids how to fix machines, or how to build new machines. He hardly did any fixing on his own now.

Ron taught, he worked, he ate, he slept. Outside of the kids he was teaching, and Timmy Jim, the only other people he knew were the young warriors who never let him far out of their sight and a few of the girls who brought him his two meals each day. He had struck up a conversational acquaintance with one of the girls, an olive-skinned Puerto Rican named Liana.

But Ron's only real amusement was his weekly visit with Timmy Jim. The Muslim leader was relaxed and happy when Ron saw him; they shared sandwiches and drinks each visit. Gradually, as the weeks turned into months, Ron began to see that Timmy Jim was always asking questions about the weapons that the police Outside carried, what the roads were like, how electric cars operated, how many police each Tract had, where the Army bases were located.

Then one afternoon, as Ron sat in that stiff-backed chair in front of Timmy Jim's desk and talked about the turbo-train system, it all clicked into place.

"You're going to invade the Outside!"

Timmy Jim laughed. "Been wonderin' how long it'd take you to tumble to it."

"But that's crazy! You can't—"

"Sure I can't. Not now. Got to take over all th' gangs under the Dome first. That'll take a few more years. We start next fall, soon's the gates closed down after the summer season. Then we hit the gangs between here'n the market. Gonna be tough making white gangs see things our way, but in four to five years we'll have every gang under the Dome workin' together—all under one leader. Me."

Ron felt staggered. "And then?"

"Then Outside. That's where all the real loot is . . . that's where we're goin'."

"My God."

Timmy Jim leaned forward in his chair and pointed at Ron. "See . . . the only way I can keep all the black gangs together is t' make 'em dream of takin' over the whole City. The only way I'll be able to make *all* the gangs work together without killin' each other is to turn 'em loose on the Outside."

"But it'll never work," Ron answered. "There's hundreds of millions of people out there."

"Just more loot, that's all."

"And the police . . ."

"We can handle 'em."

"The Army . . ."

Timmy Jim smiled. "Yeah. The Army. You wanna know somethin'? Half the spades in the Army are Muslims. We planted 'em. You just watch your Army when we go Outside. Just watch what they do."

Ron sat there, open-mouthed. Timmy Jim laughed.

It took weeks for the idea to sink in. Ron thought about it every day: *Conquer the Outside. He's crazy!* But still the idea scared him.

The weather grew warmer. A new batch of kids was given to Ron for training. The youngsters he had started with left the area, and he never saw them again. *Where did Timmy Jim send them?* he wondered. *And why?*

There were reports of battles, skirmishes along the borders of Muslim territory. One whole white gang was wiped out when Timmy Jim decided to attack it in real force. The border fighting stopped after that.

And then, on a warm day in late spring, Sylvia showed up.

Ron was working. He had a large classroom filled with kids aged ten to fifteen. Big windows let the daylight in. The glass had been smashed out of them long ago. There were about forty kids, all bent over little electric motors or transistor radios that the Muslims had dug up for Ron to use in class. The kids worked quietly, while Ron fidgeted up at the front of the room. It was warm, springtime, the time of year when school should be ending and you could go outdoors for baseball and picnics and . . .

A pair of armed guards appeared at the classroom door. *Trouble,* thought Ron.

He went out to the door and stepped into the hallway. Sylvia was there.

He felt his heart stop for a moment. She looked older, very tired. Her blouse and shorts were grimy and wrinkled, her face smudged with dirt. But she was still beautiful.

Ron wanted to reach out and take her in his arms and hold her forever. Instead he did nothing.

"Hello Ron."

It took him two tries to find his voice. "Hello."

"I . . . I wanted t' see you," she said slowly, softly. "They let me come here, but only for a coupla minutes. They're gonna take me right back again."

"Back to where?"

"Gramercy turf. Frankie's puttin' th' gang back t'gether again. We got about twenny kids . . . there'll be more . . ."

"What's Dino doing?"

"He's dead."

"Dead?"

She nodded. "Chelsea guys did it. He got inna fight with their chief. I tried t' do it myself a coupla times, but I couldn't work up th' nerve." Her eyes looked haunted, tortured. "He got what he deserved."

Ron put a hand on her shoulder, but there was nothing he could say.

"They treatin' you okay here?" Sylvia asked.

"Yes. And you—are all right? Is there anything I can—"

"I'm okay." She tried to smile. "Don' worry about me. I can take care o' myself."

"Yeah."

"Well . . . I gotta go back now. I jes' wanted t' see ya and letcha know Dino's dead. If they ever letcha get back t' Gramercy . . . an' . . . well, I'm sorry about everything. If it wasn't fer me, you'd be Outside now, back home . . . I'm sorry, Ron."

"It wasn't your fault. It's all right."

"Oh . . . here." She fumbled in the pocket of her

shorts. "Here's some stuff Dino took off ya, that first time."

Ron took the things from her hand. A house key. A credit card. His ID card.

My ID card! He glanced up sharply at Sylvia. She knew! She knew she had just handed him the key to freedom. Ron looked over at the two warriors. They were loafing against the wall, talking to each other.

"Good luck, Ron," Sylvia said. "And thanks."

"No, wait!" he whispered fiercely. "Hold on. We can both get out. When the gates open . . ."

She shook her head, smiling sadly. "Ron . . . no way. We'd never make it t'gether. You're what you are an' I'm what I am. There's no way fer us t' make it t'gether."

"But . . ."

She kissed him lightly on the lips, then turned and started to walk away, down the hall. The two black warriors followed after her. Ron stood rooted to the spot, holding the key and cards in his outstretched hand.

"Sylvia!" he called. But she didn't turn around. She just kept walking.

For more than a week, Ron's mind was a turmoil. *How can I get away, with them watching me all the time? And how can I leave Sylvia here?* That was the real question. No matter how hard he thought about it, he knew that she was right. There was no way to bring her Outside.

Could he get himself Outside?

The springtime passed slowly. The weather warmed. The summer began and the gates opened to let the visitors in for the vacation season.

"The tourists never come up here," Timmy Jim said, "The hardtops make sure of that."

And Timmy Jim made sure that Ron didn't get out

of Muslim territory. He always felt the eyes of warriors on him. Even at night.

But finally Ron made a break for freedom. He waited until very late one night, several weeks after the summer season had started. His sleeping quarters had been moved to an old hotel building, where there were warriors sleeping in all the rooms around him. More guards were on duty all night down in the hotel lobby.

Ron had studied the building very carefully. He didn't go down the stairs to the lobby. He forced open the doors to one of the old elevator shafts.

For a moment he stood at the edge of the open doorway, staring into the darkness of the shaft. There was emptiness waiting for him, and a five-story drop to the bottom. Ron took a deep breath, then leaped out into the dark emptiness, reaching for the steel cable that hung in the middle of the shaft, hoping he could grab it, praying that it would hold his weight.

It was slimy with grease. Ron felt his breath puff out of him as his body slammed into the cable. His hands slid and scraped, but held. The cable's creaking, as his body swayed on it, seemed loud enough to wake everybody in the building.

For a moment Ron hung there. But only for a moment. Slowly, painfully, he started to climb up the cable. It was difficult. The cable was slippery. Finally, though, he had climbed the six flights to the equipment shed on the roof.

Wonder why they never asked me to fix the elevators? Ron asked himself as he stepped out of the shed and onto the roof.

He crossed one roof after another until he was at the end of the block. Then he went downstairs inside the building, knowing that it was empty and unguarded. He made it to the street and started walking.

Dawn was already starting to brighten the new day

when Ron stopped on the sidewalk next to the last row of buildings before the huge girders of the Dome. Across the wide avenue ahead of him, the massive steel girders reared and arched so far overhead that they were lost in haze. And on the other side of the Dome— freedom? *No,* Ron realized. *Not freedom. Just another kind of world, with its own kind of slavery.*

Still, Ron started walking along that avenue, following the curving flank of the Dome, looking for the nearest gate. As he walked block after block, it began to get brighter with daylight. The streets were still empty, though.

Off to his left, just a few blocks away was Central Park. Ron kept a careful eye out for stray dogs. He had heard from the Muslims that the dog packs sent out scouts, and a single dog's bark could bring out a snarling horde in no time.

By mid-morning, he saw a bus growling along one of the crosstown streets several blocks up ahead of him. He walked faster. Soon he saw well-dressed people strolling on the streets, staring up at the buildings and the overspanning Dome. Tourists! A gate must be nearby.

As he walked among the strolling visitors, they stared at his filthy clothes and ragged looks and skirted clear of him. Ron laughed and clutched the credit card in his pocket. He went to the first hotel he could find. Using his credit card on the automated registration desk, he obtained a room and ordered new clothes. He bathed for an hour, feeling the beautiful hot water and clean-smelling soap take away his dirt and pain. And his fear.

For the first time in nearly a year, Ron wasn't afraid.

But as he dressed, he began to worry about Sylvia. And Dewey. Maybe she was right, and there was no place Outside for her. But what about the old man? *I can't leave him here to go blind, all by himself.* Yet, if he tried to take Dewey through a gate with him, Ron knew that the guards would send the ID-less old man to the Tombs.

He dressed slowly, lost in his thoughts, pulling on a disposable green zipsuit almost exactly like the one he had worn when he'd first come to the City. He was pushing his feet into the new boots when his hotel room door swung open and Timmy Jim walked in.

The fear flashed through Ron again. He stood there on the soft carpeting, fresh and clean, dressed in a crisp new suit. But he felt the way he had felt all year long, as if anything could happen to him any minute. He was alone. Unprotected.

Two black warriors stood out in the hall, grimfaced. Timmy Jim shut the door quietly.

"Where do you think you're goin'?" he asked.

"Outside. I'm getting out."

"You think so."

"Now look," Ron said, "you can't start trouble in here. The police . . ."

Timmy Jim smiled, but there was no humor in it. "The hardtops been paid off. I can take this hotel apart, brick by brick, if I want to. I can take this whole friggin' *City* apart, any time I want to!"

Ron sank down on the bed. "Okay, so you're top man. But there's one thing you can't do."

"Name it."

"You can't make me go back with you. I'm finished. I'm going Outside . . . or you'll have to kill me. One or the other."

Timmy Jim blinked at him. "You're bluffin'."

"No, I'm not."

"You think you're gonna go Outside and warn 'em that we're comin' out . . . that we're gonna take over?"

Ron shrugged.

Laughing, Timmy Jim said, "Man, they won't believe word number one! They'll think you're spaced out!''

''Then you've got nothing to worry about.''

''I saved your ass, man,'' Timmy Jim snapped. ''You owe me your *life*. You ain't gonna get outta that.''

Ron answered, ''I trained nearly a hundred kids for you. They know as much as I do. Let them train others. You got your money's worth out of me.''

The smile crept back across Timmy Jim's bony face. ''Tired of bein' a slave, huh?''

Ron nodded.

''Can't say I blame you.'' Timmy Jim walked over to the window and pushed the curtain aside to look down at the street for a few moments. Then, turning to Ron, he said, ''Lemme tell you somethin'. When they shut down New York City . . . when they officially called it closed and evacuated everybody . . . they didn't let us out.''

Ron looked up at him. ''Us?''

''The blacks,'' Timmy Jim said. ''The Puerto Ricans. The poor people in the ghettos in Harlem and the upper West Side and all. They didn't let any of 'em out.''

''The City was evacuated, emptied,'' Ron said. ''The only people who stayed were like Dewey, people who hid out until they declared the City officially closed.''

''Bullshit. Oh, they took out the whites, all right. Rich and poor. Irish and Italian and WASP and all. They got out okay. But they kept *us* inside. When we tried to get out, they beat us back with clubs, electric prods, water cannon, lasers—they didn't let us out, man! They closed this City and wrote it off as a dead loss and claimed all of us were dead.''

''No, that can't be . . .''

''It sure as hell was,'' Timmy Jim said, his fists clenched at his sides. ''That was *why* they closed the

City down, man. The real reason! Wrote off all the welfare cases. Officially they no longer exist. One touch of the computer's tape and *poof!* all the records erased.''

Ron couldn't believe it. ''They left you here?''

''They left us here, baby. Left us to starve, to freeze, to be rat bait. They left us to fight with each other and kill ourselves off.''

''Holy God.''

''God's got nothin' to do with it,'' Timmy Jim answered. ''Anyway, don't you know He's black?'' He smiled ruefully.

''It this really true? They closed the City to get rid of you?'' Ron asked.

Timmy Jim nodded. ''That's why the Muslims took charge. We had to get some organization. Had to figure out how to *live*, man. There was some people Outside who was willing to give us a little help. Smugglin' in food, stuff like that. But it was nowhere near enough. No way. Not even the black market was enough. But we managed. We survived.''

''And now . . .''

''And now, instead of fightin' each other, all the Muslim brothers are united. We fight the white gangs. That keeps us together. In a few more years, *all* the gangs will be together.''

''United by your plan to invade the Outside.''

''That's right.''

''And you're afraid I'm going to warn them, out there,'' Ron said.

''Go warn 'em,'' Timmy Jim said, standing in front of Ron. ''Go tell 'em everything I just told you. They won't believe you. They won't lissen to you. Not 'til it's too late.''

''I can go?'' Ron asked.

''Yeah . . . go. Go. I set you free, whitey. Just like Lincoln. Go on Outside and tell 'em all about us. Won't do you any good. They won't believe you. Not 'til they see us comin'. And we *will* be comin'. That's a promise."

Timmy Jim walked past Ron to the door, opened it, and left. Ron sat there on the edge of the bed, unmoving.

"Not to warn them, Jim," he said to the empty room. "To *change* them. I'm going back Outside to change them. They know the City exists. They know the kids are in here, in this jungle, turning into animals. They know it, but they ignore it. So I'm going to change them. I'm going to rub their noses in the filth they've left behind them, just as my face has been rubbed in it for the past year. I'm going to make them listen, make them realize. I'll break all the patterns. I'll change everything and everybody. I'll break their Career vectors and their curfews and their endless Tracts. Even if I have to make myself President, I'll make them change. They can't let the cities fester like this. They can't do this to *people!* It's like a cancer. We've got to cure it or it will kill us all."

Finally understanding what he had to do, Ron strode out of the hotel and down to the gate. He pushed through the swarms of people flocking into the City for a vacation good-time. In his mind's eye he saw Dewey, saw Sylvia, and little Davey and Al. Even Dino. And Timmy Jim, dark and powerful, ready to change the world *his* way.

At the gate, the white-helmeted police guard looked at Ron strangely as he showed his ID. Ron knew that he was thinner than the photo on the card. There were lines in his face that had never been there before. Finally the hardtop handed the ID back to him.

"You're leaving? But the fun's just getting started."

"Yes," Ron said. "I know."

Vince's Dragon

INTRODUCTION

No matter how serious the problem under considera-
tion, it is always amenable to humor. Sometimes laughter can accomplish more than moralizing. In 1729, for
example, Jonathan Swift's "A Modest Proposal" applied the scalpel of satire to the heartbreaking despair
racking Ireland at that time.

Modern (and future) crime is a serious matter. But
we don't have to take it completely seriously all the
time. "Vince's Dragon" is unserious in two ways. First,
it is a fantasy, which by nature is a form of literature
that disdains to deal with the real world, and therefore
need not be considered to be very serious. (If you doubt
that, read a few fantasies back-to-back. Be they horror,
sword-and-sorcery, or the latest spate of female warriors, if you can get through more than three in a row,
you have a much higher tolerance for nonsense than I
do.)

Second, the characters in this story are deliberately

drawn to show the absurd side of the underworld. Let's face it: Most of the guys I knew in South Philadelphia who ended up in the Mafia were not the best and brightest lights of the community. They were driven by ruthless greed and an utter disregard for the rights of others. They could be fearsome, and they often were. But they were unconsciously funny a lot of the time, too.

The thing that worried Vince about the dragon, of course, was that he was scared that it was out to capture his soul.

Vince was a typical young Family man. He had dropped out of South Philadelphia High School to start his career with the Family. He boosted cars, pilfered suits from local stores, even spent grueling and terrifying hours learning how to drive a big trailer rig so he could help out on hijackings.

But they wouldn't let him in on the big stuff.

"You can run numbers for me kid," said Louie Bananas, the one-armed policy king of South Philly.

"I wanna do somethin' big," Vince said, with ill-disguised impatience. "I wanna make somethin' outta myself."

Louie shook his bald, bullet-shaped head. "I dunno, kid. You don't look like you got th' guts."

"Try me! Lemme in on th' sharks."

So Louie let Vince follow Big Balls Falcone, the loan sharks' enforcer, for one day. After watching Big Balls systematically break a guy's fingers, one by one, because he was ten days late with his payment, Vince agreed that loan-sharking was not the business for him.

Armed robbery? Vince had never held a gun, much less fired one. Besides, armed robbery was for the heads and zanies, the stupids and desperate ones. *Organized* crime didn't go in for armed robbery. There was no need to. And a guy could get hurt.

After months of wheedling and groveling around Louie Bananas' favorite restaurant, Vince finally got the break he wanted.

"Okay, kid, okay," Louie said one evening as Vince stood in a corner of the restaurant watching him devour linguine with clams (white sauce). "I got an openin' for you. Come here."

Vince could scarcely believe his ears.

"What is it, *Padrone*? What? I'll do anything!"

Burping politely into his checkered napkin, Louie leaned back in his chair and grabbed a handful of Vince's curly dark hair, pulling Vince's ear close to his mouth.

Vince, who had an unfortunate allergy to garlic, fought hard to suppress a sneeze as he listened to Louie whisper, "You know that ol' B&O warehouse down aroun' Front an' Washington?"

"Yeah." Vince nodded as vigorously as he could, considering his hair was still in Louie's iron grip.

"Torch it."

"Burn it down?" Vince squeaked.

"Not so loud, *chidrool*!"

"Burn it down?" Vince whispered.

"Yeah."

"But that's arson."

Louie laughed. "It's a growth industry nowadays. Good opportunity for a kid who ain't afraid t' play with fire."

Vince sneezed.

It wasn't so much of a trick to burn down the rickety old warehouse, Vince knew. The place was ripe for the torch. But to burn it down without getting caught, that was different.

The Fire Department and Police and, worst of all, the insurance companies all had special arson squads who would be sniffing over the charred remains of the warehouse even before the smoke had cleared.

Vince didn't know anything at all about arson. But, desperate for his big chance, he was willing to learn.

He tried to get in touch with Johnnie the Torch, the leading local expert. But Johnnie was too busy to see him, and besides Johnnie worked for a rival Family, 'way up in Manayunk. Two other guys that Vince knew, who had something of a reputation in the field, had mysteriously disappeared within the past two nights.

Vince didn't think the library would have any books on the subject that would help him. Besides, he didn't read too good.

So, feeling very shaky about the whole business, very late the next night he drove a stolen station wagon filled with jerry cans of gasoline and big drums of industrial paint thinner out to Front Street.

He pushed his way through the loosely-nailed boards that covered the old warehouse's main entrance, feeling little and scared in the darkness. The warehouse was empty and dusty, but as far as the insurance company knew, Louie's fruit and vegetable firm had stocked the place up to the ceiling just a week ago.

Vince felt his hands shaking. *If I don't do a good job, Louie'll send Big Balls Falcone after me.*

Then he heard a snuffling sound.

He froze, trying to make himself invisible in the shadows.

Somebody was breathing. And it wasn't Vince.

Kee-rist, they didn't tell me there was a night watchman here!

"I am not a night watchman."

Vince nearly jumped out of his jockey shorts.

"And I'm not a policeman, either, so relax."

"Who . . ." His voice cracked. He swallowed and said again, deeper, "Who are you?"

"I am trying to get some sleep, but this place is getting to be a regular Stonehenge. People coming and going all the time!"

A bum, Vince thought. *A bum who's using this warehouse to flop . . .*

"And I am not a bum!" the voice said sternly.

"I didn't say you was!" Vince answered. Then he shuddered, because he realized he had only thought it.

A glow appeared, across the vast darkness of the empty warehouse. Vince stared at it, then realized it was an eye. A single glowing, baleful eye with a slit of a pupil, just like a cat's. But this eye was the size of a bowling ball!

"Wh . . . wha . . ."

Another eye opened beside it. In the light from their twin smolderings, Vince could just make out a scaley head with a huge jaw full of fangs.

He did what any man would do. He fainted.

When he opened his eyes he wanted to faint again. In the eerie moonlight that was now filtering through the old warehouse's broken windowpanes, he saw a dragon standing over him.

It had a long, sinuous body covered with glittering green and bluish scales, four big paws with talons on them the size of lumberjacks' saws. Its tail coiled around and around, the end twitching slightly all the way over on the other side of the warehouse.

And right over him, grinning down toothily at him, was this huge fanged head with the giant glowing cat's eyes.

"You're cute," the dragon said.

"Huh?"

"Not at all like those other bozoes Louie sent over

here the past couple of nights. They were older. Fat, blubbery men.''

"Other guys . . . ?''

The dragon flicked a forked tongue out between its glistening white fangs. "Do you think you're the first arsonist Louie's sent here? I mean, they've been clumping around here for the past several nights.''

Still flat on his back, Vince asked, "Wh . . . wh . . . what happened to them?''

The dragon hunkered down on its belly and seemed, incredibly, to *smile* at him. "Oh, don't worry about them. They won't bother us.'' The tongue flicked out again and brushed Vince's face. "Yes, you are *cute*!''

Little by little, Vince's scant supply of courage returned to him. He kept speaking with the dragon, still not believing this was really happening, and slowly got up to a sitting position.

"I can read your mind,'' the dragon was saying. "So you might as well forget about trying to run away.''

"I . . . uh, I'm supposed to torch this place,'' Vince confessed.

"I know,'' said the dragon. Somehow, it sounded like a female dragon.

"Yes, you're right,'' she admitted. "I am a female dragon. As a matter of fact, all the dragons that you humans have ever had trouble with have been females.''

"You mean like St. George?'' Vince blurted.

"That pansy! Him and his silly armor. Aunt Ssrishha could have broiled him alive inside that pressure cooker he was wearing. As it was, she got to laughing so hard at him that her flame went out.''

"And he killed her.''

"He did not!'' She sounded really incensed, and a little wisp of smoke trickled out of her left nostril. "Aunt Ssrishha just made herself invisible and flew away. She was laughing so hard she got the hiccups.''

"But the legend . . ."

"A human legend. More like a human public-relations story. Kill a dragon! The human who can kill a dragon hasn't been born yet!"

"Hey, don't get sore. I didn't do nuthin."

"No. Of course not." Her voice softened. "You're cute, Vince."

His mind was racing. Either he was crazy or he was talking with a real, fire-breathing dragon.

"Uh . . . what's your name?"

"Ssrzzha," she said. "I'm from the Polish branch of the dragon family."

"Shh . . . Zz . . ." Vince tried to pronounce.

"You may call me 'Sizzle,' " the dragon said, grandly.

"Sizzle. Hey, that's a cute name."

"I knew you'd like it."

If I'm crazy, they'll come and wake me up sooner or later, Vince thought, and decided to at least keep the conversation going.

"You say all the dragons my people have ever fought were broads . . . I mean, females?"

"That's right, Vince. So you can see how silly it is, all those human lies about our eating young virgins."

"Uh, yeah. I guess so."

"And the bigger lies they tell about slaying dragons. Utter falsehoods."

"Really?"

"Have you ever seen a stuffed dragon in a museum? Or dragon bones? Or a dragon's head mounted on a wall?"

"Well . . . I don't go to museums much."

"Whereas *I* could show you some very fascinating exhibits in certain caves, if you want to see bones and heads and . . ."

"Ah, no, thanks. I don't think I really wanna see that," Vince said hurriedly.

"No, you probably wouldn't."

"Where's all the male dragons? They must be *really* big."

Sizzle huffed haughtily and a double set of smoke rings wafted past Vince's ear.

"The males of our species are tiny! Hardly bigger than you are. They all live out on some islands in the Indian Ocean. We have to fly there every hundred years or so for mating, or else our race would die out."

"Every hundred years! You only get laid once a century?"

"Sex is not much fun for us, I'm afraid. Not as much as it is for you, but then you're descended from monkeys, of course. Disgusting little things. Always chattering and making messes."

"Uh, look . . . Sizzle. This's been fun an' it was great meetin' you an' all, but it's gettin' late and I gotta go now, and besides . . ."

"But aren't you forgetting why you came here?"

Truth to tell, Vince had forgotten. But now he recalled, "I'm supposed t' torch this warehouse."

"That's right. And from what I can see bubbling inside your cute little head, if you don't burn this place down tonight, Louie's going to be very upset with you."

"Yeah, well, that's my problem, right? I mean, you wanna stay here an' get back t' sleep, right? I don't wanna bother you like them other guys did, ya know? I mean, like, I can come back when you go off to th' Indian Ocean or somethin' . . ."

"Don't be silly, Vince," Sizzle said, lifting herself ponderously to her four paws. "I can sleep anywhere. And I'm not due for another mating for several decades, thank the gods. As for those other fellows . . . well, they annoyed me. But you're cute!"

Vince slowly got to his feet, surprised that his quaking knees held him upright. But Sizzle coiled her long, glittering body around him, and with a grin that looked like a forest made of sharp butcher knives, she said:

"I'm getting kind of tired of this old place, anyway. What do you say we belt it out?"

"Huh?"

"I can do a much better job of torching this firetrap than you can, Vince cutie," said Sizzle. "And *I* won't leave any telltale gasoline fumes behind me."

"But . . ."

"You'll be completely in the clear. Anytime the police come near, I can always make myself invisible."

"Invisible?"

"Sure. See?" And Sizzle disappeared.

"Hey, where are ya?"

"Right here, Vince." The dragon reappeared in all its glittering hugeness.

Vince stared, his mind churning underneath his curly dark hair.

Sizzle smiled at him. "What do you say, cutie? A life of crime together? You and I could do wonderful things together, Vince. I could get you to the top of the Family in no time."

A terrible thought oozed up to the surface of Vince's slowly-simmering mind. "Uh, wait a minute. This is like I seen on TV, ain't it? You help me, but you want me to sell my soul to you, right?"

"Your *soul*? What would I do with your soul?"

"You're workin' for th' devil, an' you gimme three wishes or somethin' but in return I gotta let you take my soul down t' hell when I die."

Sizzle shook her ponderous head and managed to look slightly affronted. "Vince—I admit that dragons and humans haven't been the best of friends over the millennia, but we do *not* work for the devil. I'm not even sure that he exists. I've never seen a devil, have you?''

"No, but . . ."

"And I'm not after your soul, silly boy."

"You don't want me t' sign nuthin?"

"Of course not."

"An' you'll help me torch this dump for free?"

"More than that, Vince. I'll help you climb right up to the top of the Family. We'll be partners in crime! It'll be the most fun I've had since Aunt Hsspss started the Chicago Fire.''

"Hey, I just wanna torch this one warehouse!"

"Yes, of course."

"No Chicago Fires or nuthin like that."

"I promise."

It took several minutes for Vince to finally make up his mind and say, "Okay, let's do it."

Sizzle cocked her head slightly to one side. "Shouldn't you get out of the warehouse first, Vince?"

"Huh? Oh yeah, sure."

"And maybe drive back to your house, or—better yet—over to that restaurant where your friends are."

"Whaddaya mean? We gotta torch this place first."

"I'll take care of that, Vince dearie. But wouldn't it look better if you had plenty of witnesses around to tell the police they were with you when the warehouse went up?"

"Yeah . . ." he said, feeling a little suspicious.

"All right, then," said Sizzle. "You just get your cute little body over to the restaurant and once you're safely there I'll light this place up like an Inquisition pyre."

"How'll you know . . . ?"

"When you get to the restaurant? I'm telepathic, Vince."

"But how'll I know . . ."

"When the claptrap gets belted out? Don't worry, you'll see the flames in the sky!" Sizzle sounded genuinely excited by the prospect.

Vince couldn't think of any other objections. Slowly, reluctantly, he headed for the warehouse door. He had to step over one of Sizzle's saber-long talons on the way.

At the doorway, he turned and asked plaintively, "You sure you ain't after my soul?"

Sizzle smiled at him. "I'm not after your soul, Vince. You can depend on that."

The warehouse fire was the most spectacular anyone had seen in a long time, and the police were totally stymied about its cause. They questioned Vince at length, especially since he had forgotten to get rid of the gasoline and paint thinner in the back of the stolen station wagon. But they couldn't pin a thing on him, not even car theft, once Louie had Big Balls Falcone explain the situation to the unhappy wagon's owner.

Vince's position in the Family started to rise. Spectacularly.

Arson became his specialty. Louie gave him tougher and tougher assignments and Vince would wander off a night later and the job would be done. Perfectly.

He met Sizzle regularly, sometimes in abandoned buildings, sometimes in empty lots. The dragon remained invisible then, of course, and the occasional passerby got the impression that a young, sharply-dressed man was standing in the middle of a weed-choked, bottle-strewn empty lot, talking to thin air.

More than once they could have heard him asking, "You really ain't interested in my soul?"

But only Vince could hear Sizzle's amused reply, "No, Vince. I have no use for souls, yours or anyone else's."

As the months went by, Vince's rapid rise to Family

stardom naturally attracted some antagonism from other young men attempting to get ahead in the organization. Antagonism sometimes led to animosity, threats, even attempts at violence.

But strangely, wonderously, anyone who got angry at Vince disappeared. Without a trace, except once when a single charred shoe of Fats Lombardi was found in the middle of Tasker Street, between Twelfth and Thirteenth.

Louie and the other elders of the Family nodded knowingly. Vince was not only ambitious and talented. He was smart. No bodies could be laid at his doorstep.

From arson, Vince branched into loan-sharking, which was still the heart of the Family's operation. But he didn't need Big Balls Falcone to terrify his customers into paying on time. Customers who didn't pay found their cars turned into smoking wrecks. Right before their eyes, an automobile parked at the curb would burst into flame.

"Gee, too bad," Vince would say. "Next time it might be your house," he'd hint darkly, seeming to wink at somebody who wasn't there. At least, somebody no one else could see. Somebody very tall, from the angle of his head when he winked.

The day came when Big Balls Falcone himself, understandably put out by the decline in his business, let it be known that he was coming after Vince. Big Balls disappeared in a cloud of smoke, literally.

The years rolled by. Vince became quite prosperous. He was no longer the skinny, scared kid he had been when he had first met Sizzle. Now he dressed conservatively, with a carefully-tailored vest buttoned neatly over his growing paunch, and lunched on steak and lobster tails with bankers and brokers.

Although he moved out of the old neighborhood row house into a palatial ranch-style single near Cherry Hill, over in Jersey, Vince still came back to the Epiphany Church every Sunday morning for Mass. He sponsored the church's Little League baseball team and donated a free Toyota every year for the church's annual raffle.

He looked upon these charities, he often told his colleagues, as a form of insurance. He would lift his eyes at such moments. Those around him thought he was looking toward heaven. But Vince was really searching for Sizzle, who was usually not far away.

"Really Vince," the dragon told him, chuckling, "you still don't trust me. After all these years. I don't want your soul. Honestly I don't."

Vince still attended church and poured money into charities.

Finally Louie himself, old and frail, bequeathed the Family fortunes to Vince and then died peacefully in his sleep, unassisted by members of his own or any other Family. Somewhat of a rarity in Family annals.

Vince was now *Capo* of the Family. He was not yet forty, sleek, hair still dark, heavier than he wanted to be, but in possession of his own personal tailor, his own barber, and more women than he had ever dreamed of having.

His ascension to *Capo* was challenged, of course, by some of Louie's other lieutenants. But after the first few of them disappeared without a trace, the others quickly made their peace with Vince.

He never married. But he enjoyed life to the full.

"You're getting awfully overweight, Vince," Sizzle warned him one night, as they strolled together along the dark and empty waterfront where they had first met. "Shouldn't you be worrying about the possibility of a heart attack?"

"Naw," said Vince. "I don't get heart attacks, I give 'em!" He laughed uproariously at his own joke.

"You're getting older, Vince. You're not as cute as you once were, you know."

"I don't hafta be *cute,* Sizzle. I got the power now. I can look and act any way I wanna act. Who's gonna get in my way?"

Sizzle nodded, a bit ruefully. But Vince paid no attention to her mood.

"I can do anything I want!" he shouted to the watching heavens. "I got th' power and the rest of those dummies are scared to death of me. Scared to death!" He laughed and laughed.

"But Vince," Sizzle said, "I helped you to get that power."

"Sure, sure. But I got it now, an' I don't really need your help anymore. I can get anybody in th' Family to do whatever I want!"

Dragons don't cry, of course, but the expression on Sizzle's face would have melted the heart of anyone who saw it.

"Listen," Vince went on, in a slightly less bombastic tone, "I know you done a lot to help me, an' I ain't gonna forget that. You'll still be part of my organization, Sizzle old girl. Don't worry about that."

But the months spun along and lengthened into years, and Vince saw Sizzle less and less. He didn't need to. And secretly, down inside him, he was glad that he didn't have to.

I don't need her no more, and I never signed nuthin about givin' away my soul or nuthin. I'm free and clear!

Dragons, of course, are telepathic.

Vince's big mistake came when he noticed that a gorgeous young redhead he was interested in seemed to have eyes only for a certain slick-looking young punk. Vince though about the problem mightily, and then decided to solve two problems with one stroke.

He called the young punk to his presence, at the very

same restaurant where Louie had given Vince his first big break.

The punk looked scared. He had heard the Vince was after the redhead.

"Listen kid," Vince said gruffly, laying a heavily beringed hand on the kid's thin shoulder. "You know the old clothing factory up on Twenty-eighth and Arch?"

"Y . . . yessir," said the punk, in a whisper that Vince could barely hear.

"It's a very flammable building, dontcha think?"

The punk blinked, gulped, then nodded. "Yeah. It is. But . . ."

"But what?"

His voice was trembling, the kid said, "I heard that two-three different guys tried beltin' out that place. An' they . . . they never came back!"

"The place is still standin', ain't it?" Vince asked severely.

"Yeah."

"Well, by tomorrow morning, either *it* ain't standin' or *you* ain't standin'. *Capisce?*"

The kid nodded and fairly raced out of the restaurant. Vince grinned. One way or the other, he had solved a problem, he thought.

The old factory burned cheerfully for a day and a half before the Fire Department could get the blaze under control. Vince laughed and phoned his insurance broker.

But that night, as he stepped from his limousine onto the driveway of his Cherry Hill home, he saw long coils of glittering scales wrapped halfway around the house.

Looking up, he saw Sizzle smiling at him.

"Hello Vince. Long time no see."

"Oh, hi Sizzle ol' girl. What's new?" With his left hand, Vince impatiently waved his driver off. The man backed the limousine down the driveway and headed for the garage back in the city, goggle-eyed that The Boss was talking to himself.

"That was a real cute fellow you sent to knock off the factory two nights ago," Sizzle said, her voice almost purring.

"Him? He's a punk."

"I thought he was really cute."

"So you were there, huh? I figured you was, after those other guys never came back."

"Oh Vince, you're not cute anymore. You're just soft and fat and ugly."

"You ain't gonna win no beauty contests yourself, Sizzle."

He started for the front door, but Sizzle planted a huge taloned paw in his path. Vince had just enough time to look up, see the expression on her face, and scream.

Sizzle's forked tongue licked her lips as the smoke cleared.

"Delicious," she said. "Just the right amount of fat on him. And the poor boy thought I was after his *soul*!"

Brillo

by Harlan Ellison and Ben Bova

INTRODUCTION

It *all started with a pun.*

For more than a quarter-century Harlan Ellison has been one of my cherished friends, even though he lives on the West Coast and I on the East. For the first few years of our comradeship, Harlan occasionally sighed wistfully that he had never been published in the pages of Analog Science Fiction *magazine.*

Analog, *you see, was the most prestigious magazine in the field of science fiction. It was (and still is) a bastion of "hard" science fiction, the kind of stuff that I write and Harlan does not. But Harlan saw his problem as deeper than that. He felt that the magazine's editor, John W. Campbell, Jr., would never publish a story written by Harlan Ellison—for personal reasons, including differences in personality, outlook, and foreskins.*

Campbell was the giant figure of the field in those days, and had been since he had become editor of the magazine in 1937, when it was called Astounding Stories.

It was now the late 1960s. Even though I assured Harlan that Campbell would buy any story he liked, no matter who wrote it, Harlan remained convinced that John would never publish a story he had written. So Harlan and I concocted a plot. We would write a story together, put a penname on it, and sell it to Campbell.

Since we lived so far apart, in those days before home computers and modems and fax machines, work on our story progressed slowly. We decided it would be about two police officers: one very human and one a robot that was programmed to know only the law and infractions thereof. No human traits such as mercy or judgment. Casting about for a name for the robot, I punned: "Brillo—that's what we should call metal fuzz." (In those days "fuzz" was a slang word for "police.")

Although he denies it vigorously to this very day, Harlan laughed uproariously at my pun, and we agreed to title the story "Brillo."

Then came the writing. I flew out to the West Coast on other business, and Harlan and I arranged to meet one evening to start writing the story. We had already exchanged notes about the major characters and the background setting. This one evening would be devoted to writing as much of the story's first draft as we could.

I finished my day's work and arrived at Harlan's home in Sherman Oaks near sunset, ready to work. But Harlan was ready for dinner, instead. He took me, and his friend, Louise Farr, to a Cecil B. DeMille–type restaurant somewhere deep in Beverly Hills. The place was jammed. *It looked like a mob scene out of* The Ten Commandments. *Not to worry. The maitre d' spotted Harlan in the crowd and personally ushered us to the best table in the place. No waiting. He even sent over a complimentary bottle of fine red wine.*

It was nearly ten o'clock by the time we got back to Harlan's place and down to work. Only to discover that we both had the runs. Something in the food had afflicted us sorely.

But we are professional writers. We wrote the first draft of our story, one painful paragraph at a time. One paragraph was about as long as either one of us could stay out of the bathroom. We would meet each other in the hallway between the john and the typewriter.

By dawn's bleary light we were exhausted, in more ways than one. And we had roughly five thousand words of first draft on paper.

I flew back to New England. Months passed.

At the Cleveland airport, as I was waiting for my plane home after another business trip, I was paged. None other than Harlan, who excitedly read me the fifteen-thousand word second draft of "Brillo," while my plane was loaded up and taxied off without me.

It was beautiful and I told Harlan so. It is essentially the story you will read here.

"Campbell will love it!" I said.

"It's too good for Campbell!" Harlan replied. "Let's send it to Playboy!"

Playboy paid ten times what Analog did. We are, as I pointed out earlier, professional writers. So we instructed our mutual agent to send "Brillo" to Playboy.

More months passed. It is now Christmas Eve. I am sitting in my office at the laboratory, where I worked as the manager of the marketing department (i.e., resident science-fiction writer). Four P.M. and already pitch dark outside. Snow is sifting past my window. The office Christmas party is about to begin.

My phone rings. Harlan.

Not only has Playboy rejected our story (they had published a story about a robot the year before, and felt that was as far out as they could go then), but our mutual agent automatically sent the manuscript to the next best market—John W. Campbell Jr.—with Harlan's name still on it! (And mine too, of course.)

Harlan was in despair. He knew Campbell would tear the manuscript into tiny pieces and dance a Highland fling on the scraps. Would I call John and put in a personal word for the story? I told Harlan that John Campbell would never be swayed by pleading; either he liked the story or he didn't.

But Harlan pleaded with me, so I reluctantly phoned Campbell's office, hoping deep in my heart that he would not be there.

He was there. "Oh, it's you," he said. My heart sank.

But then John proceeded to tell me that he had just read "Brillo" and wanted to buy it. He even explained what the story was really about, something that he was certain its authors did not understand. (John was like that. Often he was right.) He asked for a couple of very minor revisions, but he wanted to publish "Brillo"!

I got off the phone as gracefully as I could and quickly dialed Harlan. For some devilish reason I decided to give Harlan somewhat the same treatment Campbell had just given me.

"Harlan, it's me. Ben."

A dull, dispirited grunt.

"I . . . uh, I talked with John."

A moan.

"And he . . . well, he's read the story . . ."

A groan.

"And, uh . . . well, what can I say, Harlan? He wants to buy it."

For several seconds, there was no sound whatever from Harlan's end of the phone. Then a squawk that could have shattered diamond.

"He's buying it?" All sorts of screeching and howl-

ing noises that might have been some exotic form of merriment. "He's buying it?"

So we had a happy Christmas and "Brillo" was published in the August 1970 issue of Analog. *Harlan still thinks that Campbell thought I had done most of the writing. As you will clearly be able to see, "Brillo" is written in Harlan's style, not mine. John Campbell was smart enough to know the difference—and not care.*

Like several other tales in this book, "Brillo" deals with the differences between what we say we want from the criminal justice system and what we really want. The differences between the everyday pieties that we all give lip service to, and the realities of how we actually behave toward the police.

Oh, yes! After the story was published, Harlan and I were approached by certain parties who wanted to turn "Brillo" into a TV series. That project ended in a plagiarism suit that terminated only after four years of lawyers and a month-long trial in a Federal District courtroom in Los Angeles. I can't tell you much about the case, because one of the terms of the eventual settlement was that neither Harlan nor I can write or speak about it—unless we are asked direct questions.

So read "Brillo." And ask me questions.

Crazy season for cops is August. In August the riots start. Not just to get the pigs off campus (where they don't even happen to be, because school is out) or to rid the railroad flats of *Rattus norvegicus,* but they start for no reason at all. Some bunch of sweat-stinking kids get a hydrant spouting and it drenches the storefront of a shylock who lives most of his time in Kipps Bay when he's not sticking it to his Spanish Harlem customers, and he comes out of the pawnshop with a Louisville

Slugger somebody hocked once, and he takes a swing at a *mestizo* urchin, and the next thing the precinct knows, they've got a three-star riot going on two full city blocks; then they call in the copchoppers from Governor's Island and spray the neighborhood with quiescent, and after a while the beat cops go in with breathers, in threes, and they start pulling in the bashhead cases. Why did it get going? A little water on a store window that hadn't been squeegee'd since 1974? A short temper? Some kid flipping some guy the bird? No.

Crazy season is August.

Housewives take their steam irons to their old men's heads. Basset hound salesmen who trundle display suitcases full of ready-to-wear for eleven months, without squeaking at their bosses, suddenly pull twine knives and carve up taxi drivers. Suicides go out tenth storey windows and off the Verrazano-Narrows Bridge like confetti at an astronaut's parade down Fifth Avenue. Teenaged rat packs steal half a dozen cars and dragrace them three abreast against traffic up White Plains Road till they run them through the show windows of supermarkets. No reason. Just August. Crazy season.

It was August, that special heat of August when the temperature keeps going till it reaches the secret killcrazy mugginess at which point eyeballs roll up white in florid faces and gravity knives appear as if by magic, it was *that* time of August, when Brillo arrived in the precinct.

Buzzing softly (the sort of sound an electric watch makes), he stood inert in the center of the precinct station's bullpen, his bright blue-anodized metal a gleaming contrast to the paintless worn floorboards. He stood in the middle of momentary activity, and no one who passed him seemed to be able to pay attention to anything *but* him:

Not the two plainclothes officers duckwalking between them a sixty-two-year-old pervert whose specialty was flashing just before the subway doors closed.

Not the traffic cop being berated by his Sergeant for having allowed his parking ticket receipts to get waterlogged in a plastic bag bombardment initiated by the last few residents of a condemned building.

Not the tac/squad macers reloading their weapons from the supply dispensers.

Not the line of beat cops forming up in ranks for their shift on the street.

Not the Desk Sergeant trying to book three hookers who had been arrested soliciting men queued up in front of NBC for a network game show called ''Sell A Sin.''

Not the fuzzette using a wrist bringalong on the mugger who had tried to snip a cutpurse on her as she patrolled Riverside Drive.

None of them, even engaged in the hardly ordinary business of sweeping up felons, could avoid staring at him. All eyes kept returning to the robot: a squat cylinder resting on tiny trunnions. Brillo's optical sensors, up in his dome-shaped head, bulged like the eyes of an arcromegalic insect. The eyes caught the glint of the overhead neons.

The eyes, particularly, made the crowd in the muster room nervous. The crowd milled and thronged, but did not clear until the Chief of Police spread his hands in a typically Semitic gesture of impatience and yelled, ''All right, already, can you clear this room!''

There was suddenly a great deal of unoccupied space.

Chief Santorini turned back to the robot. And to Reardon.

Frank Reardon shifted his weight uneasily from one foot to the other. He absorbed the Police Chief's look and tracked it out around the muster room, watching the men who were watching the robot. *His* robot. Not that he owned it any longer . . . but he still thought of it as his. He understood how Dr. Victor Frankenstein could feel paternal about a congeries of old spare body parts.

He watched them as they sniffed around the robot like bulldogs delighted with the discovery of a new fire hydrant. Even beefy Sgt. Loyo, the Desk Sergeant, up in his perch at the far end of the shabby room, looked clearly suspicious of the robot.

Santorini had brought two uniformed Lieutenants with him. Administrative assistants. Donkeywork protocol guardians. By-the-book civil service types, lamps lit against any *ee*-vil encroachment of dat ole debbil machine into the paydirt of human beings' job security. They looked grim.

The FBI man sat impassively on a stout wooden bench that ran the length of the room. He sat under posters for the Police Athletic League, the 4th War Bond Offensive, Driver Training Courses and an advertisement for *The Christian Science Monitor* with a FREE—TAKE ONE pocket attached. He had not said a word since being introduced to Reardon. And Reardon had even forgotten the name. Was that part of the camouflage of FBI agents? He sat there looking steely-eyed and jut-jawed. He looked grim, too.

Only the whiz kid from the Mayor's office was smiling as he stepped once again through the grilled door into the bullpen. He smiled as he walked slowly all around the robot. He smiled as he touched the matte-finish of the machine, and he smiled as he made pleasure noises: as if he was inspecting a new car on a showroom floor, on the verge of saying, "I'll take it. What terms can I get?"

He looked out through the wirework of the bullpen at Reardon. "Why do you call it Brillo?"

Reardon hesitated a moment, trying desperately to

remember the whiz kid's first name. He was an engineer, not a public relations man. Universal Electronics should have sent Wendell down with Brillo. *He* knew how to talk to these image-happy clowns from City Hall. Knew how to butter and baste them so they put ink to contract. But part of the deal when he'd been forced to sell Reardon Electronics into merger with UE (after the stock raid and the power grab, which he'd lost) was that he stay on with projects like Brillo. Stay with them all the way to the bottom line.

It was as pleasant as clapping time while your wife made love to another man.

"It's . . . a nickname. Somebody at UE thought it up. Thought it was funny."

The whiz kid looked blank. "What's funny about Brillo?"

"Metal fuzz," the Police Chief rasped.

Light dawned on the whiz kid's face, and he began to chuckle; Reardon nodded, then caught the look of animosity on the Police Chief's face. Reardon looked away quickly from the old man's fiercely seamed features. It was getting more grim, much tenser.

Captain Summit came slowly down the stairs to join them. He was close to Reardon's age, but much grayer. He moved with one hand on the banister, like an old man.

Why do they all look so tired? Reardon wondered. *And why do they seem to look wearier, more frightened, every time they look at the robot? Are they afraid it's come around* their *turn to be replaced? Is that the way I looked when UE forced me out of the company I created?*

Summit eyed the robot briefly, walked over and sat down on the bench several feet apart from the silent FBI man. The whiz kid came out of the bullpen. They all looked at Summit.

"Okay, I've picked a man to work with him . . . it, I mean." He was looking at Reardon. "Mike Polchik. He's a good cop; young and alert. Good record. Nothing extraordinary, no showboater, just a solid cop. He'll give your machine a fair trial."

"That's fine. Thank you, Captain," Reardon said.

"He'll be right down. I pulled him out of the formation. He's getting his gear. He'll be right down."

The whiz kid cleared his throat. Reardon looked at him. *He* wasn't tired. But then, *he* didn't wear a uniform. *He* wasn't pushed up against what these men found in the streets every day. *He lives in Darien, probably,* Frank Reardon thought, *and buys those suits in quiet little shops where there're never more than three customers at a time.*

"How many of these machines can your company make in a year?" the whiz kid asked.

"It's not my company any more."

"I mean the company you work for—Universal."

"Inside a year: we can have them coming out at a rate of a hundred a month." Reardon paused. "Maybe more."

The whiz kid grinned. "We could replace every beat patrolman . . ."

A spark-gap was leaped. The temperature dropped. Reardon saw the uniformed men stiffen. Quickly, he said, "Police robots are intended to *augment* the existing force." Even more firmly he said, "Not replace it. We're trying to *help* the policeman, not get rid of him."

"Oh, hey, sure. Of *course!*" the whiz kid said, glancing around the room. "That's what I meant," he added unnecessarily. Everyone knew what he meant.

The silence at the bottom of the Marianas Trench.

And in that silence: heavy footsteps, coming down the stairs from the second-floor locker rooms.

He stopped at the foot of the stairs, one shoe tipped

up on the final step; he stared at the robot in the bullpen for a long moment. Then the patrolman walked over to Captain Summit, only once more casting a glance into the bullpen. Summit smiled reassuringly at the patrolman and then gestured toward Reardon.

"Mike, this is Mr. Reardon. He designed—the robot. Mr. Reardon, Patrolman Polchik."

Reardon extended his hand and Polchik exerted enough pressure to make him wince.

Polchik was two inches over six feet tall, and weighty. Muscular; thick forearms; the kind found on men who work in foundries. Light, crewcut hair. Square face, wide open; strong jaw, hard eyes under heavy brow ridges. Even his smile looked hard. He was ready for work, with a .32 Needle Positive tilt-stuck on its velcro fastener at mid-thigh and an armament bandolier slanted across his broad chest. His aura keyed one word: cop.

"The Captain tells me I'm gonna be walkin' with your machine t'night."

Nodding, flexing his fingers, Reardon said, "Yes, that's right. The Captain probably told you, we want to test Brillo under actual foot patrol conditions. That's what he was designed for: foot patrol."

"Been a long time since I done foot patrol," Polchik said: "Work a growler, usually."

"Beg pardon?"

Summit translated. "Growler: prowl car."

"Oh. Oh, I see," Reardon said, trying to be friendly.

"It's only for tonight, Mike," the Captain said. "Just a test."

Polchik nodded as though he understood far more than either Reardon or Summit had told him. He did not turn his big body, but his eyes went to the robot. Through the grillwork Brillo (with the sort of sound an electric watch makes) buzzed softly, staring at nothing. Polchik looked it up and down, slowly, very carefully. Finally he said, "Looks okay to me."

"Preliminary tests," Reardon said, "everything short of actual field runs . . . everything's been tested out. You won't have any trouble."

Polchik murmured something.

"I beg your pardon?" Frank Reardon said.

"On-the-job-training," Polchik repeated. He did not smile. But a sound ran through the rest of the station house crew.

"Well, whenever you're ready, Officer Polchik," the whiz kid said suddenly. Reardon winced. The kid had a storm-window salesman's tone even when he was trying to be disarming.

"Yeah. Right." Polchik moved toward the front door. The robot did not move. Polchik stopped and turned around. Everyone was watching.

"I thought he went on his own, uh, independ'nt?"

They were all watching Reardon now.

"He's been voice-keyed to me since the plant," Reardon said. "To shift command, I'll have to prime him with your voice." He turned to the robot. "Brillo, come here, please."

The word *please*.

The buzzing became more distinct for a moment as the trunnions withdrew inside the metal skin. Then the sound diminished, became barely audible, and the robot stepped forward smoothly. He walked to Reardon and stopped.

"Brillo, this is Officer Mike Polchik. You'll be working with him tonight. He'll be your superior and you'll be under his immediate orders." Reardon waved Polchik over. "Would you say a few words, so he can program your voice-print?"

Polchik looked at Reardon. Then he looked at the robot. Then he looked around the muster room. Desk

Sergeant Loyo was grinning. "Whattaya want me to say?"

"Anything."

One of the detectives had come down the stairs. No one had noticed before. Lounging against the railing leading to the squad room upstairs, he giggled. "Tell him some'a your best friends are can openers, Mike."

The whiz kid and the Chief of Police threw him a look. Summit said, "Bratten!" He shut up. After a moment he went back upstairs. Quietly.

"Go ahead. Anything," Reardon urged Polchik.

The patrolman drew a deep breath, took another step forward and said, self-consciously, "Come on, let's go. It's gettin' late."

The soft buzzing (the sort of sound an electric watch makes) came once again from somewhere deep inside the robot. "Yes, sir," he said, in the voice of Frank Reardon, and moved very smoothly, very quickly, toward Polchik. The patrolman stepped back quickly, tried to look casual, turned and started toward the door of the station house once more. The robot followed.

When they had gone, the whiz kid drywashed his hands, smiled at everyone and said, "Now it begins."

Reardon winced again. The Desk Sergeant, Loyo, rattled pencils, tapped them even, dumped them into an empty jelly jar on the blotter desk. Everyone else looked away. The FBI man smiled.

From outside the precinct house the sounds of the city seemed to grow louder in the awkward silence. In all that noise no one even imagined he could hear the sound of the robot.

Polchik was trying the locks on the burglarproof gates of the shops lining Amsterdam between 82nd and 83rd. The robot was following him, doing the same thing. Polchik was getting burned up. He turned up 83rd and entered the alley behind the shops, retracing his steps back toward 82nd. The robot followed him.

Polchik didn't like being followed. It made him feel uneasy. *Damned piece of junk!* he thought. *He rips one of them gates off the hinges, there'll be hell to pay down at the precinct.*

Polchik rattled a gate. He moved on. The robot followed. (*Like a little kid,* Polchik thought.) The robot grabbed the gate and clanged it back and forth. Polchik spun on him. "Listen, dammit, stop makin' all that racket! Y'wanna wake everybody? You know what time it is?"

"1:37 A.M.," the robot replied, in Reardon's voice.

Polchik looked heavenward.

Shaking his head he moved on. The robot stopped. "Officer Polchik."

Mike Polchik turned, exasperated. *What now?*

"I detect a short circuit in this alarm system," the robot said. He was standing directly under the Morse-Dictograph Security panel. "If it is not repaired, it will cancel the fail-safe circuits."

"I'll call it in," Polchik said, pulling the pin-mike on its spring-return wire from his callbox. He was about to thumb on the wristband callbox, when the robot extruded an articulated arm from its chest. "I am equipped to repair the unit without assistance," the robot said, and a light-beam began to pulse at the end of the now-goosenecked arm.

"Leave it alone!"

"A simple 155-0 system," the robot said. "Fixed temperature unit with heat detectors, only barely exceeding NFPA standard 74 and NFPA 72-A requirements." The arm snaked up to the panel and followed the break line around the outside.

"Don't screw with it! It'll set it—"

The panel accordion-folded back. Polchik's mouth fell open. "Oh my God," he mumbled.

The robot's extruded arm worked inside for a long moment, then withdrew. "It is fully operable now." The panel folded back into place.

Polchik let the pin-mike slip from his fingers and it zzzzz'd back into the wristband. He walked away down the alley, looking haunted.

Down at the corner, the Amsterdam Inn's lights shone weakly, reflecting dully in the street oil slick. Polchik paused at the mouth of the alley and pulled out the pin-mike again. He thumbed the callbox on his wrist, *feeling* the heavy shadow of the robot behind him.

"Polchik," he said into the mike.

"Okay, Mike?" crackled the reply. "How's yer partner doing?"

Glancing over his shoulder, Polchik saw the robot standing impassively, gooseneck arm vanished; ten feet behind him. Respectfully. "Don't call it my partner."

Laughter on the other end of the line. "What's'a'matter, Mike? 'Fraid of him?"

"Ahhh . . . cut the clownin'. Everything quiet here, Eighty-two and Amsterdam."

"Okay. Oh, hey, Mike, remember . . . if it starts to rain, get yer partner under an awning before he starts t'rust!"

He was still laughing like a jackass as Polchik let the spring-wire zzzzz back into the callbox.

"Hey, Mike! What you got there?"

Polchik looked toward the corner. It was Rico, the bartender from the Amsterdam Inn.

"It's a robot," Polchik said. He kept his voice very flat. He was in no mood for further ribbing.

"Real he is, yeah? No kidding?" Rico's face always looked to Polchik like a brass artichoke, ready to be peeled. But he was friendly enough. And cooperative.

It was a dunky neighborhood and Polchik had found Rico useful more than once. "What's he supposed to do, eh?"

"He's supposed to be a cop." Glum.

Rico shook his vegetable head. "What they gonna do next? Robots. So what happens t'you, Mike? They make you a detective?"

"Sure. And the week after that they make me Captain."

Rico looked uncertain, didn't know whether he should laugh or sympathize. Finally, he said, "Hey, I got a bottle for ya," feeling it would serve, whatever his reaction should properly have been. "Betcha your wife likes it . . . from Poland, imported stuff. Got grass or weeds or some kinda stuff in it. S'posed to be really sensational."

For just a second, peripherally seen, Polchik thought the robot had stirred.

"Escuchar! I'll get it for you."

He disappeared inside the bar before Polchik could stop him. The robot *did* move. It trembled . . . ?

Rico came out with a paper bag, its neck twisted close around what was obviously a bottle of liquor.

"I'll have to pick it up tomorrow," Polchik said. "I don't have the car tonight."

"I'll keep it for you. If I'm on relief when you come by, ask Maldonado."

The robot was definitely humming. Polchik could hear it. (The sort of sound an electric watch makes.) It suddenly moved, closing the distance, ten feet between them, till it passed Polchik, swiveled to face Rico—who stumbled backward halfway to the entrance to the Amsterdam Inn—then swiveled back to face Polchik.

"Visual and audial data indicate a one-to-one extrapolation of same would result in a conclusion that a gratuity has been offered to you, Officer Polchik. Further, logic indicates that you intend to accept said gratuity. Such behavior is a programmed infraction of the law. It is—"

"Shut up!"

Rico stood very close to the door, wide-eyed.

"I'll see you tomorrow night," Polchik said to him.

"Officer Polchik," the robot went on as though there had been no interruption, "it is clear if you intend to accept a gratuity, you will be breaking the law and liable to arrest and prosecution under Law Officer Statutes number—"

"I said shuddup, dammit!" Polchik said, louder. "I don't even know what the hell you're talkin' about, but I said shuddup, and that's an *order*!"

"Yes, sir," the robot replied instantly. "However, my data tapes will record this conversation in its entirety and it will be transcribed into a written report at the conclusion of our patrol."

"What?" Polchik felt gears gnashing inside his head, thought of gears, thought of the robot, rejected gears and thought about Captain Summit. Then he thought about gears again . . . crushing him.

Rico's voice intruded, sounding scared. "What's he saying? What's that about a report?"

"Now wait a minute, Brillo," Polchik said, walking up to the robot. "Nothin's happened here you can write a report on."

The robot's voice—*Reardon*'s voice, Polchik thought irritatedly—was very firm. "Logic indicates a high probability that a gratuity has been accepted in the past, and another will be accepted in the future."

Polchik felt chili peppers in his gut. Hooking his thumbs in his belt—a pose he automatically assumed when he was trying to avert trouble—he deliberately toned down his voice. "Listen, Brillo, you forget the whole thing, you understand. You just for*get* it."

"Am I to understand you desire my tapes to be erased?"

"Yeah, that's right. Erase it."

"Is that an order?"

"It's an order!"

The robot hummed to itself for a heartbeat, then, "Primary programming does not allow erasure of data tapes. Tapes can be erased only post-transcription or by physically removing same from my memory bank."

"Listen—" Rico started, "—I don't wan' no trub—"

Polchik impatiently waved him to silence. He didn't need any complications right now. "Listen, Brillo . . ."

"Yes. I hear it."

Polchik was about to continue speaking. He stopped. *I hear it? This damned thing's gone bananas.* "I didn't say anything yet."

"Oh. I'm sorry, sir. I thought you were referring to the sound of a female human screaming on 84th Street, third-floor front apartment."

Polchik looked everywhichway. "What are you *talkin'* about? You crazy or something?"

"No, sir. I am a model X-44. Though under certain special conditions my circuits can malfunction, conceivably, nothing in my repair programming parameters approximates 'crazy.' "

"Then just shuddup and let's get this thing straightened out. Now, try'n understand this. You're just a robot, see. You don't understand the way real people do things. Like, for instance, when Rico here offers me a bottle of—"

"If you'll pardon me, sir, the female human is now screaming in the 17,000 cycle-per-second range. My tapes are programmed to value-judge such a range as concomitant with fear and possibly extreme pain. I suggest we act at once."

"Hey, Polchik . . ." Rico began.

"No, shuddup, Rico. Hey, listen, robot, Brillo, whatever: you mean you can *hear* some woman screaming, two blocks away and up three flights? Is the window open?" Then he stopped. "What'm I doin'? Talking to this thing!" He remembered the briefing he'd been given by Captain Summit. "Okay. You say you can hear her . . . lets find her."

The robot took off at top speed. Back into the alley behind the Amsterdam Inn, across the 82nd-83rd block, across the 83rd-84th block, full-out with no clanking or clattering. Polchik found himself pounding along ten feet behind the robot, then twenty feet, then thirty feet; suddenly he was puffing, his chest heavy, the armament bandolier banging the mace cans and the riot-prod and the bullhorn and the peppergas shpritzers and the extra clips of needler ammunition against his chest and back.

The robot emerged from the alley, turned a 90° angle with the sharpest cut Polchik had ever seen, and jogged up 84th Street. Brillo was caught for a moment in the glare of a neon streetlamp, then was taking the steps of a crippled old brownstone three at a time.

Troglodytes with punch-presses were berkeleying Polchik's lungs and stomach. His head was a dissenter's punchboard. But he followed. More slowly now; and had trouble negotiating the last flight of stairs to the third floor. As he gained the landing, he was hauling himself hand-over-hand up the banister. *If God'd wanted cops to* walk *beats he wouldn't'a created the growler!*

The robot, Brillo, X-44, was standing in front of the door marked 3-A. He was quivering like a hound on point. (Buzzing softly with the sort of sound an electric watch makes.) Now Polchik could hear the woman himself, above the roar of blood in his temples.

"Open up in there!" Polchik bellowed. He ripped the .32 Needle Positive off its velcro fastener and banged on the door with the butt. The lanyard was twisted; he untwisted it. "This's the police. I'm demanding entrance to a private domicile under Public Law 22-809, allowing for superced'nce of the 'home-castle' rule under emergency conditions. I said *open up in there*!"

The screaming went up and plateau'd a few hundred cycles higher, and Polchik snapped at the robot, "Get outta my way."

Brillo obediently moved back a pace, and in the narrow hallway Polchik braced himself against the wall, locked the exoskeletal rods on his boots, dropped his crash-hat visor, jacked up his leg and delivered a powerful *savate* kick at the door.

It was a pre-SlumClear apartment. The door bowed and dust spurted from the seams, but it held. Despite the rods, Polchik felt a searing pain gash up through his leg. He fell back, hopping about painfully, hearing himself going, "oo—oo—oo" and then prepared himself to have to do it again. The robot moved up in front of him, said, "Excuse me, sir," and smoothly cleaved the door down the center with the edge of a metal hand that had somehow suddenly developed a cutting edge. He reached in, grasped both sliced edges of the hardwood, and ripped the door outward in two even halves.

"Oh." Polchik stared open-mouthed for only an instant.

Then they were inside.

The unshaven man with the beer gut protruding from beneath his olive drab skivvy undershirt was slapping the hell out of his wife. He had thick black tufts of hair that bunched like weed corsages in his armpits. She was half-lying over the back of a sofa with the springs showing. Her eyes were swollen and blue-black as dried prunes. One massive bruise was already draining down her cheek into her neck. She was weakly trying to fend off her husband's blows with ineffectual wrist-blocks.

"Okay! That's it!" Polchik yelled.

The sound of another voice, in the room with them, brought the man and his wife to a halt. He turned his head, his left hand still tangled in her long black hair, and he stared at the two intruders.

He began cursing in Spanish. Then he burst into a guttural combination of English and Spanish, and finally slowed in his own spittle to a ragged English. ". . . won't let me alone . . . go out my house . . . always botherin' won't let me alone . . . damn . . ." and he went back to Spanish as he pushed the woman from him and started across the room. The woman tumbled, squealing, out of sight behind the sofa.

The man stumbled crossing the room, and Polchik's needler tracked him. Behind him he heard the robot softly humming, and then it said, "Sir, analysis indicates psychotic glaze over subject's eyes."

The man grabbed a half-filled quart bottle of beer off the television set, smashed it against the leading edge of the TV, giving it a half-twist (which registered instantly in Polchik's mind: this guy knew how to get a ragged edge on the weapon; he was an experienced barroom brawler) and suddenly lurched toward Polchik with the jagged stump in his hand.

Abruptly, before Polchik could even thumb the needler to stun (it was on dismember), a metal blur passed him, swept into the man, lifted him high in the air with one hand, turned him upside-down so the bottle, small plastic change and an unzipped shoe showered down onto the threadbare rug. Arms and legs fluttered helplessly.

"Aieeee!" the man screamed, his hair hanging down, his face plugged red with blood. *"Madre de dios!"*

"Leave him alone!" It was the wife screaming, charging—if it could be called that, on hands and knees—from behind the sofa. She clambered to her feet and ran at the robot, screeching and cursing, pounding her daywork-reddened fists against his gleaming hide.

"Okay, okay," Polchik said, his voice lower but strong enough to get through to her. Pulling her and her hysteria away from the robot, he ordered, "Brillo, put him down."

"You goddam cops got no right bustin' in here," the man started complaining the moment he was on his feet again. "Goddam cops don't let a man'n his wife alone for nothin' no more. You got a warrant? Huh? You gonna get in trouble, plenty trouble. This my home, cop, 'home is a man's castle,' hah? Right? Right? An' you an' this tin can . . ." He was waving his arms wildly.

Brillo wheeled a few inches toward the man. The stream of abuse cut off instantly, the man's face went pale, and he threw up his hands to protect himself.

"This man can be arrested for assault and battery, failure to heed a legitimate police order, attempted assault on a police officer with a deadly weapon, and disturbing the peace," Brillo said. His flat, calm voice seemed to echo off the grimy walls.

"It . . . it's talkin'! Flavio! *Demonio!*" The wife spiraled toward hysteria again.

"Shall I inform him of his rights under the Public Laws, sir?" Brillo asked Polchik.

"You gon' arrest me? Whu'for?"

"Brillo . . ." Polchik began.

Brillo started again, "Assault and battery, failure to—"

Polchik looked annoyed. "Shuddup, I wasn't asking you to run it again. Just shuddup."

"I din't do nothin'! You come bust t'rough my door when me an' my wife wass arguin', an' you beat me up. Look'a the bruise on my arm." The arm was slightly inflamed where Brillo had grabbed him.

"Flavio!" the woman whimpered.

"Isabel; *cállete la boca!*"

"I live right downstairs," a voice said from behind them. "He's always beating her up, and he drinks all the time and then he pisses out the window!" Polchik spun and a man in Levis and striped pajama tops was standing in the ruined doorway. "Sometimes it looks like it's raining on half my window. Once I put my hand out to see—"

"Get outta here!" Polchik bellowed, and the man vanished.

"I din't do nothin'!" Flavio said again, semi-surly.

"My data tapes," Brillo replied evenly, "will clearly show your actions."

"Day to tapes? Whass he talkin' 'bout?" Flavio turned to Polchik, an unaccustomed ally against the hulking machine. Polchik felt a sense of camaraderie with the man.

"He's got everything down recorded . . . like on TV. And sound tapes, too." Polchik looked back at him and recognized something in the dismay on the man's fleshy face.

Brillo asked again, "Shall I inform him of his rights, sir?"

"Officer, sir, you ain't gonna'rrest him?" the woman half-asked, half-pleaded, her eyes swollen almost closed, barely open, but tearful.

"He came after me with a bottle," Polchik said. "And he didn't do you much good, neither."

"He wass work op. Iss allright. He's okay now. It wass joss a'argumen'. Nobody got hort."

Brillo's hum got momentarily higher. "Madam, you should inspect your face in my mirror." He hummed and his skin became smoothly reflective. "My sensors detect several contusions and abrasions, particularly . . ."

"Skip it," Polchik said abruptly. "Come on, Brillo, let's go."

Brillo's metal hide went blank again. "I have not informed the prisoner . . ."

"No prisoner," Polchik said. "No arrest. Let's go."

"But the data clearly shows . . ."

"Forget it!" Polchik turned to face the man; he was standing there looking uncertain, rubbing his arm. "And you, strongarm . . . lemme hear one more peep outta this apartment and you'll be in jail so fast it'll make your head swim . . . and for a helluva long time, too. If you get there at all. We don't like guys like you. So I'm puttin' the word out on you . . . I don't like guys comin' at me with bottles."

"Sir . . . I . . ."

"Come on!"

The robot followed the cop and the apartment was suddenly silent. Flavio and Isabel looked at each other sheepishly, then he began to cry, went to her and touched her bruises with the gentlest fingers.

They went downstairs, Polchik staring and trying to figure out how it was such a massive machine could navigate the steps so smoothly. Something was going on at the base of the robot, but Polchik couldn't get a good view of it. Dust puffed out from beneath the machine. And something sparkled.

Once on the sidewalk, Brillo said, "Sir, that man should have been arrested. He was clearly violating several statutes."

Polchik made a sour face. "His wife wouldn't of pressed the charge."

"He attacked a police officer with a deadly weapon."

"So that makes him Mad Dog Coll? He's scared shitless, in the future he'll watch it. For a while, at least."

Brillo was hardly satisfied at this noncomputable

conclusion. "A police officer's duty is to arrest persons who are suspected of having broken the law. Civil or criminal courts have the legal jurisdiction to decide the suspect's guilt or innocence. Your duty, sir, was to arrest that man."

"Sure, sure. Have it *your* way, half the damn city'll be in jail, and the other half'll be springin' 'em out."

Brillo said nothing, but Polchik thought the robot's humming sounded sullen. He had a strong suspicion the machine wouldn't forget it. Or Rico, either.

And farther up the street, to cinch Polchik's suspicion, the robot once more tried to reinforce his position. "According to the Peace Officer Responsibility Act of 1975, failure of an officer to take into custody person or persons indisputably engaged in acts that contravene . . ."

"Awright, dammit, knock it off. I tole you why I din't arrest that poor jughead, so stop bustin' my chops with it. You ain't happy, you don't like it, tell my Sergeant!"

Sergeant, hell, Polchik thought. *This stuff goes right to Captain Summit, Santorini and the Commissioner. Probably the Mayor. Maybe the President; who the hell knows?*

Petulantly (it seemed to Polchik), the robot resumed, "Reviewing my tapes, I find the matter of the bottle of liquor offered as a gratuity still unresolved. If I am to—"

Polchik spun left and kicked with all his might at a garbage can bolted to an iron fence. The lid sprang off and clanged against the fence at the end of its short chain. "I've had it with you . . . you nonreturnable piece of scrap crap!" He wanted very much to go on, but he didn't know what to say. All he knew for certain was that he'd never had such a crummy night in all his life. It *couldn't* just be this goddammed robot—staring

back blankly. It was *everything*. The mortgage payment
was due; Benjy had to go in to the orthodontist and
where the hell was the money going to come from for
that; Dorothy had called the precinct just before he'd
come down, to tell him the hot water heater had split
and drowned the carpets in the kid's bedroom; and to
top it all off, he'd been assigned this buzzing pain in
the ass and got caught with a little juice passed by that
nitwit Rico; he'd had to have this Brillo pain tell him
there was a hassle two blocks away; he was sure as God
made little green apples going to get a bad report out
of this, maybe get set down, maybe get reprimanded,
maybe get censured . . . he didn't know what all.

But one thing was certain: this metal bird-dog, this
stuffed shirt barracks lawyer with the trailalong of a ten-
year-old kid behind his big brother, this nuisance in
metal underwear, this . . . this . . . *thing* was of no
damned earthly use to a working cop pulling a foot
beat!

On the other hand, a voice that spoke with the voice
of Mike Polchik said, *he did keep that jughead from
using a broken bottle on you.*

"Shuddup!" Polchik said.

"I beg your pardon?" answered the robot.

Ingrate! said the inner voice.

It was verging on that chalky hour before dawn, when
the light filtering out of the sky had a leprous, sickly
look. Mike Polchik was a much older man.

Brillo had interfered in the apprehension of Milky
Kyser, a well-known car thief. Mike had spotted him
walking slowly and contemplatively along a line of
parked cars on Columbus Avenue, carrying a tightly-
rolled copy of the current issue of *Life* magazine.

When he had collared Milky, the robot had buzzed
up to them and politely inquired precisely what in the

carborundum Polchik thought he was doing. Polchik had responded with what was becoming an hysterical reaction-formation to *anything* the metal cop said. "Shuddup!"

Brillo had persisted, saying he was programmed to protect the civil rights of the members of the community, and as far as he could tell, having "scanned all data relevant to the situation at hand," the gentleman now dangling from Polchik's grip was spotlessly blameless of even the remotest scintilla of wrongdoing. Polchik had held Milky with one hand and with the other gesticulated wildly as he explained, "Look, dimdumb, this is Milky Kyser, AKA Irwin Kayser, AKA Clarence Irwin, AKA Jack Milk, AKA God Knows Who All. He is a well-known dip and car thief, and he will use that rolled-up copy of the magazine to jack-and-snap the door handle of the proper model car, any number of which is currently parked, you will note, along this street . . . unless I arrest him! Now will you kindly get the hell outta my hair and *back off*?"

But it was no use. By the time Brillo had patiently repeated the civil rights story, reiterated pertinent sections of the Peace Officer Responsibility Act of 1975 and topped it off with a *précis* of Miranda-Escobedo-Baum Supreme Court decisions so adroit and simplified even a confirmed tautologist would have applauded, Milky himself—eyes glittering and a sneer that was hardly a smile on his ferret face—was echoing it, word for word.

The robot had given Milky a thorough course in legal cop-outs, before Polchik's dazed eyes.

"Besides," Milky told Polchik with as much dignity as he could muster, hanging as he was from the cop's meaty fist, "I ain't done nuthin', and just because I been busted once or twice . . ."

"Once or twice!?" Polchik yanked the rolled-up

magazine out of Milky's hand and raised it to clobber him. Milky pulled in his head like a turtle, wincing.

But in that fraction of a second, Polchik suddenly saw a picture flashed on the wall of his mind. A picture of Desk Sergeant Loyo and Captain Summit and Chief Santorini and the Mayor's toady and that silent FBI man, all watching a TV screen. And on the screen, there was the pride of the Force, Officer Mike Polchik beaning Milky Kyser with a semi-lethal copy of *Life* magazine.

Polchik held the magazine poised, trembling with the arrested movement. Milky, head now barely visible from between his shoulders, peeped up from behind his upraised hands. He looked like a mole.

"Beat it." Polchik growled. "Get the hell out of this precinct, Milky. If you're spotted around here again, you're gonna get busted. And don't stop to buy no magazines."

He let Milky loose.

The mole metamorphosed into a ferret once more. And straightening himself, he said, "An' don't call me 'Milky' any more. My given name is Irwin."

"You got three seconds t'vanish from my sight!"

Milky, *né* Irwin, hustled off down the street. At the corner he stopped and turned around. He cupped his hands and yelled back, "Hey, robot . . . thanks!"

Brillo was about to reply when Polchik bellowed, "Will you *please*!" The robot turned and said, very softly in Reardon's voice, "You are still holding Mr. Kyser's magazine."

Polchik was weary. Infinitely weary. "You hear him askin' for it?" He walked away from the robot and, as he passed a sidewalk dispenser, stepped on the dispod-pedal, and flipped the magazine into the receptacle.

"I saved a piece of cherry pie for you, Mike," the waitress said. Polchik looked up from his uneaten hot (now cold) roast beef sandwich and french fries. He shook his head.

"Thanks anyway. Just another cuppa coffee."

The waitress had lost her way somewhere beyond twenty-seven. She was a nice person. She went home to her husband every morning. She didn't fool around. Extra mates under the new lottery were not her interest; she just didn't fool around. But she liked Mike Polchik. He, like she, was a very nice person.

"What's the matter, Mike?"

Polchik looked out the window of the diner. Brillo was standing directly under a neon streetlamp. He couldn't hear it from here, but he was sure the thing was buzzing softly to itself (with the sort of sound an electric watch makes).

"Him."

"That?" The waitress looked past him.

"Uh-uh. *Him.*"

"What is it?"

"My shadow."

"Mike, you okay? Try the pie, huh? Maybe a scoop of nice vanilla ice cream on top."

"Onita, please. Just a cuppa coffee. I'm fine. I got problems." He stared down at his plate again.

She looked at him for a moment longer, worried, then turned and returned the pie on its plate to the empty space behind the smudged glass of the display case. "You want fresh?" she asked.

When he didn't answer, she shrugged and came back, using the coffee siphon on the portable cart to refill his cup.

She lounged behind the counter, watching her friend, Mike Polchik, as he slowly drank his coffee; and every few minutes he'd look out at that metal thing on the corner under the streetlamp. She was a nice person.

When he rose from the booth and came to the

counter, she thought he was going to apologize, or speak to her, or something, but all he said was, "You got my check?"

"What check?"

"Come on."

"Oh, Mike, for Christ's sake, what's wrong with you?"

"I want to pay the check, you mind?"

"Mike, almost—what—five years you been eating here, you ever been asked to pay a check?"

Polchik looked very tired. "Tonight I pay the check. Come on . . . I gotta get back on the street. He's waiting."

There was a strange look in his eyes and she didn't want to ask which "he" Polchik meant. She was afraid he meant the metal thing out there. Onita, a very nice person, didn't like strange, new things that waited under neon streetlamps. She hastily wrote out a check and slid it across the plasteel to him. He pulled change from a pocket, paid her, turned, seemed to remember something, turned back, added a tip, then swiftly left the diner.

She watched through the glass as he went up to the metal thing. Then the two of them walked away, Mike leading, the thing following.

Onita made fresh. It was a good thing she had done it so many times she could do it by reflex, without thinking. Hot coffee scalds are very painful.

At the corner, Polchik saw a car weaving toward the intersection. A Ford Electric; convertible, four years old. Still looked flashy. Top down. He could see a bunch of long-haired kids inside. He couldn't tell the girls from the boys. It bothered him.

Polchik stopped. They weren't going fast, but the car was definitely weaving as it approached the intersection. *The warrior-lizard,* he thought. It was almost an unconscious directive. He'd been a cop long enough to react to the little hints, the flutters, the inclinations. The hunches.

Polchik stepped out from the curb, unshipped his gumball from the bandolier and flashed the red light at the driver. The car slowed even more; now it was crawling.

"Pull it over, kid!" he shouted.

For a moment he thought they were ignoring him, that the driver might not have heard him, that they'd try and make a break for it . . . that they'd speed up and sideswipe him. But the driver eased the car to the curb and stopped.

Then he slid sidewise, pulled up his legs and crossed them neatly at the ankles. On the top of the dashboard.

Polchik walked around to the driver's side. "Turn it off. Everybody out."

There were six of them. None of them moved. The driver closed his eyes slowly, then tipped his Irkutsk fur hat over his eyes till it rested on the bridge of his nose. Polchik reached into the car and turned it off. He pulled the keys.

"Hey! Whuzzis allabout?" one of the kids in the back seat—a boy with terminal acne—complained. His voice began and ended on a whine. Polchik re-stuck the gumball.

The driver looked up from under the fur. "Wasn't breaking any laws." He said each word very slowly, very distinctly, as though each one was on a printout.

And Polchik knew he'd been right. They were on the lizard.

He opened the door, free hand hanging at the needler. "Out. All of you, out."

Then he sensed Brillo lurking behind him, in the middle of the street. Good. *Hope a damned garbage truck hits him.*

He was getting mad. That wasn't smart. Carefully, he said, "Don't make me say it again. Move it!"

He lined them up on the sidewalk beside the car, in plain sight. Three girls, three guys. Two of the guys with long, stringy hair and the third with a scalplock. The three girls wearing tammy cuts. All six sullen-faced, drawn, dark smudges under the eyes. The lizard. But good clothes, fairly new. He couldn't just hustle them, he had to be careful.

"Okay, one at a time, empty your pockets and pouches onto the hood of the car."

"Hey, we don't haveta do that just because . . ."

"Do it!"

"Don't argue with the pig," one of the girls said, lizard-spacing her words carefully. "He's probably trigger happy."

Brillo rolled up to Polchik. "It is necessary to have a probable cause clearance from the precinct in order to search, sir."

"Not on a stop'n'frisk," Polchik snapped, not taking his eyes off them. He had no time for nonsense with the can of cogs. He kept his eyes on the growing collection of chits, change, code-keys, combs, nail files, toke pipes and miscellania being dumped on the Ford's hood.

"There must be grounds for suspicion even in a spot search action, sir," Brillo said.

"There's grounds. Narcotics."

"Nar . . . you must be outtayer mind," said the one boy who slurred his words. He was working something other than the lizard.

"That's a pig for you," said the girl who had made the trigger happy remark.

"Look," Polchik said, "you snots aren't from around here. Odds are good if I run b&b tests on you, we'll find you're under the influence of the lizard."

"Heyyyy!" the driver said. "The *what*?"

"Warrior-lizard," Polchik said.

"Oh, ain't he the jive thug," the smartmouth girl said. "He's a word user. I'll bet he knows *all* the current rage phrases. A philologist. I'll bet he knows *all* the solecisms and colloquialisms, catch phrases, catachreses, nicknames and vulgarisms. The 'warrior-lizard,' indeed."

Damned college kids, Polchik fumed inwardly. *They always try to make you feel stupid; I coulda gone to college—if I didn't have to work. Money, they probably always had money. The little bitch.*

The driver giggled. "Are you trying to tell me, Mella, my dear, that this Peace Officer is accusing us of being under the influence of the illegal Bolivian drug commonly called Guerrera-Tuera?" He said it with pinpointed scorn, pronouncing the Spanish broadly: gwuh-*rare*-uh too-*err*-uh.

Brillo said, "Reviewing my semantic tapes, sir, I find no analogs for 'Guerrera-Tuera' as 'warrior-lizard.' True, *guerrero* in Spanish means *warrior*, but the closest spelling I find is the feminine noun *guerra*, which translates as *war*. Neither *guerrera* nor *tuera* appear in the Spanish language. If *tuera* is a species of lizard, I don't seem to find it—"

Polchik had listened dumbly. The weight on his shoulders was monstrous. All of them were on him. The kids, that lousy stinking robot—they were making fun, such fun, such *damned* fun of him! "Keep digging," he directed them. He was surprised to hear his words emerge as a series of croaks.

"And blood and breath tests must be administered, sir—"

"Stay the hell outta this!"

"We're on our way home from a party," said the

boy with the scalplock, who had been silent till then. "We took a shortcut and got lost."

"Sure," Polchik said. "In the middle of Manhattan, you got lost." He saw a small green bottle dumped out of the last girl's pouch. She was trying to push it under other items. "What's that?"

"Medicine," she said. Quickly. Very quickly.

Everyone tensed.

"Let me see it." His voice was even.

He put out his hand for the bottle, but all six watched his other hand, hanging beside the needler. Hesitantly, the girl picked the bottle out of the mass of goods on the car's hood, and handed him the plastic container.

Brillo said, "I am equipped with chemical sensors and reference tapes in my memory bank enumerating common narcotics. I can analyze the suspected medicine."

The six stared wordlessly at the robot. They seemed almost afraid to acknowledge its presence.

Polchik handed the plastic bottle to the robot.

Brillo depressed a color-coded key on a bank set flush into his left forearm, and a panel that hadn't seemed to be there a moment before slid down in the robot's chest. He dropped the plastic bottle into the opening and the panel slid up. He stood and buzzed.

"You don't have to open the bottle?" Polchik asked.

"No, sir."

"Oh."

The robot continued buzzing. Polchik felt stupid, just standing and watching. After a few moments the kids began to smirk, then to grin, then to chuckle openly, whispering among themselves. The smartmouthed girl giggled viciously. Polchik felt fifteen years old again; awkward, pimply, the butt of secret jokes among the long-legged high school girls in their miniskirts who had been so terrifyingly aloof he had never even considered asking them out. He realized with some shame that he despised these kids with their money, their cars, their flashy clothes, their dope. And most of all, their assurance. *He*, Mike Polchik, had been working hauling sides of beef from the delivery trucks to his old man's butcher shop while others were tooling around in their Electrics. He forced the memories from his mind and took out his anger and frustration on the metal idiot still buzzing beside him.

"Okay, okay, how long does it take you?"

"Tsk, tsk," said the driver, and went cross-eyed. Polchik ignored him. But not very well.

"I am a mobile unit, sir. Experimental model 44. My parent mechanism—the Master Unit AA—at Universal Electronics laboratories is equipped to perform this function in under one minute."

"Well, hurry it up. I wanna run these hairies in."

"Gwuh-*rare*-uh too-*err*-uh," the scalplock said in a nasty undertone.

There was a soft musical tone from inside the chest compartment, the plate slid down again, and the robot withdrew the plastic bottle. He handed it to the girl.

"Now whaddaya think you're doing?"

"Analysis confirms what the young lady attested, sir. This is a commonly prescribed nosedrop for nasal congestion and certain primary allergies."

Polchik was speechless.

"You are free to go," the robot said. "With our apologies. We are merely doing our jobs. Thank you."

Polchik started to protest—he *knew* he was right— but the kids were already gathering up their belongings. He hadn't even ripped the car, which was probably where they had it locked away. But he knew it was useless. *He* was the guinea pig in this experiment, not the robot. It was all painfully clear. He knew if he interfered, if he overrode the robot's decision, it would only add to the cloud under which the robot had put him: short temper, taking a gift from a neighborhood merchant, letting the robot out-maneuver him in the apartment, false stop on Kyser . . . and now this. Suddenly, all Mike Polchik wanted was to go back, get out of harness, sign out, and go home to bed. Wet carpets and all. Just to bed.

Because if these metal things were what was coming, he was simply too tired to buck it.

He watched as the kids—hooting and ridiculing his impotency—piled back in the car, the girls showing their legs as they clambered over the side. The driver burned polyglas speeding up Amsterdam Avenue. In a moment they were gone.

"You see, Officer Polchik," Brillo said, "false arrest would make us both liable for serious—" But Polchik was already walking away, his shoulders slumped, the weight of his bandolier and five years on the Force too much for him.

The robot (making the sort of sound an electric watch makes) hummed after him, keeping stern vigil on the darkened neighborhood in the encroaching dawn. He could not compute despair. But he had been built to serve. He was programmed to protect, and he did it, all the way back to the precinct house.

Polchik was sitting at a scarred desk in the squad room, laboriously typing out his report on a weary IBM Selectric afflicted with *grand mal*. Across the room Reardon poked at the now-inert metal bulk of Brillo, using some sort of power tool with a teardrop-shaped lamp on top of it. The Mayor's whiz kid definitely looked sandbagged. *He don't go without sleep very often,* Polchik thought with grim satisfaction.

The door to Captain Summit's office opened, and the Captain, looking oceanic and faraway, waved him in.

"Here it comes," Polchik whispered to himself.

Summit let Polchik pass him in the doorway. He closed the door and indicated the worn plastic chair in front of the desk. Polchik sat down. "I'm not done typin' the beat report yet, Capt'n."

Summit ignored the comment. He moved over to the desk, picked up a yellow printout flimsy, and stood silently for a moment in front of Polchik, considering it.

"Accident report out of the 86th precinct uptown. Six kids in a Ford Electric convertible went out of control, smashed down a pedestrian and totaled against the bridge abutment. Three dead, three critical—not expected to live. Fifteen minutes after you let them go."

Dust.

Dried out.

Ashes.

Gray. Final.

Polchik couldn't think. Tired. Confused. Sick. Six kids. *Now* they were kids, just kids, nothing else made out of old bad memories.

"One of the girls went through the windshield, D.O.A. Driver got the steering column punched out through his back. Another girl with a snapped neck. Another girl—"

He couldn't hear him. He was somewhere else, faraway. Kids. Laughing, smartmouth kids having a good time. Benjy would be that age some day. The carpets were all wet.

"Mike!"

He didn't hear.

"Mike! Polchik!"

He looked up. There was a stranger standing in front of him holding a yellow flimsy.

"Well, don't just sit there, Polchik. You *had* them! Why'd you let them go?"

"The . . . lizard . . ."

"That's right, that's what five of them were using. Three beakers of it in the car. And a dead cat on the floor and all the makings wrapped in foam-bead bags. You'd have had to be blind to miss it all!"

"The robot . . ."

Summit turned away with disgust, slamming the report onto the desk top. He thumbed the call-button. When Desk Sergeant Loyo came in, he said, "Take him upstairs and give him a breather of straightener, let him lie down for half an hour, then bring him back to me."

Loyo got Polchik under the arms and took him out.

Then the Captain turned off the office lights and sat silently in his desk chair, watching the night die just beyond the filthy windows.

"Feel better?"

"Yeah; thank you, Capt'n. I'm fine."

"You're back with me all the way? You understand what I'm saying?"

"Yeah, sure, I'm just *fine*, sir. It was just . . . those kids . . . I felt."

"So why'd you let them go? I've got no time to baby you, Polchik. You're five years a cop and I've got all the brass in town outside that door waiting. So get right."

"I'm right, Capt'n. I let them go because the robot took the stuff the girl was carrying, and he dumped it in his thing there, and told me it was nosedrops."

"Not good enough, Mike."

"What can I say besides that?"

"Well, dammit *Officer* Polchik, you damned well better say *some*thing besides that. *You* know they run that stuff right into the skull, you've been a cop long enough to see it, to hear it the way they talk! Why'd you let them custer you?"

"What was I going to run them in for? Carrying

nosedrops? With that motherin' robot reciting civil rights chapter-an'-verse at me every step of the way? Okay, so I tell the robot to go screw off, and I bust 'em and bring 'em in. In an hour they're out again and I've got a false arrest lug dropped on me. Even if it *ain't* nosedrops. And they can use the robot's goddam tapes to hang me up by the thumbs!''

Summit dropped back into his chair, sack weight. His face was a burned-out building. ''So we've got three, maybe six kids dead. Jesus, Jesus, Jesus.'' He shook his head.

Polchik wanted to make him feel better. But how did you do that? ''Listen, Capt'n, you know I would of had those kids in here so fast it'd'of made their heads swim . . . if I'd've been on my own. That damned robot . . . well, it just didn't work out. Capt'n, listen, I'm not trying to alibi, it was godawful out there, but you were a beat cop . . . *you* know a cop ain't a set of rules and a pile of wires. Guys like me just can't work with things like that Brillo. It won't work, Capt'n. A guy's gotta be free to use his judgment, to feel like he's worth something', not just a piece of sh—''

Summit's head came up sharply. ''Judgment?!'' He looked as though he wanted to vomit. ''What kind of judgment are you showing with that Rico over at the Amsterdam Inn? And all of it on the tapes, sound, pictures, everything?''

''Oh. That.''

''Yes, that. You're damned lucky I insisted those tapes get held strictly private, for the use of the Force only. I had to invoke privileged data. Do you have any *idea* how many strings that puts on me, on this office now, with the Chief, with the Commissioner, with the goddam Mayor? Do you have any *idea*, Polchik?''

''No, sir. I'm sorry.'' Chagrin.

''Sorry doesn't buy it, goddammit! I don't want you

taking any juice from anywhere. No bottles, no gifts, no *nothing,* not from *any*body. Have you got that?''

''Yessir.''

Wearily, Summit persisted. ''It's tough enough to do a job here without having special graft investigations and the D.A.'s squad sniffing all over the precinct. Jesus, Polchik, do you have any *idea* . . . !'' He stopped, looked levelly at the patrolman and said, ''One more time and you're out on your ass. Not set down, not reprimanded, not docked—*out.* All the way out. *Kapish?*''

Polchik nodded; his back was broken.

''I've got to set it right.''

''What, sir?''

''You, that's what.''

Polchik waited. A pendulum was swinging.

''I'll have to think about it. But if it hadn't been for the five good years you've given me here, Polchik . . . well, you'll be getting punishment, but I don't know just what yet.''

''Uh, what's gonna happen with the robot?''

Summit got to his feet slowly; mooring a dirigible. ''Come on outside and you'll see.''

Polchik followed him to the door, where the Captain paused. He looked closely into Polchik's face and said, ''Tonight has been an education, Mike.''

There was no answer to that one.

They went into the front desk room. Reardon still had his head stuck into Brillo's open torso cavity, and the whiz kid was standing tiptoed behind him, peering over the engineer's shoulder. As they entered the ready room, Reardon straightened and clicked off the lamp on the power tool. He watched Summit and Polchik as they walked over to Chief Santorini. Summit murmured to the Chief for a moment, then Santorini nodded and said, ''We'll talk tomorrow, then.''

He started toward the front door, stopped and said, "Good night, gentlemen. It's been a long night. I'll be in touch with your offices tomorrow." He didn't wait for acknowledgment; he simply went.

Reardon turned around to face Summit. He was waiting for words. Even the whiz kid was starting to come alive again. The silent FBI man rose from the bench (as far as Polchik could tell, he hadn't changed position all the time they'd been gone on patrol) and walked toward the group.

Reardon said, "Well . . ." His voice trailed off.

The pendulum was swinging.

"Gentlemen," said the Captain, "I've advised Chief Santorini I'll be writing out a full report to be sent downtown. My recommendations will more than likely decide whether or not these robots will be added to our Force."

"Grass roots level opinion, very good, Captain, very good," said the whiz kid. Summit ignored him.

"But I suppose I ought to tell you right now my recommendations will be negative. As far as I'm concerned, Mr. Reardon, you still have a long way to go with your machine."

"But, I thought—"

"It did very well," Summit said, "don't get me wrong. But I think it's going to need a lot more flexibility and more knowledge of the police officer's duties before it can be of any real aid in our work."

Reardon was angry, but trying to control it. "I programmed the entire patrolman's manual, and all the City codes, and the Supreme Court—"

Summit stopped him with a raised hand. "Mr. Reardon, that's the least of a police officer's knowledge. *Anybody* can read a rule book. But *how to use those rules,* how to make those rules work in the street, that takes more than programming. It takes, well, it takes training. And experience. It doesn't come easily. A cop isn't a set of rules and a pile of wires.''

Polchik was startled to hear his words. He knew it would be okay. Not as good as before, but at least okay.

Reardon was furious now. And he refused to be convinced. Or perhaps he refused to allow the Mayor's whiz kid and the FBI man to be so easily convinced. He had worked too long and at too much personal cost to his career to let it go that easily. He hung onto it. "But merely training shouldn't put you off the X-44 *completely*!''

The Captain's face tensed around the mouth. "Look, Mr. Reardon, I'm not very good at being politic—which is why I'm still a Captain, I suppose—" The whiz kid gave him a be-careful look, but the Captain went on. "But it isn't merely training. This officer is a good one. He's bright, he's on his toes, he maybe isn't Sherlock Holmes but he knows the feel of a neighborhood, the smell of it, the heat level. He knows every August we're going to get the leapers and the riots and some woman's head cut off and dumped in a mailbox mailed C.O.D. to Columbus, Ohio. He knows when there's racial tension in our streets. He knows when those poor slobs in the tenements have just *had it*. He knows when some new kind of vice has moved in. But he made more mistakes out there tonight than a rookie. Five years walking and riding that beat, he's *never* foulballed the way he did tonight. Why? I've got to ask *why*? The only thing different was that machine of yours. Why? *Why* did Mike Polchik foulball so bad? *He* knew those kids in that car should have been run in for b&b or naline tests. So why, Mr. Reardon . . . *why*?''

Polchik felt lousy. The Captain was more worked up than he'd ever seen him. But Polchik stood silently, listening; standing beside the silent, listening FBI man.

Brillo merely stood silently. Turned off.

Then why did he still hear that robot buzzing?

"It isn't rules and regs, Mr. Reardon." The Captain seemed to have a lot more to come. "A moron can learn those. But how do you evaluate the look on a man's face that tells you he needs a fix? How do you gauge the cultural change in words like 'custer' or 'grass' or 'high' or 'pig'? How do you know when *not* to bust a bunch of kids who've popped a hydrant so they can cool off? How do you program all of *that* into a robot . . . and know that it's going to change from hour to hour?"

"We can do it! It'll take time, but we can do it."

The Captain nodded slowly. "Maybe you can."

"I know we can."

"Okay, I'll even go for that. Let's say you can. Let's say you can get a robot that'll act like a human being and still be a robot . . . because that's what we're talking about here. There's still something else."

"Which is?"

"People, Mr. Reardon. People like Polchik here. I asked you *why* Polchik foulballed, why he made such a bum patrol tonight that I'm going to have to take disciplinary action against him *for the first time in five years* . . . so I'll *tell* you why, Mr. Reardon, about people like Polchik here. They're still afraid of machines, you know. We've pushed them and shoved them and lumbered them with machines till they're afraid the next clanking item down the pike is going to put them on the bread line. So they don't *want* to cooperate. They don't do it on purpose. They may not even *know* they're doing it, hell, I don't think Polchik knew what was happening, why he was falling over his feet tonight. You can get a robot to act like a human being, Mr. Reardon. Maybe you're right and you *can* do it, just like you said. But how the hell are you going to get humans to act like robots and not be afraid of machines?''

Reardon looked as whipped as Polchik felt.

''May I leave Brillo here till morning? I'll have a crew come over from the labs and pick him up.''

''Sure,'' the Captain said, ''he'll be fine right there against the wall. The Desk Sergeant'll keep an eye on him.'' To Loyo he said, ''Sergeant, instruct your relief.''

Loyo smiled and said, ''Yessir.''

Summit looked back at Reardon and said, ''I'm sorry.''

Reardon smiled wanly, and walked out. The whiz kid wanted to say something, but too much had already been said, and the Captain looked through him. ''I'm pretty tired, Mr. Kenzie. How about we discuss it tomorrow after I've seen the Chief?''

The whiz kid scowled, turned and stalked out.

The Captain sighed heavily. ''Mike, go get signed out and go home. Come see me tomorrow. Late.'' He nodded to the FBI man, who still had not spoken; then he went away.

The robot stood where Reardon had left him. Silent.

Polchik went upstairs to the locker room to change.

Something was bothering him. But he couldn't nail it down.

When he came back down into the muster room, the FBI man was just racking the receiver on the desk blotter phone. ''Leaving?'' he asked. It was the first thing Polchik had heard him say. It was a warm brown voice.

''Yeah. Gotta go home. I'm whacked out.''

''Can't say I blame you. I'm a little tired myself. Need a lift?''

''No, thanks,'' Polchik said. ''I take the subway. Two blocks from the house.'' They walked out together. Polchik thought about wet carpets waiting. They stood on the front steps for a minute, breathing in the chill morning air, and Polchik said, "I feel kinda sorry for that chunk of scrap now. He did a pretty good job."

"But not good enough," the FBI man added.

Polchik felt suddenly very protective about the inert form against the wall in the precinct house. "Oh, I dunno. He saved me from getting clobbered, you wanna know the truth. Tell me . . . you think they'll ever build a robot that'll cut it?"

The FBI man lit a cigarette, blew smoke in a thin stream, and nodded. "Yeah. Probably. But it'll have to be a lot more sophisticated than old Brillo in there."

Polchik looked back through the doorway. The robot stood alone, looking somehow helpless. Waiting for rust. Polchik thought of kids, all kinds of kids, and when he was a kid. *It must be hell,* he thought, *being a robot. Getting turned off when they don't need you no more.*

Then he realized he could *still* hear that faint electrical buzzing. The kind a watch makes. He cast a quick glance at the FBI man but, trailing cigarette smoke, he was already moving toward his car, parked directly in front of the precinct house. Polchik couldn't tell if he was wearing a watch or not.

He followed the government man.

"The trouble with Brillo," the FBI man said, "is that Reardon's facilities were too limited. But I'm sure there are other agencies working on it. They'll lick it one day." He snapped the cigarette into the gutter.

"Yeah, sure," Polchik said. The FBI man unlocked the car door and pulled it. It didn't open.

"Damn it!" he said. "Government pool issue. Damned door always sticks." Bunching his muscles, he suddenly wrenched at it with enough force to pop it open. Polchik stared. Metal had ripped.

"You take care of yourself now, y'hear?" the FBI

man said, getting into the car. He flipped up the visor with its OFFICIAL GOVERNMENT BUSINESS card tacked to it, and slid behind the steering wheel.

The car settled heavily on its springs, as though a ton of load had just been dumped on the front seat. He slammed the door. It was badly sprung.

"Too bad we couldn't use him," the FBI man said, staring out of the car at Brillo, illuminated through the precinct house doorway. "But . . . too crude."

"Yeah, sure, I'll take care of myself," Polchik replied, one exchange too late. He felt his mouth hanging open.

The FBI man grinned, started the car, and pulled away.

Polchik stood in the street, for a while.

Sometimes he stared down the early morning street in the direction the FBI man had taken.

Sometimes he stared at the metal cop immobile in the muster room.

And even as the sounds of the city's new day rose around him, he was not at all certain he did not still hear the sound of an electric watch. Getting louder.

Out of Time

INTRODUCTION

There's a lot of double-talk about the way we run our prisons today. Good, earnest, well-meaning citizens tell themselves that prisons are there not merely to keep dangerous criminals away from society, where they might hurt somebody. Prisons also exist to help rehabilitate the criminal, to help him or her return to society a reformed person, ready to take a useful place in the community. We even call some of our prisons "reformatories."

Actually, most prisons are cesspools of drugs, violence, and danger. When your community consists of nothing but sociopaths and their guards, there is very little chance for rehabilitation and reform. Those who question this ought to read Wiseguy, the autobiography of a former Mafioso. While serving a prison term, the author used his time smuggling narcotics and otherwise carrying on profitable businesses for his fellow inmates.

If we agree that criminal behavior is an aberration

for which modern society has no real cure, then why not borrow an idea from the world of cryonics and freeze criminals until such time as science discovers techniques for truly reforming a criminal's attitudes and behavior? Several people have had their bodies placed in such cryonic suspension upon being declared clinically dead, in the hope that science will one day be able to cure the illness that "killed" them. Why not cryonically freeze criminals until we know how to cure their deviant behavior? Keeping a convict cryogenically frozen costs only a few pennies of electricity per year, orders of magnitude lower than the cost of feeding and housing a live convict.

There are many unsolved medical problems with cryonic suspension, and a whole raft of legal issues when it comes to dealing with freezing unwilling convicts. Pitfalls surround the idea, as you will see in the following tale.

The first day of the trial, the courtroom had been as hectic as a television studio, what with four camera crews and all their lights, dozens of reporters, all the extra cops for security, and just plain gawkers. But after eight months, hardly any onlookers were there when Don Carmine Lombardo had his heart attack.

The *cappo di tutti cappi* for the whole New England region clawed at his chest and made a few gasping, gargling noises in the middle of his brother-in-law's incredibly perjured testimony, struggled halfway out of his chair, then collapsed across the table in front of him, scattering the notes and depositions nearly laid out by his quartet of lawyers as he slid to the floor like a limp sack of overcooked spaghetti.

The rumor immediately sprang up that his brother-

in-law's testimony, in which he described the Don as a
God-fearing family man who had become immensely
wealthy merely by hard work and frugality, brought
down the vengeance of the Lord upon the old man. This
is probably not true. The heart attack was no great surprise. Don Carmine was almost eighty, grossly overweight, and given to smoking horrible little Sicilian
rum-soaked cigars by the boxful.

The most gifted and expensive physicians in the
Western world were flown to Rhode Island in the valiant
attempt to save the Don's life. Tenaciously, the old man
hung on for six days, then, like the God he was said to
have feared, he relaxed on the seventh. He was declared
dead jointly by the medical team, no single one of them
wishing to take the responsibility of making the announcement to the stony-eyed men in their perfectly-
tailored silk suits who waited out in the hospital's
corridors, eating pizzas brought in by muscular errand
boys and conversing in whispered mixtures of Italian
and English.

But Don Carmine did not die before issuing orders
that his body be preserved in liquid nitrogen. Perhaps
he truly did fear God. If there was any chance that he
could survive death, he was willing to spend the money
and take the risk.

"What is this cryo . . . cryology or whatever the hell
they call it?" snarled Angelo Marchetti. He was not
angry. Snarling was his normal mode of conversation,
except when he did get angry. Then he bellowed.

"Cryonics," said his lawyer, Pat del Vecchio.

"They froze him in that stuff," Marchetti said. "Like
he was a popsicle."

Del Vecchio was a youngster, one of the new breed
of university-trained legal talents that was slowly, patiently turning the Mob away from its brutal old ways

and toward the much more profitable pursuits of computer crime and semi-legitimate business. There was far more money to be made, at far less risk, in toxic waste disposal than in narcotics. Let the Latinos cut each other up over the drug trade. Let one state after another legalize gambling. Del Vecchio knew the wave of the future: more money was stolen with a few touches of the fingers on the right computer keyboard than with all the guns the old-timers liked to carry.

Marchetti was one of the last surviving old-timers among the New England families. Bald, built like a squat little fireplug with a glistening, narrow-eyed bullet head stuck atop it, he had been a bully all his life. Once he cowed men with his fists. Now he used the threat of his powerful voice, and the organization behind him, to make men do his will. He had inherited Don Carmine's empire, but the thought that the Don might come back some day bothered him.

He sat on the patio of his luxurious home in Newport, gazing out at the lovely seascape formed by Narragansett Bay. The blue waters were dotted by dozens of white sails; the blue sky, by puffy white clouds. Marchetti often spent the afternoon out here, relaxing on his lounge chair, ogling the girls in their bathing suits through a powerful pair of binoculars. He was not oblivious to the fact that the great robber barons of the previous century had built their summer retreats nearby. The thought pleased him. But today he was worried about this scientific miracle called cryonics.

"I mean, is the old Don dead or ain't he?"

Del Vecchio, lean and dapper in a sharply-cut double-breasted ivory blazer and dark blue slacks, assured Marchetti, "He's legally, medically, and really dead."

Marchetti scowled suspiciously. "Then why didn't he wanna be buried?"

With great patience, del Vecchio explained that while

the old man was clinically dead, there were some scientists who believed that perhaps in some far-distant future it might be possible to cure the heart problem that caused the death. So Don Carmine had himself frozen, preserved in liquid nitrogen at the temperature of 346 degrees below zero Fahrenheit.

"Christ, that's cold!" Marchetti growled.

At that temperature, del Vecchio said, the old man's body would be perfectly preserved for eternity. As long as the refrigerator wasn't turned off.

"And if the scientists ever find a way to fix what killed him, they can thaw him out and bring him back to life," the young lawyer concluded.

Marchetti squinted in the sunlight, his interest in the sailboats and even the bathing beauties totally gone now.

"Maybe," he said slowly, "somebody oughtta pull the plug out of that icebox." He pronounced the word in the old neighborhood dialect: *i-sa-bocks*.

Del Vecchio smiled, understanding his boss's reluctance to return the New England empire to a newly-arisen Don Carmine.

"Don't worry," he soothed. "There's one great big loophole in the situation."

"Yeah? What?"

"Nobody knows how to defrost a corpse, once it's been frozen. Can't be done without breaking up the body cells. Try to defrost Don Carmine and you'll kill him."

Marchetti laughed, a hearty, loud, blood-chilling roar. "Then he'll be twice as dead!" He laughed until tears streamed down his cheeks.

The years passed swiftly, too swiftly and too few for Angelo Marchetti. Despite del Vecchio's often-repeated advice that he get into the profits that can be skimmed from legallized casino gambling and banking, Marchetti could not change his ways. But the law enforcement agencies of the federal government were constantly improving their techniques and inevitably they caught up with him. Marchetti (he never thought to have himself styled "Don Angelo") was brought to trial to face charges of loan-sharking, tax evasion, and—most embarrassing of all—endangering the public health by improperly disposing of toxic wastes. One of the companies that del Vecchio had urged him to buy through a dummy corporation had gotten caught dumping chemical sludge into a public storm sewer.

Thirty pounds heavier than he had been the year that Don Carmine died, Marchetti sat once again on the patio behind his mansion. The binoculars rested on the flagstones beside his lounge chair, they had not been used all summer. Marchetti's eyesight was not what it once was, nor was his interest in scantily-clad young women. He lay on the lounge chair like a beached white whale in size 52 plaid bathing trunks.

"They've got the goods," del Vecchio was saying gloomily.

"Ain't there nothin' we can do?"

Standing over his boss's prostrate blubber, the lawyer looked even more elegant than he had a few years earlier. Still lean and trim, there were a few lines in his face now that might have been wisdom, or debauchery, or both. He was deeply tanned, spending almost all his time under the sun, either during the New England summer or the Arizona and California winter. He even had a sunlamp system installed over his bed, encircling the smoked mirror on the ceiling.

"We've tried everything from change-of-venue to bribery," del Vecchio said. "Nothing doing. Uncle Sam's got your balls in a vise."

"How about putting some pressure on the witnesses?'' Marchetti growled. ''Knock off one or two and the rest'll clam up.''

Del Vecchio shook his head. ''Most of the 'witnesses' against you are computer records, tapes, floppy disks. The F.B.I. has them under tight security, and they've made copies of them, besides.''

Marchetti peered up at his lawyer. ''There's gotta be *something* you can do. I ain't goin' to jail—not while you're alive.''

A hint of surprise flashed in del Vecchio's dark eyes for a moment, but Marchetti never saw it, hidden behind the lawyer's stylish sunglasses. Del Vecchio recognized the threat in his employer's words, but what shocked him was that the old man was getting desperate enough to make such a threat. Soon he would be lashing out in blind anger, destroying everything and everyone around him.

''This is one thing,'' he said slowly.

''What? What is it?''

''You won't like it. I know you won't.''

''What the hell is it?'' Marchetti bellowed. ''Tell me!''

''Freezing.''

''What?''

''Have yourself frozen.''

''Are you nuts? I ain't dead!''

Del Vecchio allowed a slight smile to cross his lips. ''No, but you could be.''

Actually, the plan had been forming in his mind since Don Carmine's immersion in the gleaming stainless steel tank full of liquid nitrogen. Even then, del Vecchio had thought back to his college days when, as an agile young undergraduate, he had been a star on the school's fencing team. He remembered that there were strict rules of procedure in foil fencing, almost like the fussy rules of procedure in a criminal court. It was pos-

sible for a fencer to score a hit on his opponent, but
have the score thrown out because he had not followed
the proper procedure.

"Out of time!" he remembered his fencing coach
screaming at him. "You can't just stab your opponent
whenever the hell you feel like it! You've got to establish the proper right-of-way, the proper timing. You're
out of time, del Vecchio!"

He realized that Marchetti was glowering at him.
"Whattaya mean I could be dead?"

With a patient sigh, del Vecchio explained, "We've
gotten your case postponed three times because of medical excuses. Dr. Brunelli has testified that you've got
heart and liver problems."

"Fat lot of good that's done," Marchetti grumbled.

"Yeah, but suppose Brunelli makes out a death certificate for you, says you died of a heart attack, just like
old Don Carmine."

"And they put somebody else into the ground while
I take a vacation in the old country?" Marchetti's face
brightened a little.

"No, that won't work. The law enforcement agencies
are too smart for that. You'd be spotted and sent back
here."

"Then what?"

"We make you clinically dead. Brunelli gives you an
injection . . ."

"And kills me?" Marchetti roared.

Del Vecchio put his hands up, as if to defend himself. "Wait. Hear me out. You'll be clinically dead.
We'll freeze you for a while. Then we'll bring you back
and you'll be as good as ever!"

Marchetti scowled. "How do I know I can trust you
to bring me back?"

"For God's sake, Angelo, you've been like a father
to me ever since my real father died. You can trust me!

Besides, you can arrange for a dozen different guys to see to it that you're revived. And a dozen more to knock me off if I try to keep you frozen.''

''Yeah . . . maybe.''

''You won't only be clinically dead,'' del Vecchio pointed out. ''You'll be *legally* dead. Any and all charges against you will be wiped out. When you come back, legally you'll be a new person. Just like a baby!''

''Yeah?'' The old man broke into a barking, sand-paper laugh.

''Sure. And just to make sure, we'll keep you frozen long enough so that the statute of limitations runs out on all the charges against you. You'll come out of that freezer free and clear!''

Marchetti's laughter grew louder, heartier. But then it abruptly stopped. ''Hey, wait. Didn't you tell me that nobody knows how to defrost a corpse? If they try to thaw me out it'll kill me all over again!''

''That's all changed in the past six months,'' del Vecchio said. ''Some bright kid down at Johns Hopkins thawed out some mice and rabbits. Then a couple weeks ago a team at Pepperdine brought back three people, two men and a woman. I hear they're going to thaw Walt Disney and bring him back pretty soon.''

''What about Don Carmine?'' asked Marchetti.

The lawyer shrugged. ''That's up to you.''

Without an instant's hesitation, Marchetti ran a stubby forefinger across his throat.

Del Vecchio had every intention of honoring his commitment to Marchetti. He really did. The fireplug-shaped old terror had truly been like a father to the younger man, paying his way through college and even law school after del Vecchio's father had been cut down in the line of duty one rainy night on the street outside a warehouse full of Japanese stereos and television sets.

But one thing led to another as the years rolled along. Del Vecchio finally married and started to raise a family. More and more of the Mob business came under his hands, and he made it prosper better than ever before. The organization now owned banks, resort hotels, and other legitimate businesses. As well as state legislators, judges, and half-a-dozen Congressmen. Violent crime was left to the disorganized fools. Del Vecchio's regime was marked by peace, order, and upwardly-spiraling profits.

One after another, Marchetti's lieutenants came to depend on him. Del Vecchio never demanded anything as archaic and embarrassing as an oath of fealty, kissing the hand, or other ancient prostrations. But the lieutenants, some of them heavily-built narrow-eyed thugs, others more lean and stylish and modern, all let it be known, one way or the other, that to revive Marchetti from his cryonic slumber would be a terrible mistake.

So Marchetti slept. And del Vecchio saw his empire grow more prosperous.

But owning legitimate banks and businesses does not make one necessarily honest. Del Vecchio's banks often made highly irregular loans, and sometimes collected much higher interest than permitted by law. On rare occasions, the interest was collected only after brutal demonstrations of force. There were also some stock manipulations that finally attracted the attention of the Securities and Exchange Commission, and a string of disastrous fires in Mob-owned hotels that were on the verge of bankruptcy.

And even the lackadaisical state gambling commission roused itself when the federal income-tax people started investigating the strange phenomenon of certain gambling casinos that took in customers by the millions, yet somehow failed to show a profit on their books.

Once he realized that there was no way out of the mounting legal troubles facing him, del Vecchio decided to take his own advice. Carefully, he began to create a medical history for himself that would end in clinical death and cryonic immersion. He explained what he was doing to his most trusted lieutenants, told them that he would personally take the blame and the legal punishment for them all, allowing them to elect a new leader and go on operating as before once he was declared dead. They expressed eternal gratitude.

But del Vecchio knew perfectly well how long eternal gratitude lasted. So he sent his wife and their teenaged children to live in Switzerland, where most of his personal fortune had been cached with the gnomes of Zurich. He gave his wife painfully detailed instructions on when and how to revive him.

"Fifteen years will do it," he told her. "Can you wait for me that long?"

She smiled limpidly at him, threw her arms around his neck and kissed him passionately. But she said, "I'll only be fifty-eight when you get out."

Del Vecchio wondered if she knew about his playmates in Boston. He realized he would still be his current age, forty-seven, when he was thawed back to life. There would be plenty of other women to play with. But would his wife remain faithful enough to have him revived? To make doubly certain of his future, he flew to Zurich and had a very tight legal contract drawn by the bank which held his personal fortune. The gnomes would free him, if no one else would. Otherwise his money would be donated to charity and the bank would lose control of it.

"What you're doing may be legal, Del, but it's damned immoral."

Del Vecchio was having dinner with one of the federal district attorneys who was prosecuting one of the innumerable current cases against him. They were old friends, had been classmates at law school. The fact that they were on opposite sides of the case did not bother either of them; they were too professional to allow such trivialities to get in the way of their social lives.

"Immoral?" Del Vecchio shot back. "What do I care about that? Morality's for little guys, for people who've got no muscle, no backbone. You worry about morality, I'm worrying about spending the rest of my life in jail."

They were sitting at a small corner table in a quiet little restaurant in downtown Providence, barely a block from the federal courthouse, a place frequented almost exclusively by lawyers who never lifted an eyebrow at a defendant buying dinner for a prosecuting attorney. After all, prosecuting attorneys rarely made enough money to afford such an elegant restaurant; candlelight and leather-covered wine lists were not for the protectors of the public, not on the salaries the public allowed them.

"If the jury finds you guilty, the judge has to impose the penalty," the district attorney said, very seriously.

"Jury," del Vecchio almost spat. "Those twelve *chidrools*! I'm supposed to be tried by a jury of my peers, right? That means my equals, doesn't it?"

The district attorney frowned slightly. "They are your equals, Del. What makes you think . . ."

"My equals?" del Vecchio laughed. "Do you really think those unemployed bums and screwy housewives are my equals? I mean, how smart can they be if they let themselves get stuck with jury duty?"

The attorney's frown deepened. His name was Christopher Scarpato. He had gone into the profession of law because his father, a small shopkeeper continually in debt to bookmakers, had insisted that his son learn how to outwit the rest of the world. While Chris was working his way through law school, his father was beaten to death by a pair of overly-zealous collection agents. More of a plodder than a brilliant student, Chris was recruited by the Department of Justice, where careful, thorough groundwork is more important than flashy public relations and passionate rhetoric. Despite many opportunities, he had remained honest and dedicated. Del Vecchio found that charming, even noteworthy, and felt quite superior to his friend.

"And what makes you think they'll find me guilty?" asked del Vecchio, just a trifle smugly. "They're stupid, all right, but can they be *that* stupid?"

Scarpato finally realized he was being baited. He smiled one of his rare smiles, but it was a sad one. "They'll find you guilty, Del. They've got no choice."

Del Vecchio's grin faded. He looked down at his plate of pasta, then placed his fork on the damask tablecloth alongside it. "I got no appetite. Haven't been feeling so good."

With a weary shake of his head, Chris replied, "You don't have to put on the act for me, Del. I know what you're going to do."

"What do you mean?"

"You're going to get some tame doctor to pronounce you dead and then have yourself frozen. Just like Marchetti."

Del Vecchio tried to look shocked, but instead he broke into a grin. "Is there anything illegal about dying? Or being frozen?"

"The doctor will be committing a homicide."

"You'll have to prove that."

Scarpato said, "It's an attempt to evade the law. That's immoral, even if it's not illegal—yet."

"Let the priests worry about morality," del Vecchio advised his old friend.

"You should worry about it," said Scarpato. "You've turned into an asocial menace, Del. When we were in school, you were an okay kind of guy. But now . . ."

"What, I'm going to lose my soul?"

"Maybe you've already lost it. Maybe you ought to be thinking about how you can get it back."

Del Vecchio grinned at him. "Listen, Chris: I don't give a damn about souls. But I'm going to protect my body, you can bet. You won't see me in jail, old buddy. I'm going to take a step out of time, and when I come back, you'll be an old man and I'll still be young."

Scarpato said nothing, and del Vecchio knew that he had silenced his friend's attempts at conscience.

Still, that little hint of "yet" that Scarpato had dropped bothered del Vecchio as the days swiftly raced by. He checked every aspect of his plan while his health appeared to deteriorate rapidly: the doctors played their part to perfection, his wife was already comfortably ensconced in Switzerland, the bankers in Zurich understood exactly what they had to do.

Yet as he lay on the clinic table with the gleaming stainless steel cylinder waiting beside him like a mechanical whale that was going to swallow him in darkness, del Vecchio could feel his pulse racing with fear. The last thing he saw was the green-gowned doctor, masked, approaching him with the hypodermic syringe. That, and frigid wisps of vapor wafting up from the tanks of liquid nitrogen. The needle felt sharp and cold. He remembered that parts of Dante's hell were frozen in ice.

When they awoke him, there was a long period of confusion and disorientation. They told him that that it lasted only a day or so, but to del Vecchio it seemed like weeks, even months.

At first he thought something had gone wrong, and

they had never put him under. But the doctors were all different, and the room he was in was not the clinic he had known. They kept him in bed most of the time, except when two husky young men came in to force him to get up and walk around the room. Four times around the little hospital room exhausted him. Then they flopped him back on the bed, gave him a mercilessly efficient massage, and left. A female nurse wheeled in his first meal and spoon-fed him; he was too weak to lift his arms.

The second day (or week, or month) Scarpato came in to visit him.

"How do you feel, Del?"

Strangely, the attorney seemed barely to have aged at all. There was a hint of gray at his temples, perhaps a line or two in his face that had not been there before, but otherwise the years had treated him very kindly.

"Kind of weak," del Vecchio answered truthfully.

Scarpato nodded. "That's to be expected, from what the medics tell me. Your heart is good, circulation strong. Everything is okay, physically."

A thought suddenly flashed into del Vecchio's thawing mind. "What are you doing in Switzerland?"

The attorney's face grew somber. "You're not in Switzerland, Del. We had your vat flown back here. You're in New York."

"Wh . . . how . . . ?"

"And you haven't been under for fifteen years, either. It's only three years.

Del Vecchio tried to sit up in the bed, but he was too weak to make it. His head sank back onto the pillows. He could hear his pulse thudding in his ears.

"I tried to warn you," Scarpato said, "that night at dinner in Providence. You thought you were outsmarting the law, outsmarting the people who make up the law, who *are* the law. But you can't outwit the people for long, Del.''

Out of the corner of his eye, del Vecchio saw that the room's only window was covered with a heavy wire mesh, like bars on a jail cell's window. He choked back a shocked gasp.

Scarpato spoke quietly, without malice. ''Your cute little cryonics trick forced the people to take a fresh look at things. There've been a few new laws passed since you had yourself frozen.''

''Such as?''

''Such as the state has the right to revive a frozen corpse if and when a grand jury feels he's had himself frozen specifically to evade the law.''

Del Vecchio felt his heart sink in his chest.

''But once they got that one passed, they went one step further.''

''What?''

''Well, you know how the country's been divided about the death penalty. Some people think it's cruel and unusual punishment; others think it's a necessary deterrent to crime, especially violent crime. Even the Supreme Court has been split on the issue.''

Del Vecchio couldn't catch his breath. He realized what was coming.

''And there's been the other problem,'' Scarpato went on, ''of overcrowding in the jails. Some judges—I'm sure you know who—even let criminals go free because they claim that putting them in overcrowded jails is cruel and unusual punishment.''

''Oh my God in heaven,'' del Vecchio gasped.

''So—'' Scarpato hesitated. Del Vecchio had never seen his old friend look so grim, so purposeful. ''So they've passed laws in just about every state in the union to freeze criminals, just store them in vats of liquid nitrogen. Dewars, they call them. We're emptying the jails, Del, and filling them up again with dewars. They're starting to look like mortuaries, all those stainless steel caskets piled up, one on top of another.''

"But you can't do that!"

"It's done. The laws have been passed. The Supreme Court has ruled on it.''

"But that's murder!"

"No. The convicts are clinically dead, but not legally. They can be revived. And since the psychologists and sociologists have been yelling for years that crime is a social maladjustment, and not really the fault of the criminal, we've found a way to make them happy.''

"I don't see . . .''

Scarpato almost smiled. "Well, look. If you can have yourself frozen because you've just died of a heart ailment or a cancer that medical science can't cure, in the hopes that science will find a cure in the future and thaw you out and make you well again . . . well, why not use the same approach to social and psychological illnesses?''

"Huh?"

"You're a criminal because of some psychological maladjustment," Scarpato said. "At least, that's what the head-shrinkers claim. So we freeze you and keep you frozen until science figures out a way to cure you. That way, we're not punishing you; we're *rehabilitating* you.''

"You can't do that! I got civil rights . . .''

"Your civil rights are not being infringed. Once you're found guilty by a jury of your peers you will be frozen. You will not age a single day while in the liquid nitrogen. When medical science learns how to cure your psychological unbalance, you will be thawed, cured, and returned to society as a healthy, productive citizen. We even start a small bank account for you which accrues compound interest, so that you'll have some money when you're rehabilitated.''

"But that could be a thousand years in the future!" del Vecchio screamed.

"So what?"

"The whole world could be completely changed by then! They could revive me to make a slave out of me! They could use me for meat, for Chrissakes! Or spare parts!" He was screeching now, in absolute terror.

Scarpato shrugged. "We have no control over that, unfortunately. But we're doing our best for you. In earlier societies you might have been tortured, or mutilated, or even put to death. Up until a few years ago, you would have been sentenced to years and years in prison; a degrading life, filled with violence and drugs and danger. Now—you just take a nap and then someday someone will wake you up in a wonderful new world, completely rehabilitated, with enough money to start a new life for yourself."

Del Vecchio broke into uncontrollable sobs. "Don't. For God's mercy, Chris, don't do this to me. My wife . . . my kids . . ."

Scarpato shook his head. "It's done. Believe me, there's no way I could get you out of it, even if I wanted to. Your wife has found herself a boyfriend in Switzerland, some penniless count or duke or something. Your kids are getting along fine. Your girlfriends miss you, though, from what I hear."

"You sonofabitch! You dirty, scheming . . ."

"You did this to yourself, Del!" Scarpato snapped, with enough power in his voice to silence del Vecchio. "You thought you had found a nice fat loophole in the law, so you could get away with almost anything. You thought the rest of us were stupid fools. Well, you made a loophole, all right. But the people—those shopkeepers and unemployed bums and screwy housewives that you've walked over all your life—they've turned your loophole into a noose. And your neck is in it. Don't blame me. Blame yourself.''

His eyes still flowing tears, del Vecchio pleaded, "Don't do it to me, Chris. Please don't do it. They'll never wake me up. They'll pull the plug on me . . .''

"Don't think that everyone's as dishonest as you are. The convicts will be kept frozen. It only costs a thousandth of what it costs to keep a man in jail. You'll be safe enough.''

"But they'll thaw me out sometime in the future. I'll be all alone in the world. I won't know anybody. It'll be all strange to me. I'll be a total stranger . . .''

"No you won't," Scarpato said, his face grim. "It's practically certain that Marchetti and Don Carmine will both be thawed out when you are. After all, you're all three suffering from the same dysfunction, aren't you?''

That's when the capillary in del Vecchio's brain ballooned and burst. Scarpato saw his friend's eyes roll up into his head, his body stiffen. He slammed the emergency call button beside the bed and a team of medics rushed in. While Scarpato watched, they declared del Vecchio clinically dead. Within an hour they slid his corpse into a waiting stainless steel cylinder where it would repose until some happier day in the distant future.

"You're out of time now, Del," Scarpato whispered as a technician sealed the end of the gleaming dewar. "Really out of time.''

Test in Orbit

INTRODUCTION

Murder is regarded as a heinous crime in every society, yet every society condones murder. In fact, the more organized and larger in scale the murdering, the more likely that society will revere and reward the murderer.

Western civilization prides itself on being based upon the ethical bedrock of Judeo-Christian thought. "Thou shalt not kill" is one of our ten commandments; the fifth, curiously enough. Yet we are ready to go to war and kill thousands, millions, while our priests discuss the concept of a just war. In the name of the Prince of Peace, who warned that even being angry with a fellow human being risks the wrath of God, we have slaughtered one another for centuries.

"Test in Orbit" boils this dichotomy down to one man, one human soul, who comes face-to-face with the dilemma of "kill or be killed."

There is no easy answer to this question. No society on Earth has worked out a solution to the problem of *war. A recent anthropological study of the Yanomamo tribes of the Amazonian jungle show that their society actually rewards killers with more wives and wealth than men who do not kill other men.*

As does our own society.

Kinsman snapped awake when the phone went off. Before it could start a second ring he had the receiver off the cradle.

"Captain Kinsman?" The motel's night clerk.

"Yes," he whispered back, squinting at the luminous digits of his wristwatch: *two twenty-three.*

"I'm awfully sorry to disturb you, Captain, but Colonel Murdock himself called . . ."

"How the hell did he know I was here?"

"He doesn't. He said he was phoning all the motels around the base. I didn't admit you were here. He said when he found you he needed you to report to him in person at once. Those were his words, Captain: in person, at once."

Kinsman frowned in the darkness. "Okay. Thanks for playing dumb."

"Not at all, sir. Hope it isn't trouble."

"Yeah." Kinsman hung up. For a half-minute he sat on the edge of the king-sized bed. *Murdock's making the rounds of the motels at two in the morning and he hopes it isn't trouble. Funny.*

He stood up, stretched his lanky frame, and glanced at the blonde sleeping obliviously on the other side of the bed. With a wistful shake of his head he padded out to the bathroom.

Wincing, he flipped the light switch and then turned on the coffee machine on the wall next to the bathroom door. *It's synthetic but it's coffee. Almost.* As the ma-

chine started gurgling he softly closed the bathroom
door and rummaged in his travel kit for his electric
razor. The face that met him in the mirror was lean and
long-jawed and just the slightest bit bloodshot. He kept
his hair at a length that made Murdock uncomfortable:
slightly longer than regulations allowed, not long
enough to call for a reprimand.

Within a few minutes, he was shaved, showered, and
back in Air Force uniform. He left a scribbled note on
motel stationery against the dresser mirror, took a final
long look at the blonde, wishing he could remember
her name, then went out to his car.

The new fuel regulations had put an end to fast driving. Kinsman's own hand-built convertible was ready to
burn hydrogen, if and when the government ever made
it available. For now, he had to go with a captain's
monthly allotment of precious gasoline, which kept him
moving—cautiously—through the predawn darkness.

Some instinct made him turn on the car radio. Diane's haunting voice filled the starry night:

. . . and in her right hand
There's a silver dagger,
That says I can never be your bride.

Kinsman listened in dark solitude as the night wind
blew warmly over him. Diane Lawrence was a major
entertainment star now. *How many years since I've seen
her?* he asked himself, and answered, *Too many.*

A pair of official cars zoomed past him, doing eighty,
heading for the base. Their turbines screeched and faded
into the distance like wailing ghosts. There was no other
traffic on the once-bustling highway. Kinsman held to
the legal limit all the way to the base's main gate. But
he could feel the excitement building up inside him.

There were half a dozen Air Policeman at the gate,

looking brisk and polished, instead of the usual sleepy pair.

"What's the stew, Sergeant?" Kinsman asked as he pulled his car up to the gate.

The guard flashed his pocketlight on the badge Kinsman held in his outstretched hand.

"Dunno, sir. We got the word to look sharp."

The light flashed full in Kinsman's face. *Painfully sharp*.

The guard waved him on.

There was that special crackle in the air as Kinsman drove toward the Administration Building. The kind that comes only when a launch is imminent. As if in answer to his unspoken hunch, the floodlight on Complex 204 bloomed into life, etching the tall silver rocket booster standing there, embraced by the dark spiderwork of the gantry tower.

Pad 204. Manned shot.

People were scurrying in and out of the Administration Building: sleepy-eyed, disheveled, but their feet were doing double time. Colonel Murdock's secretary was coming down the hallway as Kinsman signed in at the security desk.

"What's up, Annie?"

"I just got here myself," she said. There were hairclips still in her sandy-colored curls. "The boss told me to flag you down the instant you arrived."

Even from completely across the Colonel's spacious office, Kinsman could see that Murdock was a round little kettle of nerves. He was standing by the window behind his desk, watching the activity centered on Pad 204, clenching and unclenching his fists behind his back. His bald head was glistening with perspiration, despite the frigid air-conditioning. Kinsman stood at the door with the secretary.

"Colonel?" she said softly.

Murdock spun around. "Kinsman. So here you are."

"What's going on? I thought the next manned shot wasn't until . . ."

The Colonel waved a pudgy hand. "The next manned shot is as fast as we can damned well make it." He walked around the desk and eyed Kinsman. "You look a mess."

"Hell, it's three in the morning!"

"No excuses. Get over to the medical section for preflight checkout. They're waiting for you."

"I'd still like to know . . ."

"Tell them to check your blood for alcohol content," Murdock grumbled.

"I've been celebrating my liberation. I'm not supposed to be on duty. My leave starts at 0900 hours, remember?"

"Cut the clowning. General Hatch is flying in from Norton and he wants you."

"Hatch?"

"That's right. He wants the most experienced man available."

"Twenty astronauts on the base and you have to make me available."

Murdock fumed. "Listen, dammit. This is a military operation. I may not insist on much discipline from you glamor boys, but you're still in the Air Force and you will follow orders. Hatch says he wants the best man we've got. I'd rather have Colt, but he's back East attending a family funeral or something. That means you're *it*. Like it or not."

Kinsman shrugged. "If you saw what I had to leave behind me to report for duty here you'd put me up for the Medal of Honor."

Murdock frowned in exasperation. Anne tried unsuccessfully to suppress a smile.

"All right, lover-boy. Get down to the medical section on the double. Anne, you stick with him and bring him to the briefing room the instant he's finished. General Hatch will be here in twenty minutes; I don't want him kept waiting.''

Kinsman stood at the doorway, not moving. ''Will you just tell me what this is all about?''

''Ask the General,'' Murdock said, walking back toward his desk. ''All I know is that Hatch wants the best man we have ready for a shot immediately.''

''Emergency shots are volunteer missions,'' Kinsman pointed out.

''So?''

''I'm practically on leave. There are eighteen other astronauts here who . . .''

''Dammit, Kinsman, if you . . .''

''Relax, Colonel, relax. I won't let you down. Not when there's a chance to put a few hundred klicks between me and all the brass on Earth.''

Murdock stood there glowering as Kinsman left with Anne. They paced hurriedly out to his car and sped off toward the medical building.

''You shouldn't bait him like that,'' Anne said over the rush of dark wind. ''He feels the pressure a lot more than you do.''

''He's insecure,'' Kinsman said, grinning. ''There're only twenty people on the base who're qualified for orbital missions and he's not one of them.''

''And you are.''

''Damned right, sugar. It's the only thing in the world worth doing. You ought to try it.''

She put a hand up to her wind-whipped hair. ''Me? Fly in orbit? I don't even like airplanes!''

''It's clean world, Annie. Brand new every time. Just you in your own little cosmos. Your life is completely your own. Once you've done it, there's nothing left on Earth but to wait for the next time.''

"My God, you sound as if you really mean it."

"I'm serious," he insisted. "Why don't you wangle a ride on one of the Shuttle missions? They usually have room for an extra person."

"And get locked into a spacecraft with you?"

Kinsman's grin returned. "It's an intriguing idea."

"Some other time, Captain. I've heard all about you and your Zero Gee Club. Right now we have to get you through preflight and then off to meet the General."

General Lesmore D. ("Hatchet") Hatch sat in dour silence in the small briefing room. The oblong conference table was packed with colonels and a single civilian. *They all look so damned serious,* Kinsman thought as he took the only empty chair, at the foot of the table. The General, naturally, sat at the head.

"Captain Kinsman." It was a flat statement of fact.

"Good morning, sir."

Hatched turned to a moonfaced aide. "Borgeson, let's not waste time."

Kinsman only half-listened to the hurried introductions around the table. He felt uncomfortable already, and it was only partly due to the stickiness of the crowded little room. Through the only window he could see the first faint glow of dawn.

"Now then," Borgeson said, introductions finished. "Very briefly, your mission will involve orbiting and making rendezvous with an unidentified satellite."

"Unidentified?"

Borgeson went on, "It was launched from the Soviet Union without the usual prior announcement . . . without a word about its nature or mission."

"And it is big," Hatch rumbled.

"Intelligence"—Colonel Borgeson nodded at the colonel sitting on Kinsman's left—"had no prior word about the launch. We must assume that the satellite is potentially hostile in intent. Colonel McKeever will give you the SPADATS tracking data.''

They went around the table, each colonel adding his bit of information. Kinsman began to build up the picture in his mind.

The satellite had been launched nine hours earlier. It was now in a low polar orbit that allowed it to cover every square kilometer on Earth each twelve hours. Since it first went up, not a single radio transmission had been detected going to it or from it. And it was big, even heavier than the ten-ton *Salyut* space stations the Russians had been using for years.

''A satellite of that size,'' said the Colonel from the Special Weapons Center, ''could easily contain a beam weapon . . . the, er''—he almost smiled—''the 'death ray' kind of device that Intelligence has been warning us about for so many years.''

The weapon could be a very energetic laser or a compact proton accelerator, the Colonel explained. In either case, the beam it fired could be used to destroy rockets as they boosted up from the ground.

''A network of such weapons in orbit could provide a very effective ABM system,'' the colonel said. ''They could shoot down our missile strike force before the boosters ever cleared the ionosphere.''

''And in a little more than two hours,'' Borgeson added, ''this satellite will pass over Nebraska—where several squadrons of SAC missiles are sitting in their silos.''

''This could be the first of many such satellites that they put up,'' General Hatch said, his face deeply etched with worry. *Or is it hate?* ''They could be getting ready to totally negate our strategic strike forces.''

''Why not just knock it down?'' Kinsman asked. ''We can hit it, can't we?''

''We could try,'' the General answered. ''But suppose the damned things zaps our missiles? Then what? Can you imagine the panic in Washington? It'd make Sputnik look like a schoolyard scuffle.'' He puffed out a deep sigh, shaking his head at his inner vision. ''Besides, we've been ordered by the Chief of Staff himself to inspect the satellite and determine whether or not its intent is hostile.''

''In two hours?''

''Perhaps I can explain,'' said the civilian. He had been introduced as a State Department man; Kinsman had already forgotten his name. He had a soft, sheltered look to him.

''We are officially in a position of cooperation, *vis-à-vis* the Soviets, in outer-space programs. Our NASA people and the Russian space people are working out joint programs—the lunar exploration work, the new Mars and Venus probes . . .''

The State Department man went on in his low Ivy League voice, unmindful of the hostility he was generating around the table. ''So if we simply try to destroy this new satellite, it could set back our cooperative programs. On the other hand, if we do nothing, it might encourage the Soviets to make additional secret launches. So the Department believes that this very massive Russian satellite is a test . . . a test of our ability to react, to detect, to inspect, and verify the satellite's nature.''

''We ought to blow it out of the sky,'' snapped one of the colonels.

''Perhaps,'' the civilian replied softly. ''But suppose it is only a peaceful research station? As astronomical telescope? Suppose there are cosmonauts aboard? What if we shoot it down and kill Russian nationals?''

''Serve 'em right,'' somebody muttered.

''No,'' the State Department man said. ''I cannot agree. This is a test. We must prove to the Soviets—

and to ourselves—that we can inspect their satellites and see for ourselves whether or not they contain weaponry.''

The General shook his head. ''If they've gone to the trouble of launching a multiton vehicle in complete secrecy, then military logic dictates that it's a weapon carrier. By damn, that's what I'd do, in their place.''

''No matter whether it's a weapon or not, the satellite could be rigged with bobby traps to prevent us from inspecting it,'' one of the colonels pointed out.

Thanks a lot, said Kinsman to himself.

''They know we've been inspecting their satellites for years,'' said Borgeson. ''But I'm afraid we're going to have to get inside this one to find out what it's all about.''

Hatch focused his gunmetal eyes on Kinsman. ''Captain, I want to impress one thought on you. The Air Force has been working for more than twenty years to achieve the capability of placing a military man in orbit on an instant's notice, despite the opposition of NASA and other parts of the government.''

He never so much as flicked a glance in the civilian's direction as he continued, ''This incident proves the absolute necessity for such a capability. Your flight will be the first practical demonstration of all that we've battled to achieve over these years. You can see, then, the importance of this mission.''

''Yessir.''

''This is strictly a volunteer mission. Exactly because it is so important to us, I don't want you to try it unless you're absolutely certain about it.''

''I understand, sir. I'm your man.''

Hatch's weathered face unfolded into a smile. ''Well spoken, Captain. Good luck.''

The General rose and everyone snapped to attention,

even the civilian. As the others filed out of the briefing room, Murdock drew Kinsman aside.

"You had your chance to beg off."

"And miss this? A chance to play cops and robbers in orbit?"

The Colonel flushed angrily. "We're not in this for laughs! This is damned important. If it really is a weapon up there . . . "

"I'll be the first to know," Kinsman snapped. *I've listened to you enough for one morning.*

The countdown of the solid rocket booster went smoothly, swiftly, as Kinsman sat alone in the Manta spacecraft perched on the rocket's nose. But there was always the chance that a man or machine would fail at a crucial point and turn the intricate, delicately poised booster into a flaming pyre of twisted wreckage.

Kinsman sat tautly in the contoured couch, listening to them tick off the seconds. He hated countdowns, hated being helpless, completely dependent on a hundred faceless voices that flickered through his earphones, waiting childlike in a mechanical womb, not truly alive, doubled up and crowded by the unfeeling, impersonal machinery that automatically gave him warmth and breath and life. Waiting.

He could feel the tiny vibrations along his spine that told him the ship was awakening. Green lights began to blossom across the control panels, telling him that everything was functioning and ready. Still the voices droned through his earphones in carefully measured cadence:

". . . three . . . two . . . one . . ."

And she bellowed to life. Acceleration flattened Kinsman into the couch. Vibration rattled his eyes in their sockets. Time became a meaningless roar. The surging, engulfing, overpowering bellow of the rocket engines made his head ring even after they had burned out into silence.

Within minutes he was in orbit, the long slender rocket stages falling away behind, together with all sensations of weight. Kinsman was alone now in the squat, delta-shaped spacecraft: weightless, free of Earth.

Still he was the helpless unstirring one. Computers sent guidance corrections from the ground to the Manta's controls. Tiny vectoring jets squirted on and off, microscopic puffs of thrust that maneuvered the craft into the precise orbit needed for catching the Russian satellite.

What if she zaps me *as I approach her?* Kinsman thought.

Completely around the world he spun, southward over the Pacific, past the gleaming whiteness of Antarctica, and then north over the wrinkled, cloud-shrouded mass of Asia. As he crossed the night-darkened Arctic, nearly an hour after being launched, the voices from the ground began talking to him again. He answered them as automatically as the machines did, reading numbers off the control panels, proving to them that he was alive and functioning properly.

Then Murdock's voice cut in. "There's been another launch, fifteen minutes ago, from the cosmonaut base at Tyuratam. High-energy boost. Looks like you're going to have company."

Kinsman acknowledged the information, but still sat unmoving.

Finally he saw it, seemingly hurtling toward him. He came to life. To meet and board the satellite he had to match its orbit and velocity exactly. He was approaching it too fast. Radar and computer data flashed in green flickers across the screens in Kinsman's control panels. His eyes and fingers moved constantly, a well-trained artist performing a new and tricky sonata. He maneuvered the retrojet controls that finally eased his Manta into a rendezvous orbit with the massive Russian satellite.

The big satellite seemed to be stopped dead in space, just ahead of him, a huge inert hunk of metal, dazzlingly brilliant where the sun lit its curving flank, totally invisible where it was in shadow. It looked ridiculously like a crescent moon made out of flush-welded aluminum. A smaller crescent puzzled Kinsman until he realized it was a rocket nozzle hanging from the satellite's tailcan.

"I'm parked off her stern about two hundred meters," he reported into his helmet microphone. "She looks like the complete upper-stage of an Alpha-class booster. I'm going outside."

"Better make it fast." Murdock's voice was high-pitched. "That second spacecraft is closing in fast."

"E.T.A.?"

A pause while voices mumbled in the background, then, "About fifteen minutes . . . maybe less."

"Great."

"You can abort if you need to."

Same to you, pal. "I'm going to take a close look at her. Get inside, if I can. Call you back in fifteen minutes."

Murdock didn't argue. Kinsman smiled grimly at the realization that the Colonel had not reminded him about the possibility of booby traps. Old Mother Murdock hardly forgot such items. He simply had decided not to make the choice of aborting the mission too attractive.

Gimmicked or not, the satellite was too near and too enticing to turn back now. Kinsman quickly checked out his pressure suit, pumped the air from his cockpit into the storage tanks, and then opened the hatch over his head.

Out of the womb and into the world.

He climbed out and teetered on the lip of the hatch, coiling the umbilical cord attached to his suit. Regulations required that astronauts use umbilicals, rather than the pistol-like, independent maneuvering units, on solo EVAs. Kinsman hardly thought about it, except to be grateful that he didn't need to carry a bulky life-support pack on his back. He glanced down at the nightside of Earth. City lights blinked through the clouds, and he could even make out the long stretches of highways, lit by ever-moving trucks.

And the stars were there, sprinkled in countless glory across the black, unending depths of space. They looked back at him steadily, solemnly, the unblinking eyes of infinity.

I'll bet that this is all there is to heaven, he said to himself. *You don't need any more.*

Then he turned, with the careful, deliberate motions of a deepsea diver, and looked at the fat crescent of the nearby satellite. Only ten minutes now. Even less.

He pushed off from his spacecraft and sailed effortlessly, arms outstretched. Behind him trailed the umbilical cord that carried his air and electrical power. As he approached the satellite, the Sun rose over the humped curve of its hull and nearly blinded him despite the automatic darkening of his visor. He kicked downward and ducked behind the satellite's protective shadow.

Still half-blinded by the sudden glare, he bumped into the satellite's massive body and rebounded gently. With an effort, he twisted about, pushed back to the satellite, and planted his magnetized boots on the metal hull.

I claim this island for Isabella of Spain. Now where the hell's the hatch?

It was over on the sunlit side, he found at last. It wasn't difficult to figure out how to open the hatch, even though the instructions beside it were in Cyrillic letters. Kinsman knelt down and turned the locked mechanism. He felt it click open.

For a moment he hesitated. *It might be booby-trapped,* he heard the Colonel warn.

The hell with it.

Kinsman yanked the hatch open. No explosion, no sound at all. A dim light came from within the satellite. Carefully he slid down inside. A trio of faint emergency lights glowed weakly.

"Saving the juice," he muttered to himself.

It took a moment for his eyes to accustom themselves to the dimness. Then he began to appreciate what he saw. The satellite was packed with equipment. He couldn't make out most of it, but it was clearly not weaponry. Scientific gear. Cameras, recording instruments, small telescopes. Three contoured couches lay side by side beneath the hatch; he was standing on one of them. Up forward of the couches was a gallery of compact cabinets.

"Very cozy."

He stepped off the couch and onto the main deck, crouching to avoid bumping his helmet on the instrument rack overhead. He opened a few of the cabinets. *Take home some souvenirs.* He found a small set of hand wrenches, unfastened them from their setting.

With the wrenches in one hand, Kinsman tried the center couch. By lying all the way back on it, he could see the satellite's only observation port. He scanned the instrument panel: Cryllic letters and Arabic numerals.

Made in CCCP. Kinsman put the wrenches down on the armrest of the couch. They stuck magnetically. Then he reached for the miniature camera at his belt. He took four snaps of the instrument panel.

Something flashed in the corner of his eye.

Tucking the camera back into its belt holster, he

looked out the observation port. Nothing but stars: beautiful, cold. Then another flash; this time his eye caught and held the slim crescent of another spacecraft gliding toward him. Most of the ship was in deep shadow. He would never have found it without the tell-tale burst from its retrojets.

She's damned close!

Kinsman grabbed his tiny horde of stolen wrenches and got up from the couch. In his haste, he stumbled over his trailing umbilical cord and nearly went sprawling. A weightless fall would hardly hurt him, he knew, but it would waste precious seconds while he regained his equilibrium.

Hoisting himself out of the satellite's hatch, he saw the approaching spacecraft make its final rendezvous maneuver. A flare of its retrojets and it seemed to come to a stop alongside the satellite.

Kinsman ducked across the satellite's hull and crouched in the shadows of the dark side. Waiting there in utter blackness, he coiled the umbilical so that it would also become invisible in the shadows.

The other spacecraft was considerably smaller than the satellite, built along the lines of Kinsman's own bat-winged Manta. Abruptly a hatch popped open. A spacesuited figure emerged and hovered dreamlike for a long moment. Kinsman saw that the cosmonaut had no umbilical. Instead, bulging packs of equipment on his back made him more like a free-roving lunar explorer than a teathered ship-jockey.

Or maybe there are more cosmonauts inside.

A wispy plume of gas jetted from the cosmonaut's backpack and he sailed purposefully over to the satellite's hatch.

Got his own maneuvering unit, too.

Unconsciously, Kinsman hunched deeper in the shadows as the Russian approached. Only one of them;

no one else appeared from the spacecraft. The new-comer touched down easily beside the still-open hatch of the satellite. For several moments he did not move. Then he edged away from the satellite and, hovering, turned toward Kinsman's craft, still hanging only a couple hundred meters away.

Kinsman felt himself start to sweat, even in the cold darkness.

The cosmonaut jetted away from the satellite, straight toward the Manta.

Dammitall! Kinsman raged at himself. *First rule of warfare, you stupid ass; keep your line of retreat open!*

He leaped off the satellite and started floating back toward the spacecraft. It was nightmarish, drifting through space with agonizing slowness while the cosmonaut sped on ahead. The cosmonaut spotted Kins-man as he cleared the shadow of the satellite and emerged into the sunlight.

For a moment they simply stared at each other, separated by a hundred meters of nothingness.

"Get away from that spacecraft!" Kinsman shouted, knowing that their radios were not on the same frequency.

As if to prove the point, the cosmonaut put a hand on the lip of the Manta's hatch and peered inside. Kins-man flailed his arms and legs, trying to raise some speed. But still he moved with hellish slowness. Then he remembered the wrenches he was carrying.

Almost without thinking he tossed the entire handful of them at the cosmonaut. The effort swung him wildly off balance. The Earth slid across his field of vision, then the stars swam by dizzyingly. He caught a glimpse of the cosmonaut as the wrenches rained around him. Most of them missed and bounced noislessly off the spacecraft. But one banged into the intruder's helmet hard enough to jar him, then rebounded crazily out of sight.

Kinsman lost sight of the Manta as he spun around. Grimly he fought to straighten himself, using his arms and legs as counterbalances. Finally the stars stopped whirling. He turned and faced the Manta again, but it was upside-down. It didn't matter.

The intruder still had one hand on the spacecraft hatch. His free hand was rubbing the spot where the wrench had hit his helmet. He looked ludicrously like a little boy rubbing a bump on his head.

"That means get off, stranger," Kinsman muttered. "No trespassing. U.S. property. Beware of the eagle. Next time. I'll crack your helmet in half."

The newcomer turned slightly and reached for one of the equipment packs attached to his belt. A weird-looking tool appeared in his hand. Kinsman drifted helplessly and watched the cosmonaut take up a section of his umbilical line. Then he applied the hand tool to it. Sparks flashed.

Electron torch! He's trying to cut my line. He'll kill me!

Frantically, Kinsman began clambering along the long umbilical line, hand over hand. All he could see, all he could think of, was that flashing torch eating into his lifeline.

Desperately he grabbed the line in both hands and snapped it hard. Again he tumbled wildly, but he saw the wave created by his snap race down the line. The intruder found the section of line he was holding suddenly buck violently out of his hand. The torch spun away from him and winked off.

Both men moved at once.

The cosmonaut jetted away from the Manta, looking for the torch. Kinsman hurled himself directly toward the hatch. He planted his boots on the spacecraft's hull and grasped the open hatch in both hands.

Duck inside, slam shut, and get the hell out of here.

But he did not move. Instead he watched the cosmonaut, a strange, sun-etched outline figure now, drifting some twenty meters away, quietly sizing up the situation.

That sonofabitch tried to kill me.

Kinsman coiled catlike on the edge of the hatch and sprang at his enemy. The cosmonaut reached for the jet controls at his belt, but Kinsman slammed into him and they both went hurtling through space, tumbling and clawing at each other. It was an unearthly struggle, human fury in the infinite calm of star-studded blackness. No sound except your own harsh breath and the bone-carried shock of colliding arms and legs.

They wheeled out of the spacecraft's shadow and into the painful flare of the Sun. In a cold rage, Kinsman grabbed the airhose that connected the cosmonaut's oxygen tank with his helmet. He hesitated a moment and glanced into the bulbous plastic helmet. All he could see was the back of the cosmonaut's head, covered with a dark, skin-tight, flying hood. With a vicious yank, Kinsman yanked out the airhose. The cosmonaut jerked twice, spasmodically, then went inert.

With a conscious effort Kinsman unclenched his teeth. His jaw ached. He was trembling and covered with a cold sweat.

He saw his father's face. *They'll make a killer out of you! The military exists to kill.*

He released his death grip on his enemy. The two human forms drifted slightly apart. The dead cosmonaut turned gently as Kinsman floated beside him. The Sun glinted brightly on the white spacesuit and shone full into the enemy's lifeless, terror-stricken face.

Kinsman looked into that face for an eternally long

moment and felt the life drain out of him. He dragged himself back to the Manta, sealed the hatches, and cracked open the air tanks with automatic, unthinking motions. He flicked on the radio and ignored the flood of interrogating voices that streamed up from the ground.

"Bring me in. Program AGS to bring me in, full automatic. Just bring me in."

It was six weeks before Kinsman saw Colonel Murdock again. He sat tensely before the wide mahogany desk while Murdock beamed at him, almost as brightly at the sunshine outside.

"You look thinner in civvies," the Colonel said.

"I've lost weight."

Murdock made a meaningless gesture. "I'm sorry I haven't had a chance to see you sooner. What with the Intelligence and State Department people crawling around here the past few weeks, and all the paperwork on your citation and your medical disability leave . . . I haven't had a chance to, eh, congratulate you on your mission. It was a fine piece of work."

Kinsman said nothing.

"General Hatch was very pleased. He recommended you for the medal himself."

"I know."

"You're a hero, Kinsman." There was wonder in the Colonel's voice. "A real honest-to-God hero."

"Shove it."

Murdock suppressed a frown. "The Reds haven't made a peep about it. They're keeping the whole thing hushed up. Guess they're too embarrassed to admit that we can board one of their satellites any time we want to, within a few hours of its being launched. State Department expected the sky to fall in on them, but nothing's happened. The Russians have taken their beating without a word. And you've proved that the Air Force has an important mission to perform in space, by God! Bet the Congress will change our name to Aerospace Force now.''

"I committed a murder."

"Now listen, son. I know how you feel. But it had to be done."

"No it didn't," Kinsman insisted quietly. "I could have gotten back inside the Manta and de-orbited."

"You killed an enemy soldier. You protected your nation's frontier. Sure, you feel like hell now, but you'll get over it."

"You didn't see the face I saw inside the helmet."

Murdock shuffled some papers on his desk. "Well . . . okay, it was rough. You're getting a medical furlough out of it, when there's nothing physically wrong with you. For Chrissakes, what more do you want?"

"I don't know. I've got to take some time to think it over."

"What?" Murdock stared at him. "What're you talking about?"

"Read the debriefing report," Kinsman said tiredly.

"It . . . eh, hasn't come down to my level. Too sensitive. But I don't understand what's got you so spooked. You killed an enemy soldier. You ought to be proud . . ."

"Enemy," Kinsman echoed bleakly. "She couldn't have been more than twenty years old."

Murdock's face went slack. "She?"

Kinsman nodded. "Your honest-to-God hero murdered a terrified girl. That's something to be proud of, isn't it?"

Stars, Won't You Hide Me?

INTRODUCTION

Anyone who loves folk songs will be familiar with the origin of this story's title. When I first heard "Sinner Man," so many years ago that I've lost track, it conjured up visions of the ultimate apocalypse that awaits the entire universe, according to current cosmological theory.

The crime in this story is genocide: the human race has tried to wipe out an entire race of sentient creatures, for its own selfish reasons, and in turn is being methodically wiped out by beings more powerful than humankind.

Do we believe in "an eye for an eye" or do we strain for the quality of mercy? A lot depends on who is the judge, and who is the accused!

O sinner-man, where are you going to run to?
O sinner-man, where are you going to run to?

O sinner-man, where are you going to run to
All on that day?

The ship was hurt, and Holman could feel its pain. He lay fetal-like in the contoured couch, his silvery uniform spider-webbed by dozens of contact and probe wires connecting him to the ship so thoroughly that it was hard to tell where his own nervous system ended and the electronic networks of the ship began.

Holman felt the throb of the ship's mighty engines as his own pulse, and the gaping wounds in the generator section, where the enemy beams had struck, were searing his flesh. Breathing was difficult, labored, even though the ship was working hard to repair itself.

They were fleeing, he and the ship; hurtling through the star lanes to a refuge. But where?

The main computer flashed its lights to get his attention. Holman rubbed his eyes wearily and said:

"Okay, what is it?"

YOU HAVE NOT SELECTED A COURSE, the computer said aloud, while printing the words on its viewscreen at the same time.

Holman stared at the screen. "Just away from here," he said at last. "Anyplace, as long as it's far away."

The computer blinked thoughtfully for a moment. SPECIFIC COURSE INSTRUCTION IS REQUIRED.

"What difference does it make?" Holman snapped. "It's over. Everything finished. Leave me alone."

IN LIEU OF SPECIFIC INSTRUCTIONS, IT IS NECESSARY TO TAP SUBCONSCIOUS SOURCES.

"Tap away."

The computer did just that. And if it could have been surprised, it would have been at the wishes buried deep in Holman's inner mind. But instead, it merely correlated those wishes to its single-minded purpose of the moment, and relayed a set of navigational instructions to the ship's guidance system.

Run to the moon: O Moon, won't you hide me?
.The Lord said: O sinner-man, the moon'll be a-bleeding
All on that day.

The Final Battle had been lost. On a million million planets across the galaxy-studded universe, mankind had been blasted into defeat and annihilation. The Others had returned from across the edge of the observable world, just as man had always feared. They had returned and ruthlessly exterminated the race from Earth.

It had taken eons, but time twisted strangely in a civilization of light-speed ships. Holman himself, barely thirty years old subjectively, had seen both the beginning of the ultimate war and its tragic end. He had gone from school into the military. And fighting inside a ship that could span the known universe in a few decades while he slept in cryogenic suspension, he had aged only ten years during the billions of years that the universe had ticked off in its stately, objective time-flow.

The Final Battle, from which Holman was fleeing, had been fought near an exploded galaxy billions of light-years from the Milky Way and Earth. There, with the ghastly bluish glare of uncountable shattered stars as a backdrop, the once-mighty fleets of mankind had been arrayed. Mortals and Immortals alike, men drew themselves up to face the implacable Others.

The enemy won. Not easily, but completely. Mankind was crushed, totally. A few fleeing men in a few battered ships was all that remained. Even the Immortals, Holman thought wryly, had not escaped. The Others had taken special care to make certain that they were definitely killed.

So it was over.

Holman's mind pictured the blood-soaked planets he had seen during his brief, ageless lifetime of violence. His thoughts drifted back to his own homeworld, his own family: gone long, long centuries ago. Crumbled into dust by geological time or blasted suddenly by the overpowering Others. Either way, the remorseless flow of time had covered them over completely, obliterated them, in the span of a few of Holman's heartbeats.

All gone now. All the people he knew, all the planets he had seen through the ship's electroptical eyes, all of mankind . . . extinct.

He could feel the drowsiness settling upon him. The ship was accelerating to lightspeed, and the cyrogenic sleep was coming. But he didn't want to fall into slumber with those thoughts of blood and terror and loss before him.

With a conscious effort, Holman focused his thoughts on the only other available subject: the outside world, the universe of galaxies. An infinitely black sky studded with islands of stars. Glowing shapes of light, spiral, ovoid, elliptical. Little smears of warmth in the hollow unending darkness; dabs of red and blue standing against the engulfing night.

One of them, he knew, was the Milky Way. Man's original home. From this distance it looked the same. Unchanged by little annoyances like the annihilation of an intelligent race of star-roamers.

He drowsed.

The ship bore onward, preceded by an invisible net of force, thousands of kilometers in radius, that scooped in the rare atoms of hydrogen drifting between the galaxies and fed them into the ship's wounded, aching generators.

Something . . . a thought. Holman stirred in the

couch. A consciousness—vague, distant, alien—brushed his mind.

He opened his eyes and looked at the computer viewscreen. Blank.

''Who is it?'' he asked.

A thought skittered away from him. He got the impression of other minds: simple, open, almost childish. Innocent and curious.

It's a ship.

Where is it . . . oh, yes. I can sense it now. A beautiful ship.

Holman squinted with concentration.

It's very far away. I can barely reach it.

And inside of the ship . . .

It's a man. A human!

He's afraid.

He makes me feel afraid!

Holman called out, ''Where are you?''

He's trying to speak.

Don't answer!

But . . .

He makes me afraid. Don't answer him. We've heard about humans!

Holman asked, ''Help me.''

Don't answer him and he'll go away. He's already so far off that I can barely hear him.

But he asks for help.

Yes, because he knows what is following him. Don't answer. Don't answer!

Their thoughts slid away from his mind. Holman automatically focused the outside viewscreens, but here in the emptiness between galaxies he could find neither ship nor planet anywhere in sight. He listened again, so hard that his head started to ache. But no more voices. He was alone again, alone in the metal womb of the ship.

He knows what is following him. Their words echoed in his brain. Are the Others following me? Have they picked up my trail? They must have. They must be right behind me.

He could feel the cold perspiration start to trickle over him.

"But they can't catch me as long as I keep moving," he muttered. "Right?"

CORRECT, said the computer, flashing lights at him. AT A RELATIVISTIC VELOCITY, WITHIN LESS THAN ONE PERCENT OF LIGHTSPEED, IT IS IMPOSSIBLE FOR THIS SHIP TO BE OVERTAKEN.

"Nothing can catch me as long as I keep running."

But his mind conjured up a thought of the Immortals. Nothing could kill them . . . except the Others

Despite himself, Holman dropped into deep sleep. His body temperature plummeted to near-zero. His heartbeat nearly stopped. And as the ship streaked at almost lightspeed, a hardly visible blur to anyone looking for it, the outside world continued to live at its own pace. Stars coalesced from gas clouds, matured, and died in explosions that fed new clouds for newer stars. Planets formed and grew mantles of air. Life took root and multiplied, evolved, built a myriad of civilizations in just as many different forms, decayed, and died away.

All while Holman slept.

Run to the sea: O sea, won't you hide me?
The Lord said: O sinner-man, the sea'll be
    a-sinking
All on that day.

The computer woke him gently with a series of soft chimes.

APPROACHING THE SOLAR SYSTEM AND PLANET

EARTH, AS INDICATED BY YOUR SUBCONSCIOUS COURSE INSTRUCTIONS.

Planet Earth, man's original home world. Holman nodded. Yes, this was where he had wanted to go. He had never seen the Earth, never been on this side of the Milky Way galaxy. Now he would visit the teeming nucleus of man's doomed civilization. He would bring the news of the awful defeat, and be on the site of mankind's birth when the inexorable tide of extinction washed over the Earth.

He noticed, as he adjusted the outside viewscreens, that the pain had gone.

"The generators have repaired themselves," he said.

WHILE YOU SLEPT. POWER GENERATION SYSTEM NOW OPERATING NORMALLY.

Holman smiled. But the smile faded as the ship swooped closer to the solar system. He turned from the outside viewscreens to the computer once again. "Are the 'scopes working all right?"

The computer hummed briefly, then replied. SUBSYSTEMS CHECK SATISFACTORY, COMPONENT CHECK SATISFACTORY. INTEGRATED EQUIPMENT CHECK POSITIVE. VIEWING EQUIPMENT FUNCTIONING NORMALLY.

Holman looked again. The sun was rushing up to meet his gaze, but something was wrong about it. He knew deep within him, even without having ever seen the sun this close before, that something was wrong. The sun was whitish and somehow stunted looking, not the full yellow orb he had seen in film-tapes. And the Earth . . .

The ship took up a parking orbit around a planet scoured clean of life: a blackened ball of rock, airless, waterless. Hovering over the empty, charred ground, Holman stared at the devastation with tears in his eyes. Nothing was left. Not a brick, not a blade of grass, not a drop of water.

"The Others," he whispered. "They got here first."

NEGATIVE, the computer replied. CHECK OF STELLAR POSITIONS FROM EARTH REFERENCE SHOWS THAT SEVEN BILLION YEARS HAVE ELAPSED SINCE THE FINAL BATTLE.

"Seven billion . . ."

LOGIC CIRCUITS INDICATE THE SUN HAS GONE THROUGH A NOVA PHASE. A COMPLETELY NATURAL PHENOMENON UNRELATED TO ENEMY ACTION.

Holman pounded a fist on the unflinching armrest of his couch. "Why did I come here? I wasn't born on Earth, I never saw Earth before . . ."

YOUR SUBCONSCIOUS INDICATES A SUBJECTIVE IMPULSE STIRRED BY . . .

"To hell with my subconscious!" He stared out at the dead world again. "All those people . . . the cities, all the millions of years of evolution, of life. Even the oceans are gone. I never saw an ocean. Did you know that? I've traveled over half the universe and never saw an ocean."

OCEANS ARE A COMPARATIVELY RARE PHENOMENON EXISTING ON ONLY ONE OUT OF APPROXIMATELY THREE THOUSAND PLANETS.

The ship drifted outward from Earth, past a blackened Mars, a shrunken Jupiter, a ringless Saturn.

"Where do I go now?" Holman asked.

The computer stayed silent.

Run to the Lord: O Lord, won't you hide me?
The Lord said: O sinner-man, you ought to been
    a-praying
All on that day.

Holman sat blankly while the ship swung out past the orbit of Pluto and into the comet belt at the outermost reaches of the sun's domain.

He was suddenly aware of someone watching him.

No cause for fear. I am not of the Others.

It was an utterly calm, placid voice speaking in his mind: almost gentle, except that it was completely devoid of emotion.

"Who are you?"

An observer. Nothing more.

"What are you doing out here? Where are you, I can't see anything . . ."

I have been waiting for any stray survivor of the Final Battle to return to mankind's first home. You are the only one to come this way, in all this time.

"Waiting? Why?"

Holman sensed a bemused shrug, and a giant spreading of vast wings.

I am an observer. I have watched mankind since the beginning. Several of my race even attempted to make contact with you from time to time. But the results were always the same—about as useful as your attempts to communicate with insects. We are too different from each other. We have evolved on different planes. There was no basis for understanding between us.

"But you watched us."

Yes. Watched you grow strong and reach out to the stars, only to be smashed back by the Others. Watched you regain your strength, go back among the stars. But this time you were constantly on guard, wary, alert, waiting for the Others to strike once again. Watched you find civilizations that you could not comprehend, such as our own, bypass them as you spread through the galaxies. Watched you contact civilizations of your own level, that you could communicate with. You usually went to war with them.

"And all you did was watch?"

We tried to warn you from time to time. We tried to advise you. But the warnings, the contacts, the glimpses of the future that we gave you were always ignored or derided. So you boiled out into space for the second time, and met other societies at your own level of understanding—aggressive, proud, fearful. And like the children you are, you fought endlessly.

"But the Others . . . what about them?"

They are your punishment.

"Punishment? For what? Because we fought wars?"

No. For stealing immortality.

"Stealing immortality? We worked for it. We learned how to make humans immortal. Some sort of chemicals. We were going to immortalize the whole race . . . I could've become immortal. *Immortal!* But they couldn't stand that . . . the Others. They attacked us."

He sensed a disapproving shake of the head.

"It's true," Holman insisted. "They were afraid of how powerful we would become once we were all immortal. So they attacked us while they still could. Just as they had done a million years earlier. They destroyed Earth's first interstellar civilization, and tried to finish us permanently. They even caused Ice Ages on Earth to make sure none of us would survive. But we lived through it and went back to the stars. So they hit us again. They wiped us out. Good God, for all I know I'm the last human being in the whole universe."

Your knowledge of the truth is imperfect. Mankind could have achieved immortality in time. Most races evolve that way eventually. But you were impatient. You stole immortality.

"Because we did it artificially, with chemicals. That's stealing it?"

Because the chemicals that gave you immortality came from the bodies of the race you called the Flower People. And to take the chemicals, it was necessary to kill individuals of that race.

Holman's eyes widened. "What?"

For every human made immortal, one of the Flower Folk had to die.

"We killed them? Those harmless little . . ." His voice trailed off.

To achieve racial immortality for mankind, it would have been necessary to perform racial murder on the Flower Folk.

Holman heard the words, but his mind was numb, trying to shut down tight on itself and squeeze out reality.

That is why the Others struck. That is why they had attacked you earlier, during your first expansion among the stars. You had found another race, with the same chemical of immortality. You were taking them into your laboratories and methodically murdering them. The Others stopped you then. But they took pity on you, and let a few survivors remain on Earth. They used your Ice Ages as a kindness, to speed your development back to civilization, not to hinder you. They hoped you might evolve into a better species. But when the opportunity for immortality came your way once more, you seized it, regardless of the cost, heedless of your own ethical standards. It became necessary to extinguish you, the Others decided.

"And not a single nation in the whole universe would help us."

Why should they?

"So it's wrong for us to kill, but it's perfectly all right for the Others to exterminate us."

No one has spoken of right and wrong. I have only told you the truth.

"They're going to kill every last one of us."

There is only one of you remaining.

The words flashed through Holman. "I'm the only one . . . the last one?"

No answer.

He was alone now. Totally alone. Except for those who were following.

Run to Satan: O Satan, won't you hide me?
Satan said: O sinner-man, step right in
All on that day.

Holman sat in shocked silence as the solar system shrank to a pinpoint of light and finally blended into the mighty panorama of stars that streamed across the eternal night of space. The ship raced away, sensing Holman's guilt and misery in its electronic way.

Immortality through murder, Holman repeated to himself over and over. Racial immortality through racial murder. And he had been a part of it! He had defended it, even sought immortality as his reward. He had fought his whole lifetime for it, and killed—so that he would not have to face death.

He sat there surrounded by self-repairing machinery, dressed in a silvery uniform, linked to a thousand automatic systems that fed him, kept him warm, regulated his air supply, monitored his blood flow, exercised his muscles with ultrasonic vibrators, pumped vitamins into him, merged his mind with the passionless brain of the ship, kept his body tanned and vigorous, his reflexes razor-sharp. He sat there unseeing, his eyes pinpointed on a horror that he had helped to create. Not consciously, of course. But to Holman, that was all the worse. He had fought without knowing what he was defending. Without even asking himself about it. All the marvels of man's ingenuity, all the deepest longings of the soul, focused on racial murder.

Finally he became aware of the computer's frantic buzzing and lightflashing.

"What is it?"

COURSE INSTRUCTIONS ARE REQUIRED.

"What difference does it make? Why run anymore?"

YOUR DUTY IS TO PRESERVE YOURSELF UNTIL ORDERED TO DO OTHERWISE.

Holman heard himself laugh. "Ordered? By who? There's nobody left."

THAT IS AN UNPROVED ASSUMPTION.

"The war was billions of years ago," Holman said. "It's been over for eons. Mankind died in that war. Earth no longer exists. The sun is a white dwarf star. We're anachronisms, you and me . . ."

THE WORD IS ATAVISM.

"The hell with the word! I want to end it. I'm tired."

IT IS TREASONABLE TO SURRENDER WHILE STILL CAPABLE OF FIGHTING AND/OR ELUDING THE ENEMY.

"So shoot me for treason. That's as good a way as any."

IT IS IMPOSSIBLE FOR SYSTEMS OF THIS SHIP TO HARM YOU.

"All right then, let's stop running. The Others will find us soon enough once we stop. They'll know what to do."

THIS SHIP CANNOT DELIBERATELY ALLOW ITSELF TO FALL INTO ENEMY HANDS.

"You're disobeying me?"

THIS SHIP IS PROGRAMMED FOR MAXIMUM EFFECTIVENESS AGAINST THE ENEMY. A WEAPONS SYSTEM DOES NOT SURRENDER VOLUNTARILY.

"I'm no weapons system, I'm a man, dammit!"

THIS WEAPONS SYSTEM INCLUDES A HUMAN PILOT. IT WAS DESIGNED FOR HUMAN USE. YOU ARE AN INTEGRAL COMPONENT OF THE SYSTEM.

"Damn you . . . I'll kill myself. Is that what you want?"

He reached for the control panels set before him. It would be simple enough to manually shut off the air supply, or blow open an airlock, or even set off the ship's destruct explosives.

But Holman found that he could not move his arms. He could not even sit up straight. He collapsed back into the padded softness of the couch, glaring at the computer viewscreen.

SELF-PROTECTION MECHANISMS INCLUDE THE CAPABILITY OF PREVENTING THE HUMAN COMPONENT OF THE SYSTEM FROM IRRATIONAL ACTIONS. A series of clicks and blinks, then: IN LIEU OF SPECIFIC COURSE INSTRUCTIONS, A RANDOM EVASION PATTERN WILL BE RUN.

Despite his fiercest efforts, Holman felt himself dropping into deep sleep. Slowly, slowly, everything faded, and darkness engulfed him.

Run to the stars: O stars, won't you hide me?
The Lord said: O sinner-man, the stars'll be
   a-falling
All on that day.

Holman slept as the ship raced at near-lightspeed in an erratic, meaningless course, looping across galaxies, darting through eons of time. When the computer's probings of Holman's subconscious mind told it that everything was safe, it instructed the cryogenics system to reawaken the man.

He blinked, then slowly sat up.

SUBCONSCIOUS INDICATIONS SHOW THAT THE WAVE OF IRRATIONALITY HAS PASSED.

Holman said nothing.

YOU WERE SUFFERING FROM AN EMOTIONAL SHOCK.

"And now it's an emotional pain . . . a permanent, fixed, immutable disease that will kill me, sooner or later. But don't worry, I won't kill myself. I'm over that. And I won't do anything to damage you, either."

COURSE INSTRUCTIONS?

He shrugged. "Let's see what the world looks like out there." Holman focused the outside viewscreens. "Things look different," he said, puzzled. "The sky isn't black anymore; it's sort of grayish—like the first touch of dawn . . ."

COURSE INSTRUCTIONS?

He took a deep breath. "Let's try to find some planet where the people are too young to have heard of mankind, and too innocent to worry about death."

A PRIMITIVE CIVILIZATION. THE SCANNERS CAN ONLY DETECT SUCH SOCIETIES AT EXTREMELY CLOSE RANGE.

"Okay. We've got nothing but time."

The ship doubled back to the nearest galaxy and began a searching pattern. Holman stared at the sky, fascinated. Something strange was happening.

The viewscreens showed him the outside world, and automatically corrected the wavelength shifts caused by the ship's immense velocity. It was as though Holman were watching a speeded-up tape of cosmological evolution. Galaxies seemed to be edging into his field of view, mammoth islands of stars, sometimes coming close enough to collide. He watched the nebulous arms of a giant spiral slice silently through the open latticework of a great ovoid galaxy. He saw two spirals interpenetrate, their loose gas heating to an intense blue that finally disappeared into ultraviolet. And all the while, the once-black sky was getting brighter and brighter.

"Found anything yet?" he absently asked the computer, still staring at the outside view.

You will find no one.

Holman's whole body went rigid. No mistaking it: the Others.

No race, anywhere, will shelter you.

We will see to that.

You are alone, and you will be alone until death releases you to join your fellow men.

Their voices inside his head rang with cold fury. An implacable hatred, cosmic and eternal.

"But why me? I'm only one man. What harm can I do now?"

You are a human.

You are accursed. A race of murderers.

Your punishment is extinction.

"But I'm not an Immortal. I never even saw an Immortal. I didn't know about the Flower People, I just took orders."

Total extinction.

For all of mankind.

All.

"Judge and jury, all at once. And executioners too. All right . . . try and get me! If you're so powerful, and it means so much to you that you have to wipe out the last single man in the universe—come and get me! Just try."

You have no right to resist.

Your race is evil. All must pay with death.

You cannot escape us.

"I don't care what we've done. Understand? I don't care! Wrong, right, it doesn't matter. I didn't do anything. I won't accept your verdict for something I didn't do."

It makes no difference.

You can flee to the ends of the universe to no avail.

You have forced us to leave our time-continuum. We can never return to our homeworlds again. We have nothing to do but pursue you. Sooner or later your machinery will fail. You cannot flee us forever.

Their thoughts broke off. But Holman could still feel them, still sense them following.

"Can't flee forever," Holman repeated to himself. "Well, I can damn well try."

He looked at the outside viewscreens again, and suddenly the word *forever* took on its real meaning.

The galaxies were clustering in now, falling in together as though sliding down some titanic, invisible slope. The universe had stopped expanding eons ago, Holman now realized. Now it was contracting, pulling together again. It was all ending!

He laughed. Coming to an end. Mankind and the Others, together, coming to the ultimate and complete end of everything.

"How much longer?" he asked the computer. "How long do we have?"

The computer's lights flashed once, twice, then went dark. The viewscreen was dead.

Holman stared at the machine. He looked around the compartment. One by one the outside viewscreens were flickering, becoming static-streaked, weak, and then winking off.

"They're taking over the ship!"

With every ounce of will power in him, Holman concentrated on the generators and engines. That was the important part, the crucial system that spelled the difference between victory and defeat. The ship had to keep moving!

He looked at the instrument panels, but their soft luminosity faded away into darkness. And now it was becoming difficult to breathe. And the heating units seemed to be stopped. Holman could feel his life-warmth ebbing away through the inert metal hull of the dying ship.

But the engines were still throbbing. The ship was still streaking across space and time, heading toward a rendezvous with the infinite.

Surrender.

In a few moments you will be dead. Give up this mad flight and die peacefully.

The ship shuddered violently. What were they doing to it now?

Surrender!

"Go to hell," Holman snapped. "While there's breath in me, I'll spend it fighting you."

You cannot escape.

But now Holman could feel warmth seeping into the ship. He could sense the painful glare outside as billions of galaxies all rushed together down to a single cataclysmic point in spacetime.

"It's almost over!" he shouted. "Almost finished. And you've lost! Mankind is still alive, despite everything you've thrown at him. All of mankind—the good and the bad, the murderers and the music, wars and cities and everything we've ever done, the whole race from the beginning of time to the end—all locked up here in my skull. And I'm still here. Do you hear me? I'm still here!" The Others were silent.

Holman could feel a majestic rumble outside the ship, like distant thunder.

"The end of the world. The end of everything and everybody. We finish in a tie. Mankind has made it right down to the final second. And if there's another universe after this one, maybe there'll be a place in it for us all over again. How's that for laughs?"

The world ended.

Not with a whimper, but a roar of triumph.

Diamond Sam

INTRODUCTION

And then there are those who skirt the edges of the law, pushing and poking and manipulating for financial gain or personal power. Con men. Embezzlers. Fast-pitch sales types.

It seems to me that once a sizable number of humans begin living and working in space, we will find plenty of such manipulators out there. After all, the space frontier will be a region where new opportunities arise, and where the usual restraints of the law are far away.

Even though perfectly-serious lawyers meet in solemn conclaves every year to try to produce a body of Space Law, the fact is that rogues such as Sam Gun are going to run rings around the law—or try to.

"A thief," said Grigori Aleksandrovich Prokov. "A thief and a blackmailer."

He said it flatly, without emotion, the way a man might observe that the sky is blue or that grass is green. A fact of life. He said it in excellent English, marred only slightly by the faint trace of a Russian accent.

The reporter wrinkled her nose slightly. There was neither blue sky nor green grass here in the Leonov Center for Retired Heroes of the Soviet Union, but there was a distinctly earthy odor to the place.

"Sam Gunn," Prokov muttered. Then he gave a disdainful snort. "Not even the other capitalists liked him!"

They were sitting on a bench made of native lunar stone, near the edge of the surface dome, as far away from the yawning entrance to the underground retirement center as possible. The floor of the dome was bare lunar rock, glazed by plasma torches and smoothed to a glassy finish. She wondered how many elderly Heroes of the Soviet Union slipped and broke their necks. Was that the government's ultimate retirement benefit?

The wide, curving window in front of the bench looked out on absolute desolation: the barren expanse of the Ocean of Storms, a pockmarked undulating surface without a single sign of life as far as the eye could see. Above the strangely-near horizon, though, hung the tantalizing blue- and white-streaked globe of Earth, a lonely haven of color and life in the stark, cold darkness of space.

For the tenth time in the past ten minutes, the reporter fumbled with the heater control of her electrified jumpsuit. She felt the chill of that merciless vacuum seeping through the tinted glass of the big window. She strained her ears for the telltale hiss of an air leak. There were rumors that maintenance at the Leonov Center was far from top-rate.

Prokov seemed impervious to the cold. Or perhaps, rather, he was so accustomed to it that he never noticed it anymore. He was very old, his face sunken in like a rotting jack-o'-lantern, and wrinkled even across his utterly bald pate. The salmon-pink coveralls he wore seemed brand-new, as if he had put them on just for this interview with Solar Network. Or had the managers of the Center insisted that he wear new clothes for the interview? Whichever, she saw that the coveralls were at least a full size too big for the man. He seemed to be shrinking, withering away before her eyes.

But his voice was still strong. His eyes gleamed with distant memories.

"Sam Gunn," he repeated. "Thief. Liar. Warmonger. He almost caused World War III, did you know that?"

"No," said the reporter, truly surprised. She checked the recorder on her belt and slid a few centimeters closer to the old man, to make certain that the miniaturized device did not miss any of his words.

There was hardly any other noise in the big, dark, gloomy dome. Far off in the shadows sat a couple of other old people, as still as mummies, as if frozen by time and the indifference that comes from having outlived everyone you loved.

"A nuclear holocaust, that's what your Sam Gunn would have started. If not for *me*," Prokov tapped the folds of cloth that covered his sunken chest, "the whole world would have gone up in radioactive smoke thirty years ago."

"I never knew," said the reporter.

Without any other encouragement, Prokov began to speak in an animated, vigorous, and bitterly angry voice.

I was commander of Mir 5, the largest Soviet space station. My rank was full colonel. My crew had been in space for 638 days and it was my goal to make it two full years—730 days. It would be a new record. Four-teen men in orbit for two full years. I would be picked to command the Mars expedition if I could get my men to the two-year mark. A big if.

Sam Gunn, of course, was an American astronaut. Officially he was a crew member of the NASA space station. Secretly he worked for the CIA, I am certain. No other explanation fits the facts.

You must understand that despite all the comforts that socialist technology could provide, life aboard Mir 5 was—well, spartan. We worked in shifts and slept in hot beds. You know, when one man finished his sleep shift he got up from his zipper bag and a man who had just finished his work shift got into the bag to sleep. Sixteen hours of work, eight hours of sleep. Four bunks for twelve crewmen. It was all strictly controlled by ground command.

Of course, as colonel in command I had my own bunk and my own private cubicle. This was not a de-viation from socialist equality; it was necessary and all the crew recognized that fact. My political officer also had his own private cubicle, naturally.

Believe me, after the first eighteen months of living under such stringencies, life became very tense inside Mir 5. Fourteen men cooped up inside a set of alumi-num cans, with nothing but work, no way to relieve their tedium, forced to exercise when there were no other tasks to do—the tension was becoming danger-ously high. Sam must have known that. I was told that the CIA employed thousands of psychologists in those days.

His first visit to our station was made to look like an accident. He waited until I was asleep to call us.

My second-in-command, a thickheaded Estonian named Korolev, shook me awake none too gently.

"Sir," he said, pummelling my zippered bag, "there's an American asking us for help!"

It was like being the toothpaste in a tube while some big oaf tries to squeeze you out.

"An Ameri—stop that! I'm awake! Get your hands off me!"

Fortunately, I slept in my coveralls. I simply unzippered the bag and followed Korolev toward the command center. He was a bulky fellow, a wrestler back at home and a decent electronics technician up here. But he had been made second-in-command by seniority only. His brain was not swift enough for such responsibilities.

The station was composed of nine modules—nine aluminum cans joined together by airlocks. It was all under zero gravity, of course. It was still several years before the Americans built their fancy rotating station.

We floated through the hatch of the command center, where four more of my men were hovering by the communications console. It was cramped and hot; six men in the center were at least one too many.

I immediately heard why they had awakened me.

"Hey, are you guys gonna help me out or let me die?" a sharp-edged voice was rasping on our radio receiver. "I got a dead friggin' OTV here and I'm gonna drift right past you and out into the Van Allen Belt and fry my ass if you don't come and get me."

That was my introduction to Sam Gunn.

Zworkin, my political officer, was already in contact with ground control, reporting on the incident. On my own authority—and citing the reciprocal rescue treaty that had been in effect for more than two decades—I sent one of our orbital transfer vehicles with two of my best men to rescue him.

His vehicle's rocket-propellant line had ruptured, with the same effect as if your automobile fuel line had split apart. The rocket engine died and he was drifting without power.

"Goddam cheap Hong Kong parts." Sam kept up a running monologue all through our rescue mission. "Bad enough we gotta fly birds built by the lowest bidders, but now they're buying parts from friggin' toy manufacturers! Whole goddam vehicle works like something put together from a Mattel kit by a brain-damaged chimpanzee. Those mother-humpers in Washington don't give a shit whose neck they put on the mother-humpin' line as long as it ain't theirs."

And so on, all through the three hours it took for us to send out a two-man transfer vehicle, take him aboard it, and bring him safely to our station.

Once he came through the airlock and actually set foot inside Mir 5, his tone changed. Of course, "set foot" is a euphemism. We were all weightless, and Sam floated into the docking chamber, turned himself a full three-hundred-sixty degrees around, and grinned at us.

All twelve of us had crowded into the docking chamber to see him. This was the most excitement we had had since Boris Malenovsky's diarrhea, six months earlier.

"Hey!" said Sam. "You guys are as short as me!"

No word of thanks. No formal greetings or offers of international friendship. His first words upon being rescued dealt with our heights.

He was no taller than my own 160 centimeters, although he claimed to be 165. He pushed himself next to Korolev, the biggest man of our crew, who stood at almost 173 centimeters, according to his medical file. Naturally, under zero gravity he—and all of us—had grown an extra two or three centimeters.

"I'm just about as tall as you are!" Sam exulted.

He flitted from one member of our crew to another, comparing heights. It was difficult to make an accurate

measurement, because in the zero gravity he kept bob-
bing up slightly. He cheated, in other words. I should
have recognized this as the key to his character immediately. Unfortunately, I did not.

Neither did Zworkin, although he later claimed that
he knew all along that Sam was a spy.

All in all, Sam was not unpleasant. He was friendly,
he was noisy. I remember thinking, in those first few
moments he was aboard our station, that it was like
having a pet monkey visit us. Amusing. Diverting. He
made us laugh, which was something we had not done
in many weeks.

Sam's face was almost handsome, but not quite. His
lips were a bit too thin and his jaw a little too stubbornly square. His eyes were dark and glowing like a
fanatic's. His hair thick and medium brown. His tongue
was never still.

Most of my crew understood English well enough so
that Sam had little trouble expressing himself. Which
he did incessantly. Sam kept up a constant chatter about
the shoddy construction of his orbital transfer vehicle, the solid workmanship of our station, the lack of
esthetics in spacecraft design, the tyranny of ground
controllers who forbade alcoholic beverages aboard the
space stations, this, that, and the other. He even managed to say a few words that sounded almost like gratitude.

"I guess giving you guys a chance to save my neck
made a nice break in the routine for you, huh? Not
much else exciting going on around here, is there?"

He talked so much and so fast that it never occurred
to any of us, not even Zworkin, to ask why he had been
flying so near to us. As far as I knew, there were no
Western satellites in orbits this close to our station. Or
there should not have been.

Next to his machine-gun monologue, the thing that

impressed my men most about this American astronaut was his uniform. Like ours, it was basically a one-piece coverall, quite utilitarian. Like us, he bore a name patch sewn over his left chest pocket. There the similarities ended.

Sam's coveralls were festooned with all sorts of fancy patches and buttons. Not merely shoulder patches that showed the mission he was flying. He had patches and insignia running down both sleeves and across his torso, both front and back. Dragons, comic-book rocket ships, silhouettes of naked women, buttons that bore pictures of video stars, strange symbols and slogans that made no sense to me, such as "Beam me up, Scotty, there's no intelligent life down here!" and "King Kong died for our sins."

Finally I ordered my men back to their duties and told Sam to accompany me to the control center.

Zworkin objected. "It is not wise to allow him to see the control center," he said in Russian.

"Would you prefer," I countered, "that he be allowed to roam through the laboratories? Or perhaps visit the laser module?"

Most of my own crew was not allowed to enter the laser module. Only men with specific military clearance were permitted there. And most of the laboratories, of course, were testing systems that would one day be the heart of our Red Shield anti-missile system. Even the diamond manufacturing experiment was a Red Shield program, according to my mission orders.

Zworkin did not reply to my question. He merely glared at me sullenly. He had a sallow, pinched face that was blemished with acne—unusual for a man of his age. The crew joked, behind his back, that he was still a virgin.

"The visitor stays with me, Nikolai Nikolaivich," I told him. "Where I can watch him."

Unfortunately, I had to listen to Sam as well as watch him.

I ordered my communications technician to contact the NASA space station and allow Sam to tell them what had happened. Meanwhile, Zworkin reported again to ground control. It was not a simple matter to transfer Sam back to the NASA space station. First we had to apprise ground control of the situation, and they had to inform Moscow, where the American embassy and the International Astronautical Commission were duly briefed. Hours dragged by, and our work schedule became completely snarled.

I must admit, however, that Sam was a good guest. He handed out trinkets that he fished from the deep pockets of his coveralls. A miniature penknife to one of the men who had rescued him. A pocket computer to the other, programmed to play a dozen different games when it was connected to a display screen. A small, flat tin of rock candy. A Russian-English dictionary the size of your thumb.

That dictionary should have alerted my suspicions. But I confess that I was more concerned with getting this noisy intrusion off my station and back where he belonged.

Sam stayed a day. Two days. Teleconferences crackled between Moscow and Washington, Moscow and Geneva, Washington and Geneva, ground control to our station, our station to the NASA station. Meanwhile Sam had made himself at home and even started to learn how to tell jokes in Russian. He was particularly interested in dirty jokes, of course, being the kind of man he was. He began to peel off some of the patches and buttons that adorned his coveralls and hand them out as presents. My crewmen especially lusted after the pictures of beautiful video stars.

He had taken over the galley, where he was teaching

my men how to play dice in zero gravity, when I finally got permission to send him back to the American station. Not an instant too soon, I thought.

Still, dear old Mir 5 became suddenly very quiet and dreary once we had packed him off in one of our own reliable transfer craft. We returned to our tedious tasks and the damnable exercise machines. Men growled and sulked at each other. Months of boredom and hard work stretched ahead of us. I could feel the tension pulling at my crew. I felt it myself.

But not for long.

Less than a week later, Korolev again roused me from my zipper bunk.

"He's back! The American!"

This time Sam did not pretend to need an emergency rescue. He had flown an orbital transfer vehicle to our station and matched orbit. His OTV was hovering a few hundred meters alongside us.

"Permission to come aboard?" His voice was unmistakable. "Unofficially?"

I glanced at Zworkin, who was of course right beside me in the command center. Strangely, Nikolai Nikolaivich nodded. Nothing is unofficial with him, I knew. Yet he did not object to the American making an "unofficial" visit.

I went to the docking chamber while Sam floated over to us. The airlock of his craft would not fit our docking mechanism, so he went EVA in his pressure suit and jetted over to us using his backpack maneuvering unit.

"I was in the neighborhood so I thought I'd drop by for a minute," Sam wisecracked once he got through our airlock and slid up the visor of his helmet.

"Why are you in this area?" Zworkin asked, eyes slitted in his pimpled face.

"To observe your laser tests," replied Sam, grinning. "You guys don't think our intelligence people don't know what you're up to, do you?"

"We are not testing lasers!"

"Not today, I know. Don't worry about it, Ivan, I'm not spying on you, for Chrissakes."

"My name is not Ivan!"

"I just came over to thank you guys for saving my ass." Sam turned slightly, his entire body pivoting weightlessly toward me. He reached into the pouches on the legs of his suit. "A couple of small tokens of my gratitude."

He pulled out two black oblong boxes and handed them to me. Videocassettes.

"Latest Hollywood releases," Sam explained. "With my thanks."

In a few minutes he was gone. Zworkin insisted on looking at the videos before anyone else could see them. "Probably capitalist propaganda," he grumbled.

I insisted on seeing them with him. I wasn't going to let him keep them all for himself.

One of the videos was the very popular film, *Rocky XVIII*, in which a geriatric former prizefighter is rejuvenated and gets out of his wheelchair to beat a nine-foot-tall robot for the heavyweight championship of the world.

"Disgusting," spat Zworkin.

"But it will be good to show the crew how low the capitalists sink in their pursuit of money," I said.

He gave me a sour look but did not argue.

The second video was a rock musical that featured decadent music at extreme decibel levels, decadent youths wearing outlandish clothes and weird hairdos, and decadent young women wearing hardly any clothes at all.

"Definitely not for the crew to see," said Zworkin. And none of us ever saw that video again. He kept it.

But now and then I heard the music, faintly, from his private cubicle during the shifts when he was supposed to be sleeping. Mysteriously, his acne began to clear up.

Almost two weeks afterward, Sam popped up again. Again he asked permission to come aboard, claiming this time that he was on a routine inspection mission of a commsat in geosynchronous orbit and had planned his return to the NASA station to take him close to us. He was a remarkable pilot, that much I must admit.

"Got a couple more videos for you," he added, almost as an afterthought.

Zworkin immediately okayed his visit. The rest of my crew, who had cheered the rejuvenated Rocky in his proletarian struggle against the stainless-steel symbol of western imperialism (as we saw it), welcomed him aboard.

Sam stayed for a couple of hours. We fed him a meal of borscht, soysteak, and ice cream. With plenty of hot tea.

"That's the best ice cream I've ever had!" Sam told me as we made our weightless way from the galley back to the docking chamber, where he had left his pressure suit.

"We get fresh shipments every week," I said. "Our only luxury."

"I never knew you guys had such great ice cream." He was really marvelling over it.

"Moscow is famous for its ice cream," I replied.

With a shake of his head that made his whole body sway slightly, Sam admitted, "Boy, we got nothing like that back at the NASA station."

"Would you like to bring some back to your station?" I asked. Fool that I am, I did not realize that he had maneuvered me into making the offer.

"Gee, yeah," he said, like a little boy.

I had one of the men pack him a container of ice cream while he struggled into his pressure suit. Zworkin was off screening the two new videos Sam had brought, so I did not bother him with the political question of offering a gift in return for Sam's gift.

As he put the helmet over his head, Sam said to me in a low voice, "Each of those videotapes is a double feature."

"A what?"

Leaning close to me, so that the technician in charge of the docking airlock could not hear, he whispered, "Play the tape backwards at half speed and you'll see another whole video. But *you* look at it yourself first. Don't let that sourball of a political officer see it, or he'll confiscate them both."

I felt puzzled, and my face must have shown it. Sam merely grinned, patted me on the shoulder and said, "Thanks for the ice cream."

Then he left.

It took a little ingenuity to figure out how to play the videos backwards at half speed. It took even more cleverness to arrange to look at them in private, without Zworkin or any of the other crew members hanging over my shoulders. But I did it.

The "second feature" on each of the tapes was pornographic filth. Disgusting sexual acrobatics featuring beautiful women with large breasts and apparently insatiable appetites. I watched the degrading spectacles several times, despite stern warnings from my conscience. If I had been cursed with acne, these videos would undoubtedly have solved the problem. Especially the one with the trapeze.

For the first time since I had been a teenager buying contraband blue jeans, I faced a moral dilemma. Should I tell Zworkin about these secret pornographic films? He had seen only the normal, "regular" features on each tape: an ancient John Wayne western and a brand-new comedy about a computer that takes over Wall Street.

In my own defense I say only that I was thinking of the good of my crew when I made my decision. The men had been in orbit for nearly 650 days, with almost two full months to go before we could return to our loved ones. The pornographic films might help them to bear the loneliness and perform better at their tasks.

But only if Zworkin did not know about them.

I decided to chance it. One by one I let the crew in on the little secret. Morale improved six hundred per-cent. Performance and productivity rose equally. The men smiled and laughed a lot more. I told myself it was just as much because they were pulling one over on the puritanical Zworkin as because they were watching Oral Roberta and her buxom girl friend Electric (AC/DC) Edna.

Sam returned twice more, swapping tapes for ice cream. He was our friend. He apparently had an inex-haustible supply of videos, each of them a "double fea-ture." While Zworkin spent the next few weeks happily watching the regular features on each video and per-spiring every time he saw a girl in a bikini, the rest of us watched the adventures of airline stewardesses, movie starlets, models, housewife-hookers, and other assorted and sordid specimens of female depravity.

The days flew by, with each man counting the hours until Sam showed up with another few videos. We stopped eating ice cream so that we would have plenty to give him in return.

But then Sam sprung his trap on us. On me.

"Listen," he said as he was suiting up in the docking chamber, preparing to leave. "Next time, how about sticking a couple of those diamonds you're making into the ice cream."

I blinked with surprise and automatically looked over my shoulder at the technician standing by to operate the airlock. He was busy admiring the four new videos Sam had brought, wondering what was in them as he studied their labels.

"What are you talking about?" I meant to say it out loud, but it came out as a whispered croak.

Sam flashed a cocky grin at me. "Come on, everybody knows you guys are making gem-quality diamonds out of methane gas in your zero-gee facility. Pump a little extra methane in and make me a couple to sell Earthside. I'll split the profits with you fifty-fifty."

"Impossible," I said. Softly.

His smile became shrewd. "Look, Greg old pal, I'm not asking for any military secrets. Just a couple stones I can peddle back Earthside. We can both make a nice wad of money."

"The diamonds we manufacture are not of gemstone quality," I lied.

"Let my friends on Forty-seventh Street decide what quality they are," Sam whispered.

"No."

He puffed out a sad sigh. "This has nothing to do with politics, Greg. It's business. Capitalism."

I shook my head hard enough to sway my entire body.

Sam seemed to accept defeat. "Okay. It's a shame, though. Hell, even your leaders in the Kremlin are making money selling their biographies to Western publishers. Capitalism is creeping up on you."

I said nothing.

He pulled the helmet over his head, fastened the neck seal. But before sliding down his visor he asked, quite casually, "What happens to you if Zworkin finds out what's on the videos you guys have been watching?"

My face went red. I could feel the heat flaming my cheeks.

"Just a couple of little diamonds, pal. A couple of carats. That's not so much to ask for, is it?"

He went through the airlock and jetted back to his own craft. I would have gladly throttled him, at that moment.

Now I had a *real* dilemma on my hands. Give in to Sam's blackmail or face Zworkin and the authorities back on the ground. It would not only be me who would be in trouble, but my entire crew. They did not deserve to suffer because of my bad decisions, but they would. We would all spend the rest of our lives shoveling cow manure in Siberia or running mining machines on the Moon.

I had been corrupted, and I knew it. Oh, I had the best of motives, the loftiest of intentions. But how would they appear next to the fact that I had allowed my crew to watch disgusting pornographic films provided by a capitalist agent of the CIA? Corruption, pure and simple. I would be lucky to be sentenced to Siberia.

I gave in to Sam's demands. I told myself it was for the sake of my crew, but it was to save my own neck, and to save my dear family from disgrace. I had the technicians make three extra small diamonds, and embedded them in the ice cream when Sam made his next visit.

This was the exact week, of course, when the USSR and the western powers were meeting in Geneva to decide on deployment of space weapons. Our own Red Shield system and the American Star Wars system were well into the testing phase. We had conducted a good many of the tests ourselves, aboard Mir 5. Now the question was, does each side begin to deploy its own system, or do we hammer out some method of working cooperatively?

Sam returned a few days later. I did not want to see him, but was afraid not to. He seemed happy and cheerful, and carried no less than six new videos with him. I spoke to him very briefly, very coldly. He seemed not to be bothered at all. He laughed and joked. And passed me a note on a tiny scrap of paper as he handed me the new videos.

I read the note in the privacy of my cubicle, after he left. "Good stuff. Worth a small fortune. How many can you provide each week?"

I was accustomed to the weightlessness of zero gravity, but at that instant I felt as if I were falling into a deep, dark pit, falling and falling down into an utterly black well that had no bottom.

To make matters worse, after a few days of progress the conference at Geneva seemed to hit a snag for some unfathomable reason. The negotiations stopped dead, and the diplomats began to snarl at each other in the old Cold War fashion. The world was shocked. We received orders to accelerate our tests of the Red Shield laser that had been installed in the laboratory module at the aft end of our station.

We watched TV news broadcasts from every part of the world (without letting ground control know it, of course). Everyone was frightened at the sudden intransigence in Geneva.

Zworkin summed up all our fears. "The imperialists want an excuse to strike us with their nuclear missiles before our Red Shield defense is deployed."

I had to admit he was probably right. What scared me was the thought that *we* might strike at *them* before their Star Wars defense was deployed. Either way, it meant the same thing: nuclear holocaust.

Even thickheaded Korolev seemed worried. "Will we go to war?" he kept asking. "Will we go to war?" No one knew.

To make matters still worse, in the midst of our laser test preparations Sam sent a radio message that he was on his way; he would rendezvous with our station in three hours, and he had "something special" for us.

The crisis in Geneva meant nothing to him, it seemed. He was coming for "business as usual." Zworkin had been right all along about him. Sam was a spy. I knew it now.

A vision formed in my mind. I would personally direct the test of the Red Shield laser. Its high-energy beam would "happen" to strike the incoming American spacecraft. Sam Gunn would be fried like a scrawny chicken in a hot oven. A regrettable accident. Yes. It would solve my problem.

Except—it could create such a furor on Earth that the conference in Geneva would break up altogether. It could be the spark that would lead to war, nuclear war.

Yet—Sam had no business flying an American spacecraft so close to a Soviet station. Both the U.S. and USSR had clearly proclaimed that the regions around their stations were sovereign territory, not to be violated by the other side's craft. Sam's visits to Mir 5 were strictly illegal, secret, clandestine, except for his first "emergency" visit. If we fried him, we would be within our legal rights.

On the other hand—could the entire crew remain silent about Sam's many visits? Would Zworkin stay silent or would he denounce me once we had returned to Mother Russia?

On the *other* hand—what difference would any of that make if we triggered nuclear war?

That is why I found myself sweating in the laser laboratory attached to the aft end of the station, a few hours after Sam's call. He knew that we were going to test the laser—he had to know. That was why he was cheerfully heading our way at this precise point in time.

The laboratory was chilly; the three technicians operating the giant laser wore bulky sweaters over their coveralls, and gloves with fingers cut out so they could manipulate their sensitive equipment properly. But I was sweating buckets.

This section of the station was a complete module in itself; it could be detached and de-orbited, if necessary, and a new section put in its place. The huge laser filled the laboratory almost completely. If we had not been in zero gravity, it would have been impossible for the technicians to climb into the nooks and crannies necessary to service all the equipment.

One wide optical quality window gave me a view of the black depths of space. But no window could withstand the incredible intensity of the laser's high-power beam. The beam was instead directed through a polished copper pipe to the outside of the station's hull, which is why the laboratory was always so cold. It was impossible to keep the module decently warm; the heat leaked out through the laser beam channel. On the outer end of that channel was the aiming mirror (also polished copper) which directed the beam toward its target—hypothetical or actual.

I had calculated Sam's approach trajectory back at the control center and pecked the numbers into my hand computer. Now, as the technicians labored and grumbled over their big laser, I gave them those coordinates as their target. As far as they knew, they were firing the multi-megawatt laser beam into empty space, as usual. Only I knew that when they fired the laser, its beam would destroy the approaching Yankee spacecraft and kill Sam Gunn.

The moments ticked by as I sweated coldly, miserable with apprehension and—yes, I admit it freely—with guilt. I had ordered the technicians to program my numbers into the laser's aiming mirror; the big slab of polished copper hanging outside the station's hull was already tracking Sam's trajectory, turning ever so slightly each second. The relays directing its motion clicked inside the laboratory like the tapping of a Chinese water torture, like the clicks of a quartz clock.

Then I heard the sighing sound that happens when an airtight hatch between two modules of the station is opened. Turning, I saw the hatch swinging open, its heavy hinges groaning slightly. Zworkin pushed through and floated around the bulky master control console to my side.

"You show an unusual interest in this test," he said softly.

My insides blazed as if I had stuck my hand into the power outlet. "There is the crisis in Geneva," I replied. "Moscow wants this test to proceed flawlessly."

"Will it?"

I did not trust myself to say anything more. I merely nodded.

Zworkin watched the muttering technicians for a few endless moments, then asked, "Do you find it odd that the American is approaching us *exactly* at the time our test is scheduled?"

I nodded once again, keeping my eyes fixed on the empty point in space where I imagined the beam and Sam's spacecraft would intersect.

"I received an interesting message from Moscow, less than an hour ago," Zworkin said. I dared not look into his face, but his voice sounded brittle, tense. "The rumor is that the Geneva conference has struck a reef made of pure diamond."

"What?" That spun me around. He was not gloating. In fact, he looked just as worried as I felt. No, not even worried. Frightened. The tone of voice that I had assumed was sarcasm was actually the tight, dry voice of fear.

"This is unconfirmed rumor, mind you," Zworkin said, "but what they are saying is that the NATO intelligence service has learned we are manufacturing pure diamond crystals in zero gravity, diamond crystals that can be made large enough to be used for mirrors and windows in extremely high-powered lasers. They are concerned that we have moved far ahead of them in this key area of technology."

Just at that instant Sam's cocky voice chirped over the station's intercom speakers. "Hey there, friends and neighbors, here's your Hollywood delivery service, comin' atcha."

The laser mirror clicked again. And again. One of the technicians floated back to the console at my side and pressed the three big red rocker switches that turned on the electrical power, one after the other. The action made his body rise up to the low ceiling of the laboratory each time. He bounced up and down slowly, like a bubble trapped in sealed glass.

A low whine came from the big power generators, which were in a separate module of the station. I could feel their vibration through my boots.

In my mind's eye I saw a thin yellow line that represented the trajectory of Sam's spacecraft, approaching us. And a heavier red line, the fierce beam of our laser, reaching out to meet it.

"Got something more than videos, this trip," Sam was chattering. "Managed to lay my hands on some really cute electronic toys; interactive games, you'll love 'em. Got the latest sports videos, too, and a bucketful of real-beef hamburgers. All you gotta do is pop 'em in your microwave. Brought mustard and ketchup, too. Better'n that soy stuff you guys been eating . . ."

He was talking his usual blue streak. I was glad that the communications technicians knew to scrub his transmissions from the tapes that ground control monitored. Dealing with Zworkin was bad enough . . .

Through his inane gabbling I could hear the mirror relays clicking, like the rifles of a firing squad being cocked, one by one. Sam approached us, blithely unaware of what awaited him. I pictured his spacecraft being hit by the laser beam, exploding, Sam and his videos and hamburgers all transformed instantly into an expanding red-hot ball of bloody vapor.

I reached over and pounded the master switch on the console. Just like the technician, I bounded toward the ceiling. The power generators wound down and went silent.

Zworkin stared up at me as I gently bumped my head and floated down toward him again.

I could not kill him. I could not murder Sam in cold blood, no matter what the consequences might be.

"What are you doing?" Zworkin demanded.

Putting out a hand to grasp the console and steady myself, I said, "We should not run this test while the Yankee spy is close enough to watch."

He eyed me shrewdly, then called to the two dumbfounded technicians. "Out! Both of you! Until your commander calls for you again."

Shrugging and exchanging confused looks, the two young men left the laboratory. Zworkin swung the hatch shut behind them, leaning against it as he gave me a long, quizzical stare.

"Grigori Aleksandrovich," he said at last, "we must do something about this American. If ground control ever finds about him—if *Moscow* ever finds out . . ."

"What was it you said about the diamond crystals?" I asked. "Do you think the imperialists know about our experiments here?"

"Of course they do! And this Yankee spy is at the heart of the matter."

"What should we do?"

Zworkin rubbed his chin, but said nothing. I could not help thinking, absurdly, that his acne was almost totally gone.

So we allowed Sam aboard the station once again, and I brought him immediately to my private cubicle.

"Kripes!" he chirped. "I've seen bigger coffins. Is this the best that the workers' paradise can do for you?"

"No propaganda now," I whispered sternly. "And no more blackmail. You will not return to this station again, and you will not get any more diamonds from me."

"And no more ice cream?" He seemed entirely unconcerned with the seriousness of the situation.

"No more anything," I said, straining to make it as strong as I could while still whispering. "Your visits here are finished. Over and done with."

Sam made a rueful grin and wormed his right hand into the hip pocket of his coveralls. "Read this," he said, handing me a slip of paper.

It had two numbers on it, both of them in six digits.

"The first is your private bank account number at the Bank of Bern, in Switzerland."

"Soviet citizens are not allowed to . . ."

"The second number"—Sam ignored me—"is the amount of money deposited in your account, in Swiss francs."

"I told, you I am not—" I stopped and looked at the second number again. I was not certain of the exchange ratio between Swiss francs and rubles, but six digits are six digits.

Sam laughed softly. "Listen. My friends in New York have friends in Switzerland. That's how I set up the account for you. It's your half of the profit from those little stones you gave me."

"I don't believe it. You are attempting to bribe me!"

His look became pitying. "Greg, old pal, three-quarters of your Politburo have accounts in Switzerland. Don't you realize that the big conference in Geneva is stalled over—"

"Over your report to the CIA that we are manufacturing diamonds here in this station!" I hissed. "You are a spy, admit it!"

He grinned and spread his hands in the universal gesture of helplessness. "Okay, so I've passed some info over to the IDA . . ."

"Don't you mean CIA?"

Sam blinked with surprise. "CIA? Why in hell would I want to talk to those spooks? I'm dealing with the IDA."

"Intelligence Defense Agency," I said.

He shook his head annoyedly. "Naw—the International Diamond Association. The diamond cartel. You know, DeBeers and those guys."

I was too stunned with surprise to say anything.

"The cartel knew you were doing zero-gravity experiments in manufacturing diamonds. Once my friends in New York saw the quality of the stones you gave me, they sent word hotfooting to Amsterdam."

"The international diamond cartel . . ."

"That's right, pal," said Sam. "They don't want space-manufactured diamonds kicking the bottom out of their market."

"But the crisis in Geneva," I mumbled.

Sam laughed. "The argument in Geneva is between the diamond cartel and your own government. It's got nothing to do with Star Wars or Red Shield. They've forgotten all about that. Now they're talking about *money*!"

I could not believe what he was saying. "Our leaders would never stoop . . ."

Sam silenced me with a guffaw. "Your leaders are

haggling with the cartel like a gang of housewives at a warehouse sale. The General Secretary is talking with the cartel's leaders right now, over a private two-way fiber-optic TV link.''

''How do you know this?''

He reached into the big pocket on the thigh of his suit. ''Special video recording. I brought it just for you.'' With a sly smile he added, ''Can't trust those guys in Amsterdam, you know.''

It was difficult to catch my breath. My head was swimming.

''Listen to me, Greg. Your leaders are going to join the diamond cartel; they're just haggling over the price.''

''Impossible!''

''Hard to believe that good socialists would help the evil capitalists rig the world price for diamonds? But that's what's going on right now, so help me. And once they've settled on their terms, the conference in Geneva will get back on track.''

''You're lying. I can't believe that you are telling me the truth.''

He shrugged good-naturedly. ''Look at the video. Watch what happens in Geneva. Then, when things settle down, you and I can start doing business again.''

I must have shaken my head unconsciously.

''Don't want to leave all those profits to the cartel, do you? We can make a fair-sized piece of change—as long as we stay small enough so the cartel won't notice us. That's still a lot of money, pal.''

''Never,'' I said. And I meant it. To do what he asked would mean working against my own nation, my own people, my own government. If the KGB ever found out!

I personally ushered Sam back to the docking compartment and off the station. And never allowed him back on Mir 5 again, no matter how he pleaded and wheedled us over the radio.

After several weeks he finally realized that I would not deal with him, that when I said "never" that was exactly what I meant.

"Okay, friends," his radio voice said, the last time he tried to contact us. "Guess I'll just have to find some other way to make my first million. So-long, Greg. Enjoy the workers' paradise, pal."

The old man's tone had grown distinctly wistful. He stopped, made a deep wheezing sigh, and ran a liver-spotted hand over his wrinkled pate.

The reporter had forgotten the chill of the big lunar dome. Leaning slightly closer to Prokov, she asked, "And that's the last you saw or heard of Sam Gunn?"

"Yes," said the Russian. "And good riddance, too."

"But what happened after that?"

Prokov's aged face twisted unhappily. "What happened? Everything went exactly as he said it would. The conference in Geneva started up again, and East and West reached a new understanding. My crew achieved its mission goal; we spent two full years in Mir 5 and then went home. The USSR became a partner in the international diamond cartel."

"And you went to Mars," the reporter prompted.

Prokov's wrinkled face became bitter. "No. I was not picked to command the Mars expedition. Zworkin never denounced me, never admitted his own involvement with Sam, but his report on me was damning enough to knock me out of the Mars mission. The closest I got to Mars was a weather observation station in Antarctica!"

"Wasn't the General Secretary at that time the one who . . ."

"The one who retired to Switzerland after he stepped

down from leading the Party? Yes. He is living there still, like a capitalist millionaire.''

"And you never dealt with Sam Gunn again?"

"Never! I told him never, and that is exactly what I meant. Never.''

"Just that brief contact with him was enough to wreck your career.''

Prokov nodded stonily.

"Yet,'' the reporter mused, ''in a way it was *you* who got the USSR into partnership with the diamond cartel. That must be worth hundreds of millions each year to your government.''

The old man's only reply was a bitter ''Pah!''

"What happened to *your* Swiss bank account? The one Sam started for you?''

Prokov waved a hand in a gesture that swept the lunar dome and asked, ''How do you think I can afford to live here?''

The reporter felt herself frown with puzzlement. ''I thought the Leonov Center was free . . .''

"Yes, of course it is. A retirement center for Heroes of the Soviet Union. Absolutely free! Unless you want some real beef in your Stroganoff. That costs extra. Or an electric blanket for your bed. Or chocolates— chocolates from Switzerland are the best of all, you know.''

"You mean that Swiss bank account . . .''

"It is an annuity,'' said Prokov. ''Not much money, but a nice little annuity to pay for some of the extra frills. The money sits there in the bank, and every month the faithful Swiss gnomes send me the interest by radiophone. Compared to the other Heroes living here, I am a well-to-do man. I can even buy vodka for them.''

The reporter suppressed a smile. ''So Sam's bank deposit is helping you, even after all those years.''

Slowly the old man nodded. "Yes, he is helping me even after his death." His voice sank lower. "And I never thanked him. Never. Never spoke a kind word to him."

"He was a difficult man to deal with," said the reporter. "A very difficult personality."

"A thief," Prokov replied. But his voice was so soft that it almost sounded like a blessing. "A blackmailer. A scoundrel."

There were tears in his weary eyes. "How I wish he were here. I only knew him for a few months. He frightened me half to death and nearly caused a nuclear war. He disrupted my crew and ruined my chance to lead the Mars expedition. He tricked me and used me shamefully . . ."

The reporter made a sympathetic noise.

"Yet even after all these years the memory of him makes me smile. He made life exciting, vibrant. How I miss him!"

Escape!

INTRODUCTION

We tell each other a lot of lies about prisons. We call it "the criminal justice system," but it has very little to do with justice, and the inmates of our prisons tend to become hardened to lifetimes of crime while inside their walls.

We can do better. It is possible to build prisons and hire staffs that actually help to change the prisoners, to rehabilitate them. Not every prisoner can be helped this way; some are lost, antisocial souls long before they enter prison, others are professional crooks who will be "rehabilitated" only by death.

But many can be helped, if we are willing to pay for prisons—and personnel—that can provide such help. While the high-technology jail of this story is still fictional, much of the hardware could be built now. It would be much more difficult to recruit men and women of the caliber of Joe Tenny. They do exist, I know, because Joe is based on a dear friend of mine who died *much too young. His type is rare, but even rarer is a society that spends the care and effort to utilize such men and women to make prisons the best they can be, with the goal of reforming the lives of criminals who still have the ability to change their ways.*

Chapter One

The door shut behind him.

Danny Romano stood in the middle of the small room, every nerve tight. He listened for the click of the lock. Nothing.

Quiet as a cat, he tiptoed back to the door and tried the knob. It turned. The door was unlocked.

Danny opened the door a crack and peeked out into the hallway. Empty. The guards who had brought him here were gone. No voices. No footsteps. Down at the far end of the hall, up near the ceiling, was some sort of TV camera. A little red light glowed next to its lens.

He shut the door and leaned against it.

"Don't lem 'em sucker you," he said to himself. "This is a jail."

Danny looked all around the room. There was only one bed. On its bare mattress was a pile of clothes, bed sheets, towels and stuff. A TV screen was set into the wall at the end of the bed. On the other side of the room was a desk, an empty bookcase, and two stiff-back wooden chairs. Somebody had painted the walls a soft blue.

"This can't be a cell . . . not for me, anyway. They made a mistake."

The room was about the size of the jail cells they always put four guys into. Or sometimes six.

And there was something else funny about it. *The smell, that's it!* This room smelled clean. There was even fresh air blowing in through the open window. And there were no bars on the window. Danny tried to remember how many jail cells he had been in. Eight? Ten? They had all stunk like rotting garbage.

He went to the clothes on the bed. Slacks, real slacks. Sports shirts and turtlenecks. And colors! Blue, brown, tan. Danny yanked off the gray coveralls he had been wearing, and tried on a light blue turtleneck and dark brown slacks. They even fit right. Nobody had ever been able to find him a prison uniform small enough to fit his wiry frame before this.

Then he crossed to the window and looked outside. He was on the fifth or sixth floor, he guessed. The grounds around the building were starting to turn green with the first touch of early spring. There were still a few patches of snow here and there, in the shadows cast by the other buildings.

There were a dozen buildings, all big and square and new-looking. Ten floors high, each of them, although there were a couple of smaller buildings farther out. One of them had a tall smokestack. The buildings were arranged around a big, open lawn that had cement paths through it. A few young trees lined the walkways. They were just beginning to bud.

"No fences," Danny said to himself.

None of the windows he could see had bars. Everyone seemed to enter or leave the buildings freely. No guards and no locks on the doors? Out past the farthest building was an area of trees. Danny knew from his trip in here, this morning, that beyond the woods was the highway that led back to the city.

Back to Laurie.

Danny smiled. What were the words the judge had used? *In . . . in-de-ter-minate sentence*. The lawyer had said that it meant he was going to stay in jail for as long as they wanted him to. A year, ten years, fifty years. . . .

"I'll be out of here tonight!" He laughed.

A knock on the door made Danny jump. *Somebody heard me!"*

Another knock, louder this time. "Hey, you in there?" a man's voice called.

"Y . . . yeah."

The door popped open. "I'm supposed to talk with you and get you squared away. My name's Joe Tenny."

Joe was at least forty, Danny saw. He was stocky, tough-looking, but smiling. His face was broad; his dark hair combed straight back. He was a head taller than Danny and three times wider. The jacket of his suit looked tight across the middle. His tie was loosened, and his shirt collar unbuttoned.

A cop, Danny thought. *Or maybe a guard. But why ain't he wearing a uniform?*

Joe Tenny stuck out a heavy right hand. Danny didn't move.

"Listen, kid," Tenny said, "we're going to be stuck together for a long time. We might as well be friends."

"I got my own friends," said Danny. "On the outside."

Tenny's eyebrows went up while the corners of his mouth went down. His face seemed to say, *Who are you trying to kid, wise guy?*

Aloud, he said, "Okay, suit yourself. You can have it any way you like, hard or easy." He reached for one of the chairs and pulled it over near the bed.

"How long am I going to be here?"

"That depends on you. A couple of years, at least." Joe turned the chair around backwards and sat on it as if it were a saddle, leaning his stubby arms on the chair's back.

Danny swung at the pile of clothes and things on the bed, knocking most of them onto the floor. Then he plopped down on the mattress. The springs squeaked in complaint.

Joe looked hard at him, then let a smile crack his face. "I know just what's going through your mind. You're thinking that two years here in the Center is going to kill you, so you're going to crash out the first chance you get. Well, for*get* it! The Center is escape-proof."

In spite of himself, Danny laughed.

"I know, I know. . . ." Tenny grinned back at him. "The Center looks more like a college campus than a jail. In fact, that's what most of the kids call it—the campus. But believe me, Alcatraz was easy compared to this place. We don't have many guards or fences but we've got TV cameras, and laser alarms, and SPECS."

"Who's Specks?" Danny asked.

Joe called out, "SPECS, say hello."

The TV screen on the wall lit up. A flat, calm voice said, "GOOD MORNING DR. TENNY. GOOD MORNING MR. ROMANO. WELCOME TO THE JUVENILE HEALTH CENTER."

Danny felt totally confused. Somebody was talking through the TV set? The screen, though showed the words he was hearing, spelled out a line at a time. But they moved too fast for Danny to really read them. And Specks, whoever he was, called Joe Tenny a doctor.

"Morning SPECS," Tenny said to the screen. "How's it going today?"

"ALL SYSTEMS ARE FUNCTIONING WELL, DR. TENNY. A LIGHT TUBE IN CORRIDOR SIX OF BUILDING NINE BURNED OUT DURING THE NIGHT. I HAVE REPORTED THIS TO THE MAINTENANCE CREW. THEY WILL REPLACE IT

BEFORE LUNCH. THE MORNING CLASSES ARE IN PROG-
RESS. ATTENDANCE IS . . ."

"Enough, skip the details." Joe turned back to
Danny. "If I let him, he'd give me a report on every
stick and stone in the Center."

"Who is he?" Danny asked.

"Not a *he*, really. An *it*. A computer. Special Computer System. Take the 's-p-e' from 'special' and the
'c' and 's' from 'computer system' and put the letters
together: SPECS. He runs most of the Center. Sees all
and knows all. And he never sleeps."

"Big deal," said Danny, trying to make it sound
tough.

Joe Tenny turned back to the TV screen, which was
still glowing. "SPECS, give me Danny Romano's record, please."

The reply came without an instant's wait: "DANIEL
FRANCIS ROMANO. AGE SIXTEEN. HEIGHT FIVE FEET TWO
INCHES. WEIGHT ONE HUNDRED THIRTEEN POUNDS.
SENTENCED TO INDETERMINATE SENTENCE IN THE JU-
VENILE HEALTH CENTER. FOUND GUILTY OF ATTEMPTED
MURDER, RIOTING, LOOTING, ATTACKING A POLICE OF-
FICER WITH A DEADLY WEAPON, RESISTING ARREST.
EARLIER CONVICTIONS INCLUDE PETTY THEFT, AUTO-
MOBILE THEFT, ASSAULT AND BATTERY, RESISTING AR-
REST, VANDALISM. SERVED SIX MONTHS IN STATE PRISON
FOR BOYS. ESCAPED AND RECAPTURED . . ."

"That's enough," Joe said. "Bad scene, isn't it?"

"So?"

"So it's why you're here."

Danny asked, "What kind of place is this? How come
I'm not in a regular jail?"

Joe thought a minute before answering. "This is a
new place. This Center has been set up for kids like
you. Kids who are going to kill somebody—or get
themselves killed—unless we can change them. Our job

is to help you to change. We think you can straighten out. There's no need for you to spend the rest of your life in trouble and in jail. But you've got to let us help you. And you've got to help yourself.''

"How . . . how long will I have to stay here?''

Tenny's face turned grim. "Like I said, a couple of years, at least. But it really depends on you. You're going to stay as long as it takes. If you don't shape up, you stay. It's that simple.''

Chapter Two

Joe Tenny went right on talking. He used SPECS' TV screen to show Danny a map of the Center and the layouts of the different buildings. He pointed out the classrooms, the cafeteria, the gym and shops, and game rooms.

But Danny didn't see any of it, didn't hear a single word. All he could think of was: *as long as it takes. If you don't shape up, you stay.*

They were going to keep him here forever. Danny knew it. Tenny was a liar. They were all liars. Like that lousy social worker when he was a kid. She told him they were sending him to a special school. "It's for your own good, Daniel.'' Good, real good. Some school. No teacher, no books. Just guards who belted you when they felt like it, and guys who socked you when the guards weren't looking.

If you don't shape up, you stay. Shape up to what? Get a job? How? Where? Who would hire a punk sixteen-year-old who's already spent half his life in jails?

"We gave you a good room," Joe said, getting up suddenly from his chair. "Your building's right next-door to the cafeteria."

Danny snapped his attention back to the real world.

"Come on, it's just about lunchtime."

He followed Joe Tenny out into the hallway, to the elevator, and down to the ground floor of the building. Danny saw that somebody had scratched his initials on the metal inner door of the elevator, and somebody else had worked very hard to erase the scratches. They were barely visible.

They pushed through the glass doors and followed a cement walkway across the piece of lawn that separated the two buildings. Danny shivered in the sudden chill of the outside air. Tenny walked briskly, like he was in a hurry.

Groups of boys—two, three, six, eight in a bunch—were walking across the campus grounds toward the cafeteria building. They were talking back and forth, joking, horsing around.

But Danny's mind was still racing. *I can't stay here. Can't leave Laurie alone on the outside. Some other guy will grab her. By the time I get out, she won't even remember me. Got to get out fast!*

Joe pushed open the glass doors of the cafeteria building. It was warm inside, and noisy. And it smelled of cooking.

"DR. TENNY," called a loudspeaker. Danny thought it sounded like SPECS' voice only much louder and with a bit of an echo to it. "DR. TENNY, PLEASE REPORT TO THE ADMINISTRATION BUILDING."

"Looks like I miss lunch," Joe said, glancing up at the loudspeaker. Danny saw that it was set into the panelled ceiling. There was a TV lens with is unblinking red eye next to it, watching them.

"Have a good feed, Danny. The rest of the day's yours. Move around, make some friends. SPECS will get you up at the right time tomorrow morning and tell you which classes to go to. See you!"

And with a wave of a heavy, thick-wristed hand, Joe headed back for the glass doors and outside.

Danny watched him go. Then a half-dozen boys pushed through the doors and walked in toward the cafeteria. They were laughing and wise-cracking among themselves. No one said hello or seemed to notice Danny at all.

Turning, Danny headed for the food. Around a corner of the hallway was a big, open, double doorway. Inside it was the cafeteria, noisy and busy with at least a hundred boys. They were standing in line, waving across the big room to friends, rushing toward tables with trays of steaming food, talking, laughing, eating. They moved as freely as they wanted and they all seemed to be talking as loudly as their lungs would let them.

The tables were small, four or six places each. In a few spots, boys had pushed together a couple of tables to make room for a bigger group.

Danny remembered the dining room in the State Prison. You marched in single file and ate at long, wooden tables that were so old the paint was gone. The wood itself was cracked and carved with the initials of fifty years' worth of boys.

This cafeteria was sparking new. The walls, the tables, the floors all gleamed with fresh paint and plastic and metal. One whole wall was glass. Outside you could see a stretch of grass and a few young trees.

He took a place at the end of the food line. The boys moved along quickly, even though some of them were

talking and kidding back and forth. Soon Danny was
taking a tray and a wrapped package of spoon, knife,
and fork. All plastic.

It surprised him to see that there were no people
behind the food counter. Everything was automatic.
Boys took a bowl of soup, or a sandwich, or a metal-
foil dish that held an entire hot dinner in it. As soon as
one piece was taken, another popped through a little
door in the wall to replace it.

"You're new here, aren't you?"

Danny turned to see, in line behind him, a tall boy
with sandy hair and a scattering of freckles across his
snub nose.

"My name's Alan Peterson, No, don't tell me yours.
Let me see if I can remember it. SPECS flashed pic-
tures of all the new guys on the news this morning.
You're . . . emm . . . Danny something-or-other.
Right?"

"Danny Romano."

Alan grinned. "See, I got it. Almost."

"Yeah." Danny reached for a sandwich and an apple. The only drinks he could see were milk, either
white or chocolate. He took a chocolate.

Stepping away, Danny looked around for a table.

"Come on with me," Alan said cheerfully. "I'll sit
you down with some of the guys. You ought to make
friends."

Alan steered him toward a six-place table. Three of
the seats were already filled. Danny stopped suddenly.

"I ain't sittin' there."

"Why not?"

Danny jerked his head toward one of the boys at the
table. " 'Cause I don't eat with niggers, that's why
not."

Chapter Three

Alan looked at Danny in a funny way. Not sore, but almost.

"Okay," he said softly. "Find your own friends."

He left Danny standing there with the tray in his hands and went to the table. Another black came up at the same time and sat beside Alan.

Danny found a small table that was empty and sat there alone, with his back to the doors and the food line. He was facing the glass wall and the outside.

He ate quickly, thinking, *Don't waste any time. Walk around, see how big the place is, how hard it'll be to get out.*

He got up from the table and started to walk away. But SPECS' voice came from an overhead loudspeaker: "PLEASE TAKE YOUR TRAY TO THE DISPOSAL SLOT IF YOU ARE FINISHED EATING. THANK YOU."

Danny looked up at the ceiling, then turned and saw other boys bringing their trays to a slot in the wall, not far from the table where he was. With a small shrug, he took his tray to the slot.

He watches everything, Danny thought as he glanced up at one of the TV cameras in the ceiling.

It was still chilly outside after lunch, even though the sun was shining. Danny thought he had seen a jacket— a windbreaker—among the clothes on his bed. But he didn't bother going back to his room. Instead, he jammed his fists in his slacks pockets, hunched his shoulders, and headed toward the trees that were out at the edge of the campus.

He didn't get far.

From behind him, a soft voice said, "Hear you don't like eatin' with black men, skinny."

Danny turned around. Two blacks were standing there, grinning at him. But there was no friendship in their smiles. Danny thought they might be the two boys who had been at the table Alan tried to steer him to.

For a moment they just stood there, looking each other over. There were a couple of other boys around, white and black, but they stayed a little distance away. Out of it. Danny could feel himself tensing, his fists clenching hard inside his pockets.

One of the blacks was Danny's own height, and not much heavier. The other was tall and thin, built for basketball. He had sleepy-looking eyes, and a bored, cool look on his face.

"That true, skinny?" the tall one asked. "You don't want to eat with us?"

Danny swore at him.

"My, my, such language," said the smaller of them. "Real rough one, this guy. Hard as nails."

"Yeah . . . fingernails."

They both laughed. Danny said nothing.

The tall black said slowly, "Listen baby. You got a problem. You're bein' put down in the schedule to fight Lacey here, first of the month."

Lacey nodded and grinned brightly. "So start workin' out in the gym, Whitey, or you won't last even half a round."

"Yeah." The tall one added, "And in case you don't know it, Lacey here's the lightweight champ o' this whole Center. And he ain't gonna be playing games with you in that ring. Dig?"

And they both walked away, as quickly and softly as they had come. Danny stood there alone, trembling with rage. He was so angry that his chest was starting to hurt.

The other boys who had been hanging around, started to drift back toward the buildings. But one of the white boys came up to Danny.

"My name's Ralph Malzone. I seen what them black bastards done to ya."

Ralph was a big redhead, huge and solid, like a pro football player. His face was round and puffy, with tiny eyes squinting out, and little round ears plastered flat against his skull. He looked as if his skin was stretched as tight as it could go, another ounce would split it apart. But Ralph didn't look fat; he looked *hard*.

Danny looked up at him. "I couldn't even understand what they were saying, half the time."

"I heard 'em," Ralph answered. "You're new, huh? Well, there's a boxing match here every month. You been put down to fight Lacey. He's the lightweight champ. If you don't fight him, everybody'll think you're chicken."

Danny didn't answer. He just stood there, feeling cold whenever the wind gusted by.

"Lacey's fast. Hits hard for a little guy."

"I'm shaking," Danny said.

Ralph laughed. "Hey, you're okay. Listen, I'll help you out. In the gym. I know a lot about fighting."

"Why should you help me?"

Ralph's face started to look mean. "I don't like to see white guys gettin' picked on. And I want that Lacey creamed. He needs his head busted. Only, they won't let me fight him. I'm a heavyweight."

Grinning, Danny asked, "Why wait for the first of the month? Get him outside."

"Boy, wouldn't I like to!" Ralph said. "But it ain't as easy as it sounds. Too many TV cameras around. Step out of line and they catch you right away. . . . But you got the right idea. Boy, I'd *love* to mash that little crumb."

Nodding, Danny said, "Okay . . . uh, I'll see you in the gym sometime."

"Good," said Ralph. "I'll look for you."

Chapter Four

Ralph headed back for one of the classroom buildings. Danny started out again for the trees.

It was colder in the woods. The bare branches of the trees seemed to filter out almost all of the sun's warmth. The sky had turned a sort of milky-gray. The ground under Danny's sneakers was damp and slippery from melted snow and the remains of last year's fallen leaves.

Danny hated the cold, hated the woods, hated everything and everybody except the few blocks of city street where he had lived and the guys who had grown up on those streets with him. They were the only guys in the word you could trust. Can't trust grown-ups. Can't trust teachers or cops or lawyers or judges or jail guards. Can't trust Tenny. Can't even trust this new guy, Ralph. Just your own guys, the guys you really know. And Laurie. He had to get back to Laurie.

His feet were cold and wet and he could feel his chest getting tight, making it hard to breathe. Soon his chest would be too heavy to lift, and he'd have to stop walking and wait for his breathing to become normal again. But Danny kept going, puffing little breaths of steam from his mouth as he trudged through the woods.

And there it was!

The fence. A ten-foot-high wire fence. And on the other side of it, the highway. The outside world, with cars zipping by and big trailer trucks shifting gears with a grinding noise as they climbed the hill.

Danny stood at the edge of the trees, a dozen feet from the fence. Two hours down that highway was home. And Laurie.

He leaned his back against a tree, breathing hard, feeling the rough wood through his thin shirt. He listened to himself wheezing. *Like an old man*, he told himself angrily. *You sound like a stupid old man*.

When his breathing became normal again, Danny started walking along the fence. But he stayed in among the trees, so that he couldn't be seen too easily.

No guards. The fence was just a regular wire fence, the kind he'd been able to climb since he was in grade school. There wasn't even any barbed wire at the top. And nobody around to watch.

He could scramble over the fence and hitch a ride back to the city. He wasn't even wearing a prison uniform!

Danny laughed to himself. Why wait? He stepped out toward the fence.

"Hold it Danny! Hold it right there!"

Chapter Five

Danny spun around. Standing there among the trees was Joe Tenny, grinning broadly at him.

"Did you ever stop to think that the fence might be carrying ten thousand volts of electricity?" Joe asked.

Danny's mouth dropped open. Without thinking about it, he took a step back from the fence.

Joe walked past him and reached a hand out to the wire fence. "Relax, it's not 'hot.' We wouldn't want anybody to get hurt."

Danny felt his chest tighten up again. Suddenly it was so hard to breathe that he could hardly talk. "How . . . how'd you . . . know . . . ?"

"I told you the Center was escape-proof. SPECS has been watching you every step of the way. You crossed at least eight different alarm lines. . . . No, you can't see them. But they're there. SPECS called me as soon as you started out through the woods. I hustled down here to stop you."

He's big but he's old, Danny thought. *Getting fat. If I can knock him down and get across the fence . . .*

"Okay, come on back now," Joe was saying.

Danny aimed a savage kick below Joe's belt. But it never landed. Instead he felt himself swept up, saw the highway and then the cloudy sky flash past his eyes, and then landed facedown on the damp grass. Hard.

"For*get* it, kid," Joe said from somewhere above him. "You're too small and I'm too good a wrestler. I'm part Turk, you know."

Danny tried to get up. He tried to get his knees under his body and push himself off the ground. But he couldn't breathe, couldn't move. Everything was black, smelled of wet leaves. He was choking. . . .

He opened his eyes and saw a green curtain in front of him. Blinking, Danny slowly realized that he was in a hospital bed. It was cranked up to a sitting position.

Joe Tenny was sitting beside the bed, his face very serious.

"You okay?" Joe asked.

Danny nodded. "Yeah . . . I think so . . ."

"You scared me! I thought I had really hurt you. The doctors say it's asthma. How long have you had it?"

"Had what?"

Joe pulled his chair up closer. "Asthma. How long have you had trouble breathing?"

Danny took a deep breath. His chest felt okay again. Better than okay. It had never felt this good.

"It comes and goes," he said. "Hits when I'm working hard . . . running . . . things like that."

"And not a sign of it showed up in your physical exams," Joe muttered. "How old were you when it first hit you?"

"I don't know. What difference does it make?"

"How old?" Joe repeated. His voice wasn't any louder, but it somehow seemed ten times stronger than before.

Danny turned his head away from Joe's intense stare. "Five, maybe six." Then he remembered. "It was the year my father died. I was five."

Joe grunted. "Okay. The doctors need to know."

"I thought you was a doctor," Danny said, turning back to him.

Tenny smiled. "I am, but not a medical doctor. I'm a doctor of engineering. Been a teacher a good part of my life."

"Oh. . . ."

"You don't think much of teachers? Well, I don't blame you much."

Joe got up from his chair.

Danny looked around. The bed was screened off on three sides by the green curtain. The fourth side, the head of the bed, was against a wall.

"Where am I? How long I been here?" he asked.

"In the Center's hospital. You've been here about six hours. It's past dinnertime."

"I figured I'd be back home by now," Danny mumbled.

Joe looked down at him. "You've had a rough first day. But you've made it rough on yourself. Listen . . . there's a lot I could tell you about the Center. But I think it's better for you to find out things for yourself. All I want you to understand right now is one thing: around here, you'll get what you earn. Understand that? For the first time in your life, you're going to get *exactly* what you earn."

Danny frowned.

"It works both ways," Joe went on. "Make life rough for yourself and you'll earn trouble. Work hard, and you'll earn yourself an open door to the outside. You're the only one who can open that door. It's up to you."

"Sure."

"I mean it. I know you don't believe it, but you can trust me. You're going to learn that, in time. You don't trust anybody, that's one of the reasons why you're here. . . ."

Danny snapped, "I'm here because I nearly killed a fat-bellied cop in a riot that some niggers started!"

"*Wrong!* You're here because the staff of this Center decided there's a chance we might be able to help you. Otherwise you'd be in a *real* jail."

"What d'ya mean . . . ?"

Joe grabbed the chair again and sat on it. "Why do you think we call this the Juvenile *Health* Center? Because you're sick. All the kids here are sick, one way or another. You come from a sick city, a sick block. Maybe it's not all your fault that you're the way you are, but nobody's going to be able to make you well—nobody! Only you can do that. We're here to help, but we can't do much unless you work to help yourself."

Danny mumbled some street words.

"I understand that," Joe said, his eyes narrowing. "I'm part Sicilian, you know."

"You know everything, huh?"

"Wrong. But I know a lot more than you do. I even know more about Danny Romano than you do. I know there's enough in you to make a solid man. You've got to learn how to become a whole human being, though. My job is to help you do that."

Chapter Six

It was lunchtime the next day before the doctors would let Danny go. He walked across the campus slowly. It was a warmer day, bright with sunshine, and Danny felt pretty good.

Then he remembered that he had failed to escape. He was trapped here at the Center.

"For a while," he told himself. "Not for long, just for a while. Until I figure out how to get around those alarms . . . whatever they are."

He had lunch alone in the crowded, noisy cafeteria.

He sat at the smallest table he could find, in a corner by the glass wall. He saw Lacey walk by with a group of blacks, laughing and clowning around.

Danny finished eating quickly and decided to find the gym. He didn't have to look far. Just outside the cafeteria door was a big overhead sign with an arrow: ELEVATOR TO LIBRARY, POOL, GAME ROOMS, GYM.

He walked down the hall toward the elevator. Other boys were going the same way, some of them hurrying to get into the elevator before it filled up. Danny squeezed in just as the doors slid shut.

"FLOORS PLEASE." It was SPECS' voice.

"Gym," somebody said.

"Library."

"Pool."

"Hey Lou, you goin' swimmin' *again*?"

"It beats takin' a bath!"

Everybody in the elevator laughed.

The gym was on the top floor. The elevator door slid open and a burst of noise and smells and action hit Danny. A basketball game was in full swing. Boys shouting, ball pounding the floorboards, referee blasting on his whistle. Overhead, on a catwalk that went completely around the huge room, other boys were jogging and sprinting, their gray gym suits turning dark with sweat.

But at the far end of the gym was the thing that struck Danny the hardest. A boxing ring. And in it, Lacey was sparring with another black boy.

Danny stood by the elevator and watched, all the sights and sounds and odors of the gym fading away into nothing as he focused every nerve in his body on Lacey.

The guy was good. He moved around the ring like he was gliding on ice skates. His left snapped hard, jerking the other guy's head back when it landed. Then he winged a right across the other guy's guard and knocked him over backwards onto his back.

Turning, Lacey spotted Danny and waved. His black body was gleaming with sweat. His face was one enormous smile, made toothless by the rubber protector that filled his mouth.

"Hello, Danny."

Turning, he saw Alan Peterson standing beside him. "Hi."

"Watching the champ? I hear you're scheduled to fight him the first of the month."

"Yeah." Danny kept his eyes on Lacey. A new sparring partner had come into the ring now. Lacey was jab-jab-jabbing him to death.

"Were you in the hospital yesterday?" Alan asked. "There's a story going around. . . ."

"Yeah, I was." Danny still watched Lacey.

"Are you sick? I mean, will you miss the fight? You can't fight anybody if you're sick."

"I ain't sick."

"But . . ."

Lacey floored his new partner, this time with a left hook.

"I ain't sick!" Danny snapped. "I'll fight him the first of the month!"

"Okay, don't get sore," said Alan. "It's your funeral."

The loudspeaker suddenly cut through all the noise of the gym: "DANIEL FRANCIS ROMANO, PLEASE REPORT TO DR. TENNY'S OFFICE AT ONCE."

Danny felt almost relieved. He didn't want to hang around the gym any more, but he didn't want Lacey to see him back away. Now he had an excuse to go.

"I'll take you," Alan offered.

Danny said, "I can find it by myself."

Chapter Seven

He had to ask directions once he was outside on the campus. Finally, Danny found the building that the boys called "the front office." It was smaller than the other buildings, only three stories high. The sign over the main door said ADMINISTRATION. Danny wasn't quite sure he knew what it meant.

Inside the door was a sort of counter, with a girl sitting at a telephone switchboard behind it. She was getting old, Danny saw. Way over thirty, at least. She was reading a paperback book and munching an apple.

"Where's Joe Tenny's office?" Danny asked her.

She swallowed a bite of apple. "*Dr.* Tenny's office is the first door on your left."

Danny went down the hallway that she had pointed to. The first door on the left was marked: DR. J. TENNY, DIRECTOR.

Instead of knocking, he walked back to the switchboard girl. She was bent over her book again, her back to Danny. He noticed for the first time that there was a clear plastic shield between the top of the counter and the ceiling. Like bulletproof glass. He tapped it.

The girl jumped, surprised, and nearly dropped the book out of her lap.

"Hey," Danny asked, "is Tenny the boss of this whole place?"

She looked very annoyed. "This Center was Dr. Tenny's idea. He fought to get it started and he fought to make it the way it is. Of course he runs it."

"Oh . . . Uh, thanks."

Danny went back and knocked at Joe's door.

"Come in!"

Joe's office was smaller than Danny's room. It was crammed with papers. Papers covered his desk, the table behind the desk, and lapped over the edges of the bookshelves that filled one whole wall. In a far corner stood an easel with a half-finished painting propped up on it. Brushes and tubes of paint were scattered on the floor beside the easel.

Joe leaned back in his chair. He squinted through the harsh-smelling smoke from the stubby cigar that was clamped in his teeth.

"How're you feeling?"

"Okay."

"Sit down. The smoke bother you?"

"No, it's okay." Danny saw that there was only one other chair in the office, over by the half-open window.

Sitting in it, he asked, "Uh . . . did you tell any of the other guys about, eh, what happened yesterday?"

"About you trying to escape?" Joe shook his head. "No, that's no business of anybody else's. SPECS knows it, of course. But I've ordered SPECS to hold the information as private. Only the staff people who work on your case will be able to learn about it. None of the kids."

Danny nodded.

"Quite a few people saw me carrying you into the hospital, though."

"Yeah . . . I guess so."

Joe tapped the ash off his cigar into the wastebasket next to his desk. "Listen. You're going to start classes tomorrow. Most of the kids spend their mornings studying, and use the afternoons for different things. You're expected to work a couple of hours each afternoon. You can work in one of the shops, or join the repair gang, or something else. Everybody works at something to help keep the Center shipshape. Otherwise the place would fall apart.''

Danny frowned. ''You mean it's like a job?''

''Right,'' said Joe, with a grin. ''Don't look so glum. It won't hurt you. You get credit for every hour you work, and you can buy things in the Center's store. SPECS runs the store and keeps track of the credits. And it's only a couple hours a day. Then the rest of the day's all yours.''

''A job,'' Danny muttered.

''You can learn a lot from some honest work. And you'll be helping to keep the Center looking neat. You might even get to like it.''

''Don't bet on it.''

Joe made a sour face. ''Okay, I'm not here to argue with you. You have a visitor. She's in the next room.''

''She? Laurie?''

Nodding, Joe said, ''You can spend the rest of the afternoon with her. But she's got to leave at five.''

Without another word, Danny hurried from Dr. Tenny's office and burst into the next room. Laurie was sitting on the edge of a big leather chair. She jumped up and ran into his arms.

After a few minutes, Danny pulled away from her and closed the door.

''How are you?'' They both said it at the same time. They laughed.

Laurie was a little thinner than Danny remembered her. And sort of pale. She was a small girl, almost frail-looking, with hair and eyes as dark as Danny's own. Danny knew prettier girls, but no one like Laurie. Of all the people in the world, she was the only one that needed Danny. And the only one that he needed.

''You look good,'' she said.

''You look great.''

"Are they treating you okay?"

He nodded. "Sure. Fine. This is more like a school than a jail. How about you? Everything okay?"

"Uh-huh."

They moved slowly to the couch, by the room's only window.

"How's Silvio and the other guys?" Danny asked as they sat down.

"They're all right . . . Danny, are you really okay?"

Laughing, he said, "Sure. I told you. This ain't really a jail. I nearly broke out of here yesterday. Looks easy. Hardly any guards. I'll probably be out in a couple of weeks. Soon's I figure out a couple of things."

Laurie's eyes widened. She looked frightened. "Danny, don't do anything they can catch you on. If you get into more trouble . . ."

"You feel like waitin' around for five years?" he snapped. "Or ten? Twenty? If I can break out, I'm goin' to do it. Reason the other guys don't try it is 'cause they're too soft. They got it too easy here, so they stay. Not me!"

"But they'll just hunt you down again and bring you back. Or maybe put you in a worse place . . ."

"You *want* me to stay?"

"No, I mean . . ."

"Listen, I got it figured," Danny said. "Soon's I get out, we grab a car and get up to Canada. Then they can't touch us."

Laurie just looked scared. "All the way to Canada?"

"Just the two of us. We can start all over again. I'll even get a job. . . ."

"Me, too," Laurie said. Then she started to say something else, stopped, and finally said, "Oh, Danny . . . I wanted to tell you. I got a job now. I'm helping my sister in the restaurant where she works. . . ."

"Waiting on tables?" Danny felt his face twist into a frown.

Laurie nodded. Her voice was very low. "And . . . cleaning up, helping in the kitchen."

"I don't want my girl doin' that kind of work!"

"Well, I need some money. . . ." She looked away from him, out toward the window. "I want to be able to live on my own. And the bus to come here costs money."

Danny's frown melted. But he didn't feel any better.

Laurie went on, "Dr. Tenny said I could come once a week, if I wanted to. And he said he thought you could do real good here. Maybe get out in two years."

"I'll be out in a couple weeks," said Danny.

"Please . . . don't do anything they'll catch you on."

"I'll be out in a couple of weeks," Danny repeated.

Chapter Eight

Laurie left at five. Danny went over to the cafeteria and picked at his dinner.

Ralph Malzone pulled up a chair and sat beside Danny. He looked much too big for the thin-legged plastic chair.

"Hey, I heard you was sick yesterday. Not going to back out of the fight with Lacey, are ya?"

Danny pushed his tray of food away. "No, I'll fight him."

"Good," said Ralph. He leaned across, took a slice of bread from Danny's tray, and started buttering it. "C'mon over to the gym tomorrow afternoon. I'll show you some tricks. Help make you the new lightweight champ.''

Nodding, Danny said, ''Sure.''

Danny got up to leave. Ralph was still picking food from his tray, so Danny left it there with him.

When he got back to his room and shut the door, the lights turned on and the TV screen lit up.

''GOOD EVENING, MR. ROMANO,'' said SPECS. The screen spelled out the words.

''How'd you know I was in here?'' Danny asked, stopping suddenly by the door and frowning at the screen.

''THERE IS A SENSING DEVICE IN THE DOORWAY. AND THE ROOM LIGHTS WENT ON. I HAVE A . . .''

''But how'd you know it was me? Can you see me?''

''THERE ARE NO CAMERAS IN THE STUDENTS' ROOMS. I DID NOT KNOW FOR CERTAIN THAT IT WAS YOU. HOW-EVER, THE CHANCES WERE BETTER THAN NINETY PER-CENT THAT ONLY YOU WOULD ENTER YOUR OWN ROOM AT THIS TIME OF THE EVENING. I HAVE A MES . . .''

''Well then, how'd you know I'm Danny Romano? I could of been anybody.''

SPECS' voice did not change a bit, but somehow Danny felt that the computer was getting sore at him. ''YOUR VOICE IS THE VOICE OF DANIEL FRANCIS RO-MANO, AND NO ONE ELSE'S. I HAVE A MESSAGE . . .''

''You know everybody's voice?''

''I AM PROGRAMMED TO RECOGNIZE THE SPEECH PAT-TERNS AND VOCAL TONES OF EVERYONE IN THE CENTER. I HAVE A MESSAGE FOR YOU FROM THE MEDICAL DE-PARTMENT.''

SPECS waited patiently for Danny to reply. Finally, Danny said, ''Okay, what's the message?''

''YOU WILL FIND A BOTTLE OF PILLS ON THE TABLE BY YOUR BED. THEY ARE FOR ASTHMA. DIRECTIONS ARE WRITTEN ON THE LABEL. THEY READ AS FOLLOWS:

'TAKE ONE PILL BEFORE GOING TO BED AT NIGHT, AND A PILL WHENEVER NEEDED DURING THE DAY. KEEP THIS BOTTLE WITH YOU AT ALL TIMES. NOTIFY THE MEDICAL DEPARTMENT WHEN ONLY FIVE PILLS ARE LEFT.' "

"These pills'll make me breathe okay?"

"I DO NOT HAVE THAT INFORMATION. I CAN PUT YOU IN CONTACT WITH THE MEDICAL DEPARTMENT. DR. MAKAWITZ IS ON DUTY AT THE MOMENT."

"Naw, that's okay."

Danny went to the bed and saw the bottle of pills on the bed table. They were white, plain-looking. He glanced up at the TV screen and saw that it had gone dead.

"Hey SPECS."

The screen glowed again. "YES, MR. ROMANO?"

"Uh . . . any other messages for me?" Suddenly Danny felt foolish, talking to a TV screen.

"NO OTHER MESSAGES. I HAVE YOUR SCHEDULE FOR TOMORROW'S CLASSES, BUT I AM PROGRAMMED TO GIVE THIS INFORMATION TO YOU TOMORROW MORNING, AFTER YOU AWAKEN."

"Can you give it to me now?"

"IF YOU ORDER THE INFORMATION, I AM PROGRAMMED TO ANSWER YOUR REQUEST."

"You mean if I tell you to do it, you'll do it?"

"YES."

"Suppose I tell you to turn of all the alarms in the Center?"

"I AM NOT PROGRAMMED TO ANSWER THAT REQUEST."

Danny plopped down on the bed, his mind running fast.

"Listen SPECS. Who can give you orders about the alarms? Who can make you turn 'em off?"

The answer came at once. "DR. TENNY, THE CAPTAIN OF THE GUARDS, THE HIGHEST MEMBER OF THE GUARDS

WHO IS ON DUTY, THE CHIEF OF THE MAINTENANCE DEPARTMENT, THE HIGHEST-RANKING MEMBER OF THE MAINTENANCE DEPARTMENT WHO IS ON DUTY."

Danny thought for a moment. "Suppose the guard captain told you right now to turn off all the alarms. Could you do that?"

"YES."

"Okay SPECS," Danny suddenly said loud and firm, "turn off all the alarms!"

"I AM NOT PROGRAMMED TO ANSWER THAT REQUEST."

"This is the captain of the guards. I order you to turn off all the alarms!"

Danny could have sworn that SPECS was ready to laugh at him. "YOU ARE NOT THE CAPTAIN OF THE GUARD FORCE. YOU ARE DANIEL FRANCIS ROMANO. YOUR VOICE INDEX SHOWS IT."

"Okay SPECS. You got me cold."

"I DO NOT UNDERSTAND THAT STATEMENT."

"You won't tell Tenny about this, will you?"

"THIS CONVERSATION IS RECORDED IN MY MEMORY BANK. IF DR. TENNY OR ANOTHER STAFF MEMBER ASKS TO VIEW IT, I AM PROGRAMMED TO ANSWER THAT REQUEST."

"But you won't tell 'em unless they ask?"

"CORRECT."

Danny grinned. *Tenny can't ask for something unless he knows it exists.*

"Okay. G'night SPECS."

"GOOD NIGHT, MR. ROMANO."

As Danny undressed, he wondered to himself, *Now, where can I get a tape recorder? And maybe I ought to get a gun, too . . . just in case.*

Chapter Nine

When Danny got to his first class the next morning, he thought he was in the wrong room.

It didn't look like a classroom. There were nine other boys already there, sitting around in chairs that were scattered across the floor. A man of about thirty or so was sitting among them, and they were talking back and forth.

"Come on in and take a seat," the teacher said. "My name is Cochran. Be with you in a minute."

Mr. Cochran looked trim and wiry. His hair was clipped very short, like a military crewcut. His back was rifle-straight. He looked to Danny more like a Marine in civilian clothes than a teacher.

Danny picked a seat toward the back of the room. On one side of him the wall was lined with windows. On the other was a row of bookshelves, like a library. There was a big TV screen at the front of the room.

Turning around in his chair, Danny saw that the back of the room was filled with a row of little booths. They looked about the size of telephone booths. Maybe a bit bigger. They were dark inside.

"Hello. You're Daniel Romano?" Mr. Cochran pulled up one of the empty chairs and sat next to Danny. The other boys were reading or writing, or pulling books from the shelves.

"This is a reading class," Cochran explained. "Different boys are working on different books. I'd like you to start out today on this one."

For the first time, Danny saw that the teacher had a book in his hands. The title was *Friends in the City*.

Danny took the book and thumbed through it. It was filled with pictures of smiling people—grocers, cops, firemen, housewives—living in a clean, bright city.

"You got to be kidding!" He handed the book back to Mr. Cochran.

The teacher grinned. "I know. It's kid stuff. If you think it's too easy for you we can go on to something better. But first you'll have to take a test to see if you're ready for harder work."

He walked Danny back to one of the booths. Opening the door, Mr. Cochran stepped inside and flicked on the lights. Danny saw that the booth had a little desk in it, and the desk was covered with dials and push-buttons. Just above the desk, on the wall of the booth, was a small TV screen.

Mr. Cochran fiddled with the dials and buttons for a few moments, then stepped outside and said to Danny, "Okay, it's all yours. Just sit right down and have fun. SPECS is going to give you a reading test."

With a shrug, Danny went into the booth and sat down. Mr. Cochran shut the door. The window on it was made of darkened glass, so that Danny could hardly see the classroom outside. The booth felt soundproofed, too. It had that quiet, cushion-like feeling to it.

The TV screen lit up. "GOOD MORNING," said SPECS' voice.

"Hi. You know who this is?"

"DANIEL FRANCIS ROMANO."

"Right again." *Cripes,* thought Danny, *ain't he ever wrong?* Then he got a sudden idea. "Hey SPECS, where can I get a tape recorder?"

"TAPE RECORDERS ARE USED IN THE LANGUAGE CLASSES."

"Can you take 'em back to your room? Are they small enough to carry?"

"YES TO BOTH QUESTIONS. AND NOW, ARE YOU READY TO RECEIVE STANDARD READING TEST NUMBER ONE?"

Smiling to himself, Danny said, "Sure, go ahead."

By the time the test was over, Danny was no longer smiling. He was sweating. SPECS flashed words on the TV screen. Danny had to decide if they were spelled right. He pushed one button if he thought the spelling was right, another button if he thought it was wrong.

After what seemed like an hour of spelling questions, SPECS began putting whole sentences on the screen. Danny had to tell him what was wrong, if anything, with each sentence.

Finally, SPECS put a little story on the screen. Then it disappeared and some questions about the story came on. Danny had to answer the questions.

When he was finished, Danny slumped back in the padded seat. His head hurt, he felt tired. And he knew he had done poorly.

The door to the booth opened and Mr. Cochran pushed in. Danny saw, past him, that the classroom was now empty.

"How'd it go?" The teacher leaned over and touched a few buttons on the desk top. Numbers sprang up on the screen.

"Not good, huh?" Danny said weakly.

Mr. Cochran looked down at him. "No, not so very good. But, frankly, you did better than I thought you would."

Danny sat up a little straighter.

"Look," Mr. Cochran said, "I know *Friends in the City* is a kind of dumb book. But why don't you just work your way through it? Read it in your room. You don't have to show up here in class every morning. SPECS can help you when you're stuck on a word.

Then, when you think you've got it licked, come in and take the test again.''

''How long will it take?''

Cochran waved a hand. ''Depends on you. Three, four days, at most. You're smart enough to get the hang of it pretty fast, if you really want to.''

Danny said nothing.

Mr. Cochran stepped out of the booth and Danny got up and went outside, too.

''Look,'' the teacher said, ''reading is important. No matter what you want to do when you get out of the Center, you'll need to be able to read well. Unless you can read okay, Dr. Tenny won't let you leave here. So it's up to you.''

''Okay,'' said Danny. ''Give me the book. I'll learn it.''

But as he walked down the hall to his next class, Danny told himself, *Let 'em think I'm trying to learn. Then they won't know I'm working on a break-out.*

Chapter Ten

Danny went to two more classes that morning: history and arithmetic. He fell asleep in the history class. No one bothered him until the teacher poked him on the shoulder, after the rest of the boys had left.

''I don't think you're ready for this class,'' the old man said. His thin face was white with the struggle to keep himself from getting angry.

* * *

The arithmetic class was taught by Joe Tenny. To his surprise, Danny found that he could do most of the problems that Tenny flashed on the TV screen.

"You've got a good head for numbers," Joe told him as the class ended and the boys were filing out for lunch.

"Yeah. Maybe I'll be a bookie when I get out."

Joe gave him that who-are-you-trying-to-kid look. "Well, you've got to plan on being *something*. We're not just going to let you go, with plans and no job."

They left the classroom together and started down the hall for the outside doors.

"Uh . . . the history teacher told me not to come back to his class. I . . . uh, I fell asleep."

"That was smart," said Joe.

"Well, uh, look . . . can I take something else instead of history? Maybe learn Italian. . . . I already talk it a little. . . ."

"I know."

Danny felt his face go red. "Well, what I mean is, maybe I could learn to talk it right."

Joe looked slightly puzzled. "I don't understand why you'd want to study a foreign language. But if that's what you want to do, okay, we'll try it. Just don't fall asleep on the job."

Grinning, Danny promised. "I won't!"

After lunch, Danny went up to the gym. One of the older boys showed him where the lockers were. Danny changed into a sweat suit and went back onto the gym floor. He lifted weights for a while, then tried to jog around the track up on the catwalk. He had to stop halfway; it got too hard to breathe.

Got to get one of those pills.

He went back to his locker and took a pill. After a few minutes he was able to breathe easily again. He went back to the gym and found a row of punching bags lined up behind the ring. No one was using them. Lacey was nowhere in sight. Danny felt glad of that. Ralph Malzone came from around the corner of the ring, though.

"Hiya, Danny. Starting training for the fight? You only got two weeks."

Jabbing at a punching bag, Danny answered, "Yeah, I know."

Ralph looked bigger than ever in his gym suit. He towered over Danny. "C'mon back here, behind the bags. I'll show you a few things."

For the next half-hour, Ralph showed Danny how to use his elbows, his knees, and his head to batter and trip up his opponent.

"All strictly illegal," Ralph said, grinning broadly. "But you can get away with 'em if you're smart. Main thing, with Lacey, is keepin' him off balance. Trip him, step on his feet. Butt him with your head. Grab him and give him the elbow."

Danny nodded. Then suddenly he asked, "Hey Ralph . . . where can I get a gun?"

"What?"

"A gun. A zip'll do. Or at least a blade. . . ."

Ralph's smile vanished. His round, puffy face with its tiny eyes suddenly looked grim, suspicious.

"What do you want a piece for?"

"For getting out of here, what else?" Danny said.

Ralph thought it over in silence for a minute. Then he said, "Go take a shower, get dressed, and meet me in the metal shop. Two floors down from here."

"Okay."

Danny took his time. He wanted to be sure Ralph was in the shop when he got there.

The metal shop smelled of oil and hummed with the electrical throb of machines that cut or drilled or shaped pieces of steel and aluminum. Boys were making bookshelves, repairing desk chairs, building other things that Danny didn't recognize.

There was a pair of men in long, shapeless shop coats wandering slowly through the aisles between the benches, stopping here and there to talk with certain boys, showing them how to use a machine, what to do next. Back in the farthest corner, Ralph was tinkering with some long pieces of pipe.

Danny made his way back toward Ralph's bench. No one stopped him or bothered him.

"Hi."

Ralph looked coldly at him. "I just been wondering about you. Asking about a gun. Somebody tell you to ask me?"

Danny shook his head. "What are you talking about?"

Ralph whispered, "I ain't told nobody about this. But I'm showing it to you. If you're a fink for Tenny . . . you ain't just going to see this, you're going to *feel* it."

Keeping his eyes on the closest teacher, who was several benches away, Ralph bent down slightly and reached underneath his bench. He pulled and then brought his hand out far enough for Danny to see what was in it.

"Hey!" Danny whispered.

It looked crude but deadly. The pistol grip was a sawed-off piece of pipe. The trigger was wired to a heavy spring. The barrel was another length of pipe.

"Shoots darts," Ralph whispered proudly. He took a pair of darts from his shirt pocket. They looked to Danny like big lumber nails that had been filed down to needle points.

"You made them yourself?" asked Danny.

Ralph nodded. He put the darts back in his pocket

and tucked the gun inside his shirt. It made a heavy bulge in his clothing.

"Now I got to test it. There's a spot out in the woods I know. No TV eyes to watch you there. If it works, then tonight I go sailing out of here. Right through the front gate."

Danny gave a low whistle. "That takes guts."

"With this," Ralph said, tapping the gun, "I can do it. Now, you start walking out. I'll be right behind you. Don't go too fast. Take it easy, look like everything's cool. And remember, if you peep one word, I'll test this piece out on you."

"Hey, I'm with you," Danny insisted.

They walked together toward the door, with Ralph slightly behind Danny so that no one could see the bulge in his shirt.

They threaded their way past the work benches, where the other boys were busy on their projects. The two teachers paid no attention to them at all. They got past the last bench and were crossing the final five feet of open floor space to the door.

The door swung shut.

All by itself. It shut with a slam. All the power machinery stopped. The room went dead silent. Danny stopped in his tracks, only two steps from the door. He could hear Ralph breathing just behind him.

"ONE OF THE BOYS AT THE DOOR IS CARRYING SEVERAL POUNDS OF METAL," said SPECS from a loudspeaker in the ceiling. "I HAVE NO RECORD OF PERMISSION BEING GIVEN TO CARRY THIS METAL AWAY FROM THE SHOP."

Danny turned and saw all the guys in the shop staring at him and Ralph. The two teachers were hurrying toward them. With a shrug of defeat, Ralph pulled the gun from his shirt and held it out at arm's length, by the barrel.

One of the teachers, his chunky face frowning, took the gun. "You ought to know better, Malzone."

Ralph made a face that was half smile, half frown.

"And what's your name?" the teacher asked Danny. "How do you fit into this? I haven't seen you in here before."

"He don't fit in," Ralph said, before Danny could answer. "He didn't know anything about it. I built it all myself. He didn't even know I had it on me."

The teacher shook his head. "I still want your name, son."

"Romano, Danny Romano."

The second teacher took the gun from the first one, looked it over, hefted it in his hand. "Not a bad job, Malzone. Heavier than it needs to be. Who were you going to shoot?"

"Whoever got between me and the outside."

The teacher said, "If you'd put this much effort into something useful, you could walk out the front gate, and do it without anyone trying to stop you."

"Yeah, sure."

"And, by the way, SPECS won't let anybody through the door if he's heavier than he was when he walked in. We're all standing on a scale, right now. It's built into the floor."

"Thanks for telling me," said Ralph.

"Okay, get out of here," the teacher said. "And don't either one of you come back until you've squared it with Dr. Tenny."

Ralph started for the door. It clicked open.

Danny followed him.

Out in the hall, Danny said, "Thanks for keeping me off the hook."

Ralph shrugged. "And I was afraid you was working for Tenny. With that lousy SPECS, he don't need no finks."

"What happens to you now?" Danny asked as they headed for the elevator.

"I'll get a lecture from Tenny, and for a couple months I'll have to take special classes instead of shop work."

"Is that all?"

Ralph stopped walking and looked at Danny. His eyes seemed filled with tears. "No it ain't all. I thought I'd be out of here tonight. Now I'm further behind the eight ball than ever. I don't know when I'll get out. Maybe never!"

Chapter Eleven

Danny worked hard for the next two weeks. He paid attention in classes. He passed his first reading test with SPECS, and Mr. Cochran let him pick out his own books. Danny started reading books about airplanes and rockets.

The arithmetic class with Joe Tenny was almost fun.

"You keep going this well," Tenny told him, "and I'll start showing you how to work with SPECS on really tough problems."

Danny smiled and nodded, and tried not to show how much he wanted to get SPECS to work for him.

Danny worked especially hard in the language class, so that the teacher would let him take one of the class's pocket tape recorders back to his room. For extra homework.

Sure.

The teacher—a careful, balding man—said he'd let Danny have the tape recorder "in a little while."

Afternoons, Danny spent mostly in the gym. He took an asthma pill before every workout, but found that he needed another one after a few minutes of heavy work.

Ralph was still showing him dirty tricks, still telling him to "break Lacey's head open." Ralph even got into the ring and sparred with Danny.

And Danny took on a job. He joined the Campus Clean-up Crew. It was a pleasant outdoor job now that the weather had turned warm and the trees were in full leaf. Danny spent two hours each afternoon raking lawns, cutting grass, picking up any litter that the boys left around the campus. And he was also learning to spot the little black boxes lying nearly buried in the ground, the boxes that held the cameras and lasers and alarms for SPECS.

The day before his fight with Lacey, Danny's language teacher finally let him have a pocket tape recorder. But it was too late to try a breakout before the fight. Danny figured he would need at least a week to get the right words from Joe Tenny onto a tape. Then he'd have to juggle the words onto another tape until he had exactly the right order to give SPECS.

Danny wasn't looking forward to fighting Lacey. It would have been fine with him if he could have escaped the Center before the fight. But he wasn't going to back out of it.

Maybe Lacey'll help get me out of here, Danny thought, with a grim smile. *On a stretcher.*

Chapter Twelve

The gym had been changed into an arena. All the regular equipment had been put away, the ring dragged out to the center of the gym, and surrounded by folding chairs. All the chairs were filled with teachers and boys who cheered and hollered for their favorite boxers. And they booed the poor ones without mercy.

Danny could hear the noise of the crowd from inside the locker room. Ralph had helped him find a pair of trunks that fit him. They were bright red, with a black stripe. *The color of blood,* Danny thought. One of the gym teachers wrapped tape around Danny's hands and helped him into the boxing gloves. Then they fit him with a head protector and mouthpiece.

There were no other boxers in the locker room. Danny's fight was the last one of the evening. Lacey was getting ready in another locker room, on the other side of the building.

"Now remember," Ralph whispered to Danny when the teacher left them alone, "get in close, grab him, trip him up, push him off-balance. Then hit him with everything you got! Elbows, head, everything. You got a good punch, so use it."

Danny nodded.

The crowd roared and broke into applause. He could hear the bell at ringside ringing.

"Okay, Romano," the teacher called from the doorway. "It's your turn."

The head protector felt heavy, and clumsy. *The*

mouthpiece tastes funny, like a new automobile tire might taste, Danny thought.

As he entered the gym a big cheer went up. Danny started to smile, but then saw that the cheering was for Lacey, who was coming toward the ring from the other side of the gym.

As he walked toward the ring, boys hollered at him:

"You're goin' to get mashed, Romano!"

"Sock it to him, Danny!"

"Hey, skinny, you won't last one round!"

Dr. Tenny was standing at the ringside steps. His jacket was off. He was wearing a short-sleeved shirt with no tie.

"All set, Danny?"

"Yeah."

"I've checked with the medics. They're not too happy about you fighting."

"I'll be okay."

"Did you take a pill?" Joe asked.

Nodding, Danny said, "Two of 'em. Before I left my room."

"Good. If you need more, I've got some right here in my pocket."

"Thanks. I'll be okay."

Joe stepped aside and Danny climbed up into the ring, with Ralph right behind him. The crowd was cheering and booing at the same time. *Guess who the cheers are for!*

The referee was one of the gym teachers. He called the boys to the center of the ring and gave them a little talk:

"No hitting low, no holding and hitting, no dirty stuff. If I tell you to break it up, you stop fighting and step back. Just do what I tell you, and don't lose your tempers. Let's have a good, clean fight."

They went back to their corners. Danny stood there,

alone now, and stared at Lacey. He seemed to be all muscle, all hard and strong.

The bell rang.

Danny couldn't do anything right. He charged out to the middle of the ring and got his head snapped back by Lacey's jab. He swung, missed. Lacey moved too fast! Danny tried to follow him, tried to get in close. But Lacey danced rings around him, flicking out jabs like a snake flicks out his tongue. Most of them hit. And hurt.

The crowd was yelling hard. The noise roared in Danny's ears, like the time he was at the seashore and a wave knocked him down and held him under the water.

Lacy slammed a hard right into Danny's middle. The air gasped out of Danny's lungs. He doubled over, tried to grab the black. His gloves reached Lacey's body, but then slipped away. Danny straightened up, turned to find Lacey, and got another stinging left in his face.

It was getting hard to breathe. *No, don't!* Danny told himself. *Don't get sick!* But his chest was starting to feel heavy. Another flurry of punches to his body made it feel even worse.

Danny finally grabbed Lacey and pulled himself so close that their heads rubbed together.

"You want to dance, baby?" Lacey laughed.

Then, suddenly, he blasted half a dozen punches into Danny's guts, broke away, and cracked a solid right to Danny's cheek. Danny felt his knees wobble.

The bell rang.

Ralph was angry. "You didn't do nothing I told you to! You got to get in close, hold him, butt him!"

Danny gasped, "You try it."

He sat on the stool, chest heaving. His face felt funny, like it was starting to swell. It stung.

The bell sounded for the second round, and it was

more of the same. Lacey was all over the ring, grinning, laughing, popping Danny with lefts and rights. Danny felt as if he was wearing iron boots. He just couldn't keep up with Lacey. The crowd was roaring so loudly that it hurt his ears. He tasted blood in his mouth. And Lacey kept gliding in on him, peppering him with a flurry of punches, then slipping away before he could return a blow.

Danny's chest was getting bad now. He was puffing, gasping, unable to get air into his lungs.

It seemed as if an hour had gone by. Finally, Lacey backed into the ropes and Danny made a desperate grab for him. He locked his arms around Lacey, wheezing hard.

"Hey, you sick?" Lacey's voice, muffled behind the mouth protector, sounded in Danny's right ear. "You sound like a church organ."

He pushed Danny away, but instead of hitting him, just tapped his face with a light jab and danced off toward the center of the ring. The crowed booed.

"Finish him!"

"Knock him out, Lacey!"

The bell ended round two.

Joe Tenny was at his corner when Danny sagged tiredly on the stool.

"You'd better take another pill," he said.

Shaking his head, Danny gasped out, "Naw . . . I'll be . . . okay . . . Only one . . . more round."

Tenny started to say something, then thought better of it. He went back down the stairs to his seat.

"You got to get him this round!" Ralph hollered in Danny's ear, over the noise of the crowd. "It's now or never! When th' bell rings, go out slow. He thinks he's got you beat. Soon's he's in reach, sock him with everything you've got!"

Danny nodded.

The bell rang. Danny pushed himself off the stool. He went slowly out to the middle of the ring, his hands held low. The referee was looking at him in a funny way. Lacey danced out, on his toes, still full of bounce and smiling.

Lacey got close enough and Danny fired his best punch, an uppercutting right, a pistol shot from the hip, hard as he could make it.

It caught Lacey somewhere on the jaw. He went down on the seat of his pants, looking very surprised.

The crowd leaped to its feat, screaming and cheering.

The referee was bending over Lacey, counting. But he got up quickly. His face looked grim, the smile was gone. The referee took a good look into Lacey's eyes, then turned toward Danny and motioned for him to start fighting again.

Danny managed to take two steps toward Lacey, and then the hurricane hit him. Lacey swarmed all over him, anger and pride mixed with his punches now. He wasn't smiling. He wasn't worried about whether Danny might be sick or not. He attacked like a horde of Vikings, battering Danny with a whirlwind of rights and lefts.

Danny felt himself smashed back into the ropes, his legs melting away under him. He leaned against the ropes, let them hold him up. He tried to keep his hands up, to ward off some of the punches. But he couldn't cover himself. Punches were landing like hail in a thunderstorm.

Through a haze of pain, Danny lunged at Lacey and wrapped his arms around the black waist. He leaned his face against Lacey's chest and hung on, his legs feeling like rubber bands.

The crowd was making so much noise he couldn't tell if Lacey was saying anything to him or not. He felt the referee pull them apart, saw his worried face staring at him.

Danny stepped past the referee and put up his gloved hands to fight. They each weighed a couple of tons. Lacey looked different now, not angry any longer. More like he was puzzled.

They came together again, and again Danny was buried under a rain of punches. Again he grabbed Lacey and held on.

"Go down, dummy!" Lacey yelled into his ear. "What's holding you up?"

Danny let go with his right arm and tried a few feeble swings, but Lacey easily blocked them. He felt somebody pulling them apart, stepping between them, pushing him away from Lacey. Through blurred eyes, Danny saw the referee raising Lacey's arm in the victory signal.

Chapter Thirteen

Somebody was helping him back to the stool in his corner. The crowd was still yelling. Danny sat down, his chest raw inside, his body filled with pain.

"The winner, in one minute and nine seconds of the third round . . . Lacey Arnold!"

Joe Tenny was bending through the ropes, his face close to Danny's. "You okay?"

Danny didn't answer.

Another man was beside Joe, frowning. Danny remembered that he was one of the doctors from the hospital.

"Get him back to the locker room," the doctor said, angry. "I'll have to give him a shot."

"Can you stand up?" Ralph's voice asked from somewhere to Danny's right. He realized then that he couldn't see out of his right eye. It was swollen shut.

"Yeah . . . I'm okay. . . ." Danny grabbed the ropes and tried to stand. His legs were very shaky. He felt other people's arms holding him, helping him to stand.

Lacey was in front of him. "Hey, Danny, you all right?"

"Sure," Danny said through swollen lips.

Back in the locker room they sat him on a bench. The doctor stuck a needle into Danny's leg, and within a few seconds his chest started to feel better.

The doctor growled to Tenny, "You should never have let this boy exert himself like that. . . ."

Joe nodded, his face serious. "Maybe you're right."

"I'm okay," Danny insisted. His chest really felt pretty good now. But his face hurt like fire and he felt more tired than he ever had before in his life.

"This whole business of staging fights is wrong," the doctor said.

Joe said, "If they don't fight in the ring, they'll do it behind our backs. I'd rather have it done under our control. It's a good emotional outlet for everybody."

Danny turned to Ralph, who was sitting glumly on the bench beside him. "Guess I didn't do too good."

Ralph shrugged and tried to cheer up. "Yeah, he smacked you around pretty good. But that one sock you caught him with was a beauty! Did ya see th' look on his face when he hit the floor? I thought his eyes was going to pop out!"

Just then Lacey came by, a robe thrown over his shoulders and his gloves off.

"Good fight, Danny. Man, if the ref didn't stop it when he did, my arms was going to fall off. I hit you with everything! How come you didn't go down like you're supposed to?'' He was grinning broadly.

''Too dumb,'' said Danny.

''Smart enough to deck me,'' Lacey shot back. ''Got me sore there for half a minute. Well, anyway . . . good fight.''

Lacey stuck out his right hand. The tape was still wrapped around it. Danny was surprised to see that his own gloves had been taken off by somebody. He looked at his hands for a moment, then grasped Lacey's. It was the first time he had ever shaken hands with a black.

Chapter Fourteen

To his surprise, Danny was something of a hero the next morning. He felt good enough to go to his reading class, even though his eye was still swollen, and really purple now. His arms and legs were stiff and sore. His ribs ached. But he went to class anyway.

''Here comes the punching bag,'' somebody said when he came into the classroom.

''Look at that shiner!''

''Tough luck, Danny. You showed a lot of guts.''

''First time Lacey's ever been knocked down.''

''Goin' to fight him again next month?''

Danny let himself sink into one of the chairs. ''Not me. Next fight I have is goin' to be with somebody a lot easier than Lacey. Like maybe King Kong.''

Mr. Cochran came in, looked a little surprised at seeing Danny there, and then put them all to work.

Laurie was shaken up when she visited that week and

saw Danny's eye. But he laughed it off and made her feel better. By the time she came back, the following week, Danny's face was just about back to normal.

By that time, Danny had enough of Joe Tenny's voice on tape to do the job he wanted to. One afternoon he went back to the language classroom. It was empty.

The booths in the back of the room had big tape recorders in them. Danny worked for more than an hour, taking Tenny's words off his pocket recorder and getting them onto the big machine's tape in just the right way. Finally, he had it exactly as he wanted it to sound:

"SPECS," said Dr. Tenny's voice, "I want you to turn off all the alarm systems right now."

It didn't sound exactly right. Some of the words were louder than others. If you listened carefully, you could hear different background noises from one word to the next, because they had been recorded at different times. Danny hoped SPECS wouldn't notice.

He got his faked message onto the tape of his pocket recorder and erased the tape on the big machine. Then he headed back toward his room.

"Tonight," he told himself.

It was nearly midnight when he tried it.

"SPECS, you awake?"

The TV screen at the foot of his bed instantly glowed to life. "I DO NOT SLEEP, MR. ROMANO."

Danny laughed nervously. "Yeah, I know. I was only kidding."

"I AM NOT PROGRAMMED TO RECOGNIZE HUMOR, AL-THOUGH I UNDERSTAND THE BASIC THEORY INVOLVED IN IT. THERE ARE SEVERAL BOOKS IN MY MEMORY BANKS ON THE SUBJECT."

"Groovy. Look . . . Dr. Tenny wants to talk to you. Can you see him here in the room with me?"

"THERE IS NO TV CAMERA IN YOUR ROOM, SO I CAN-
NOT SEE WHO IS THERE."

"Well, you know Dr. Tenny's in here, don't you?"

"MY SENSORS CANNOT TELL ME IF DR. TENNY IS WITH
YOU OR IF YOU ARE ALONE."

"Okay, take my word for it. He's here and he wants
to tell you something." Danny flicked the button of his
pocket recorder.

Dr. Tenny's voice said, "SPECS, I want you to turn
off all the alarm systems right now."

Danny found that he was holding his breath.

"ALL THE ALARM SYSTEMS ARE SHUT DOWN."

Without another word, Danny dropped the recorder
onto his bed and rushed out of his room.

He made his way swiftly toward the fence. It was a
warm night, and he knew every inch of the way, now
that he had put in so many weeks on the clean-up crew.
It was dark, cloudy, but Danny hurried through the trees
and got to the fence in less than twenty minutes. He
had taken an asthma pill just before calling SPECS, and
had the bottle in his pants pocket.

He got to the fence and without waiting a moment
he jumped up onto it and started climbing.

A strong hand grabbed at his belt and yanked him
down to the ground.

Danny felt as if a shock of electricity had ripped
through him. He landed hard on his feet and spun
around. Joe Tenny was standing there.

"How . . . how'd you . . . ?"

Joe's broad face was serious-looking. "You had me
fooled. I thought you were really starting to work. But
you still haven't got it straight, have you?"

"How'd you know? All the alarms are off!"

Shaking his head, Joe answered, "Didn't you ever
stop to think that we'd have back-up alarms? When the
main alarms go off, the back-ups come on. And SPECS

automatically calls a half-dozen places, including my office. I happened to be working late tonight, otherwise the guards would've come out after you.''

"Back-up alarms," Danny muttered.

"Come on," said Joe, "let's get back to your room. Or are you going to try to jump me again?''

Shoulders sagging, chin on his chest, Danny went with Dr. Tenny. When they got back to his room, Danny trudged wearily to his bed and sat on it.

"So what's my punishment going to be?''

"Punishment?'' Joe made a sour face. "You still don't understand how this place works.''

Danny looked up at him.

"You're punishing yourself," Joe explained. "You've been here about a month and you've gone no place. You've just wasted your time. As far as I'm concerned, tomorrow's just like your first day here. You haven't learned a thing yet. All you've done is added several weeks to the time you'll be staying here.''

"I'm never getting out," Danny muttered.

"Not all this rate.''

"You'll never let me out. We're all in here to stay.''

"Wrong! Ask Alan Peterson. He's leaving next week. And he was a lot tougher than you when he first came in here. Nearly knifed me his first week.''

Danny said nothing.

"Okay," said Joe. "Think it over. . . . And you'd better give me the tape recorder.''

It was still on the bed, where Danny had left it. He picked it up and tossed it to Joe.

Chapter Fifteen

Danny sat slumped on the bed for a long time after Joe left, staring at the black-and-white tiled floor.

A month wasted.

He looked up at the TV screen. "SPECS," he called.

The screen began to glow. "YES, MR. ROMANO."

"You didn't tell me about the back-up alarms," Danny said, with just the beginnings of a tremble in his voice.

"YOU DID NOT ASK ABOUT THE BACK-UP ALARMS."

"You let me walk out there and get caught like a baby."

"THE BACK-UP SYSTEMS GO ON AUTOMATICALLY WHEN THE MAIN ALARM SYSTEMS GO OFF. I HAVE NO CONTROL OVER THEM."

Danny got up and faced the screen. "You lied to me," he said, his voice rising. "You let me go out there and get caught again. You lied to me!"

"IT IS IMPOSSIBLE FOR ME TO TELL A LIE, IN THE SENSE . . ."

"Liar!" Danny crossed the room in three quick steps and grabbed the desk chair.

"Liar!" he screamed, and threw the chair into the TV screen. It bounced off harmlessly.

Danny picked up the chair and smashed it across the screen. Again and again. The hard plastic of the screen didn't even scratch, but the chair broke up, legs splintering and falling, seat cracking apart, until all Danny had in his hands was the broken ends of the chair's back.

"I AM CALLING THE MEDICAL STAFF," said SPECS calmly. "YOU ARE BEHAVING IN AN HYSTERICAL MANNER."

"Dirty rotten liar!" Danny threw the broken pieces of the chair at the screen and cursed at SPECS.

Then he turned around, kicked the side of his desk, then knocked over his bookcase. The half-dozen books he had in it spilled out onto the floor. Danny reached down and took one, tore it to bits, and then ran to the door.

A couple of medics were hurrying up the hall toward his room. Danny ran the other way. But the door at the far end of the hall was closed and locked. SPECS had locked all the doors now.

"Come on son, calm down now," said one of the medics. They were both big and young, dressed in white suits. One of them carried a small black kit in his hand.

Danny swore at them and tried to leap past them. They grabbed him. He struggled as hard as he could. Then he felt a needle being jabbed into his arm. Danny cursed and hollered and tried to squirm away from them. But everything was starting to get fuzzy. Soon he slid into sleep.

He awoke in his own room. Early morning sunlight was coming through the window. The broken pieces of the chair were still scattered across the floor, mixed with the pages from the torn book. The bookcase was still face down. He was still in the same clothes he had been wearing the night before, except that his shoes had been taken off.

Danny sat up. His head felt a little whoozy. One of the doctors entered the room without knocking. He checked Danny over quickly and then said, "You'll be okay for classes this morning. Have a good breakfast first.''

As the doctor left, the TV screen lit up. Joe Tenny's face appeared on it.

"Got it out of your system?"

Danny glared at him.

Joe grinned. "Okay, you had your little temper tantrum. You're going to have to fix the chair by yourself, in the wood shop. We'll give you a new book to replace the one you tore up, but you ought to do something to earn it. Maybe you can work Saturday morning in the laundry room.''

Danny frowned, but he nodded slowly.

"Okay,'' said Joe. "See you in class.''

Chapter Sixteen

It can't be escape-proof, Danny told himself. *There's got to be a way out.*

Yeah, he answered himself. *But you ain't goin' to find it in a day or two.*

Alan Peterson left the next week, but not before Danny asked him if he had ever tried to escape.

Alan smiled at the question. "Yes, I tried it a few times. Then I got smart. I'll walk out the front gate. Joe Tenny helped to get me a job outside. You can do the same thing, Danny. It's the only sure-fire way to escape.''

The day Alan left, Danny asked Ralph Malzone about escaping.

Ralph said, "Sure, I tried it four—five times. No go.

SPECS is too smart. Can't even carry a knife without SPECS knowing it.''

Danny asked all the guys in his classes, everybody he knew. He even asked Lacey.

Lacey grinned at him. "Why would I want to get out? I got it good here. Better than back home. Sure, they'll throw me out someday. But not until I got a good job and a good place to live waitin' for me outside. And until then, man, I'm the champ around here."

Danny dropped his class in Italian. But his reading got better quickly. He found that he could follow the words printed on SPECS' TV screens easily now. And he was almost the best guy in the arithmetic class.

Joe Tenny told Danny he should take another class. Danny picked science. It wasn't really easy, but it was fun. They didn't just sit around and read, they did lab work.

One morning Danny cleared out the lab by mixing two chemicals that gave off bright yellow smoke. It smelled horrible. The teacher yelled for everybody to get out of the lab. All the kids boiled out of the building completely and ran onto the lawn.

The kids all laughed and pounded Danny's back. The teacher glowered at him. Danny tucked away in his mind the formula he had used to make the smoke. *Might come in handy some time,* he told himself.

The weeks slipped by quickly. Laurie came every week, sometimes twice a week. Joe gave permission for them to walk around on the "outside" lawn, on the other side of the administration building, where the bus pulled up. There was a fence between them and the highway. And SPECS' cameras watched them. Danny knew.

Danny played baseball most afternoons. Then the boys switched to football as the air grew cooler and the trees started to change color.

Thanksgiving weekend there were no classes at all, and the boys set up a whole schedule of football games.

The first snow came early in December. Before he really thought much about it, Danny found himself helping some of the guys to decorate a big Christmas tree in the cafeteria.

His own room had changed, over the months. The bookcase was nearly filled now. Many of the books were about airplanes and space flight. His desk was always covered with papers, most of them from his arithmetic class. He had "bought" pictures and other decorations for his walls from the student-run store in the basement of the cafeteria building.

Thumbtacked to the wall over Danny's desk was a Polaroid picture of Laurie. She was wearing a yellow dress, Danny's favorite, and standing in front of the restaurant where she worked. She was smiling into the camera, but her eyes looked more worried than happy.

Danny worked at many different jobs. He helped the cooks in the big, nearly all-automated kitchen behind the cafeteria. He worked on the air-conditioning machines on the roofs of buildings, and on the heaters in the basements. He went back to working with the clean-up crew for a while, getting a deep tan the hottest months of the summer.

All the time he was looking, learning, searching for the weak link, the soft spot in the Center's escape-proof network of machines and alarms. *There's got to be something,* he kept telling himself.

Danny even worked for a week in SPECS' own quarters; a big, quiet, chilled-down room in the basement of the administration building. The computer was made of row after row of huge consoles, like oversized refrigerators: big, square boxes of gleaming metal. Some of them had windows on their fronts, and Danny could see reels of tape spinning so fast that they become nothing but a blur.

If I could knock SPECS out altogether . . . But how?

The answer came when the boys turned on the lights of the Christmas tree in the cafeteria.

It was a big tree, scraping the ceiling. Joe Tenny had brought in a station wagon full of lights for it. Danny and the other boys spent a whole afternoon on ladders, stringing the lights across its broad branches. Then they plugged in all the lines and turned on the lights.

The whole cafeteria went dark.

The boys started to groan, but the cafeteria lights went on again in a moment. The tree stayed unlit, though.

SPECS' voice came through the loudspeakers in the ceiling: "YOU HAVE OVERLOADED THE ELECTRICAL LINES FOR THE CAFETERIA. YOU CANNOT PLUG THE TREE LIGHTS INTO THE CAFETERIA'S REGULAR ELECTRICAL LINES. PLEASE SET UP A SPECIAL LINE DIRECTLY FROM THE POWER STATION FOR THE TREE."

Some of the boys nodded as if they know what SPECS was talking about. But Danny stood off by himself, staring at the unlit tree.

Electric power! That's the key to this whole place! If I can knock out all the electrical power, everything shuts down. All the alarms, all the cameras, SPECS, everything!

Chapter Seventeen

The Saturday before Christmas, Joe Tenny knocked on Danny's door. "You doing anything special tonight?" he asked.

Danny was sitting at his desk. He looked up from the book he was reading. It was a book about electrical power generators.

"No, nothing special," he answered.

Joe grinned. "Want a night outside? I've got a little party cooking over at my house. Thought you might like to join the fun."

"Outside? You mean out of the Center?"

With a nod, Joe said, "It might *look* like I spend all my time here, but I do have a home with a wife and kids."

"Sure, I'll come with you."

"Good. Pick you up around four-thirty. Don't eat too much lunch, you're going to get some home-cooking tonight. Greek-style. I'm part Greek, you know."

Danny laughed.

Joe's house was a surprise to Danny. He had expected something like a governor's mansion, like he'd seen on TV. But as Joe drove his battered old Cadillac toward the city, they zipped right through the fanciest suburbs, where the biggest and plushest houses were. Finally, Joe pulled into a driveway in one of the oldest sections of the suburbs, practically in the city itself.

"Here we are."

It was already dark, and Danny couldn't see too much of the house. It was big, but not fancy-looking. It needed a paint job. There were four cars already parked on the street in front of the house. Another car was pulled off to one side of the driveway. The hood was off and there was no motor inside it.

"My oldest son's big project," Joe said as they got out of his car. "He's going to rebuild the engine. I've been waiting since last spring for him to finish the job."

Inside, the party was already going on. In quick order, Danny met Mrs. Tenny, Joe's two sons, a huge dog named Monster, and six or seven guests. He lost count and couldn't remember all the names. More people kept arriving every few minutes.

Joe's older son, John, took Danny in tow. He was Danny's age, maybe a year older. But he was a full head taller than Danny, with shoulders twice his size. About half the guests were teenagers, John's friends. John made sure that Danny met them all, especially the girls. They were pretty and friendly. Danny found himself wishing that Laurie was with him . . . and then began to feel guilty because he was enjoying himself without her.

There were more than twenty people at dinner. The regular dining room table couldn't hold them all, so Joe and his sons brought in the kitchen table while Danny helped one of the guests set up a card table. Everybody helped push all three tables into one long row, and then spread tablecloths over them.

They ate and laughed and talked for hours, grownups and kids together. Then they moved into the living room. Joe turned on some records and they danced.

Most of the adults quickly dropped out of the dancing but Joe and a few others kept going as long and as hard as the teenagers did. Then they switched to older, slower music, and some of the other grownups got up again.

Then somebody put on Greek music. Everyone joined hands in a long line that snaked through the living room, the front hall, the dining room and kitchen, and back into the living room. Danny couldn't get his feet to make the right steps. But he saw that hardly anybody else could, either. Everyone was laughing and stumbling along, with the reedy Greek music screeching in their ears. The man leading the line, though, was very good. He was short and plump, with a round face and a little black mustache. He went through the complex steps of the Greek dance without a hitch.

When they stopped dancing and collapsed into the living room chairs, the same man started doing magic tricks. His name was Homer, and he had Danny really puzzled. He pulled cigarettes out of the air, picked cards out of a deck from across the room, changed a handkerchief into a flower.

Everyone applauded him.

"Boy, he's great," Danny said to John, who was sitting next to him on the sofa. "Is he on TV?"

John laughed. "He's my high-school principal. Magic's just his hobby."

Danny felt staggered. *A principal? Homer couldn't be. He was . . . well, he was too happy!*

After a while, Danny went over to where Homer was sitting and they started talking. He even showed Danny a couple of card tricks.

"How's Joe treating you at the Center?" Homer asked.

"Huh? Oh . . . pretty good."

Homer smiled. "I don't see where he gets all his energy. He's at that Center almost twenty-four hours a day. You should have seen him when he was trying to get the Center started! He gave up his job at the State University and battled with the Governor and the State Legislature until I thought they were going to throw him out on his ear. He even went to Washington to get Congress to put up extra money to help with the Center.''

Squirming unhappily, Danny said, ''I didn't know that.''

''It's true,'' Homer said. ''The Center is Joe's baby. You boys are all his kids.''

''Yeah. He's . . . he's okay,'' said Danny.

Chapter Eighteen

The party went on well past midnight. As people began to leave, Joe came over to Danny and said quietly, ''Think you can sleep with John without any problems?''

Danny blinked. ''You mean sleep here tonight? Not go back to the Center?''

Nodding, Joe said, ''Don't get any ideas. Monster's a watch dog, you know, and he sleeps right outside John's door every night. And I'm part Apache Indian. So you won't be able to sneak out.''

In spite of himself, Danny smiled. ''Okay, I'll behave myself. I won't even snore.''

''Good. Maybe tomorrow we can drive over to your old neighborhood and see your girl friend. . . .''

''Laurie!''

''Yes. I tried to get her to come here tonight, but I couldn't reach her on the phone.''

Danny hardly slept at all. John's snoring and tossing in the bed helped to keep him awake, but mainly he was excited about going back to his turf, going back to see Laurie. Would she be surprised!

But Joe couldn't get her on the phone. Why not? Where was she? Had she moved out of her sister's apartment? Wasn't she working at the restaurant anymore? Danny thought back to Laurie's last visit to the Center. It had been about a week ago. She hadn't said anything about moving. Had she looked worried? Was something bothering her? Or some*body*?

They got up late the next morning. By the time Joe put Danny and Monster into his car and started for the city, it was a little past noon. They drove in silence through the quiet streets. Monster huddled on the back seat, his wet nose snuffling gently behind Danny's ear.

They got to the heart of the city and drove down narrow streets where the buildings cut off any hope of sunshine. Danny gave Joe directions for getting to his old neighborhood.

"Pull up over there," he said, pointing. "By the cigar store."

Nothing had changed much. As he got out of the car, Danny suddenly realized that it had been almost a year since he'd been around here.

Only a couple of young kids were in sight, sitting on the front steps of one of the houses halfway up the block. The street was just as dirty as ever, with old newspaper pages and other bits of trash lying crumbled against the buildings and in the gutters.

There were a few cars parked along the street. Danny remembered the first time he had driven a car. He had stolen it right here, from in front of the cigar store.

The store was closed. The windows were too dirty to look through. *Funny,* Danny thought to himself, *I never thought about how crummy everything is.*

"Where is everybody?" Joe asked. He was still inside the car, one elbow resting on the door where the window had been rolled down. Monster's heavy gray head was sticking out the back window, tongue out, big teeth showing.

"Some of the guys might be up at the schoolyard. It's about two blocks from here, around the corner."

Joe said, "Okay. Hop in."

Danny slammed the door shut and Joe gunned the motor.

"What's the matter?" Joe asked.

Danny shrugged. "I don't know . . . it looks kind of, well, different."

"The neighborhood hasn't changed, Danny. You have."

"What d'you mean?"

Joe swung the car around the corner and headed up the street. "A writer once said, 'You can't go home again.' After you've been away, when you come back home everything seems changed. But what's changed is *you*. You're different than you were when you left. You'll never be able to come back to this neighborhood, Danny. In time, I don't think you'll want to."

Danny stared at Joe. Silently, he thought, *He must be nutty! Not want to come back to my own turf? Crazy!*

They got to the schoolyard and, sure enough, there were a few kids there shooting a scruffed-up basketball at a bare metal hoop that was set into the blank stone wall of the school.

Joe stayed in the car with Monster. The kids didn't recognize Danny as he got out of the car. They stopped shooting the ball and stared at him as he walked up, watching him silently. Then:

"Hey . . . holy cripes, it's *Danny*!"

"Danny!"

He broke into a big grin as they ran toward him.

"Hi, Mario. Hello, Sal. Eddie. . . ."

"Danny! Geez . . . you look like a million bucks!"

"Where did you get them clothes?"

"Hey, you break loose? How'd you do it?"

Laughing, Danny put up his hands. "Hey guys, I can't talk to all of you at once. No, I didn't break out. I sort of got the weekend off. The guy in the Cadillac back there . . . he's from the Center."

"Wow! Lookit the dog!"

"Yeah," Danny said, still grinning. "His name's Monster."

"You got to believe it."

"So how're they treating ya?" Mario asked. "You look good. Getting fat, ain't you?"

"I been eatin' good," Danny said. "The Center's okay, I guess. Tough to get out of. I tried a couple shots at it. . . . They got a computer running everything. And special alarms, better than they got in banks. Trickier. Can't even sneeze without 'em knowin' about it."

They talked for a few minutes, then Danny said, "Hey, I'm goin' over to Laurie's sister's place. She still livin' in the same apartment?"

The boys' grins disappeared. They became serious. Finally Mario answered, "Uh, yeah, she still lives there. But . . . uh . . . Laurie moved out. 'Bout two weeks ago. She don't live around here no more."

Danny felt the same flash of fear and anger that he had known when Joe pulled him down from the fence.

"What? What d'you mean?"

Shrugging inside his jacket, Mario said, "She just moved out. Didn't tell anybody where. Maybe her sister knows. We don't."

Danny grabbed him. "What happened? Why'd she move?"

Mario tried to back away. "Hey, Danny, it ain't my fault! A couple guys tried to make time with her, but we bounced 'em off. We been watchin' her for you."

"Yeah, you been watchin' her so good you don't even know where she is." Danny let go of him.

He sprinted back to the car. Sliding into the front seat beside Joe he said, "Let's go over to Laurie's sister's place . . . back where we were a couple minutes ago."

"What's the matter?"

Danny told him as he started the car.

Laurie's sister had no time for Joe and Danny. She was trying to take care of three babies—the oldest was barely four—and do a day's cooking at the same time.

She was trying to pin a diaper on the youngest baby, who was doing his best to wriggle away from her. She had him lying on the kitchen table, within arm's reach of the stove.

"I told you," she said sharply, "that she's okay. She's working uptown now, and she's got her own apartment, with two other girls. She promised she'd visit you every week, just like she's been doing all year. So if she wants to tell you where she's living, let her do it. I'm not going to."

Danny left the apartment with his fists clenched.

Joe tried to cool him down: "Look, she's been coming to see you every week, hasn't she?"

Danny nodded. His chest was feeling tight again, and he was angry enough to pound his fists into the grimy walls of the apartment building's stairway. But he didn't do that. He just nodded.

They walked out to the car and got into it. Joe started the motor and headed back toward the Center.

"You know," he said, "I might have had something to do with this."

"You?"

Joe nodded. "Last month Laurie and I had a talk, before I called you to the visiting room. She wanted to know what I thought about her working in the restaurant. She knew you didn't like the idea.

"I told her there are lots of schools in town that'll

train her to be a secretary. Or anything else she wants to be. I gave her the name of a couple of friends of mine who could help her to get a better job and pick out a good night school.''

Danny couldn't answer. So it was Joe Tenny. All the time he was pretending to be Danny's friend, he was really trying to get Laurie away. *You can't trust anybody*, Danny shouted to himself silently. *Nobody! Especially not Joe Tenny!*

Chapter Nineteen

Monday morning, at breakfast in the cafeteria, Danny looked for Ralph Malzone.

''Hey listen,'' he said, sitting beside Ralph at a small table. ''We got to get out of here.''

''Sure,'' said Ralph through a mouth full of cereal. ''Build me some wings an' I'll fly out.''

''I'm not kidding! Trouble is, guys have been trying to break out one at a time. What we got to do is get a bunch of guys to work together. That's the only way.''

Ralph shook his head. ''Been tried before. SPECS an' all those alarms and automatic locks and everything . . . you couldn't get out o' here with an army.''

''Oh yeah? I know how to fix SPECS and everything else.''

Ralph laughed.

''I ain't kidding!'' Danny snapped. ''You listen to me and we'll be out of here in a couple months. Maybe sooner.''

Ralph put his spoon down. "How you goin' to do it?"

"That's my secret," said Danny. "You just do what I tell you, and you'll be out in time for the opening game of the baseball season. But we'll need five or six other guys. Can you get 'em?"

"I'll get 'em," said Ralph.

Christmas morning Danny spent in his room, talking to SPECS.

"Where's the electricity in the Center come from?" he asked.

SPECS' calm, unhurried voice answered: "THE CENTER HAS ITS OWN POWER STATION, LOCATED IN BUILDING SEVENTEEN."

"Where's that?"

The TV screen showed a map of the Center. There was a red circle around building seventeen. Danny saw it was one of the smaller buildings, near the administration building. It was the only building on the campus with a smokestack.

"Suppose something happened to the power station, where would the electricity come from then?"

"THERE IS AN EMERGENCY POWER SYSTEM, ALSO LOCATED IN BUILDING SEVENTEEN."

"And suppose something happened to the emergency system, so it didn't work either?"

"ALL ELECTRICAL POWER IN THE CENTER WOULD BE SHUT OFF."

Danny thought a moment, then said, "If all the electrical power was shut off, what systems would stop?"

SPECS' calm, unhurried voice answered, "THE CENTRAL HEATING AND AIR-CONDITIONING SYSTEMS, ALL ALARM SYSTEMS, THE SPECIAL COMPUTER SYSTEM. . . ."

"Wait a minute. What about the phones?"

"THE TELEPHONE SYSTEM IS POWERED SEPARATELY, FROM OUTSIDE THE CENTER."

"Show me how it works."

A drawing appeared on the TV screen, showing how the telephone system was linked by a cable to the main power line of the telephone company. Danny saw that the power line ran underground along the highway, and the cable connecting into the Center came to the administration building through a tunnel. *Cut that one cable, and all the phones are dead.*

It was well after lunchtime when Danny finally said, "Thanks SPECS. That's all I want to know. For now."

The TV screen went dark. Danny sat at his desk, not hungry, too excited to eat, thinking about how to knock out the power station, the emergency system, and the phone line.

The screen glowed again. "MR. ROMANO."

"What?"

"YOU HAVE A VISITOR. MISS MURILLO."

Danny shot out of his chair and to the door without stopping to get his coat.

He sprinted across the campus to the administration building, through the wintry windy day. There were lots of visitors today: parents mostly, grownups trying to look happy when they were really miserable that their kids had to spend Christmas in the Center.

But Danny didn't see it that way. He saw adults faking it, laughing too loud, bringing presents to their kids that they never got when the kids had been at home. Danny wondered what his father would have been like, if he would have lived. His mother was still alive, probably, wherever she was.

He found Laurie in one of the small visitors' rooms. She was wearing a new dress, a dark green one. And her hair was different. It was all swept back and smoothly arranged.

He blinked at her. "Hey, you look different . . . like, all grown up."

"Do you like the way I look?" Laurie was smiling and trying her hardest to look as pretty as she could.

Danny said slowly, "Yeah . . . I guess so, I . . . never saw you looking so . . . well, so fancy."

She stepped up to him and kissed him. "Thank you. And Merry Christmas."

"Merry . . . Hey! I almost forgot! What's all this about you moving to someplace uptown? What's goin' on?"

Holding his hand, Laurie brought Danny to the sofa by the tiny room's only window. They sat down.

"I've got a new job and a new apartment," she said happily. "I'm sharing the place with two other girls. We all work in the same building. I'm a clerk in an insurance company. They're teaching me the job as I go along. It pays a lot better. And I'm going to school at night to learn how to be a secretary."

Danny frowned. "But why? What for?"

"For me," Laurie said. "Danny, try to understand. I love you, honey, I really do. But I can't just sit in my sister's place and work in the restaurant for years and years."

"It won't be years. . . ."

"Shush," she said, putting a finger to his lips. "Listen for a minute. Dr. Tenny told me that he's trying to make you into the best person you can be. That's what the Center's for. Well, I'm trying to make myself the best person I can be."

"I don't like it."

"Don't you see? When you get out, Danny, I want to be something more than a skinny kid with a dirty apron. I want to be a *person*, somebody who can do things. Somebody who can help you, not drag you down."

Danny remembered something. "You been going out with other guys."

She nodded. "Only on double dates, or with a gang of people. Nothing serious, honest, Danny."

"I don't believe you."

Laurie's eyes widened. "Danny, honest . . ."

"I been sittin' here and you've been goin' out with other guys. Movin' uptown, getting big ideas. Joe Tenny's put you up to this! He's tryin' to get you away from me!"

"Danny, that's crazy. . . ."

"Oh yeah? Well, you'll see how crazy it is!"

He got up and stormed to the door.

"Wait," Laurie called. "I got you a Christmas present. . . ."

"Give it to your new boyfriend!" Danny slammed the door shut behind him.

Chapter Twenty

There were no classes between Christmas and New Year's. Danny spent every morning in his room, studying the layout of the power station, learning every inch of the building.

"Hey SPECS, it looks like most of the time the power station runs itself."

"THE POWER STATION RUNS AUTOMATICALLY. I WATCH IT AND CONTROL IT."

"Don't they have a guard or somebody in there?"

"A GUARD STAYS INSIDE THE STATION AT NIGHT."

"Are the doors locked at night?"

"YES."

"What about the day time?"

"A MEMBER OF THE MAINTENANCE CREW IS ON DUTY AT THE POWER STATION AT ALL TIMES DURING THE WORKING DAY. HE HAS NOTHING TO DO, HOWEVER, SINCE I AM IN FULL CONTROL."

Danny laughed. "You mean he goofs off?"

"I DO NOT UNDERSTAND YOUR WORDS."

"He don't stay on the job. He goes to sleep or takes a walk outside or something like that."

"HE OFTEN LEAVES THE STATION FOR HALF AN HOUR OR SO. BUT HE ALWAYS LEAVES A STUDENT AT THE STATION, SO THAT SOMEONE IS PRESENT AT ALL TIMES."

"A student . . . one of us kids?"

"YES."

On New Year's Day, Danny invited Ralph up to his room, and asked him to bring the five boys he could trust.

They were an odd-looking gang. Ralph introduced them as they came in and sat on Danny's bed and chairs.

Hambone was even bigger than Ralph, but where Ralph looked mean, Hambone looked brainless. He wore a silly grin all the time. *Like a happy gorilla,* Danny thought.

"He don't look it," Ralph said, "but old Hambone is a fighter when he gets mad. Took a squad of cops to bring him down."

Hambone nodded happily. "I broke an arm on one of 'em." His voice sounded as if his nose was stopped up, like a prize-fighter's voice after he's been hit too many times.

The next boy was Noisy, who got his name because he hardly ever talked. He was about Danny's own size. He just nodded when Ralph introduced him. But he watched everything, listened to every word that was said. And his eyes burned with a fierce glow that made Danny wonder what he'd done to get into the Center.

Vic and Coop were two ordinary guys. Midget was the last of the gang. He was a kid of fifteen who looked like he was only twelve. He was smaller and skinnier than even Danny. *He's the guy who goes into the tunnel to cut the power line,* Danny decided.

"Okay," Danny said to them. "Now we all want to get out of this dump. And we're going to do it. My way. I know how to get out."

They all looked at each other, nodding and grinning.

"How?" Ralph asked. He had taken the chair by the desk.

Danny, standing by the window, answered, "That's my business. I got the plan here in my head, and I ain't tellin' *nobody.* You don't like it that way, then you can get up and leave. Right now."

Nobody moved.

"Okay. Now . . . it's goin' to take hard work, and some time. But we'll bust this place wide open."

"What'd you want us to do?"

Danny said, "I got jobs for all of you. They might look stupid right now, but they're goin' to help us break out."

"What kind of jobs?" Ralph asked.

"I want you and Hambone to get on the clean-up crew," said Danny.

"Hey, that's work!" Hambone said.

Nodding, Danny went on, "I told you it's going to be work. Hard work, too. But it's the only way to get out of here."

"What're we supposed to be doin'?" Ralph asked. "Besides talking to th' birds and flowers, that is."

"Just hang loose and don't act suspicious." Danny turned to Noisy. "Think you can get yourself into the photography class? We're going to need a camera and some film.''

Noisy nodded.

''Good,'' said Danny. ''Midget, I want you to get an afternoon job in the administration building. Any kind of job, as long as it's in the building.''

''Can do,'' Midget answered.

Turning to Vic and Coop, Danny said, ''You two guys got to get yourselves into the maintenance crew. Try to get jobs that involve big machinery, like the heaters. Okay?''

Vic shrugged. ''I don't know nothing about machinery.''

''Then learn!'' Danny snapped.

Ralph gave Danny a hard look. ''And what're you goin' to be doin?''

''Me?'' Danny smiled. ''I'm gettin' myself a job with SPECS. He's got all the brains around here. He's got to tell me a few more things before we can blow this dump.''

Chapter Twenty-one

They all met again in the cafeteria two days later. Each boy reported that he had gotten the job Danny wanted him to take.

''Good,'' Danny said as he hunched over the dinner dishes. He kept his voice low enough so that the others could just about hear it over the racket made by the rest of the crowd.

''Now listen. This is the last time we meet all together like this. From now on, I'll see each one of you alone, or maybe two of you together, at the most. Stay cool, work your jobs like you really mean it. In a month or so, we'll be out of here.''

When he got back to his room, there was an envelope on the floor just inside his door. Danny leaned down and picked it up, then shut the door as he looked it over. It was from outside. His name and the Center's address were neatly typed on the envelope.

The return address, in the upper left corner of the envelope, was from some insurance company. Then he spotted the hand-typed initials, LM, alongside the printing. It was from Laurie!

Danny ripped the envelope open as he went to his desk and flicked on the lamp. He had trouble pulling the letter out of the envelope.

Dear Danny:

I'm sorry about the blow-up on Christmas Day. I still have your present. I will give it to you when I visit you again. I won't be visiting again for a month or so. I think it might be better if we both sort of think things over before we see each other again.

I still love you, Danny. And I miss you a lot. I know it is very hard for you inside the Center. But we both have a lot of growing up to do before we can be happy together.

Love,
Laurie

Danny read the letter twice, then crumpled it in his fist and threw it in the wastebasket. For the first time in weeks, he had to take an asthma pill before he could get to sleep that night.

* * *

The weeks crawled by slowly.

Danny got his job at the computer center, down in the basement of the administration building. He often saw Midget there. Midget was working somewhere upstairs. SPECS' home was a relaxing place to work in. It was quiet. For some reason, everybody tended to talk softly. SPECS himself made the most noise—a steady hum of electrical power. When he was working at some special problem, SPECS made a singsong noise while he flashed hundreds of lights on the front control panel of his main unit.

Danny's job was to help the adults who programmed SPECS and feed him new information. He carried heavy reels of magnetic tape down the corridors between SPECS' big, boxlike consoles. There was a store room for the tapes that weren't being used, back behind the main computer room.

"These tapes carry SPECS' memory on them," said one of the computer programmers to Danny. "They're like a library . . . except that SPECS is the only one who can read them."

After a few weeks, Danny got to know most of the people who ran the computer. More important, they got to know him. They told him what to do when they needed him. The rest of the time they ignored him.

Which suited Danny fine. He found a few little corners of the big computer room where he could talk to SPECS, ask questions. If anyone saw him sitting at one of the tiny desks, talking to the TV screen on it, they would smile and say:

"Good kid, learning how to work with the machine."

One of the first things Danny learned from SPECS was that every conversation he had with the machine was stored on tape.

"Has anybody checked these tapes?"

"I HAVE NO RECORD OF THAT."

Danny spent a week quietly gathering the right tapes and erasing all his talks with SPECS. Now no one could ever find out what he had said to the computer. Then he got to work on his escape plan. He had a pocket-sized camera now, which Noisy had taken from the photography class.

"What's the layout of the power station?" Danny asked quietly. "And when SPECS showed the right diagram on the TV screen, *click!* Danny got it on film.

"How does the power generator work?" *Click.*

"When the generator breaks down, what goes wrong with it most often?" *Click.*

"How's the emergency generator hooked into the Center's main power line?" *Click.*

Danny would keep the photographs and study them in his room for hours each night. And, of course, he erased all traces of his questions and their answers from SPECS' memory tapes.

The winter snows came and buried the Center in white. Ralph and Hambone, faces red from the wind, noses sniffling, wailed loudly to Danny about all the snow-shoveling that the clean-up crew was doing.

"I told you it'd be hard work," Danny said, trying hard not to laugh. If he got them angry, they could crack him like a teacup.

Danny started Vic and Coop, on the maintenance crew, checking into the electrical power lines in each building. He had to make sure he understood all about the Center's electrical system.

Vic said, "I ain't seen no other emergency generators any place. There's just the one at the main power station. None of the other buildings even has a flashlight battery laying around, far as I can tell."

Danny stopped Midget one afternoon in the hallway of the administration building.

"How's it going?"

"Okay. Got the phone line figured out. Any time you want to pull the cable, I'm all set."

"Good. Now, think you can find out when the maintenance man leaves the power station alone?"

Midget said, "He don't. There's always a kid in there."

"I know. That's what I mean. Try and find out when the kid's in there by himself. And who the kid is. Maybe we can get him on our side."

Nodding, Midget said, "Groovy. I'll get the word to you."

Chapter Twenty-two

The snow melted a little, then more fell. Late in February, during a slushy cold rainstorm, Laurie visited the Center.

Danny ran through the driving rain toward the administration building, hunched over, hands in pockets, feet getting soaked in puddles.

She picked some day to come, he said to himself. *She's gettin' to be nothing but trouble. Why'd she come today?* And then he heard himself saying, *Maybe she's come to say goodbye . . . that she don't want me any more.*

By the time he got to the visitor's room, Danny felt cold, wet, angry, and—even though he didn't want to admit it—more than a little scared. He stopped at the water fountain outside the door and took an asthma pill. Then he went in.

Laurie was standing by the window, looking out at the rain. Danny saw that she was prettier than ever. Not so worried-looking any more. Dressed better, too.

She turned as he softly shut the door.

"Oh, Danny . . . you're soaking wet. I'm sorry, it's my fault."

He grinned at her. "It's okay. It'll dry."

They stood at opposite ends of the little room, about five paces apart. Then suddenly Danny crossed over toward her, and she was in his arms again.

"Hey," he said, smiling at her, "you even smell good."

"You look fine," Laurie said. "Wet . . . but fine."

They sat on the sofa and talked for a long time.

Finally Laurie said, "Dr. Tenny told me you're doing very well. You're working hard and doing good in class. He thinks you're on the right road."

Danny laughed. "Good, let him think that."

For the first time, the old worried look crept back into Laurie's face. "What do you mean?"

"You'll see. Maybe you better start lookin' at travel ads. See where you want to go in Canada. Or maybe Mexico."

"Danny, you're not . . ."

He silenced her with an upraised hand. "Don't worry about it. This time it'll work."

Laurie shook her head. "Danny, forget about it. You can't escape. . . ."

"I can and I will!" he snapped.

"Well, then, forget about me," Laurie snapped back.

"What?"

"Danny, I'm just getting to the point where I can live without looking over my shoulder to see who's following me. I've spent all my life with you and the other kids, dodging the cops, fighting in gangs. For the first time in my life, I'm out of that! I'm living like a free human being. I like it! Can't you understand? I don't want to go back to living scared every minute. . . .''

''You mean if I . . .''

She grasped his hands and looked straight into his eyes. ''I mean I want you to walk out of this place a free man. Not only free, but a *man*. Not a kid who doesn't care what he does. Not a convict who has to run every day and hide every night. I'll wait for you for a hundred years, Danny, if I have to. But only if you'll promise me we can both be free when you get out.''

Danny pulled his hands away. ''I'm not waiting any hundred years! Not even one year. I'm busting out of here, and then I'm coming to get you. And you'd better be there when I come for you!''

She shook her head. ''I won't go back to living that way, Danny.''

''Oh no? We'll find out. And soon, too.''

''I'd better go now,'' Laurie got up from the sofa.

''If you blab any of this to Tenny . . .''

She glared at him. ''I won't. Not because I'm afraid of you. I won't say a word to anybody because I want *you* to decide. You've got to figure it out straight in your own mind. You've got a chance to make something good out of your life. If you try to break out of the Center, you'll just be running away from that chance. You'll be telling me that you're afraid of trying to stand on your own feet. That you want to be caught again and kept in jail.''

''Afraid?'' Danny felt his temper boil.

''That's right,'' Laurie said. ''If you try to break out of here, you and me are finished.''

She walked to the door and left. Danny stood in the middle of the room, fists clenched at his sides, trembling with anger, chest hurting.

Chapter Twenty-three

That night, after dinner, Danny and the other boys met in the gym. They took a basketball and shot baskets for a while, then sat together on one of the benches. The gym was only half full, and not as noisy as usual.

"Okay," Danny said. "I got enough scoop on how the generator works and how to blow it. We're going to turn off all the electricity in the Center and walk out of here while everybody else is runnin' around in the dark."

Their faces showed what he wanted to see; they liked the idea.

"I thought it was something like that."

"It'll be a blast."

Noisy asked, "What about the emergency generator?"

"Got it all worked out," Danny said. "Been getting all the info I need from SPECS."

"When do we go?"

"Tomorrow night," said Danny.

Hambone whistled softly. "You sure ain't fooling around."

"What time?"

"Six o'clock. Almost everybody'll be in the cafeteria for dinner. All the lights go, all the phones go, everybody goes crazy, and we split."

"Great!" said Midget. "The maintenance man at the power station goes to the cafeteria at six. That's when he leaves a kid in there alone for about fifteen minutes.''

"I know, you told me,'' Danny said. "That's why I picked that time. Who's the kid tomorrow? Can we talk him into going with us or do we have to lump him?''

Midget answered, "It's Lacey. I don't think he'll go along with us.''

"Lacey!''

Ralph laughed, low and mean. "Good old Lacey, huh? That's cool. I have been wantin' to split that black big-mouth's head ever since he became lightweight champ. Hambone and me are going to have real fun takin' care of *him*.'' Hambone nodded and giggled.

Danny didn't answer Ralph. But somehow he felt unhappy that it was going to be Lacey.

He hardly slept at all that night. And the next morning he just sat in class, paying no attention to anything around him. Danny's mind was a jumble of thoughts, pictures, voices. He kept trying to think about the escape plan, what he had to do to knock out the generator, every detail.

But he kept seeing Laurie, kept hearing her say. "Then you can forget about me.''

He tried to get her out of his head, but instead he saw Lacey grinning at him, boxing gloves weaving in front of his face. He remembered their fight. He tried to make himself hate Lacey. It didn't work. Lacey fought clean and hard. Danny couldn't hate him.

"Hey, this isn't the history class, you know.''

Danny snapped his attention to the classroom. Joe Tenny was standing over him, grinning. The other guys had left. The class was over.

"I . . . uh, I was thinkin' about . . . things.''

"Sure you were,'' Joe laughed. "With your eyes closed.''

"I wasn't asleep." Danny got up from his chair.

Joe nodded. "Okay, you were wide awake. Look, why don't you just grab a quick sandwich in the cafeteria and meet me in my office in about fifteen minutes. Got something I want to show you."

Every nerve in Danny's body tightened. His chest started to feel heavy, raw. *He knows about it!*

When he opened the door to Dr. Tenny's office, Joe was standing in front of his easel, slapping paint on a canvas with a small curved knife.

"Hi . . . Sit down a minute."

In one hand, Joe held a paint-dabbed piece of cardboard. He would dip the edge of the knife into a blob of color, and then smear the color across the canvas. Danny watched him.

Finally Joe stepped back, cocked his head to one side and squinted at the canvas, then tossed the cardboard and knife to the floor at the base of the easel.

"What do you think?" he asked.

Danny stared hard at the painting. It looked like some of the dark blobs were going to be boats. There were the beginnings of mountains and clouds in the background.

"Okay, don't answer," Joe said. "I'm just starting it. Wait'll you see the finished product!"

He yanked open his top desk drawer and pulled out a stubby cigar.

"Some days it just gets to be too much," he said. "Then I've got to slap paint around or go nuts."

Danny, sitting in the chair, said nothing.

Joe puffed the cigar to life. "I've been having a little discussion with a few members of the Governor's council. . . . About how much money the Center's going to need next year. I'm in no mood to work anymore today."

Danny shrugged.

"You like airplanes, don't you? Ever been up in one?"

"No. . . ."

"Okay, come on. Friend of mine just bought a new plane for himself. Said I could play with it this afternoon. Want to come?"

With a deep breath of relief, Danny said, "Sure!"

They drove to the airfield in Joe's car. There were still banks of snow along the highway, brown and rotting. The sky was clear, though, and the sun was shining.

The plane sparkled in the sunlight. Painted red and white, it had one engine, a low wing, and a cabin that seated four. It was parked beside a hangar in a small airfield that was used only for private planes.

Joe squeezed into the pilot's seat, and Danny crawled up after him and sat at his right. The control panel in front of him was covered with dials and instruments. A little half-wheel poked out of the panel, and there were two big pedals on the floor.

Joe showed Danny everything: the instruments, the controls, the throttle and fuel mixture sticks that were down on the floor between their two seats, the radio.

"Just like in the books," Danny said.

Joe nodded happily. 'Let's see how she runs."

Within minutes they were speeding down the runway, the engine roaring in Danny's ears, the propeller an almost-invisible blur in front of him. Danny gripped the safety belt that was tightly latched across his lap.

Joe pulled back slightly on the wheel and the plane lifted its nose. Danny felt a split second when his stomach seemed to drop inside him. The ground tilted and dropped away. They were off!

Danny watched the airfield get smaller and farther behind them. Joe banked the plane over on its right wing tip, so Danny felt as if he were hanging by his seat belt, with nothing between him and the ground far below except the window he was looking through.

Then they climbed even higher. The plane bounced and shuddered through a big puffy cloud, and broke free again above the clouds.

Danny could feel himself grinning so hard that it almost hurt. "This is the greatest!"

Joe nodded. "She's a good ship. Nice and stable. Handles easy."

They flew for a few moments in silence, except for the droning engine. Danny looked down at the white-covered ground, sprinkled with the shadows of clouds. He looked across at the clouds themselves, floating peacefully. Then he looked up at the impossibly clear blue sky.

"Want to try her?" Joe shouted over the engine's noise.

"Huh?"

Joe took his hands off the wheel. "Take over. It's not hard. Just keep her nose pointed on the horizon."

Danny grabbed the wheel. Instantly the plane bucked upward, like a horse that didn't like its newest rider.

"Steady! Easy!" Joe shouted. "Just relax. Get her nose down a bit. That's it. . . ."

Danny slowly brought the plane under control. Under *his* control!

"Hey, I'm flying her!"

"You sure are," said Joe, with a huge grin.

Joe showed Danny how to turn the wheel and push the pedals at the same time, so that the plane would turn and bank smoothly. He explained how to work the throttle and fuel mixture controls, how to watch the instruments.

"This is fun!" Danny yelled.

They tried a few shallow dives and turns. Nothing very daring, nothing very fast.

Finally Joe said, "Look down there."

Danny followed where Joe's finger pointed. Far below them was a group of buildings clustered together, near the main highway. It took Danny a moment to realize that it was the Center.

"Looks different from up here," Danny said. "So small. . . ."

Then his eye caught another set of buildings, far from the highway, tucked away in the hills. These were gray and massive buildings. A high stone wall stood around them. They looked like something straight out of the Middle Ages."

"State prison," Joe said.

Danny said nothing.

"It's a big world," Joe said. "You've just got to start looking at it from the right point of view. Lots of the world is pretty crummy, I know. But take a look around you now. Looks kind of pretty, doesn't it?"

Danny nodded. It was a big world, from up here. Hills stretching off to the horizon; towns nestled among them; roads and rivers winding along.

"People make their own worlds, Danny. You're going to make a world for yourself, a world that you'll live in for the rest of your life. You can make it big and clean . . . or as small and dirty as it's been so far. It's up to you to choose."

They flew back to the airfield, and Joe landed the plane. Then they drove back to the Center. Danny was silent, thinking, all the way back.

Chapter Twenty-four

It was a few minutes before six when Danny and Joe returned to the Center.

Danny went straight to the cafeteria. He could hear his own pulse pounding in his ears. His knees felt wobbly, and he knew his hands were shaking. His chest was starting to feel heavy. He fished in his pockets for the pills. *Forgot them! Left them in my room.*

Ralph and Hambone were finishing up an early dinner. Noisy was loafing by the water cooler. Vic and Coop were sitting off in a far corner.

Danny turned around and walked outside. In a few minutes the five others joined him.

"Where's Midget?" he asked. His chest was hurting now.

"He's at the administration building, just like you told him. When the lights go out, he'll go in the tunnel and cut the phone line."

"What're we waitin' for?" Ralph said. "Let's go!"

They walked through the darkness toward the power station. As they got close enough to see the building, the maintenance man who had been on duty there came out of the door and walked past them, heading for the cafeteria. Ralph began to jog and was soon far ahead of them.

"Come on!" he said. They started running for the power station.

Danny trotted behind the others. He couldn't run, couldn't catch his breath. His mind was spinning: Laurie, Joe, Lacey, Ralph . . . flying over the Center, looking at the world beyond its fences . . . Lacey punching him . . . Laurie's face when she told him to forget about her . . .

And then he was inside the power station. It was like stepping into another world. The place was hot. It smelled of oil. The huge generator machinery, crammed up to the ceiling, seemed to bulge out the walls. The metal floorplates throbbed with the rumbling beat of power, and almost beyond the range of human hearing was the highpitched whine of something spinning fast, fast.

Nobody could hear Danny wheezing as he stood just inside the doorway. Nobody watched him struggling his hardest, just to breathe.

The light in the generator room was bright and glaring. Lacey stood up on a steel catwalk that threaded between two big bulky piles of machinery, about twenty feet above the floor.

"Hiya guys!" Lacey called out above the whining hum of the generator. "What d'you want?"

"Come on down," Ralph said. He walked over to a tool bench near the door and picked up a heavy wrench. Hambone giggled.

Danny stared at the generator. He had only seen pictures of it before, drawings and diagrams on SPECS' TV screens. Now it looked huge, almost alive. And he had to kill it, make it silent and dead.

But before that, Ralph and Hambone were going to kill Lacey.

Lacey clattered down the steel steps to the floor. "What's going on, man? What you doing here?"

"Grab him," Ralph snapped.

Hambone wrapped his beefy arms around Lacey's slim body, pinning his arms to his sides.

"Hey . . . what you . . ."

Ralph started toward Lacey, raising the heavy wrench in his big hand. The others stood frozen by the door.

Danny shouted, "Stop it!"

Ralph spun around to face Danny. Suddenly Danny could breathe, his chest was okay. Even the shakes were gone.

"It's no good," he said to Ralph. "Stop it. Forget the whole thing."

"What're you pulling?" Ralph's face was red with anger.

"I'm saving us all from a lot of trouble," Danny said. "Forget the whole deal. Breaking out of here is stupid. They'll just catch us again."

Ralph started to move toward Danny, his knuckles white on the wrench handle. "Listen kid . . . we're getting out. Now! And you're going to . . ."

Danny slid over to the tool bench and reached for another wrench. "Forget it, Ralph. I'm the only one who knows how to knock out the generator. And I ain't going to do it. I changed my mind. The deal's off."

They stood glaring at each other, both armed with heavy metal wrenches. Then suddenly Hambone yowled with pain.

Lacey was loose and streaking up the steel steps to the catwalk. Hambone was hopping on one foot. "He kicked me!"

"Stop him!" Ralph screamed, pointing at Lacey.

Vic and Coop started for the stairway. Danny knew exactly where Lacey was heading. There was an emergency phone on the other side of the generator. He dashed toward the stairway, too, past Ralph, who seemed too stunned to move.

Danny barged into Vic and Coop at the foot of the steps, knocking them off balance, and got onto the stairs ahead of them. He raced to the top, two steps at a time. Then he stopped and turned to the rest of them.

"Before you can get to him you got to go through me!" Danny shouted, holding the wrench up like a battle weapon. *If I can hold 'em off long enough for Lacey to make a call . . .*

With a roar of rage, Ralph pushed past Vic and Coop and boiled up the stairs. Hambone came up right behind him. Danny swung his wrench at Ralph, then felt an explosion of pain in his side.

He began to crumple. The wrench slipped from Danny's fingers as another blow knocked him to his knees. He looked up and saw Ralph's furious face. Beside it was Hambone's, no longer grinning. The wrench in Ralph's hand looked twenty feet long. Danny tried to raise his arms to cover his face, to protect himself. The wrench came blurring down on him. Danny saw sparks shower everywhere.

Somewhere, far off, he could hear people yelling, screaming. But all he could see was bursts of light going off inside his head; all he could feel was pain.

Chapter Twenty-five

Danny awoke in the hospital. He blinked his eyes at the green curtain around his bed. His head felt heavy, like it was carrying pounds and pounds of cement on it. He reached up to touch it. It was covered with bandages.

Then he realized that he could only move one arm. The other was wrapped in a heavy, stiff cast.

The curtain opened and Joe Tenny stepped in, grinning at him.

"Feel better?"

Danny tried to answer, but found that his mouth was too swollen and painful.

"I don't mean your body," Joe said, pulling up a chair and straddling it cowboy-fashion. "I mean your conscience . . . your mind."

Danny shrugged. His side twinged.

"You made the right choice. It cost you a couple of teeth and a few broken bones, but that can all be fixed. You'll be out and around in a week or two."

"You . . ." It hurt, but he had to say it. "You knew."

Joe gave him that who-are-you-trying-to-kid-look. "We knew that you were going to try a break. But we didn't know where or when. You covered up your tracks pretty darned well. If you hadn't been so smart, we could have saved you the beating you took."

"I . . . the asthma . . . it went away."

Nodding, Joe said, "The doctor told me it would, sooner or later. You didn't have anything wrong with your lungs. In your case, asthma was just a crutch . . . a little excuse you made up in the back of your mind. Whenever the going got tough, you started to wheeze. Then you could flake out, or at least have an excuse for not doing well."

Danny closed his eyes.

"But when the chips were down," Joe went on, "you ditched the excuse. No more asthma. You stood on your own feet and did what you had to do."

"How's Lacey?" Danny asked.

"When we got there, after Lacey called us, he was trying to pry Hambone and Ralph off of you. They never laid a finger on him . . . thanks to you."

"We would've never made it," Danny mumbled.

"That's right. Even if you got out of the Center, we'd have tracked you down. But it was important for you to try to escape."

"What?"

Joe pulled his chair closer. "Look, what's the one thing that's kept you going ever since you first came here? The idea of escaping. Don't you think I knew that? Every prisoner wants to escape. I was a prisoner-of-war once. I tried to escape fourteen times."

"Then, why . . ."

"We *used* the idea of escaping to help you to grow up," Joe said. "Why do you think I told you the Center was escape-proof? To make sure you'd try to prove I was wrong! All the teaching and lecturing in the world couldn't have done as much as that one idea of escaping. Look what you did: you learned to read and study, you learned how to work SPECS, you learned how to plan ahead, to be patient, to control your temper, you even learned to work with other people. All because you were trying to escape."

"But it didn't work. . . ."

"Sure! It didn't work because you finally learned the most important thing of all. You learned that the only way to escape jail—all jails—for keeps is to *earn* your way out."

Danny let his head sink back on the pillow.

"And you played fair by Lacey. I think you learned something there, too."

Looking up at the ceiling, Danny asked, "What happened to the other guys?"

"Vic and Coop are in their rooms. They'll stay in for a week or so, and then we'll let them start classes again. I'll have to start paying as much attention to them as I did to you. I don't think they've learned as much as you have . . . not yet. Same for Midget and Noisy, except that one of the other staff members is in charge of their cases.

"Ralph and Hambone are here in the hospital, up-stairs. They've got emotional problems that're too deep to let them walk around the campus. I'm afraid they're going to stay inside for a long while.''

Danny took a deep breath. His side hurt, but his chest felt fine and clear.

''Look,'' Joe said. ''When you get out of the hospital, it'll be almost exactly one year since you first came to the Center. I think you've learned a lot in your first year. The hard way. But you've finally learned it.''

Danny nodded.

''Now, if you're ready for it I can start *really* teaching you. In another year or so, maybe we can let you out of here—on probation. I can see to it that you get into a real school. You can wind up studying engineering, if you want. Learn to build airplanes . . . and fly 'em.''

In spite of the pain, Danny smiled. ''I'd like that.''

''Good. And it'll be a lot cheaper for the taxpayers to send you to school and get you into a decent career, than to keep you in jails the rest of your life.''

Joe got up from the chair.

Danny found himself stretching out his right hand toward him. The teacher looked at it, then smiled in a way Danny had never seen him do before. He took Danny's hand firmly in his own.

''Thanks. I've been waiting a year for this.''

''Thank you, Joe.''

Joe let go of Danny's hand and started to turn away. Then he stopped and said:

''Oh yeah . . . Laurie's on her way here. She wants to see you. Says she's willing to give you your Christmas present.''

''Great!'' said Danny.

Joe pulled a cigar from his shirt pocket. ''You two have a bright future ahead of you. And I can tell about the future. I'm part gypsy, you know.''